Praise for FALLEN GODS:

Beneath the fantasy and horror, a simmering love story brews. One that left me uneasy and completely unsure how to feel. Not because Ms. Simper failed, but because she succeeded so very, very well.
-Evie Drae, author of Beauregard and the Beast

Simper has created a brilliant combination of gruesomely dark fantasy and scorching romance. The protagonists are both so flawed, you are at once drawn to and repelled by them. Simper takes the idea of grey morality and writes it to perfection.
-The Lesbian Review

Simper has created a complex, immersive world for the series and that's not even touching on the well-developed characters or the complicated, fucked up relationship you can't help but ship anyway.
-Manic Femme Reviews

Praise for SEA AND STARS:

"If you like your fantasy with an extra dark twist, exceptional world building and deeply complex characters then reel this book in fast. You'll be hooked."
-The Lesbian Review

"The Fate of Stars, the first book in the Sea and Stars trilogy, is delightfully dark and sexy, full of lush imagery, vibrant characterization, and enough adrenaline to keep me up way past my bedtime."
-Anna Burke, award winning author of THORN and COMPASS ROSE

Praise for Carmilla and Laura:

A beautiful retelling . . . perfect for anyone who likes darker-themed romance, horror stories, or plain ol' lesbian vampires.
-The Lesbian 52

Death's Abyss

Death's Abyss

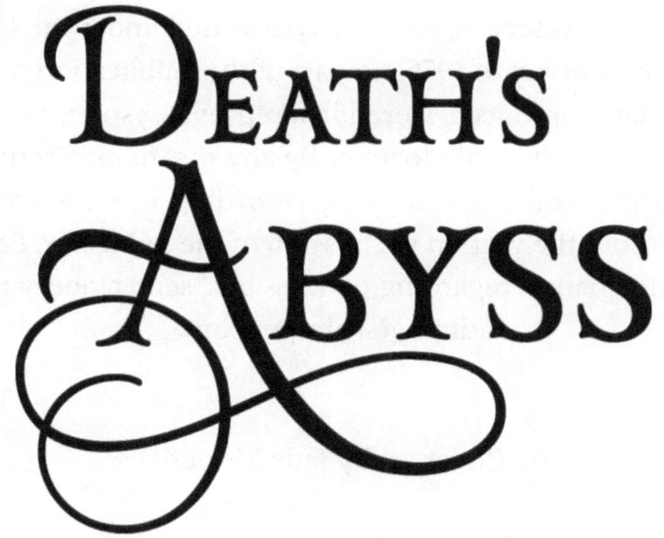

S D Simper

Includes an excerpt from the Patreon exclusive
story: *Aftermath*

For LaRae

THE Theocracy OF Sol Kareena
Tholheim
City of Light
Solvira
Neolan
Tanill
Great Fire Trenches
Yal
Kent
Stelune
Ilunnes
Iids
Contested Territory
Vaile
Tortalgan Sea
Kal'Far
Ablom
Canyon OF THE Great Mother
Moratham

*One thousand years before the Old Gods return,
a monster comes to destroy the seas.*

The whole world holds its breath.

Prologue

A shadow moved toward the undersea utopia of Stelune.

Citizens went about their day, content beneath the autumn rays of the sun, the water cool and invigorating. Shopkeepers sold their wares to wanting customers, money exchanging hands with a gentle *clink*. Protestors cried in the canals, ignored by those who gave no care to the inevitable war.

But sounds of joy and anger silenced when a great shadow appeared at the edge of the valley. A hush filled the populace as a mass of tentacles slowly undulated above the rocks. Countless suckered appendages steadily spread wide, and as it moved to cover the edges of the canyon—for its tentacles reached nearly as far—thus was revealed a gigantic, unblinking eye at its center, larger than any of the residents of Stelune and as vibrant as a second sun, though a great slit marred the center, pure black upon a golden star.

The leviathan had come

Like thunder across the sea, his voice shook the very foundation of the earth. *"This shall do."*

The silence broke; screams erupted among the merfolk.

The leviathan—Yu'Khrall, Son of Onias—descended upon the city, tentacles swooping out. Structures crumbled, spewing clouds of dust that swirled around the black appendages. Screams cut off as toppled buildings crushed their residents; fleeing merfolk were engulfed by Yu'Khrall's tentacles, carried to the center of the mass.

His beak-like mouth opened, revealing an endless void wherein the victims might rot. He consumed all he grabbed—soon, blood seeped from the edges, yet his hunger remained limitless.

Some fled, a few even managing to dodge the array of darting tentacles and escape across the valley's walls. Others cowered in crevices or within their homes, only to be exposed when the stone collapsed. Soon, blood rose from the ground, saturating the water as Yu'Khrall picked up the dead and dying and plunged them into his maw.

At the center of Stelune remained a beacon of hope—the castle stood as a final bastion among the carnage. Armored merfolk swam from its alcoves, spears in hand, only to be cast aside or grabbed by its massive appendages. One fell upon the castle's walls, destroying the outer gates with merely an idle blow.

Another, more deliberate, crushed it from the center.

Amidst the slaughter, Yu'Khrall floated down to the center of the massive valley and stretched his tentacles, able to bridge the widest part. Any movement was met with a swift end, either by being swatted into the ground, broken and bleeding, or caught and condemned to the monster's mouth.

Content, he settled upon a kingdom of rubble. Those who remained cowered.

Chapter I

The leviathan had long ago disappeared from her vision, but Tallora swam as quickly as her aching tail would allow. Although lacerated from the braided kelp that had bound her, scraped by the cave's walls, her scales had stopped bleeding in time. Her tears had staunched as well, though her heart palpitated with fear.

Yet, she swam toward the danger. She had to warn Stelune, her mother, Kal's family . . .

All she knew might be lost. And so she swam even when her lungs threatened to burst, when she swore her tail had been wrung ragged. The faintest aftertaste of rust touched her tongue, and Tallora flinched to even breathe.

Upon the horizon, the first hints of her beloved valley appeared, yet she saw no light, save from the sun. The water seemed saturated in a deep red cloud, and her limbs numbed from panic. It grew thicker as she swam, the putrid taste growing sharp.

She kept her body close to the ground, lest the creature appear and see her, though a leviathan would likely struggle to hide. She herself hid among the rocks and scattered arrays of kelp leading to the slope that ended in Stelune.

She saw nothing. Not until her face peeked over a sheer cliff face.

There it lay, its great eye having become the new center of the once beautiful city. The behemoth lay still, yet remained far taller than even the destroyed castle. Its tentacles spread out from the center, easily touching the canyon walls. The rainbow of colors had been reduced to rubble and grey dust, saturated red by the thick cloud of carnage engulfing the city. Every breath Tallora stole burned her lungs, and she'd surely be coughing out dirt and blood for days, yet she could not tear her eyes away from the horror, from that massive eye, that closed mouth, like a deformed squid, and the hundreds of pulsing tentacles, idly floating in the water.

As she watched, a serene tentacle suddenly darted out, deliberate as it grabbed a colored bit of movement in the distance and brought it to its mouth. The cloud of red pulsed as though alive. Tallora's hand covered her mouth, struck by the countless lives extinguished by this monster's actions.

All of Stelune. Thousands of innocents. By Staella's Grace, what of her momma—

"You!"

She gasped, her tears escaping into the sea as an unfamiliar voice stole her focus. Behind, she saw a man with the gaze of one who had witnessed death, pale and distant, the scales of his kelp-green tail seeping blood.

His eyes softened at her stare. "There's a group of us, not too far away. Other survivors. We'd best hurry—the blood is attracting hordes of sharks."

She could not summon words. She merely quivered as she nodded, the reality of her home and its destruction slowly crushing her heart.

The man led her away from the annihilated city. It was as he had said, that a group of merfolk had gathered at the edge of a nearby reef—entire families, with mothers hugging their children, fathers embracing the mothers, their own tears apparent, and other little children sobbing with no parent to hold them, perhaps murdered in the purging of the once-magnificent city. So many refugees, perhaps a hundred in all—

Yet, it held not a bubble to the entire populace, gone in a bloodstained morning. Tallora spotted Queen Fauln and the two princesses at the center, perhaps the cause for order among the group. Relief washed over her. Kal's family was safe.

Yet what of her own? She saw no mirrors to herself, no graying hair with pink-sheened scales. "Is this everyone?" she asked the man.

"All that we've found. There are other scouts searching the area."

She nodded, though her heart ached. "Thank you," she said, and she swam into the crowd, passing broken people, many tending to wounded folk whose blood seeped into the open sea. Some followed with their eyes, recognition in a few as they muttered her title—*The Great Survivor.*

Well, she had survived this too, though she had only witnessed the end.

The queen was surrounded by a small ensemble, to whom she spoke frantically, and Tallora overheard practical terms such as, "food," and, "shelter," and, "if we stay here and the creature rises, we'll be next."

She caught the queen's eye, however, and the monarch gasped and beckoned her forward. "You met with Solvira. What happened?"

"Queen Fauln, your husband and son are alive," Tallora said, lest the queen panic.

Relief settle upon the queen's face, and perhaps it was only years spent as a monarch that stopped her from bursting into sobs. "Thank Tortalga," Fauln said, and behind her, one of her daughters cried, with the other to consul her. "Where are they?"

Tallora clenched her fist, the pain of betrayal still lacerating her heart, even among the tragedy. "Solvira . . ." Emotion choked her throat as she recalled the bloodthirsty crowd, the murdered men. "Solvira betrayed us. They've taken your husband and Kal hostage. They aren't to be harmed, but—"

Her words cut off when the queen's expression darkened, her regal gaze spelling murder. "What?"

"They won't be harmed unless the Tortalgan Sea joins Moratham in the fight against Solvira. But Empress Dauriel lied to us—she slew the Speaker and the rest of his entourage."

"Did you not swear that Solvira's intentions were noble?" Queen Fauln said, pointed in her glare. Shame welled in Tallora's stomach, rising and threatening to suffocate her. "Did you not swear that Empress Dauriel, who captured you from your homeland, meant us no harm? I begged my husband not to go, but he felt pride at Kal's ambition. He fell for the empress' charade. I should have known you were behind it all."

Tallora shrunk, barely composed at the brutal words. "We were all deceived, your majesty."

"There are bigger problems than your betrayal to the crown. Keep your head down, lest I banish you from this party."

Then, the queen swam upward, above the small populace of people. "Everyone, listen! We shall be leaving a few scouts here to find survivors, but the rest of us will be traveling to the village of Iids, only a few hours away." Iids, like all the other villages surrounding Stelune, was but a planet to the sun in size, but perhaps it could provide for them. "Begin moving out! Any unsupervised children need a companion—do your part and help out."

The crowd stirred, like some giant awoken from sleep, slow as it roused its traumatized inhabitants. Tallora turned away from the queen, her heart torn between two terrible truths—that she was responsible for Kal and King Merl's capture, yet perhaps it might've been what saved their lives.

So few remained. Yet more still appeared, as told by three more merfolk approaching the crowd from beyond. She had yet to see her mother; perhaps she lived. Swallowing tears, Tallora clung to that hope, lest she face the reality of losing everything—her momma, her dearest friend, and . . .

The memory of Dauriel's tearful words tore at her heart. Tallora knew she should hate her; the anguish of her love's betrayal pulsed like fire through her blood. Instead, she mourned the life they couldn't live. They had disrupted fate to have even met, and the world hadn't been meant for them. Yes, she was angry, but Tallora loved her, loved her so. Anger could exist with love.

But she would never see her again; it was the only path ahead.

The crowd moved, and Tallora looked around her, noticing a pair of children, perhaps seven years old each, clinging to each other, watching the crowd with fearful eyes. Their hair bore similar shades of purple and burgundy, and each of them, both little girls, cast their eyes onto Tallora as she approached. "Come on," she said, lip trembling, but she was hardly the only one who'd lost something dear this day. So she forced a smile, watched the girls' faces soften as one took her hand, the other content to clutch who Tallora presumed was her sister.

They said nothing, for there was nothing to say. But whatever Tallora's failures, whatever her turmoil, there was a greater work to be done. Behind her eyelids, Tallora saw tentacles searching for her in the dark, saw that great eye glowing in sickly shades of yellow, but she pushed that away, vowing instead to lead these two wards to safety.

Iids held little grandeur.

Queen Fauln had sent a few able-bodied scouts ahead, so a small welcome party greeted them. "We've scavenged what accommodations we could," said an aging man. "We will at least have passable sleeping arrangements for everyone. We can discuss further plans tonight, your majesty."

Tallora held to her wards as they were escorted through a tiny village. The stone buildings were not stacked as they were in the once massive city, but spread wide near the ground. Tallora saw structured nets of fish being tended to, as well as fields of seaweed in the distance. Stelune relied on the farming villages to survive, paying them handsomely for wares—Tallora knew this, having spent a lifetime watching her mother run a shop.

Orders were shouted. Tallora listened as it was announced that the courthouse had been cleared to house refugees for the night, and that the populace had volunteered to take in any orphans in the meantime. Food awaited them. Tallora's heart bled at the kindness.

She watched Queen Fauln's eyes tear up with every word, and though they stood at odds, Tallora found her humility inspiring. These people offered all they had—and not for fear of reprimand, no, but because they sought to help their queen and the residents of the capital city.

Tallora wondered what Solvira would say, if Solvirans would do as much for their empress. Her own tears threatened to fall when the girls she'd escorted were welcomed into a family with three other children of their own, but not without a shy hug goodbye from one burgundy-haired girl. Tallora held her tight, savoring the innocent touch, knowing they both needed the embrace.

Tallora followed with the rest to the great hall of stone, built into a sea of coral. She marveled at the colors, the natural beauty of the place lovingly combined with innovation. But as Tallora lined up to receive her dinner, her name was called, "Tallora?"

She turned, her soul longing for any familiarity, but to her surprise, it was Fauln. The queen beckoned for her, and though confusion slowed her movements, she approached. "Yes, your majesty?"

"You'll be taking dinner with my family and the magistrate of Iids. Come."

Tallora followed the regal woman, who wore no finery but her small crown. Her hair bore the same shades of blue as Kal, and Tallora's heart hurt at the reminder of the dear friend she'd lost.

They swam to an isolated room, wherein dinner had already been served—the same food, the same portions as the rest. The presumed magistrate smiled at their entrance, and Tallora recognized him as the one who had met them at the city gates. Queen Fauln's daughters already sat at the table, looking exhausted but otherwise healthy.

There were a few others as well—men and women bearing the same sad smiles. "Tallora," the magistrate said, "my name is Gregor. Please have a seat." She did, watching as the rest followed. He took his own seat at the front, no food before him. "Queen Fauln says you know the fate of our king."

Tallora nodded, sparing a glance for the queen. She looked to her daughters, both of whom appeared despondent at the words. They knew too, it seemed. "I saw it for myself," she said slowly, praying this was not some sort of test. "They are alive and will remain so, but they're held captive. Solvira killed the Morathan envoy and kidnapped our rulers during what was supposed to be a peace summit."

Gregor looked to Fauln. "Of all times," he said, a tragedy lacing his words. "It seems you shall be our guiding beacon instead, your majesty."

Fauln's face held perfect stoicism, but Tallora knew she hid fury. Before she could continue, Fauln spoke. "Tallora, I would ask you something else, and I implore that you speak the truth. It will not be held against you. But my husband had been in talks with Advisor Chemon, both of them conspiring to acquire a weapon to protect us from Solvira." A certain bitterness settled into Fauln's face, and Tallora saw that she knew and had disapproved. "The time for blame is past. My husband told me of the witch they'd tortured for information. But did you know anything of the plan to awaken the leviathan?"

A hush filled the room, everyone staring at Tallora as though she'd grown a second tail. "Yes, your majesty," she replied softly. "The witch—Harbinger—couldn't speak of it because of a curse placed upon her, but when Kal and I went to Solvira, I recognized the mural on a wall in one of their halls as the same beneath the Great Fire Trenches. According to the stories, only the Heart of Silver Flame could release the monster. Your husband and Chemon knew that much, but only knew how to act when . . ." Tallora steadied her breath, the next words painful—and alarming. ". . . when Chemon was told the rest of it in a vision. Or so he claimed." She watched Fauln carefully for a reaction, for hers was ultimately the only that mattered. "I don't know whose hands they've played into and neither did he, but this was the result."

The queen nodded, understanding in the gesture.

The magistrate, however, appeared baffled. "You mean to tell me this being was awoken with the king's permission?"

"He was desperate," Fauln whispered, shame steeling her jaw, "and forgive me, but a damned fool as well." She looked back to Tallora, her previous fury having dissolved away. "Was there any mention of how to lock the leviathan away again? Any hope you can remember?"

"No," Tallora replied. "He was locked up thousands of years ago by Neoma herself. So, perhaps a prayer to Staella, but I don't know."

Fauln looked to the table, at the untouched food, and placed a hand beneath her chin. "She is as good a hope as we could ask for."

"Staella rarely interferes, as a rule," Gregor said, no judgement on his tongue. "She might provide peace, but I do not know if she could give any aid."

Tallora shut her eyes as silence settled upon the room, seeing the giant mural behind her eyelids. Dauriel had only spoken of Neoma. Perhaps that was their only hope. Within the Hall of Relics they had spoken of Yu'Khrall . . . and upon the ceiling—

"Queen Fauln," Tallora said, a plan quickly spinning as she spoke, "what of Yaleris? The dragon?"

All eyes in the room looked to her. Fauln looked intrigued. "What of him?"

"He's our protector. It's his duty beneath the seas. He wields his orb of water and ice to defend us. Surely he sleeps, but if we can awaken him, he would aid us."

Fauln nodded, visibly intrigued by the plan. "If there was ever a threat greater than Yu'Khrall, then steal my crown and beat me with it. Yaleris sleeps, but he will awaken when the need is dire."

"Send me," Tallora said, and everyone looked to her in shock. But she recalled her own adventure from long ago—when a silly fourteen-year-old girl had resolved to find the dragon with a boy she thought she loved and had studied every map she could. "I know the way, and I'll be able to leave once I've eaten— sooner, even, if that's what it takes." She looked to Gregor. "You can't spare the guards, and we're all refugees." To Queen Fauln, she added, "Let me do this. Let me redeem myself."

"Sleep first." The queen offered a lackluster smile, the exhaustion of the day settling into her features. "Eat. Rest. But I accept your offer, and should you succeed, you will be a hero to your people."

Instead of a betrayer, came the unspoken words, and Tallora nodded, though she wondered if it would be enough.

She settled into eating, her stomach suddenly starved, as the magistrate and Fauln spoke of logistics.

Chapter II ✸

Tallora hardly slept. Situated among a room full of refugees, she doubted anyone could find peace enough to sleep, given the perpetual crying of children, coughing, even rustling upon the ground.

Distracted, her mind had no time to dwell upon the tragedy before them. She had not even witnessed the great cataclysm, yet it caused her stomach to tighten, her air to constrict.

When she finally balanced upon the cusp of sleep, a voice whispered in her head, clear as day: *"Tallora, awaken!*

She opened her eyes, a chance glance to the window revealing a single glowing, yellow eye.

Though her heart leapt in fear, she realized it was not the monster she feared. "Harbinger?" she mouthed, and beyond the window, the image disappeared. In silence, Tallora sat up, those still awake following with their eyes. But she swam, her tail gentle lest she disturb the still water, and left the room, and then the courthouse.

When she looked to the window, the familiar Onian witch floated in the distance, beyond the sleepy town's borders, waving her many tentacles, beckoning for Tallora to come.

She obeyed, swimming quickly now. "Harbinger?" she said, audibly now, and once she came close, she saw that the witch bore a grimace as deep as the seafloor. One hand rested on her hip; the other—

Was nothing more than a stump. Tallora brought a hand to cover her mouth at the raw flesh, barely scarred as if cauterized. "You cut off the—"

"Well, well—Heart of Silver Flame had to get herself captured."

Fury rose in Tallora's throat; she nearly choked holding it back. "I beg your pardon?"

"Listen," Harbinger said, her smile about as sweet as putrid codfish, "I realize this is not technically your fault, but if I thought that slitting your throat would undo this mess, I would do it."

Despite the idle threat, Tallora glared, fury rising. "You listen—I just lost my entire city, most of my species, and my mother—" Her words suddenly choked, but she spat out the rest nonetheless. "And that's only in the past day. Ask me about Solvira. Ask me about Kal—I've lost *everything,* and you have the audacity to *blame* me for the very disaster I risked my life to try and stop? Fuck you, fuck your god, and *fuck* your bastard father who just *murdered my people!*"

Tallora turned on her tail, furious at the tears seeping from her eyes. The village faced her, the sleepy town hopefully not awakened by her rage.

"Tallora—"

She whirled around, glaring at Harbinger, whose face seemed permanently etched in indifference. "You'd slit my throat to undo this, but you didn't slit my throat to prevent it—don't act high and mighty now. You didn't cut off the brand until it was too late either."

"I apologize," Harbinger said curtly. "May I try again?"

Tallora crossed her arms as she glared, daring Harbinger to give her a reason to swim away.

"I want to help." She held up her stump of an arm, lip twisting into a sneer. "Perhaps I am to blame as well—if I had done this sooner, perhaps I could have warned you. But do not forget that your people did this to themselves." Tallora's chest rose in fury, but before she could spew more vitriol, Harbinger added, "Demoni Law says it is! Otherwise Onias might help, had Yu'Khrall freed himself. But King Merl sought to bring him back, and so it is your problem to deal with."

Tallora's heart sank, contemplating the wicked truth of her words. "Yes, but perhaps to fall before Neoma would do something."

"Likely, but getting an audience is difficult, hmm? Let us focus on what we can control."

"I told Queen Fauln I would go find Yaleris," Tallora said softly, her rage finally seeping away.

Harbinger's intrigue visibly spiked. "The dragon?"

"Yu'Khrall is a threat to all life beneath the seas. Yaleris has every reason to come save us."

"So we call upon a dragon wielding a Convergence Orb. I approve of this plan. How can I help?"

"It would take days for me to go on my own," Tallora said, her own hope slowly rising, "but you could take us there in a matter of hours."

Harbinger's smile revealed her shark-like teeth, vicious delight in the gesture. "I will help."

When Harbinger offered a hand, Tallora accepted, unsurprised when she was dragged into a particularly dark patch beside the sea of kelp.

The world shifted. Where there was once color and light came only shades of grey. No movement— the ocean lay utterly serene, the edges of Tallora's sight covered in fog. Yet it was as seamless as swimming through a doorway. She alone bore color, standing as a beacon among the monochromatic scenery; Harbinger's deep blue coloring shifted to grey, blending her in with the new world.

Here they were, in the world of demons. "All of Sha'Demoni fears what Yu'Khrall's return means for them," Harbinger said as they swam along. When Tallora looked back, the shadowy remains of the town were but a memory. So strange, to swim within a parallel world stretched so thin. "I do not think he would be foolish enough to attack anyone here; others are not so certain. Should he keep to himself in your world, Onias will do nothing."

In the far distance, Tallora saw a great shadow flicker along what she presumed was the surface of the sea. "Damn," the Onian said, and she gripped Tallora's arm and yanked her down.

Tallora resisted the impulse to squeak. Something inside her welled dread, that eerie, creeping feeling of being in the presence of a shark prickling at her neck. Harbinger hid them within a great crevice, the shadowed realm protecting them from sight. She held a finger to her lip as she looked up.

Tallora followed her gaze, throat seizing when she saw the monstrosity high above.

It bore a hundred tentacles, not unlike Yu'Khrall, yet instead of a single, unblinking eye, Tallora caught sight of thousands of them covering the center of its eldritch body. They blinked in the manner of an ocean wave, rolling from one side to the next, yet it moved so silently, a predator in an unfamiliar sea. She tore her gaze away, looking to Harbinger instead, and mouthed, "Leviathan?"

Harbinger met her eyes and nodded, then watched until the monster disappeared, first from above and then beyond the horizon—it took minutes, surely, yet Tallora swore she remained in stasis for hours.

"There are other leviathans in the sea," Harbinger whispered, beckoning for her to follow. "Yu'Khrall is simply the most violent of them. However, your presence will be unappreciated, given you opened his prison." Objection rose in Tallora's being, but Harbinger held up a hand. "I know, I know. If it is a consolation, they will not be so keen on me either, given he and I share blood."

Tallora stilled her tongue, contemplating the merit of asking what might be a rude question to someone currently assisting her in saving the world. However, Harbinger was largely unoffendable, she'd learned. She met her eerie gaze, mesmerized by that one eye, and asked, "Why do they hate him? And why do *you* hate him?"

"The story says that Yu'Khrall was the most powerful leviathan in Sha'Demoni—the largest, and the most vicious. Always hungry; always seeking power. He killed the leviathan Yu'Erit and became

Onias' favorite. Onias, for all his power, cannot move from his domain. He has become too large. Infinite power, but stunted in how he can wield it. And so Yu'Khrall was his best and greatest, and the other leviathans feared him—until he suddenly lost his mind."

"Lost his mind?"

"Lost his mind. He and Goddess Ilune engaged in battle for reasons I do not know, and he won—then he began rampaging across Sha'Demoni, consuming innocent denizens, but there were not enough. He came to your world and continued his carnage across the sea. That is when Neoma sealed him away." Harbinger's sneer could have rotted meat, so bitter it was. "Does that answer your question?"

She had once heard a similar tale from Dauriel. "Those are reasons to fear him, yes," Tallora replied, sensing the radiant disdain from her companion, "but none of that involves you. Is that the only reason?"

Harbinger said, "It is complicated," and fell silent. Around them, Sha'Demoni remained stagnant, the ripples behind their tails and tentacles like a tsunami on a serene beach.

Minutes passed before Harbinger spoke again. "My mother was a human. All Onians are descended from humans."

The noise of her words startled Tallora. "My ancestors were as well. We're all children of Tortalga— or Onias, in your case."

"Tortalga is an angel, and a hermit, but not a bad man. His children were brought into the world through love. But can you imagine falling into Onias' realm? You know what they say? That to gaze upon him brings even the most assured to madness?"

"You mentioned that, once."

"It is true. I have never seen my grandfather, Tallora—on the occasions I have had to directly communicate with him, I bring a mirror. The fact of the matter is, the women he impregnates literally *burst* within months of conception, leaving a little parasitic leviathan to feast on their remains."

Tallora's stomach clenched at the thought. "Staella's Grace . . ."

"A brutal beginning. Mine was not much better. Demon morality is very different than ours—some leviathans adopt Demoni Law, while others hold a conscience enough to never procreate. As for me, I distrust them all. My father is a monster; he would eat me too, if he saw me."

Tallora recalled a memory of what felt like a lifetime ago—Dauriel standing between she and General Khastra on the beach, who by all accounts was as demonic as the leviathans. Despite the sincere love between them, Khastra might have killed Dauriel then and there—something Tallora simply couldn't fathom.

"Once Yu'Khrall has rested and eaten his fill, he will move on," Harbinger continued. "For now, the uplanders are safe, but who can say, once he has rampaged across the sea."

Tallora recalled how Harbinger had used her tentacles to crawl above land as an insect; the image of Yu'Khrall doing the same caused her skin to turn to ice. "Can Onias not stop him? He'll lose his power if Yu'Khrall slays all his followers."

Harbinger shook her head. "Demonic gods cannot leave their realms, just as angels cannot either. Perhaps if we could convince another leviathan to host him, but they would surely die in the process. None would ever agree."

"Forgive me, but what about you?"

"You do not know much of channeling demonic gods, do you." Harbinger's eye surveyed the area ahead, but all the horizon seemed clear. "Channeling any god sucks the life out of you, reducing your lifespan by years—some immortals can handle it, if they have the magical capacity. In dire circumstances, a mortal can channel a god, usually for some act of heroism, though they'll perish to the god's power— then, the god is banished back to their realm. The

Speaker of Moratham is always a son of Morathma, so it is a calling, and one he may live through. Demon gods are more difficult to channel, however—they suck more life, they destroy their host, and so on. The Bringer of War is the only person who can channel Ku'Shya and live. Rumors have spread that Izthuni, the Lurker, has found an undead hostess he calls upon. To channel Onias would be a death sentence, and so no leviathan would agree to it. So why not me? Because I would die within minutes, even as an immortal."

Tallora followed Harbinger's gaze across the horizon, the eerie silence unsettling.

"So what happened with Solvira?"

Startled, Tallora looked to Harbinger, noted the curiosity in her stare. "Excuse me?"

"Earlier you said to ask about Solvira and Kal. What happened?"

The rawness of the betrayal still burned. Tallora clenched her fists as they swam. "Empress Dauriel listened to everything we told her, and instead of using it for peace, she used it as collateral. She killed the Speaker and the Morathan Envoy. She captured Kal and King Merl to hold as hostages and keep the Tortalgan Sea in line while they marched on Moratham." Bitterness stained her words, but she had nothing to hide—not from Harbinger. "Chemon discovered Dauriel and mine's true relationship and told King Merl, who gave the order. Somehow he knew what the story meant—something about a vision; I don't know. So I suppose you can be angry with me. My crime was trusting Dauriel—"

The name choked in her throat. Her nails dug into her palm as she warded away fresh tears.

"I am sorry," Harbinger said softly, the sincerity of it startling. "Y-You are the Heart of Silver Flame, so I thought she cared about . . ."

Perhaps she stopped because of how Tallora's face had twisted from pain. Tallora covered her eyes with her palms, determined to ward away the hurt. Now was not the time to fall into bed and sob—it might not ever be. But as she sucked in a painful breath, a hand gently touched her shoulder. Tallora looked up, surprised to see Harbinger looking contrite. "I apologize. I misspoke."

"You really didn't though," Tallora replied, managing a laugh, though it certainly carried a sob. "All she's ever wanted was a war with Moratham—to be known as the empress who destroyed the Desert Sands. And it isn't a crime to want to bring glory to her goddess by defeating her enemy, but she still betrayed me."

"Speak of it. We have a few more hours ahead of us."

The memory remained raw and visceral. Tallora clenched her jaw, the words painful to contemplate, but she forced herself to speak. "She does care, but she can't care more about me than she cares for her kingdom. It broke her heart to do it, but she still did it." Shaking her head, Tallora managed a gasping breath. "I don't know how I'm allowed to feel."

Their shared moments of vulnerability shone like gold—the Dauriel who could never bear children; Dauriel, who loved beautiful things yet saw no beauty in herself, who cried when they made love, who had once thrown away her life to save Tallora's—

The woman she loved was a hero. But Dauriel hadn't been born into a life meant for heroics.

As Tallora cried within Sha'Demoni, she longed for the promise they'd made—

A promise Dauriel would not accept Tallora's answer for until the betrayal was revealed. Tallora stopped, anguish stilling her tail as a sob shook her entire body. Damn Dauriel and her misguided honor.

Tallora cried in her hands, hardly cognizant to Harbinger's presence. "I-I'm sorry. It's just . . . we were going to be married. Now, I have nothing—I lost her, but I've also lost my home and my momma—"

Harbinger, her inexplicable, unexpected ally, stopped beside her and placed her stump around

Tallora's torso. The gesture, though startling, was not unappreciated. "All is not lost."

Tallora smiled, daring to briefly lean into the odd affection.

The dragon awaited. When Harbinger pulled away, Tallora forced a smile, though genuine gratitude twisted it.

"I am not useless when it comes to magic," Harbinger continued. "I know you are afraid to know your mother's fate, but I can help."

The statement wiped Tallora's expression clean. "What do you mean?"

"Once we have awakened Yaleris, I have the means to scry for her. We will either find her body or what camp of refugees she hides with. A simple spell; I am happy to do it."

Had they not just hugged, Tallora might've launched into her arms. "Harbinger, I can't—" Hope filled her, fragile and tentative, but even the smallest light could illuminate the dark. "Thank you."

"Dragon first. Come on."

In better spirits, though her world fell apart, Tallora followed Harbinger through the water.

Chapter III

Perhaps it truly was hours, but it seemed like no time at all before Harbinger announced they neared.

When she grabbed Tallora's arm, the familiar shifting of planes occurred, and Tallora was struck by the world of color. Her eyes blinked rapidly, trying to equate a land of greys to the gorgeous landscape.

A vast coral reef lay before them, filled with life, a rainbow of color spreading wide. Oblivious to the horror of Stelune, fish swam in little schools, snacking among the anemones, content in their beautiful forest beneath the sea.

The Canyon of the Great Mother awaited. Tallora and Harbinger swam on.

For not the first time, Tallora watched the beauty of the reef and its inhabitants and thought of Solvira and its gardens and vast array of animals—from sweet puppies to powerful horses. Tallora had loved the colorful insects, adored the fragile flowers growing from the earth and populating the bushes.

Tallora had loved it, even when home had shined brilliantly in her memory, even when she'd missed it with all her heart.

Yet she'd been willing to cast home aside for Dauriel. Tallora's hand touched the rough coral, careful to keep her fragile tailfin away. All the world was in disarray; Tallora had never felt so confused and afraid.

The reef stopped at a steep slope, yet no darkness permeated the deep canyon. A smile came to her face unbidden; though she could not yet see the source, she knew.

Yaleris was near. Harbinger and Tallora swam downward.

In her youth, Tallora had seen Yaleris on a festival day, where the great dragon had come to greet her people, had shyly sat aside and watched their celebration of the Goddess of Stars and her constellations.

A new work of art had been scattered across the sky—a depiction of Tortalga, an homage to their god. They had celebrated, praised her name and his, and Yaleris had blessed it, all the while wielding the same sort of orb the Solvirans had killed his sister to claim.

As they dove down the sheets of rock, Harbinger said, "You speak to him. I cannot say how he will feel about the child of a leviathan, much less the Daughter of Yu'Khrall. But he likes merfolk."

Tallora nodded, unwilling to argue, though she suspected Yaleris wouldn't give any mind to her heritage. "He's kind and gentle. But I suspect he can be fearsome too."

They reached the base of the canyon. In the distance stood a massive cave entrance. With renewed vigor, they swam quickly to the rock formation, and Tallora soon floated before it.

It hardly held a candle to the size of Yu'Khrall's prison. Not even close. The hope she'd kindled threatened to extinguish.

But Harbinger forged ahead; Tallora followed.

Light permeated the cave, illuminated by crystal-like structures upon the walls, ever shining. Tallora slowed her pace, basking in the mystical ambience, even as the cave became colder. When she brushed against one such crystal, it burned her skin—though not from heat.

Ice. Impossibly rare here in the south, yet when Tallora touched it again, she could not deny it. "How strange," she whispered, and the deeper they swam, the more ice coated the walls. It floated in the water, frost clinging to her hair and skin. Tallora had been affectionately teased her papa that her hair was like snowfall, frost upon a glacier, and as the flakes clung to her hair, she saw the truth in it and smiled.

The icicle structures became larger, more jagged. Tallora and Harbinger dodged the jutting, glowing collections of ice, and she wondered how the rest of the water did not simply freeze beside it.

When the chill became unbearable, the cave opened into a massive outcropping. Centered, fast asleep, was Yaleris.

His scales bore the same texture of ice, glittering in blues and subtle rainbow hues. Yet, his wings were more akin to fins than the wings of a bird, though Tallora knew he was capable of flight. When he exhaled his deep, sleepy breaths, the water around his nostrils froze and then dissolved, like a small cloud beneath the sea.

No, he was not so large as Yu'Khrall, but he was still many times larger than she and Harbinger, impossibly so. As Tallora approached the great behemoth, she contemplated what to say to a sleeping dragon.

She stole a stabilizing breath. "Hello?" she said aloud, but the dragon merely snored. Resisting the urge to giggle at so majestic a creature doing something so silly as *snoring*, Tallora tried again. "Yaleris! Hello?"

Nothing. He looked as content as a clown fish in an anemone. She turned to Harbinger. "Any ideas?"

The Onian approached cautiously. "This creature is older than the Convergence. Staggering to consider. They say dragons were created by the Old Gods, did you know?"

Tallora shook her head. "I don't know much of uplander religion."

"'Children of Chaos,' some call them, but only because of their creator." Harbinger swam toward the dragon's tail. "Keep away from his mouth."

Tallora obeyed, watching as Harbinger touched the tip of Yaleris' tail—

And suddenly, Tallora faced a great, sleepy eye—cerulean blue, glowing, and nearly her height. It blinked, the double-lidded eyelids moving a half-second apart. It opened its great mouth, its yawn more akin to a roar as it revealed massive fangs and a forked tongue.

He could have snapped Tallora up in a single bite, yet she felt no fear. When he finished, he rubbed his clawed hand—Paw? Fin?—against his eye and slowly sat up, keeping his gaze on Tallora all the while.

"Good morning." Yaleris said, and his scaled mouth pulled into a smile, revealing teeth as large as Tallora. The depth of his voice was from sheer volume—he spoke in a beautiful tenor. "I am confused but not unhappy to have company. I hope it was not too much trouble to get here."

Tallora resisted the urge to laugh at the odd words—what a darling thing! "It was no trouble at all. My name is Tallora, and Harbinger is by your tail."

Yaleris turned, visibly cautious as he sought Harbinger. "I so rarely see Onians," he said, and kindness shone in his words; Harbinger looked baffled. "You are welcome here, Harbinger." He returned his attention to Tallora. "Forgive me for being forward, but you must have come with a purpose."

"We did," Tallora replied, her smile faltering. "A great evil has come and threatens the seas—Yu'Khrall, Son of Onias." Recognition shone in the dragon's aged face. "He's destroyed Stelune. We're all refugees."

"By the Mother's Grace," he said, and perhaps it was a whisper, though it echoed across the icy walls. As he stood tall, Tallora saw, embedded in his scaled chest, a radiant blue orb, perfectly sized for her own palm. "I regret that I slept through Yu'Khrall's first rampage across the Tortalgan Sea. I presume you wish for my help?"

Tallora nodded. "You may be our only hope." Harbinger joined her, floating with absolute wonder on her face.

Yaleris offered a clawed hand, far larger than she or Harbinger. "I shall go. I shall also not abandon you in my home. You said you were refugees—where are the rest?"

"The queen has taken shelter with a number of us in the village of Iids," Tallora replied, wary of the gigantic, clawed appendage.

"You will have to direct me, but I will take you there."

Cautiously, Tallora swam to his claw, where a gentle, cool embrace engulfed her. Yaleris cradled both of them to his massive chest, and the ice before him parted as he swam to the smaller cave, the icy walls diminishing at his approach. He moved slowly, mindful of the two mortals held to his scaled body, and Tallora thought he might be the most magnificent creature in the realm.

She recalled Rulira, a corpse strung up in the Solviran Library, a dragon slain for Solvira's glory. The thought saddened her, that anyone might think there was glory to be found in murdering so majestic a being.

The ice receded as he swam, until Yaleris escaped the narrow cavern—narrow to him, at least. He looked down at his mortal wards. "Brace yourselves. Do not try to look ahead, lest you hurt your eyes. I know most of the way; I shall tell you when I need your expertise."

His gaze was so sweet for a reptilian creature of magic. Tallora obeyed and braced her head against his icy chest, the glittering scales each as large as her hand. She felt him stiffen.

He launched.

Water parted in a vortex, their speed impossible. Bubbles passed her peripheral. Tallora tucked her face away, content to let the dragon lead.

It must have been hours, of Yaleris travelling at the speed of Sha'Demoni.

When he slowed. Tallora felt her skin cease to press against his scales. The motions stopped, her stomach lurching. "Stretch, Tallora and Harbinger," Yaleris said, his hold releasing.

When Tallora looked about, the scenery held familiarity—these were the plants of home. She glanced back at the gigantic dragon serenely floating before them. In gentle strokes, his wings kept him stable. "Thank you," Tallora said, her tail grateful for the chance to move about.

Harbinger, however, rested against the sandy floor, her tentacles stretching every direction. "Agreed." Her curt word was punctuated with a groan.

Tallora swam to the dragon's head, facing an eye nearly as large as she. "What is the plan, Yaleris? Is there a way we can help?"

"I shall bring you two to safety first. I will then meet with the queen and express my goodwill. Hope is the most powerful force in the world, you know." So expressive, this reptilian creature; Yaleris' large eyes held visible regret. "I know the pain of loss, and I am so sorry for yours, Tallora. To lose your home must weigh heavily on your heart."

"I've heard you lost someone too." Tallora hesitated to speak the name, yet the peace in Yaleris' patient countenance never faded. She thought of the skeleton in the Hall of Relics. "Rulira?"

"We all felt her death, my brothers and sisters and I. I mourn her still."

"I lost my father as a little girl," Tallora replied, the pain of it never quite ebbing away. "And now I may have lost my mother; I don't know."

"I, too, lost my parents—my Mother and Father."

The Old Gods, Tallora realized.

"Losing a parent leaves a hollow that cannot be filled," Yaleris continued, sadness in is visage, "I don't know if the sorrow ever truly fades—I still miss them dearly."

Tallora's smile threatened to bring tears, but she felt she could unburden herself to this dragon without shame. "Thank you. I've lost everything these past few days."

"There is nothing that cannot be found again," he said, assurance in his ancient voice, "even if that nothing is something new. Though we lost my Mother and Father, the New Gods have shown that they care for humanity just as well. And look at you—you are alive, and there is nothing more beautiful than that." Though his smile showed large teeth, Tallora found it sweet. "Now, forgive me for moving this along, but I would like you to direct me to Iids."

"We aren't far, I think," Tallora said. "If you'll take me to the surface, I can read the stars and tell you."

Yaleris looked pleased, something soft in his gargantuan eyes. "Then let us go."

He gently took she and Harbinger in his claws and floated toward the surface, keeping an easy pace lest their necks be broken.

When they breached the surface, night air prickled against Tallora's face, though the dragon's chill was far icier. Yaleris released them—

Then he leapt from the water, the air causing tumultuous waves to slosh them around in the open sea. He flew across the night sky, stretching his wings, scales glittering in the moon's light.

Tallora saw the stars and their path, the way north visibly clear in the cloudless night. The sight brought her comfort, the stars and dragon both. *"Goddess Staella,"* she whispered, uncaring if Harbinger heard, *"bless Yaleris. Guide his hand. He is our hope for survival."*

She swore the stars twinkled just a bit brighter.

A roar suddenly *ripped* across the night sky. From Yaleris' throat tore a vicious cry, and from his mouth came a cloud of frost, dissipating in the air and gently floating down as snow.

She smiled. Hope was not lost. As Yaleris descended, Tallora heard a joyous laugh. "I forget what fun the air can be." He plopped rather ungracefully into the ocean, waves rippling all about, causing even

Tallora to tumble. "Sorry," she heard, and a clawed hand plucked her from the waves. She was lifted into the air, held to his face above the water. "Did you find your directions?"

"I did."

Yaleris held Harbinger up beside them, who looked rather uneasy in the air. "Then lead on, Tallora. Your knowledge of the stars is truly a gift."

He carefully sunk back down, and Tallora bid him to swim west. Yaleris obeyed, keeping she and Harbinger safe in his claws. He swam slowly this time— slow for the great dragon, rather—and Tallora directed him as the landscape passed.

Soon, Iids appeared.

A day had passed, and though night had since fallen, the sight of a great dragon approaching roused the populace. Yaleris stopped just outside the village, careful to test the terrain before plopping his gargantuan self down. He released Tallora and Harbinger, then looked to the villagers and refugees. "Hello," he said, a certain shyness in his tone. "I've been told of the tragedy that's befallen your people. I would like to help."

Tallora saw Queen Fauln break from the crowd, disbelief in her regal face. She placed a hand to her mouth as she gazed up, then swam toward his face. "Great Yaleris," she said, loud enough for Tallora to hear, "your presence is a wonderful omen."

Something touched Tallora's shoulder; Harbinger beckoned for her to follow. She looked to Yaleris and Fauln, locked in a conversation she realized wouldn't need her input, and followed Harbinger away.

She noticed, beyond, the eyes following them. Most of the populace gazed transfixed upon the dragon and his splendor, but a select few looked warily at Harbinger.

They swam away from the crowd, into the fields of kelp beyond. "What's going on?" Tallora asked, and Harbinger paused, contemplation visible in her expressive face.

"I will not stay here much longer. But I promised I would scry for your mother. We need a safe location."

Though invigorated by the renewed promise of Harbinger's help, the words felt like a knife—though not one meant for her. "You were instrumental in finding Yaleris. I'd speak for you. They would accept . . ."

When Harbinger shook her head, Tallora's words faded. They entered the field of kelp. "I gave up trying to integrate with merfolk a thousand years ago."

Tallora longed to argue, yet realized she'd stumbled onto something far deeper than mere politics or even kind sentiment. "For what it's worth," she replied softly, surprised when Harbinger stopped to face her, "I trust you."

A simple quirk of her lip, and Harbinger's morose dissipated by small degrees. "That is a very foolish thing to do. Now, have a seat."

Confused, Tallora watched as Harbinger sat herself down, buried entirely in kelp. She landed beside her, bringing the bend of her tail to her chest for balance.

"It will not cost you anything," Harbinger said, her tentacles floating idly, "but I will need to sift through your memories to feel your mother. I have not met her, so I need to know her as you did."

When Harbinger offered her one hand, Tallora accepted, her joy fading—now was the moment of truth. "Do whatever you need to do."

"Close your eyes. Do not fight; just breathe."

Tallora shut her eyes. Whatever cover the kelp provided, she swore the world behind her eyelids darkened. Harbinger's voice filled her head, yet they were foreign words, the same Demoni tongue she'd chanted at her home, when Kal was still free and Tallora's broken heart was merely cracked instead of shattered.

A strange coldness seeped against her skin, penetrating through to her blood and bones. She dared to peek, and nearly pulled away for the horror before her.

Harbinger's eye was wide open, yet it absorbed all light, a perfect, consuming black. Where she held Tallora's hand, black ichor stuck them together, slowly creeping in tendrils as it crawled up Tallora's body. It held her arms captive, and the cold crept to cover her shoulder, her neck—

She shut her eyes, a whimper escaping her lips as that same icy sensation coated her face.

And she saw . . . memories of joy. Of bittersweet moments. Of love.

"Tallora, darling, eat your krill! You silly, picky thing—"

"Your father, he . . . he—"

"You're much braver than my protective heart would like. I know the reef is beautiful at night, but that's when the sharks come out—"

A lifetime of moments flashed before her eyes. Years passed in her soul—

And then came a new vision of her mother's shop, as familiar to Tallora as her own home. Yet, unnatural darkness permeated the scene, rubble outside the window blocking the light. Her mother held her finger to her lips, to another figure—*figures*, Tallora realized—one of whom shushed a small, crying child—

Her eyes shot open. There was no ichor, no horror—merely Harbinger seated before her, frowning. "Harbinger, that was—"

"Your mother is alive," Harbinger confirmed, though there was no joy in the statement. "She's still in Stelune."

"We have to rescue her—"

"We?"

"We have to figure out how to sneak in," Tallora continued, an idea quickly blossoming. "You could take me. We sneak in through Sha'Demoni, grab her and the rest, and then we go."

Harbinger shook her head. "Yu'Khrall will know. He is a resident of Sha'Demoni, capable of shifting between the realms like myself, and he will smell you. Worse—he will *feel* me if I come too close. Not a confrontation I want. Your mother is safer staying put."

"There has to be something we can do."

"The risks are massive. If we want a hope to succeed, we need a distraction. Something very big. Like . . . a dragon-sized distraction, actually."

Tallora's grin appeared unbidden, and she nearly laughed at Harbinger's annoyed victory. "So we wait until Yaleris goes to fight him. Then, we go and save my mother."

Harbinger flopped backwards onto the ground, letting her body float serenely up. "I suppose we do."

For the first time in days, Tallora felt hope.

Chapter IV

Yaleris stayed among the populace of Iids for hours, resting in the sand as children marveled at his pearlescent scales. They refracted light in a thousand glittering colors, and he was patient with their antics, content to laugh with them.

When Tallora eventually approached, he smiled. "I'd wondered where you'd gone, Tallora."

She looked to the children, the little merfolk swimming circles around his leisurely floating tail. "Do you like children?"

"I do," he replied, and his tail suddenly lifted, the ensuing pulse of water leaving the children tumbling and giggling. "My Father always said to take time for the little ones. During his reign upon the realm, he walked among the people, letting kindness and mercy lead him. They loved him, and I learned from him to love them back."

"That's a beautiful story."

"Thank you." He looked to the small school of children, his scaly smile infectious. "Little ones, be careful—I'm going to set my tail down now."

They obeyed, and Yaleris gently placed his tail upon the seafloor. The children resumed their play.

Harbinger remained hidden outside the town, content to avoid attention. Alone, Tallora summoned her courage. "Yaleris, we wanted to warn you—Harbinger and I will be accompanying you to Stelune."

"Heavens, no!" With his claw beneath his chin, Yaleris' head stood taller than Tallora's body. "I cannot say what will happen, but I won't be able to protect you."

"Nor would we expect that. But Harbinger's magic has found my mother, but she's trapped in Stelune. Your fight with Yu'Khrall would be a perfect distraction for us to rescue her."

"Forgive me for being presumptuous, but I believe the purpose of me going to fight Yu'Khrall is the slay him."

"Yes," Tallora replied, fervent in her words, "but it's as you said—you can't protect me. You can't account for the further destruction of Stelune in Yu'Khrall's rage. My mother is trapped in her shop, and all it would take is one swipe of his tentacles to destroy it and her. But Harbinger and I can travel through Sha'Demoni. We need only minutes to get in and out, and with you there, Yu'Khrall won't notice us."

Yaleris' ensuing sigh held all the weight of the inevitable conflict. "All right. But I must wash my claws of your fate."

"I understand."

The dragon smiled once more. "Your bravery should be commended. To find me is no easy feat, and now you'll willingly swim into the battlefield to save your mother."

A blush filled her cheeks. "You'll give me a complex, if you keep saying words like that."

Yaleris laughed, and it lit up the whole world. His voice lowered, his eyes endlessly kind. "All my sisters and brothers have our own unique gifts—both elemental and in magic. I have always been a being of empathy, so while I don't know the details of your turmoil, I felt it the moment you touched me. There's something broken inside you. Something you must forgive yourself for. I'm simply telling you what I and the rest of the world see."

She hadn't been prepared for a touching moment. Tallora offered a broken smile. "Not all the world."

Yaleris shook his head. "I like you very much, Tallora, and I only met you a few hours ago. I'm confident your loved ones think the world of you."

Tallora thought of Kal and prayed it was true, that he might forgive her someday. She thought of her mother and her disapproval of her path but knew that love remained between them.

And finally, her thoughts settled on Dauriel, whose opinion she wished didn't matter, but though her heart remained shattered, there was still love there, somewhere.

As always, her heart dragged her down like an anchor.

"The time nears," Yaleris said, looking fondly toward Iids. "Won't you find your friend? I will carry you to Stelune."

As Stelune approached, anxiety welled in Tallora's stomach. The vision had said her mother lived, but what if her death came by Tallora's actions instead? What if their plan failed?

Tallora reminisced over the lifetime of memories she had hours ago witnessed—a lifetime of her mother sacrificing over and over for her only daughter.

She had to try.

When the edge of the valley appeared, Yaleris slowed, then softly landed on the ground. "I wish you both luck," he said, finality in the words. "I'll lure him out, and then you go."

Sadness brewed in Tallora's stomach from a source she could not quite name. "Thank you, Yaleris," she said softly, and beside her, Harbinger simply watched. "The seas don't deserve you."

"The seas are my duty, sweet Tallora. I shall find you in Iids, when this matter is done." With care to not sweep them aside with his wings, Yaleris floated up and slowly approached the edge of the valley.

"Tallora."

Startled, she turned to see Harbinger offering a hand. "We will be safer in Sha'Demoni," she continued, but then a great rumble stole their attention.

Yaleris roared as he swopped into the valley, a spray of ice bursting from his mouth. Throwing aside any notions of sanity, Tallora swam to the valley's wall and watched as the ice nearly hit Yu'Khrall in his single, massive eye—the leviathan managed to cover it in time; instead the elemental spray coated his tentacles. He shuddered and twitched, ice sealing the appendages together.

A furious cry split the sky. Yu'Khrall's tentacles broke their frozen bonds, enormous chunks of ice floating through the waters. Yaleris sprayed his icy stream, and again Yu'Khrall protected the eye at the center of his being. His tentacles flailed wildy, seeking the dragon, but Yaleris dodged with grace.

Tallora gasped when something touched her shoulder. "Go," Harbinger said, and Tallora accepted her hand.

The world shifted. Tallora saw grey. Yet, within Sha'Demoni remained shadows of Stelune and thus the titans clashing before them. They phased in and out of sight—Yu'Khrall's monstrous tentacles remained a real danger, even in the broken realm. Yaleris' ice sent shocks of light through the shadow world, and when a stray stream came toward them, Tallora ducked.

Harbinger, however, simply let the ice engulf her—and when it dissipated, she remained. "Yaleris is not in this world. Nothing he does can hurt us. But Yu'Khrall can, if he seeks us."

Beyond, Yu'Khrall unearthed himself, his tentacles stretching wide as he rose from the ground. *"You carry . . . something,"* Tallora heard his thunderous voice say. *"I want it."*

Yaleris said nothing, merely roared as he led Yu'Khrall from the valley.

Harbinger and Tallora swam. The scenery raced by at a nauseating speed, and before them were the main canals, shadowed and crushed by Yu'Khrall's power. "Lead the way," Harbinger said, and Tallora took her hand as she navigated the broken streets, watching them swoosh by with every motion.

It took time, her frustration rising as streets came and went, her control limited in this broken world. With it came sorrow, to see the destruction of the world she loved. "Harbinger, we keep going too fast. I can't find it."

Though visibly pained, Harbinger said, "All right," and suddenly all color reappeared.

Destruction and blood surrounded them, though most had filtered away into the ocean. Bodies floated serenely in the waters, those not yet claimed to satisfy Yu'Khrall's hunger—their bloated corpses welled nausea within Tallora.

Her tears came fast, until Harbinger yanked on her arm. *"Go,"* she spat, and Tallora obeyed, her motions methodical and possessed. "I will watch for Yaleris and Yu'Khrall and drag us to Sha'Demoni if needs be. You lead."

Tallora swam quickly through the winding canals, the deafening battle beyond the valley increasingly cataclysmic. But she knew these sights, even though horror lay between buildings, crushed by a monster's will.

But the shop approached. Tallora sped up, screeching when Harbinger suddenly pulled her back—

Color vanished. Light consumed them. Tallora flinched, but forced her breath to steady—there was no danger from ice here in Sha'Demoni. The battle remained in Stelune.

When the ice dissipated, color reappeared. The world returned to what she knew. Tallora spared a glance for the titans above them, watched as Yaleris tore at an ice-covered tentacle with his mouth and *ripped* it from Yu'Khrall's body.

A horrendous shriek filled the canyon, but the leviathan pushed on.

Tallora swam to the window, covered by rubble and rocks, but managed to catch sight of a few terrified figures. "Mom!" she said, and she matched eyes with a familiar woman.

Her mother swam to the window. "Tallora?!"

"We're going to rescue you. Stay there." She looked to Harbinger. "Sha'Demoni can't help us phase through walls, can it?"

"Actually, yes."

Convenient. The world shifted back into greys. Harbinger pulled her through the wall—and though it resisted, she fell through.

Immediately, the shop appeared, color restored as Harbinger released her. Tallora fell into a loving embrace. "Oh, Momma."

She heard quiet crying in her ear. "Tallora, my darling, how did you get here?"

As Tallora pulled away, she saw survivors watching their reunion—only a handful, five in all. "Mom, this is Harbinger," she said, gesturing to the witch. "She can take us through Sha'Demoni to get you out of here.'

Mother's eyes grew wide. "Sha'Demoni?"

"Trust us. But we have to hurry—we aren't safe here."

"What's going on out there? I swear I saw ice out the window."

"Mom, it's Yaleris." Understanding dawned upon her mother's face. "He's come to save us. But there's every chance we'll be destroyed while they fight, so we have to go."

Her mother beckoned for the others, but one resisted. "I'd rather take my chances here than in the demon world," a man said, disdain in his gaze as he looked at their Onian rescuer.

Vitriol rose in Tallora's throat, but Harbinger spoke first. "All right. Stay. The rest of you, hold hands."

The man seemed appalled to be dismissed, but the rest, however wary they appeared, joined in a circle, including a woman holding a small child. Tallora held Harbinger's hand as well as her mother's, keeping watch on the man until the world changed—he became simply a dark shadow in the corner.

"Hold tight," Harbinger said, and she led them slowly through the solid wall—but not so solid in the demonic plane. Once out, she said, "We must be fast; there is no telling what—"

"Yoon?"

"Damn." Harbinger looked up, as did the rest—

And staring at their small group was Yu'Khrall's massive eye, golden even in Sha'Demoni's monochromatic void. He phased out of sight—a glow of light engulfed him. Oh, thank every god for Yaleris!

"Tallora." Harbinger grabbed Tallora's shoulders, panic in her eyes. "Take them. I will find you."

"What?"

"He will look for me first. Not you. You can do it. Just wait beyond the valley for me to come."

Tallora placed a hand on Harbinger's and squeezed. She hated it so, but she knew the Onian was right. "Good luck."

"You better hope so. You will be trapped here if I die."

And with those soothing words, Harbinger darted away, tentacles pulsing.

Tallora said, "Stay in a line." She grabbed her mother's hand and pulled her and the rest along, keeping one eye on the battle high above.

Yaleris phased in and out of sight, more a shadow than a magnificent beast. Yet, Yu'Khrall remained constant, his eye fully visible though not turned to them—not yet. His tentacles flailed about erratically, toppling structures not quite destroyed in his rampage against Yaleris.

Rubble scattered through the water, some of the rocks twice Tallora's size. She gasped as she dodged the falling stone, forced to release her mother's hand.

Their formation broke amidst the falling rocks, but then one fell upon Tallora—

And moved through her. None of it existed in this world. "It can't hurt you!" she cried, then realized her great error.

That eye turned upon her. Tallora stared into a terrifying void.

A tentacle shot out to grab her. Tallora darted aside, knowing the effort was futile, but just as she felt the still water pulse, familiar hands pushed her aside—

The tentacle grabbed her mother. "Momma!" she screamed, and she caught her eye, that final glimpse not of fear no—but of relief. "Momma, no!"

Her momma disappeared among the mass of tentacles. Tallora felt nothing, numb as one of the refugees grabbed her arm and tugged her along. Even when they appeared at the edge of the canyon, Tallora stared beyond, the first of her tears welling in her eyes.

She watched a shadowy tentacle dart to a minute figure, a faint spot upon the grey palette of the world. A flash of light, and Yaleris appeared for a flickering moment, the spray of light engulfing the tentacle, perhaps saving Harbinger's life as it passed harmlessly through her. Yet, she disappeared again amidst the mass of tentacles, not grabbed but engulfed.

Tentacles surrounded Yaleris. The dragon bit at the appendages, but more wrapped around him, even as ice spread from his body. Yu'Khrall recoiled, but his sheer size—many times larger than the beloved dragon—enveloped Yaleris, and Tallora heard a cry of pain that echoed through both realms.

She stared, transfixed as Yaleris flickered in and out of sight, the mass of tentacles steadily surrounding his glowing light. "No," she whispered, pain in the word. "No—!"

A sickening *crack* sounded through the valley. Yaleris disappeared in Yu'Khrall's great mass. Tears welled in Tallora's eyes as Harbinger appeared. "Tallora, we should hurry."

She shook her head, then realized what Harbinger had slung over her shoulder, supported by her one arm—Tallora's momma, though bleeding and limp. When Tallora beckoned, Harbinger gently placed the woman into her arms. Her heart broke to see the mass of bruises on her mother's torso and the faint cloud of blood escaping her mouth, but when she placed a hand to her mother's throat, Tallora felt a faint pulse.

The world suddenly flashed with color. One by one, the refugees appeared, but Tallora hardly noticed—for beyond, a horrible red cloud spread above the ruins of Stelune. She caught glimpses of the corpse in Yu'Khrall's grasp, nauseating crunching sounds revealing his actions. Scales fell, as did bones as Yu'Khrall feasted upon his conquest.

Tallora sobbed at Yaleris' death, the gentle dragon having died to save them all. She saw Yu'Khrall pluck something from the corpse, an undeniable flash of blue and white glowing within one of his many appendages.

And she heard a voice that filled her with dread. *"What . . . is this?"*

Harbinger whispered, "We have to go, *now.*"

The Onian all but dragged her away, for Tallora's limbs were too numb to move.

Yu'Khrall had claimed the dragon's power.

Once away, Harbinger phased them back into Sha'Demoni. The trip was silent as they swam to Iids, the mood heavy. Tallora cried the entire way, her mom's body held to her chest, supported by her small arms and the water.

Despite her momma's rescue, all hope had vanished.

They returned to the mortal realm when Iids was in sight. Tallora noticed, for the first time, Harbinger's own thoughtful countenance, subtle anguish in the lines of her face. Tearful cries of relief sounded as the refugees swam ahead, some embracing other survivors, leaving only Tallora, the unconscious woman in her arms, and Harbinger. "Thank you for rescuing my momma," Tallora said softly, but the Onian glanced back toward Stelune.

"That orb," Harbinger whispered thoughtfully, "...they say its power is depthless. He will either be docile for a thousand years, or we are in deep trouble. Either way..." Something akin to rage twisted her visage. "We cannot let this stand."

"I don't disagree," Tallora said, her own exhaustion steadily seeping into her bones—emotional and physical, both. "But I don't know that there's anything more I can do." In her arms, her mother groaned. "I have to—"

"Go," Harbinger said, ushering her forward. "There is work yet to do. I need to commune with Onias."

"Be safe," Tallora said. "Thank you." She added a strange word, though not one she might've anticipated feeling toward the odd Onian witch. "...friend."

Harbinger's ensuing smile held a quiet, resigned sort of happiness. "You are welcome."

She left them, disappearing into the kelp beyond. Tallora immediately swam toward Iids, crying, "I need help! This woman needs help!"

A man she recognized as the magistrate—Gregor—immediately swam toward her, his eyes wide. "Follow me. We have healers who may be able to bandage her."

"I think it's internal," Tallora said, following as he swam.

Gregor said nothing for a moment, sorrow settling onto his features. "Then perhaps we can at least ease her pain."

The words welled dread into her stomach, and when they reached a crowded building, Gregor cried, "Adira! Come quickly!"

A mermaid with hair of spun gold approached. When she saw Tallora's mother, her kind gaze immediately turned calculating. "Who is she?"

"My momma," Tallora replied, and she didn't fight when Adira gently took her. "Is she . . ?"

"I don't know. But I will take what care of her I can."

Tallora longed to follow when Adira left, but knew there was one more task she must do. To Gregor, she said, "I need to speak to Queen Fauln."

"Follow me."

Fortunately, the queen sought her too. Within minutes, she spotted the familiar woman, her crown unmistakable. "I fear the worst," Fauln said, studying their appearance, "if only for your countenance."

And tearfully, Tallora told the queen all—of rescuing her mother and the rest, of Yaleris' terrible end, and of the orb's fate. "Not even Harbinger can say what will happen, now that Yu'Khrall has the orb."

"Who is Harbinger?" Fauln asked, her own eyes red as tears escaped into the ocean.

Tallora explained that too, the daughter of Yu'Khrall's role in this political affair and her hatred toward the leviathan. "She's a hero, much more than I am."

But the queen suddenly looked beyond her, and when Tallora followed her gaze, she saw an odd sight.

A small envoy of Onians, revealed by their distinct tentacles, approached the outer wall, a large, closed carriage pulled by sharks in their company. Tallora followed Queen Fauln to the gates of the city, two guards at her side. One of the Onians, his skin a deep, yet florescent red, approached, his tentacles undulating not unlike Harbinger's. "Greetings," he said, his subtle accent typical of the northerners. "I seek the one in charge."

"I am Queen Fauln of the Tortalgan Sea," she replied, her expression more confused than unpleasant.

The Onian bowed, his smile revealing pointed teeth. "Queen Fauln, I am Prince Rek'Thir of the Frigid Abyss. We have heard the tragedy that has befallen your people and wish to offer what aid we can. This is the first of many carriages of food and supplies, if you will accept them, donated from the people of our capital."

Tallora saw the guards beside Queen Fauln, their expressions wary, yet the queen appeared only touched. Her lip quivered as she spoke. "We would humbly accept, but we have nothing to offer in return."

"And we will accept nothing, save the promise of aid should this tragedy spread. My people speak of Yu'Khrall in a whisper; to hear of his return is a terrible omen for us all."

Queen Fauln offered a hand, which the Onian Prince accepted. "This is as much of a treaty as I can offer for now. But you have my word as queen that we shall be allies during this tragic time. When it has passed, I would happily open up discussions for further alliances between our people. I thank you for your kindness."

The carriage beyond came closer, and though many in the populace watched warily, the children's faces held only intrigue. Tallora offered her own smile to the Onians but saw there was little she could contribute. She wondered, bitterly, if they knew that it was her king who had released Yu'Khrall in the first place, if they would be as generous.

Instead, she darted back to what she assumed was a medical ward, pushing through the sea of people as she said, "I'm looking for Adira! Someone, please help!"

She was pointed to a room in the back, and there she saw her mother lying upon a stone slab with Adira inspecting her supine form. She looked up at Tallora's entrance. "She is conscious, but barely so. You should speak to her. I don't know how much time she has left."

Tallora trembled as she approached. "What do you mean?"

"Something has crushed her ribs, and they've likely punctured nearly everything within her. There's nothing I can do."

Tallora immediately grabbed her momma's hand, noting her distended stomach, the deep blossom of purple upon her abdomen and chest. Tears welled in her eyes as her momma's batted open. "Tallora?" she whispered, though it was airy and pained.

"Momma," she managed, though already sobs threatened to steal her voice. She idly noted Adira's departure and brought a hand to gently run through her momma's white and grey locks of hair. "Momma, I'm so sorry. I should have listened to you—"

A light squeeze on her hand stole her words. "Tallora, my world, this wasn't your fault."

Her mother didn't know the half of it, but the poignant words punctured a flood. Tears welled in her eyes and disappeared into the sea. "I love you."

"I love—" A cough stole her mother's words, and she cried out in agony. Blood seeped from her mouth. Tallora's fingers touched her face, her hair, providing whatever comfort she could.

"Don't try and speak." She met her momma's eyes, her lip trembling to see their fading light. Despite the days spent worrying for her mother's death, to face it felt like a knife between her ribs. "I'll just say what I know we're both thinking—that yes, I know you love me and that I promise to keep living and to live well and be happy—" Her voice choked to see her momma's soft smile. Her heart lay in broken pieces yet it seemed it could still shatter. "Give my love to papa. I . . . I'll see you again."

When her momma reached up to touch her, Tallora guided her hand, helping it to rest on her face. Momma's thumb drew soft lines upon it, her smile of infinite worth. Tallora whispered a soft prayer to their goddess, one she'd learned years ago at her father's passing:

> *Mother Staella, carry me*
> *Into your arms where I may be*
> *Safe and sleep upon your breast*
> *and take my final rest . . .*

Her momma's lips mouthed the words with her, until they suddenly stilled. The light faded. Her momma's hand became limp.

Tallora fell upon her momma's chest and wept.

Chapter V 🐚

The queen made the announcement of Yaleris' fate and proclaimed a day of mourning—for both the dragon and for the massacre on the city. She said it would be a holiday forevermore, that the tragedy and sacrifice should never be forgotten.

Patrols were sent to covertly watch the ruins of Stelune, to report on Yu'Khrall's activities. He appeared to be sleeping—and they prayed it was for a long while yet.

In the following days, more Onian aid arrived. Some lingered among the populace, helping to build shelters for the refugees. Tallora marveled at the distrust between their people, yet saw small miracles scattered about—watched children asking innocent questions about their tentacles, saw tentative friendships form, and, perhaps the oddest of all, saw the queen's eldest daughter chatter glowingly with Prince Rek'Thir.

It warmed Tallora's heart to watch, despite hers being so broken.

And so the village of Iids expanded in the following weeks. With the shock of the tragedy settling firmly into reality, Tallora adjusted well enough to her makeshift shelter—there was little time to mourn, with all the work to be done. She threw herself into this new adventure, finding moments of happiness in aiding her own. With heartbreak came a sense of purpose, even with the looming shadow of Yu'Khrall in the distance.

Harbinger had yet to return, but Tallora knew the witch lived in her own timeline. Her mind often wandered in quiet moments, dwelling upon what she'd lost. She thought of Kal; she prayed he was comfortable. She thought of King Merl and wondered if he knew the slaughter he'd brought.

She thought of her momma and wept lonely tears every night. It was foolish to think she might've fixed this, that something so simple as a mother's embrace could soothe the hurt, but perhaps it might've been a small boon. Instead, she spoke to no one.

Darkness pervaded the sea when the bells sounded. Tallora awoke with the rest, panic pulling her from deep sleep.

"Something's coming!" a voice cried. *"Return to your homes immediately!"*

Tallora peeked out her window and saw, in the center of town, a ship's anchor sink to the sandy floor. Queen Fauln approached; a guard swam down to meet her. "It's a ship from Moratham, your majesty. They wish to speak to you."

Tallora's heart seized at the statement. Whatever compulsion spurred her to act, she couldn't say, but she darted out the door of her little hut and cried, "Wait!"

Queen Fauln frowned at her approach. "Tallora?"

"My Queen, I . . ." Her voice faded as the guards held their spears forward, the threat apparent. "If you're going to meet with them, please be careful."

Visibly wary, the queen seemed to study her, searching for an explanation. "Do you think I shouldn't?"

"They aren't trustworthy. If they offer aid, you must ask what they expect in return."

Queen Fauln's frown deepened. "Forgive my tact, but your judgement on who is and who is not trustworthy has shown to be lacking."

Her curt words clearly said, *'Go away.'* Tallora simply offered a nod as the queen and her small envoy swam up to the ship.

Tallora returned to her hut. She laid upon the sandy floor and shut her eyes, refusing to consider who was on that ship and what it meant, praying it truly was only for aid.

But when she might've drifted off into sleep, there was a sharp knock on her wall. Tallora peeked her face out the window, only to see Queen Fauln herself meet her eye. "Your majesty—"

"They asked for you," the queen said from beyond the window. Tallora swore her heart skipped. "I told them you'd died in the destruction of the city."

In the oddest of ways, it was the greatest kindness she could have received. Tallora couldn't find her voice to express her gratitude . . . or fear.

"They blamed you for the betrayal at the summit," Queen Fauln continued, "and wanted to use you as leverage against Solvira. But while I think you're a naïve fool, I don't believe you are malicious, and if the time ever comes to condemn you for your crimes, it is my right—not theirs." Her frown remained, but her eyes seemed sad. "And you were right to advise me to ask their motives. They seemed keen to help, but when I asked if they would aid our Onian allies as well, they were hesitant. When I asked the price of an alliance, they wanted one of my daughters, so she could be given to Morathma to wed. If you and I see eye to eye on nothing else, surely you can understand why I would never sell my daughter to them—we are not so desperate as that. But I told them I would consider it. I also cannot afford to insult the ones offering the aid. Not yet."

Tallora slowly nodded, gratified when the queen's expression softened. "Did they say anything of Yu'Khrall?"

"They did not, and they were patronizing when I pushed the subject." Her sneer spoke volumes. Tallora understood well the frustration of dealing with Morathan nobles as a woman.

Beyond, Tallora watched the anchor's chain twitch and grow taut. It slowly rose, and Tallora frowned at the implications of Moratham's visit, as well as their request. Did they know the truth of Tallora's relationship with Dauriel?

Well, former relationship. Bitterness filled her at the thought.

Confusion furrowed Queen Fauln's brow. "They said they'd stay," she muttered, and she and Tallora both watched, mesmerized as the anchor disappeared. High above, the faint shadow of the ship steadily moved forward.

Realization stirred in Tallora's gut, sickness rising with it. "Queen Fauln, you knew of your husband's plot to release Yu'Khrall—Moratham wanted it too."

"My heart prays they would not have wanted this carnage," the queen whispered, but there was little hope in her voice.

"They did, but for Solvira. I don't think they'll mourn us, though, if Solvira still falls." With those words came a damning sort of knowledge—that this was their purpose. It must have been. "I think they're going to speak to Yu'Khrall. Our people couldn't reason with him, and so they'll try instead."

Horror steadily fell upon Queen Fauln's countenance. "I fear what that will mean for us."

"I'll go," Tallora said, the words stupid but the chance for any redemption one she must take. "I'll eavesdrop. Yu'Khrall has only one eye—it's powerful, but all I must do is hide beside Moratham's ship. I'll be safe." In theory, but she wouldn't cause any more worry than necessary. "And if they do spot me, they won't kill me—they want me to negotiate with Solvira, remember? I'll say I was with a different refugee camp. Nothing would be on your hands."

"You would risk your life for this?"

"I would. Let me help."

Queen Fauln shut her eyes, giving a slow nod. "Go. Return and report. I . . . I'll pray for your safe return."

Tallora left. There was no time to waste.

Ships travelled slowly, even in the best of weather—within minutes, Tallora caught up to the side of the sleek vessel, wondering if Moratham had any sort of armada. Though pieces of their land touched the ocean, they were not known for sea warfare. The ship appeared new and unseasoned, the wood still holding a subtle shine, no barnacles upon its hull. Tallora dove to the base and found a small handhold—a place the wood had not quite sealed together.

She held it, comfortable enough as the ship sailed along in the quiet night.

It left far too much time for speculation, for Tallora to shut her eyes and reflect on this new and dangerous life. In a twisted sort of way, at least Stelune's destruction meant she wouldn't be tried as a traitor—too much work to be done, and too few citizens left to bother punishing any, save the most dangerous and violent. Iids had a prison, but rapid reformations had led to many being freed.

They were comfortable. Their Onian neighbors had provided sustenance enough for months. Tallora lived a life of little finery, but at least she lived.

It was half a day before she recognized the scenery. They neared Stelune. The smell of rust remained in the air, and through the dissipating cloud of red was a docile monster, its golden eye nowhere in sight. Tallora swam around the ship, gasping when she realized they were laying anchor—she narrowly dodged the great iron emblem, watching as it slowly sank to the side of the canyon.

She surfaced in time to witness a miracle.

Dauriel had slain the Speaker—Morathma's host upon the world. But Morathma himself lived, for to slay a god was no easy feat, considered impossible by most. As Tallora peaked around the bow of the ship, she watched the final pieces of a transformation she understood now.

The man at the railing glowed like a brilliant star in the night, rapidly growing, translucent wings bursting from his back. He was beautiful, unbearably so, though upon the shiny sheen of his false image was the unmistakable pattern of scars, the source of his blasphemous name—*Snake God.*

This was Morathma, Jewel of the Desert, and as he rose into the sky, he enlarged by impossible degrees, larger than the slain Yaleris.

Tallora cowered behind the ship, hardly daring to breathe lest she be spotted. Gods were not omniscient, but even an unexpected ripple might reveal her presence to the powerful deity.

"Yu'Khrall," a great, booming voice said, calm and assured, yet bearing the power of thunder, *"awaken. We must speak."*

Staella, save me, Tallora silently prayed, and she pressed harder against the hull of the ship, stomach clenching at the pulsing waves below. They rose ever higher, and Tallora dug her nails into the soft wood, fighting tears as the ship nearly capsized. She swore she felt a caress upon her tail, and nearly screamed when the great monster surfaced—opposite the ship. She needn't face his eye to see the gentle undulations of his tentacles below the surface.

"I . . . was sleeping."

Yu'Khrall's voice brought dread unparalleled, but with those words, Tallora felt a surge of rage. Harbinger had said he might've slept a thousand years . . .

"I would have thought you'd slept long enough, Son of Onias."

Damn Morathma, Tallora thought. But she couldn't curse; all she could do was listen.

"You . . . are . . . Morathma."

"I am, indeed," the deity said. *"I seek your aid."*

Tallora did not have to see Yu'Khrall to feel the strange turn in the air, the intrigue radiating from his gargantuan figure. She knew it like the palms of her hands. *"Tell me."*

"The merfolk who woke you saw you as a weapon to wield and nothing more," Morathma said, and she strained to listen as his voice suddenly lowered. *"But I see you as you are, Son of Onias. I see the injustice done to you and would offer you pardon. I cannot break your curse, but if*

you will help me topple Solvira once and for all, I shall offer you all the sustenance you could ask for."

"I have sustenance . . . enough," Yu'Khrall replied. From the depths, he lifted a single tentacle; it bore Yaleris' orb. *"For now. But I do not trust your kind . . . angel."*

Hatred steeled Tallora's resolve as she gazed upon Morathma and his glory, speaking as an equal to Yu'Khrall—whose head floated well-enough outside the water, his single eye revealed to Morathma.

Morathma could have summoned a weapon to stab him, perhaps end the conflict once and for all. Instead, they negotiated, despite his genocide of Tallora's people.

"Solvira's goddess will come for you," Morathma said, and Tallora could not look away. *"She will come as she did in the time before, but I can help you—"*

"I do not fear Neoma." In Yu'Khrall's tentacle, the orb flashed. Ice spread around his tentacles, then dissipated into the water. *"If she slays me, I will have peace."*

"Forgive me, but I did not mean Neoma."

Tension rose. Tallora found it alarming how well the one-eyed beast could convey emotion without his words—she felt fear. *"She is . . . free?"*

"Ilune is free. She rules Solvira with the rest. And she will come."

"If she does . . . I shall consume her," Yu'Khrall bellowed, every word reverberating against the waves. *"I will not hesitate."*

"Let me help you," Morathma said, sincerity in his powerful voice. *"Her death is reward enough for me."*

"How?"

Morathma's gentle gaze was startling, if only for the stories Tallora had heard. He was a man of self-importance, yet believed every word he said, even if they were lies. *"I shall return with a plan. Resume your slumber and know that I shall take care of everything."*

"I will not." Below, Yu'Khrall's tentacles began swirling slowly, causing disarray upon the surface. *"It is as you said . . . I have slept for too long."*

Yu'Khrall sank below the water; Tallora, again, pressed herself against the hull, muttering silent prayers as he disappeared. The radiant light that was Morathma faded, but Tallora shut her eyes tight and prayed.

By Staella's Grace, what had she just witnessed?

The Morathan ship did not linger above Stelune, but Tallora returned home near sunrise. Darkness still blanketed the sky, but the barest hints of light shone at the horizon. Tallora hardly directed her descent, so exhausted she was. But the time to sleep was not yet.

She swam to the shelter where Queen Fauln was staying. Guards approached. "State your business."

"I was instructed by Queen Fauln to return and report. What I must say is of the highest importance."

She was told to wait as one disappeared inside the shelter. A few minutes later, Queen Fauln emerged, still regal despite the lingering sleep in her eyes. "Forgive me, but I'm surprised you returned at all."

"There was no danger. I managed to stay hidden. But listen."

Tallora told her all—of Yu'Khrall's reawakening, of Morathma's bargain, all she could remember. "I don't know what any of it means," she said.

"Nor do I," Queen Fauln muttered. "I know little of Solviran legends, but for Moratham to feed us from one hand and appease our oppressor with the other is an ill omen. But I also fear what Yu'Khrall will do, now that he's awake again. We should consider finding a safer home—"

A strange chill wafted through the water. Tallora gasped as sweeping sheets of *ice* approached the town. Screams rose; merfolk left their homes and fled. Parents clutched children, guards cried out orders, directing the flow of the panic. Tallora matched eyes with Queen Fauln and saw fear, until a guard swam up and dragged her away.

Ice spread across the landscape like approaching waves upon the shore, except it did not recede—it merely expanded. It stopped near the walls but spread all about, a great sea of death surrounding them.

And far away, Tallora saw a great shadow approach.

It needn't hurry.

The monster had come.

Tallora dared to glance back—a single tentacle descended upon the village. She darted for a wall, prepared to press against it should the leviathan strike. High above, Yu'Khrall's shadow blocked the night sky. *"I seek . . . your king."* The crowd continued screaming and flailing as they sought escape. A second tentacle landed outside the village. *"Cease this recklessness. Bring out your king . . . lest I crush you."*

A third tentacle landed. High above, a great eye gazed down like a second sun.

To Tallora's horror, the queen approached. She swam up from the safety of the crowd and came alone toward the behemoth. "Yu'Khrall, I am Queen Fauln. My husband is a captive of Solvira, so I shall speak in his stead."

"You shall do." Yu'Khrall's voice boomed across the sky—some people still fled, but Tallora stared transfixed at the queen, close enough to be heard, yet high in the sea. *"I have been . . . contemplative. I was freed to be a weapon, or so I was told. For what purpose?"*

Below, the panic had yet to quell. Queen Fauln floated tall, regal even in the face of death. "My husband thought you might protect us from Solvira."

"And what do you think?"

"I think he was mistaken."

Yu'Khrall was silent for a time, long enough for Tallora's blood to run cold. *"We can . . . negotiate those terms."*

Fauln visibly hesitated. "If you can swear that no more blood shall be spilled, we may speak."

"I shall consider it . . . if you accept my own terms."

"And what are those?"

One of Yu'Khrall's tentacles slowly came toward the queen, menacing for its sheer size. Within it, Tallora realized, was the dragon's orb. *"I must gather power . . . as much as possible. Pledge to me. I shall be your god. And when Solvira comes, I shall destroy them."*

Queen Fauln stared into that great eye, fear in her stance. "Let me discuss it with my populace. My advisors. I would grant you no unwilling worshippers, Yu'Khrall."

Yu'Khrall's voice rumbled against Tallora's very soul. *"I shall return upon the morrow at this time."*

Yu'Khrall withdrew his tentacles from the ground. He floated away like a stormcloud, his threat leaving a weight of dread upon the town.

Order was called for. Tallora remained by the wall, not calm but certainly not so frantic as the populace. By Staella's Grace—when had her life become this hell? Trembling, she sat herself upon the ground, resorting to the only hope she had left—she clasped her hands in prayer.

Tallora had prayed a hundred times since losing her home, yet a whisper in her soul said to speak the words again. "Goddess Staella," she whispered, recalling the goddess' visage, the benevolence of her love, "we are truly in our darkest hour. I have nothing to offer save my devotion, but I and my people beg for a blessing. We beg for your aid."

She paused, searching her soul for what words to say, when something soft whispered in her ear: *"Open your eyes."*

Tallora gasped, recoiling when she saw Harbinger inches from her ear. "A warning next time, please?"

"Little time for anything anymore." Bitterness stained every word from her tongue; Harbinger's bloodshot, golden eye was nothing less than crazed. "I spoke to Onias."

As one did. Tallora waited, gut churning.

"I meditated for a month. All I was told was one sentence: *'My word is law, forever and always.'* I do not know what that means."

Tallora's heart sunk. "But why?"

"I do not know! We have been abandoned by the gods, but we do not need them. We can change our own fate."

Harbinger trembled, and Tallora couldn't say whether she was about to scream or sob. "What are you proposing?"

"There is only one force in the realm with the naval power to fight Yu'Khrall. Solvira's arsenal of ships is the largest in the world."

Harbinger's words fell together in scattered pieces, forming a plan Tallora's stomach sickened to contemplate. "You want me to go to Solvira?"

"I do. Consider it my final gift to you."

Tallora shook her head; Harbinger's glare could melt a glacier. "I can't. Solvira won't listen—"

"Fuck your empress. Yu'Khrall is a threat to the entire world. With the power of the orb, do you think the uplanders will be safe? He seeks to be a god, if that display showed us nothing else. I am happy to damn myself to stop it, but I need your help. Solvira will at least listen long enough to understand the threat, and they will stand from their pompous asses to help."

"What are you proposing?" Tallora said, but Harbinger shook her head.

Instead, she offered a hand. "I have one last spell in me. I will tell you on the way to my home."

Lip trembling, Tallora limbs numbed. "I shouldn't. I can't. I ruined everything the last time I tried to—"

"I am not in the business of accepting no in the face of the apocalypse. I will kidnap you, so kindly come peacefully."

Tallora saw nothing but steel in Harbinger's one eye. When she accepted the Onian's hand, they shifted into Sha'Demoni's ambient chill.

"Where are we going?" Tallora asked, managing to match Harbinger's hastened speed.

"My home."

The journey would take no time at all; not at She'Demoni's pace. "Will you explain yourself, please?" Tallora swam faster, catching the Onian's eye. "What does 'one last spell' even mean?"

Harbinger continued her relentless pace. "It is a powerful spell. You'll be able to change back and forth—when fully submerged or fully out of the water."

"And what is the cost?" Tallora asked, fearing the answer.

"Nothing. Not for you."

Hardly reassuring. "What are you going to do?"

"I am not going to die."

And she said little else. Tallora had to rush to keep up.

Soon, the great cave appeared. Harbinger grabbed Tallora, color saturating the world. "Hurry," she said, and as she moved the cave illuminated in her presence, no touch required, it seemed.

Tallora still marveled at the sight, this time prepared for the approaching shadow of the beast. A shark appeared, unnaturally large, and Harbinger approached with pouted lips. "Kra'Tir, my love," she said, her hand caressing the nose of the gargantuan shark. "Will you help us?"

They each gripped the shark's fin as it bolted through the cave.

The expansive passage opened into an enormous antechamber, the glowing sconces upon the wall casting surreal light upon the small home in the center. The second shark came to welcome its partner, and Tallora smiled at their interaction, but it quickly faded when Harbinger joined them, her eye swollen and teary as she placed her hands upon them. "Defend my home," she whispered, placing kisses on their noses. "You will see me again."

"Harbinger," Tallora said, but the Onian ignored her, instead leaving her beloved guardians and bolting toward her home. Tallora followed. "Harbinger, what is going on?"

Tallora entered the home, finding it as disarrayed as before, the organized chaos hurting her mind. Drak'Thon, the little octopus, watched from the countertop, its one eye following its witch companion. Harbinger grabbed a small basket and began stuffing it with supplies—food, a few scarves, money—which she handed to Tallora. "Take these with you. The scarves will suffice well enough for clothing until you can find a tailor." She reached out and stroked Tallora's white hair, then plucked a single strand. "One more for the cauldron—"

"Harbinger!" Tallora cried, and the Onian finally stilled, her golden eye fixated upon her. "Tell me what's going on."

"The price for your transformation is a life. And so I shall give up a lifetime."

Silence settled between them. Tallora's knuckles went stark white around the basket's handle. "What?"

"I am immortal." Harbinger's word held a poignancy Tallora couldn't yet fathom. "And so to lay down my life would be too much. But I can sleep for as long—the price is a hundred years. Onias shall shelter me."

"You . . ." The word died in her throat. Tallora swallowed and forced the rest. "You can't."

"I cannot sacrifice a few years for the chance to save the sea? Do not look at me as a hero. I am a coward who does not want to touch this."

"Don't say that," Tallora pled. Harbinger's stare held a challenge, one Tallora knew she couldn't fight. "You don't have to do this. I can give you a memory, and I'll—"

"I mean it. I do not want this."

Harbinger tore her gaze away. She placed the strand of hair into the cauldron, then frantically gathered supplies from her shelves and threw them into the cauldron, no apparent method to her madness.

"You are the hero, Tallora," Harbinger said, her focus clearly elsewhere. With care, she beckoned to Drak'Thon, the tiny octopus, and placed him on her shoulder. "Perhaps not foreordained, but certainly blessed with all the potential. I am simply a woman who has seen this fall apart before. I am not on the side of good; I am afraid."

Tallora set the basket down and carefully approached, uncertain of the feeling welling in her chest. "You may not see it," she said softly, unsure if the witch even heard, "but there is goodness inside you. This sacrifice isn't cowardice—it's the part you can play, for the greater good."

Harbinger did slow, lingering as she held what appeared to be a blood red gemstone above the cauldron. "You hardly know me."

"Perhaps not." It was true, Tallora realized—Harbinger had lived for several millennia. Their friendship was but a drop in the bucket of her life. "But it doesn't mean I don't see your heart. You pretend to not care, but you care very deeply. Otherwise, you'd simply hide away, protected by Onias."

Harbinger's lip twitched, and Tallora couldn't say if it were for a smile or for tears. "Stay back. Do not look down."

Harbinger released the gem, letting it fall into the cauldron's mass.

A great explosion rocked the cave. From the cauldron emitted what appeared as a florescent, yellow flame, though they were beneath the sea. Tallora pressed herself against the wall of Harbinger's home as the Onian opened her mouth to sing.

Her lips formed guttural tones in the language Tallora had come to know as Demoni. Shadows rose, the world growing dark as the lines between worlds blurred. Brighter and brighter, the cauldron shone, the world's gravity gently pulled inside.

Harbinger's voice grew louder and louder, emanating not only from her but from the walls, then from the cave itself. A thunderous tone joined with her words, shaking Tallora to her core—something deep and dark and from below.

The walls of the home faded away, flickering in and out of sight. The world fell into a surreal, hazy mass, color desaturating as Harbinger suddenly screamed. Her chanting ended, but the thunderous voice did not.

Below, a great void opened. At the peripheral of her vision was a swirling, eldritch mass, undulating amidst a sea of black ichor. Light radiated from the center, but Tallora stared only at Harbinger, her voice having faded, her body falling limp.

She gently rocked back, eye closed as she slowly sunk down into the depths. Drak'Thon shut its eye, as limp as she. Tallora watched her descend, then caught a glimpse of hell.

Below, the void beckoned, welcoming her to join. The wailing of a thousand lost souls echoed eternal, a siren call to her senses. In the center was not a pupil, no, but a white and blinding light, radiating a wickedness that sickened her to her very soul. It seemed endless, boundless, this mass of horror.

To stare upon Onias was to descend into madness. Tallora cried out as she covered her eyes, even as a surreal touch brushed against her skin.

"You have lost so much," it whispered, but Tallora merely whimpered. *"I can protect you. Join me; forget your pain."*

He asked a question; she managed an answer. "No."

The world became quiet.

Tallora opened her eyes. She floated in Harbinger's home. All was calm.

Chapter VI

It took six days to swim to Solvira. She thought often of Harbinger and her one hundred years of sleep. She offered nightly prayers for the witch's soul, wondering if it were appropriate at all, given Onias' claim to it.

His vision haunted her dreams; she wondered if she had seen too much or was merely afraid.

A thousand times, she envisioned her confrontation with Dauriel, imagined the monarch upon her throne of glass. She spoke to herself, screaming alone into the sea at her imaginary empress, preparing her speech, ending with a plea.

It was night when Tallora finally peeked her head above the lake. The water's surface glittered in the moon's light, her own skin luminous, manifesting like her distant, angelic progenitors. Freezing cold whipped across her face, and upon the ground was ice—but gentle, a lush flurry. It brought memories of Yaleris and his cruel demise; Tallora swallowed fresh tears.

Beyond, the Glass Palace stood as a beacon against the night sky, brilliant and bright. She had never seen it at night—not like this, with the moon and stars overhead, shining as a symbol of strength.

Solvira was strong. Tallora prayed it was strong enough to save them.

In the distance were the remains of the amphitheater, but the darkness obscured the details. She swam to the lake's shore, lingering doubt manifesting as she pulled herself out of the water—

Familiar pain tore through her tailfin. Tallora shut her eyes, breathing through her distress, knowing it was temporary. Still, she cried, tears streaming down her face as a hot knife split her tail in two.

And when it faded, there were her legs. Uneasy, she tested them, finding her balance. From the basket, she withdrew Harbinger's offered scarves, wrapping one around her waist and tying it like the nets in her mother's shop. It clung to her legs, waterlogged and dripping, long enough to brush her toes. The other scarf soon covered her breasts, and though the patterns were strange, she would at least be allowed through the city's gates.

She held no fear save the bitter cold as she walked through the field toward Neolan. Though she shivered, an odd, resigned peace settled within her as she navigated the castle town. She had accepted, a second time, that she would never see Dauriel again, yet here she walked tall toward the palace. Somewhere in her mind, she wondered how she would fare facing her, but the world held greater problems than her shattered heart. Her bare feet ached against the icy stone, yet perhaps her lineage offered protection—she froze and yet did not. She passed the clothier by.

Let this business be done with. Her heart ached, but not for longing.

Before the great palace, Tallora saw two guards at their post. As she approached, she thought of her lie. "Good evening, sirs," she said politely, forcing charm into her smile. "I am Lady Stelune of . . . the Theocracy of Sol Kareena. I come seeking your general—"

"Aren't you that mermaid girl?"

Dammit. He did look familiar, now that she stared. "You must be mistaken."

The guard looked to his friend. "Doesn't she look like that mermaid who tried to break into the castle?"

The second guard frowned as he studied Tallora. "Are you?"

"If I say yes, will you let me in?"

"Aye, if you can tell me your name."

Tallora frowned, suspicious at this unexpected turn. "Tallora of Stelune, a resident of the Tortalgan Sea."

"You can pass."

Taken aback, Tallora stood her ground, skeptical as she said, "I can?"

"False mermaids are still prohibited." He looked down to her bare feet, her scattered scales easily visible. "But you match the proper description."

"Thank you," she replied, though she kept glancing back until she stepped indoors, wary of this odd reception.

The castle slept at night. Tallora wandered winding, empty halls. Surely there were patrols, servants rushing to prepare the next day's meals, but she walked alone, her path lit by sconces on the ornate walls. Her feet, numb from the cold, tapped softly against the stone. The lift was useless to her. Instead, she found the stairs.

Soon, carpeted steps cushioned her feet, plush and cozy. It seemed her thighs held the strength of her tail; though they burned, she never faltered. Instead, she recited her speech in her head, wondering idly if Dauriel would simply throw her out.

I don't care what we are. I don't care what you've done.

Bitterness rose within her. Dauriel's betrayal stung like grains of sand in her lungs.

This isn't about me. This is about the world.

Tallora's world, yes. But soon the rest. Soon Solvira with it.

If you don't act, your people will be destroyed—just like mine.

She stopped partway up, curiosity pulling at her mind. A window revealed an outdoor enclosure within the palace, and Tallora knew it like a stain upon a white sheet.

She left the staircase and wandered the familiar hall. The menagerie awaited.

Already, she saw her quarry, visible from the door as she stepped upon the outdoor stone. She passed cages of beasts, though a few were gone, including the odd insect who had clicked to hide her steps, all those months ago.

Before her was the enormous tank, the water serene—its inhabitants fast asleep behind the screen of kelp. Tallora glanced back, then pressed her hand against the water, disrupting the peaceful scene. "Kal?" she said, and thank every god—one of the figures stirred. "Kal!"

She nearly sobbed for relief—approaching within the water was her beloved friend, his mop of navy hair long enough to cover his ears. "Tallora?" he said, a smile spreading across his face. "Tallora, what are you doing here?"

"So much has happened, Kal." She pushed her arm through the magic wall, water enveloping her as she clasped Kal's hand in greeting. "Harbinger sent me. A horrible tragedy has befallen Stelune, and Solvira may be our only hope."

Worry marred the beautiful boy's face. "What do you mean?"

"They freed the leviathan." She hesitated to speak of it all—there was no time. "I can explain the details later. Your mother and sisters are safe, but Yu'Khrall destroyed Stelune. Almost everyone is dead."

It wounded her, to watch Kal's eyes as his heart broke in two. "Stelune is . . ?"

"It's gone. Harbinger and I went to find Yaleris, but . . ." Her eyes filled with tears at the memory, the kind dragon and his horrible scream. "He's dead. Yu'Khrall murdered him and stole his orb. Now Yu'Khrall seeks our pledges so that he might become a god. I'm here to beg Solvira's aid. We're already defeated."

Kal glanced back to the second sleeping figure, his own lip trembling. "I'll tell my father when he awakens. It's better he hears it from me than you."

Tallora nodded as she squeezed Kal's hand and released. "Are they treating you well?"

"It's boring, but we're fed and protected."

Regret welled in her stomach, but she swallowed her tears, finally daring to speak her heart. "Kal, I'm so sorry. I swear to you, I thought she was—"

"I know, I know," he replied, his smile undeservedly kind. "We were both tricked."

"Dauriel let me go after what happened at the summit. I made it clear I wouldn't be seeing her again—" Her voice failed, but she forced herself to press on. She clenched her fists. "Have you seen her?"

"Not since the summit."

Tallora nodded, her soul heavy at the task ahead. "What of the war?"

"I don't know anything," Kal replied, regret on his tongue, "except that their troops marched forward the day of the summit."

"Morathma came to the ocean," Tallora whispered, heart seizing at the memory. "He's making a bargain with Yu'Khrall. We were right—they have no interest in helping us. As soon as we fell, they forgot us." Tallora looked back to the door. "I should go. But I swear I'll visit again unless they throw me out." She forced a smile, but Kal's faded.

"Good luck," he said, his shattered hope returning to his eyes.

Tallora left him, resisting the urge to weep.

Here in the palace, it was so easy to forget that home was broken. Exhaustion weighed down her steps. She returned to the stairs, climbing upward until familiarity slowed her.

She knew this hall. The journey to the corridor housing Dauriel's suite felt like a thousand miles, but perhaps the empress wouldn't be there at all. Perhaps she busied herself in a study, or the library. Perhaps she trained with the general late into the night.

Yet Tallora hoped. Was she a fool to want to join Dauriel in bed? Not for sex; for comfort, for normalcy, for stability amidst the storm of her life. Her heart ached for reasons far deeper than their severance, but she had to be strong—even if the longing for a hug threatened to bring her to tears.

An ornate door stood before Tallora. She knocked, then recalled it merely led to a hallway. She twisted the knob, surprised to find it unlocked, and wondered at the blatant oversight in security.

Something odd met her ears. Something her stomach knew to sicken for before her mind could comprehend it. She took the two steps needed to traverse the small hall, the bathroom beside her, the bedroom door slightly ajar, and peeked inside.

She saw Dauriel, saw her face twisted in soft ecstasy as she knelt behind a naked woman—whose riotous pleasure had surely been what Tallora had heard. But they weren't alone. Before them, two tangled women were caught in their own lovemaking, in perfect view of the empress for her salacious tastes. The vision etched itself into Tallora's mind as she stood, frozen before the appalling scene, until Dauriel's eyes snapped open and met her own.

All pleasure faded from her countenance, replaced by horror unbound. "Tallora?"

Dauriel removed herself from the woman, struggled to step out of whatever odd device she wore at her hips, but Tallora wished to see none of it. Shock numbed her—from the cold, from her quest, from the riotous scene. She left, steps hurried as she returned to the hallway.

"Tallora!"

The desperation was reminiscent of a time long past, back when Tallora had loved Dauriel with all her heart. But she continued on her way, appall fueling her.

Soon, hurried footsteps approached. "Tallora, wait!"

Tallora stopped, and Dauriel appeared, a maroon robe wrapped around her naked body, a faint sheen of sweat at her brow. Her hair had grown in their time apart, longer in its masculine style, unmaintained, and Tallora swore she smelled alcohol on her breath. Shame colored Dauriel's visage, those silver eyes visibly struggling to meet her own.

They stared a moment. Tallora smiled curtly. "Seems you've returned to your old habits."

Dauriel said nothing. There was no magnificence in her stance, no pride.

"But don't worry. I'm not mad. I really can't be, given I have no sway on your life."

Dauriel blinked a moment too long, her eyes downcast as she said, "What are you doing here?"

"I'm half frozen to death and would like to sleep." Tallora's grin held by mere strings, certain her ire was apparent. "You seem busy, anyway. Wouldn't want to disturb you. But I'd like to request an audience with your council tomorrow."

"Come with me," Dauriel said softly. With stiffness in her steps, her stance straightened, the false airs of her station returning. Her shame hid behind a curtain of steel, and Tallora wondered at that.

She wondered a great many things, but they were quiet compared to her anger.

Dauriel led her to a bedroom Tallora remembered from long ago, the one designated as hers during her captivity, when Dauriel had slept on the floor beside her. Clean and sparse, it seemed maintained, but before Tallora could march inside and slam the door, Dauriel's words gave her pause. "I'm sorry."

Tallora's smile returned, only slightly less bitter than before. "Apology not necessary. I told you I'm not mad, remember?"

Dauriel's false pride visibly withered. She met Tallora's gaze, her hair nearly covering those silver eyes. "You didn't need to see that."

"No, I didn't. Though her tits were very nice. Better than mine, you think?" Dauriel looked like she'd been punched—a sight Tallora had seen—and her anger surged, crueler words escaping her tongue. "There are bigger problems in the world than your pride. Some of us have been through hell while you've rotted away in your nest of whores, and if you had an ounce of fucking empathy, you'd realize that my world doesn't revolve around you!"

She slammed the door. Pity looked horrendous on Dauriel, and Tallora couldn't stand to look at her.

Furious tears rose and seeped from her eyes. Tallora stalked toward the bed, resisting the urge to scream as her fists beat upon the mattress.

That arrogant *bitch!* Her audacity to apologize wounded Tallora most of all, and once enough time had passed she grabbed the pillow and screamed into it, letting the sound muffle her fury.

She shouldn't care. She didn't care! But Dauriel did as Dauriel would, all the pleasures of the world at her disposal while the rest of them burned.

"Fine," Tallora whispered, her angry tears still streaming freely. "Fill your callused heart with whores, you bastard."

She lay in bed, but her heart thumped too rapidly to sleep. She tossed and turned, her mind racing, replaying the image of Dauriel doing . . . whatever the hell she was doing with that girl. Tallora wasn't the jealous sort, but *gods* it had hurt—

It had hurt. Tallora was hurting.

She swallowed her tears, letting the bitter truth wash over her. Damn Dauriel. Damn her and her callused heart, for Tallora so dearly wanted it. Wanted it still.

Sleep would evade her a while longer, she knew. Tallora sat up, her clothing sticky from the lake's water, but though robes surely waited in the cupboards, she would accept no kindness—not yet.

She left the room. Kal had uplifted her during her last heartbreak. She resolved to find him and speak of joy. What little there was left, at least.

Her silent steps were but a whisper in the hallway. As she approached the staircase, she heard a muffled voice.

And then a quiet sob.

The door beside her led to a study. When Tallora peeked beyond the doorframe, she recognized General Khastra seated upon a couch, her hand placed upon the back of a weeping figure, faced away from the door.

Dauriel wore her same robe. In her broken stance, she cried into her hands. Tallora looked to Khastra, watched as the general met her eye but said nothing—Tallora quickly shook her head and slowly backed away.

Tallora returned to her room. She shut the door. Her own tears had long ago dried, yet she felt empty, as though she'd cried an ocean's worth.

Damn Dauriel. Damn her for letting her life fall apart.

Chapter VII

Tallora awoke to daylight blinding her through the cracked curtains and a knock at the door.

She roused herself from bed, exhaustion tugging at her eyelids from days of travel, and answered the door.

A maidservant stood there, a folded pile of clothing in her hands. "These are for you," she said, offering Tallora the bundle. "You've been invited to attend breakfast in half an hour, though you also have the option to eat in your bedroom, should you wish it."

Tallora recognized this clothing, the patterns and soft fabrics evoking old memories. "I'll be there. Thank you."

"Will you need help dressing, my lady?"

Humbling herself, Tallora nodded. The maidservant stood quietly as Tallora placed the offered clothing onto the bed and she knew it all—these were her dresses, gifted by Dauriel. She'd worn them in her final weeks in Solvira, leading to the coronation—on top was the coronation gown itself, white and gold.

Curious above all, though, was the dress she'd worn on her last visit with Kal. It had been cleaned and pressed, like the rest, yet the scent held lingering traces of something she knew—it smelled of Dauriel and her bed.

It was precisely the sort of sentimental thing she would do, to hug Tallora's dress as she tried to sleep.

She chose the coronation gown, having adored it those many months ago, and allowed the servant to help tie her into the cumbersome pieces. Content with how her hair had dried, she brushed it alone in the washroom, admiring the luxurious waves. Dauriel loved it, once sprinkling compliments like kisses.

Tallora placed the brush down, staring at her reflection in the mirror. Whatever grime coated her soul, she looked beautiful. Dauriel would think so too, and she wished she could revel in that, but discomfort brewed to remember the lewd vision of the night before. No, she shouldn't care; she couldn't care; they weren't together and so Tallora reserved no opinion on who Dauriel fucked.

Tallora swallowed a sudden rise in grief. A month ago, she had held the whole world—a marriage proposal, a future, a home, a momma who loved her . . .

Now she'd lost everything.

Soon enough, she left her room, annoyed at how the dress swooshed around her legs. She held her head high as she traversed the majestic hallways, contemplating the life she could have lived within its walls, the future she'd swum away from. The castle was a beautiful cage, and Tallora knew she'd die if she chained herself to its walls.

She descended the stairs. When she reached the dining hall, she lingered before the door, taking a steadying breath before twisting the knob.

She could face Dauriel.

Within, there was no Dauriel, but there was her father and Khastra, Magister Adrael and the rest of the council. Seated beside Prince Ilaeri was a little boy Tallora had only seen a handful of times, but Eniah Solviraes was unmistakable with his silver eyes and charming smile. No older than six, he waved as she entered. "Hello, Mermaid!"

Tallora opened her mouth to reply, but Ilaeri leaned into his son's ear and whispered something. The little boy straightened his posture and looked back to Tallora. "Hello, Tallora!" he said instead, and Tallora actually managed to smile.

"Hello, Eniah," she said, taking the empty seat across from him—and next to Khastra, thankfully.

"Hello, Mermaid," the demonic general said, far taller than Tallora, even seated. She gave no indication that she'd seen her the night before, though those glowing eyes were difficult to decipher. "I trust you slept well."

"As well as I could. I was too tired to sleep properly. I travelled for some time to come here."

Ilaeri smiled politely as he ruffled his son's hair. "Priestess Toria has spoken of unrest beneath the seas. Rumors of a monster. Is that why you've come?"

Servants filtered in, each carrying trays of food. Tallora's mouth watered at the delicious smells. "Yes," she said, shamelessly piling her plate once the food was set. She spared a glance for the priestess in question—the lovely woman sat at the other end of the table, kindness in her eyes as she met Tallora's gaze.

"Let her eat first," Khastra said, waving off the prince. "She is half-starved."

Grateful to the general, Tallora ate, content to listen to their banter. They spoke of the war, of their recent victory in the city of Ablom, and Tallora sickened to hear it. Instead, she savored the tiny, bready cakes on her plate and topped them with fruit as Dauriel had once taught, her stomach crying out for joy at each bite.

The door opened. Dauriel stepped inside, a magnificent cape sweeping behind her. Though her eyes held dark circles, she wore an embroidered black ensemble, and Tallora silently cursed her and her attractive self and that gods-damned cape. The last time they'd sat here, Dauriel had touched her beneath the table, and Tallora's body was keen to remember that.

Dauriel sat in the throne at the end of the table, unfortunately adjacent to Tallora. But she wouldn't meet her eye, instead beckoning to a servant. "Wine."

She smelled faintly of alcohol, and Tallora wondered if it were lingering from the previous night. Judging by her temperament, perhaps she hadn't stopped drinking at all.

Dauriel didn't touch the food, nor say hello. When her wine arrived, a mild sneer twisted her lip as she brought the goblet to her mouth.

The conversation resumed, with Ilaeri and Adrael debating the merits of trying to rehabilitate the displaced Morathan slaves while Khastra merely watched with some perturb. Dauriel kept to herself, and when her wine glass emptied, a servant came to refill it. No one acknowledged that Tallora's friend was held captive just a floor away.

When her stomach had filled, the delicious scents of breakfast no longer quite so enticing, Tallora politely cleared her throat. "Excuse me." Everyone's attention turned to her—including Dauriel's. "I'd like to discuss why I'm here, please." Tallora slowly stood up, too anxious to sit and give her speech. She gripped the top of her chair, daring to face Solvira's council. "Whatever you've heard, it's a thousand times worse. A leviathan has come and destroyed Stelune." No one reacted save for Khastra, whose subtle twitching frown suggested she understood. "Countless people are dead. My home was a city of thousands, and nearly all were eaten by the monster—Yu'Khrall, Son of Onias."

A hush fell upon the council—not of horror, no, but intrigue. "I went to find Yaleris, the dragon beneath the sea, to plead for him to save us. And he listened. He came to fight Yu'Khrall—" Oh, the wound was still so fresh. Tallora swallowed her sorrow. ". . . and perished. Yu'Khrall has the orb he wielded."

Tallora looked to Khastra, the one who actually understood. "Harbinger—*Yoon*—knew how to free Yu'Khrall. That's what she was trying to prevent, but . . ." She hesitated to speak the truth, unsure what the council knew. ". . . they found the way."

"What about your mother?"

Wounded at the question, Tallora turned toward the tentative voice—to Dauriel, who sipped at her wine. "She sleeps with the rest of the dead," she replied, forcibly stoic as she swallowed her pain.

Dauriel's stare lingered as she nodded, and Tallora said, "Yu'Khrall is a threat to the whole world. When I left, his new agenda was to force what remained of my people to pledge to him as a god. He won't stop there. The Onians will surely be next. Once he learns how to wield Yaleris' orb, the lands won't be safe either. I'm here to plead for Solvira's help—your navy is the most powerful in the world. You could fight him."

"If we do this—" Ilaeri's smile widened, a wicked glint in his eye. "—Solvira will keep the orb as payment."

"Fine," Tallora said, though it surely meant Solvira would rule the seas next. "There's more. Morathma himself came to speak to Yu'Khrall. He told Yu'Khrall he would help protect him from from Ilune."

Tallora didn't understand what it meant, and neither did a decent assortment of people at the table— Dauriel among them. But Khastra frowned, as did Rel, Ilune's priest. "It is not a simple thing, to kill Yu'Khrall," Khastra said. "That is why Neoma was called, years ago, to put him down."

"What would you suggest, General?" Ilaeri asked.

"I would suggest we not be arrogant. I am willing to prepare the armada, but not before we have a plan. There is also the matter of the continuing conflict in Moratham. We should consider a temporary ceasefire, given the gravity of the situation. We pretend we know nothing of their god colluding with the leviathan."

"My queen told the Morathan ship I was dead," Tallora said. "They won't suspect I'm here."

Dauriel spoke, more assured in her words. "Priestess Greyva, when we've concluded, commune with Neoma. See what wisdom she would grant us."

At the far end of the table, Priestess Greyva nodded.

"We will help," Dauriel said, calculation in her steel gaze, and the stability of her words was admirable, given her subtle slurring. "Your witch is correct—we have the greatest armada in the world. Neoma fought him an eon ago, and so it shall be Solvira's duty to stop him once more."

"Mermaid," Khastra said, "where has Yu'Khrall settled?"

"Last I saw, he had come to Iids. I don't know if he stayed."

Khastra sat back, muttering to herself about *'knots'* and *'distance'* and *'better get those damn repairs started.'*

"We shall have an official meeting this evening," Dauriel said, sipping her wine glass—now half-empty. "Father, alert Tanill that we need the ships inspected and put into good repair. Rel and Toria, send prayers to your respective goddesses—seek their wisdom as well." She stood from her throne, swaying as she escaped the table. "I adjourn this meeting. I will see you all after dinner."

And Dauriel left, wine glass still in hand. Tallora glowered at her exit, her own petulance growing.

Khastra said, "This matter will take time to resolve—must we get you back to the ocean before nightfall?"

Tallora shook her head. "Harbinger cast a spell so I could transform between being a mermaid and a human as necessary."

"A valuable gift."

"She paid a high price. A lifetime—for her, sleep for a hundred years."

Khastra merely laughed, much to Tallora's shock. "A high price for someone like you. I would love a one-hundred-year nap."

Tallora forced a smile at Khastra's enthusiasm, though the sacrifice still felt high.

"Mermaid, come with me," Khastra said, standing from the table. "I would discuss logistics with you."

She offered a hand, which Tallora accepted. With her stomach content for the first time in weeks, she followed Khastra from the dining room.

Once in the hallway, the general idly led them outdoors. The chill was far less in the morning light, the sun having melted any frost upon the ground, revealing the well-treaded earth and the corpses of plants not yet consumed. It saddened her, though she knew it was only temporary. "I've never seen winter," she whispered. "Not like this."

"It is the way of the world," Khastra replied, the jewel tones of her skin in stark contrast to the near monochromatic outdoors. "All things must die, but in death there is rebirth."

The words might've been hopeful, but Tallora thought only of her loss and felt sorrow. "There's only rebirth if there's something left," she whispered, but stopped when Khastra's large hand settled on her shoulder.

"I apologize. I am the Bringer of War, and thus a purveyor of death, but never a proponent of genocide." There was something odd in her glowing eyes—usually so unreadable—yet Tallora saw regret. "This business with Yu'Khrall is distasteful, even to me."

"Thank you," Tallora replied, a question welling in her mind. "Khastra, why does Yu'Khrall fear Ilune?"

Khastra's sorrow faded into stoicism. "Ilune fought him before."

"She lost, though." When Khastra said nothing, Tallora wrapped her arms around herself, wishing she had more layers in the frigid morning. "Did you ever speak to Ilune about freeing Yu'Khrall? You told Harbinger you would."

Khastra nodded, her next words swift and terse. "She said nothing of merit."

Tallora braced herself for her next inquiry, knowing it could be considered a blaspheme. "Do you think she might've lied?"

"No, she was honest about withholding the truth." Tallora balked at that, even as Khastra's steps paused, her hooves leaving distinctive marks behind her in the dirty snow. "Mermaid, tell me everything you know. I know where Stelune is, but where else has Yu'Khrall gone? What has he done? No information is too obsolete."

Tallora recited every vague detail she could recall as they walked through the expansive garden.

She spoke of Iids; she spoke of the destruction of Stelune—and Khastra listened, asking clinical questions regarding the death toll and the dragon's demise.

Which . . . she seemed especially enthused by. At least, by the battle itself. "I resent Yu'Khrall for having the chance to fight a dragon."

"I'll be honest," Tallora said, bitterness in the words, "I'd have rather not watched Yaleris be eaten."

"Oh, barbaric, assuredly." Something wistful overtook her elegant features, her glowing eyes distant. "But a story to tell."

Tallora decided to simply let the matter go.

She spoke instead of the orb, of Yu'Khrall's apparent fascination with it. "Well now he's learning to wield it, whatever it truly is," Tallora said, after describing the creeping ice.

"Do you not know of the Convergence Orbs?" Khastra asked, and when Tallora shook her head, she frowned thoughtfully. Tallora realized she knew so little of the demon-blooded general, no idea of her age or history. "They were created by the Old Gods and given to dragons to help in protecting and directing the ways of the world. There are six in all, and each bear their own unique power. Some say the power is depthless. This bespeaks consequences I fear we cannot foresee."

Tallora thought of the dragon skeleton in the Hall of Relics and of Dauriel's idle mention of its power stored elsewhere. "Was it a mistake, then? To call Yaleris for aid?"

Khastra shook her head. "The sea was his realm. You did precisely as you should. Though we do have a far larger problem now because of it."

Tallora spoke of Harbinger's cryptic message from Onias: *"'My word is law, forever and always.'*—I have no idea what that means."

"Let me contemplate it," Khastra replied, calculation in the words. "But please, keep speaking. You are helpful."

The morning passed as Tallora continued her account—of Moratham's bargain with Queen Fauln, and her verbatim account of Morathma and Yu'Khrall's exchange. Only once the sun hung directly above did she run out of words to say. "If I think of anything more, I'll tell you, but I think that's everything."

They stood at a far corner of the garden, well out of earshot and sight. Khastra studied a tree with no leaves, her mind clearly far away. "I shall consider what you've said, Mermaid. And I shall be studying more of Yu'Khrall's legend in the library. I regret to tell you that warfare rarely moves quickly—the war in Moratham continues, but it has been made complicated. I need only a few soldiers for the armada, thankfully—and only those who specialize in harpoons. But supplies will risk running out. And I must be present for both, at least in spirit." A sneer twisted her lip. "I despise sea warfare. I will not be stepping onto any ships. I can lead perfectly well from the shore."

A strange dismissal, from a renowned general. "Good to know," Tallora said, an amused smile at her lip.

"I know what is down there. Onias would not touch me for fear of starting a war with my mother, but it does not mean I wish to come near his realm. You saw a glimpse, and you are lucky to not have fallen into his abyss. They call it Onias' Hell for a reason."

Tallora recalled the dread that had permeated her soul and nodded.

"But even with the promise of immunity, I would not join. I cannot swim. I have hooves; I do not swim."

Except, even aside from the inherently humorous issue that her hooves would present, Khastra didn't say 'hooves.' Her accent apparently prevented it. She pronounced it *'hoofs,'* and Tallora had to bite her lip and look away to not burst into giggles.

Who was she to tell the daughter of a demon goddess that she had hilariously mispronounced as silly a word as 'hooves?'

"Mermaid, do you plan to tell Dauriel that you saw her crying, or can I breathe easy?"

Tallora returned her attention to Khastra, the impulse to laugh entirely squashed. "I . . ." She shook her head. "No. I wasn't planning on speaking with her any more than necessary."

Khastra nodded, contemplative as she continued her leisurely steps through the garden. The crisp air had warmed during their walk, the chill almost pleasant. "That would be best, unfortunately."

"And what does that mean?"

Oh, she hadn't meant to sound quite so defensive. Khastra raised an eyebrow, her steps stopping entirely. "I will tell you, but know that it is a betrayal to her trust in me to do so."

Tallora nodded, but not for a desire to help, if she were honest—truthfully, it was her inner gossip.

"Over the years, I have done everything I can to impart wisdom into her, to teach her discipline and honor and steer her away from the paths of her progenitors. When you left her to return to your home months ago, she held sorrow, but she was not defeated. I had hope that she would heal and move on." Khastra looked to the ground, an odd stance for the proud half-demon to take. "I should not tell you this, but on the day we captured your king, Dauriel disappeared. When I searched for her that night, I found her on the tallest tower of the castle, weeping as she drank from her bottle. I stayed with her and coaxed her inside because I truly feared she would jump."

It hurt, and fresh bitterness rose in Tallora's heart. To feel pity for the Empress of Solvira was not why she'd come here.

"I may be overthinking," Khastra continued, a sudden distance to her tone. "But it is a fear that haunts me. I am certain you know that Dauriel has tried to take her own life before. Perhaps she told you that I found her bleeding out. It was one of the more harrowing moments of my life, to hold someone I see as a daughter in my arms and know she is dying. She lived, and it is a miracle, but my greatest fear now is that I am too late, and I find her on the ground instead of the roof."

Khastra was not one to speak idly of anything, but she held no reservation about her sorrow—and though she did not cry, Tallora saw subtle anguish.

The general was silent a moment, the winter air as stagnant as she. When she did speak, it held resignation. "And so while I disapprove of her regressing back into paying women for their bodies, at least I have the peace of mind of knowing she is not alone at night."

"She is unwell," Khastra continued, her hooves slowly digging into the rocky ground. "I have watched generations of Solviran Royalty succumb to the madness of their bloodline, and I fear this is the beginning. She is a fool, yes. She is a belligerent, frustrating woman who lets her passions become her undoing. But I made her my responsibility years ago. I love her very much, and I beg you to leave her alone."

Tallora followed Khastra's gaze to the highest tower of the castle, glittering in the sunlight, but surely daunting at night.

"I do not mean to ignore her. I simply mean to leave her be. Consider it a kindness to me and not to her." Exhaustion weighed down Khastra's gaze, age showing in her ancient eyes.

"If she provokes me," Tallora said, "I can't say what will come out of my mouth. But somehow . . ." She remembered the shame in Dauriel's countenance and sighed. "I don't think she would. I can be cordial."

Khastra's expression visibly lightened. "Thank you, Mermaid."

They continued their pace, and Khastra spoke of kinder things as she led her back to the castle. "I have much to prepare, but I can say with assurance that you are allowed wherever you would like to go. You are a guest."

"Thank you, General," Tallora said, but as they approached the entrance to the castle, she realized someone waited.

Tallora did not know Priestess Toria well, only that they shared a mutual goddess, and so it surprised her when the beautiful woman stole her hands in her own. "Tallora, I wanted to speak to you," she said, sparing Khastra only a glance as she walked away. She wore her blonde hair in a messy sort of bun, dotted with tiny, dried flowers, the disheveled look endearing on her ethereal, ageless face. "Staella has been distant, and I fear it is from grief. I don't doubt she weeps for her and Tortalga's people. I know I do."

"Thank you," Tallora said softly, finding only sincerity in Toria's lovely features. "It's been difficult."

"And the story of Morathma coming to speak to Yu'Khrall—unbelievable." Toria shook her head, and only then did she release Tallora's hands. "There aren't nearly so many followers of Staella here as there are for Neoma, but I wanted you to know that you aren't alone here, and if you need to speak to someone who might offer comfort, you can always come to me."

"I appreciate that."

"Won't you follow me a moment? It's nearly lunch, and I thought we could share the time together."

Tallora agreed, relieved to not have to be alone.

Chapter VIII

Priestess Toria took Tallora to a private room in a high tower of the castle.

An expansive window covered a wall from floor to ceiling, offering her a view of the world without the price of winter's chill. A sheet of white covered the rooftops far below, but the city bustled all the same, little dots of people going about their day. The city extended far, barely ending at the horizon, though the outer rings seemed darker, even from her tower.

But more mesmerizing than even that was a small section of the room blocked from the sun by a curtain. Tallora saw a white bat hanging from a beam, presumably fast asleep. Goddess Staella gave bats to her uplander priestesses, and Tallora found them adorable.

"I've heard so much about you," Toria said, interrupting Tallora's staring. Lunch had been provided, and Tallora joined her at a small table. "When I first came to work at the castle, Magister Adrael told me the story of the mermaid who was stolen from the seas. What a harrowing experience. You're very strong, to have continued on."

Tallora poked the provided meat with her fork, uncertain of the species, but the small slab was dark and gamey, seeping delicious juices as she cut. "I've let go of my anger," she said, then sighed as she realized her lie. "Mostly. Regarding my kidnapping, yes. But there's plenty more to be frustrated about."

"I was appalled at Solvira's behavior at the so-called peace summit," Toria replied, her own plate filled with an identical slab of meat, as well as plants Tallora still didn't know the name of. "Only a select few members of the council knew of the eminent betrayal—perhaps they thought, as an Acolyte of Staella, that I would disapprove. They were right, of course; my goddess abhors conflict. She longs for peace."

Tallora sat back in her chair, wounded at the memory. The fresh sting of betrayal struck her. "It was awful."

"Tell me," Toria said, her smile as kind as the first glittering stars at night. "I'm trained in wounds of the heart and mind—perhaps I could help."

Tallora had spoken so little of it. She set down her utensils, knowing there was only so much she could say, even now. "I trusted Dauriel," she whispered, quickly swallowing the emotion those words wrought. "And she used me."

"The Solviraes have always been tempestuous," Toria replied. "I knew this when I accepted my position in the castle. I'd hoped I might do some good. But, keep going."

"I don't know how much they told you," Tallora continued, wrapping her arms around herself, "but Dauriel and I . . ." She shut her eyes and released a heavy sigh. "We were dear to each other. We . . . And please tell no one, because it was never spoken of, but we had wanted to marry." Her nails dug into her arms, staunching her threatened tears. "I couldn't accept. Not after what she did. She was born to be an empress, but I wasn't born to be an empress consort. My heart can't take the cost. So I ended it."

Silence lingered a moment before Toria's words gently interrupted it. "Empress Dauriel is a lost soul. Staella loves her, because Staella loves everyone, but that doesn't dismiss what she's done—and most especially what she's done to you. You must feel conflicted."

Tallora nodded.

"Staella believes in mercy, but she does not believe in being stepped on. I think you've done a brave thing, returning here to plead for help. A selfless thing. And forgive me if I'm overstepping, but I don't believe you've ever fully healed from everything Solvira did to you. Perhaps you've offered forgiveness, but you still hurt."

"You're probably right," Tallora whispered.

Toria offered a hand, and Tallora accepted, finding comfort in the familiar gesture. "Your mind is clouded, but it is never too late to find peace. Will you be returning home or staying in Solvira?"

"I'm not sure yet."

"Perhaps you might find peace among your own kind," Toria suggested. "I'm told you were close to the merfolk prince—perhaps some time spent in his company would do you well."

Tallora's smile came unbidden. "I do adore him."

"Look at you—you're glowing," the priestess said, a soft sort of joy in her countenance. "A bit of healing already."

"Honestly, he might benefit from talking to you too, if you're allowed," Tallora said, recalling his heartbreak when she'd told him the news. "He's pledged to Tortalga, but we've both just lost our home."

"Empress Dauriel has said nothing of it, so I shall make it a priority. You can tell me of that too, if you'd like."

Tallora fought to hide her sudden rise of anguish. "I've never felt so lost in my entire life. Just a few weeks ago, I had everything I could have ever wanted. I love my home, but now all I can think about is that awful cloud of blood—" She cut off her words when tears prickled in her eyes. Steeling herself, she said stiffly, "And my mom. She wasn't eaten by the monster; she died in my arms. I don't know which of my friends are dead or alive, except for Kal, who's a prisoner of war. And I know it's for the best that I left Dauriel. I hate what she's done. But I'm hurting, and I know she's hurting, and between you and me, I'm worried she'll do something to . . . to hurt herself." She couldn't speak her true fear aloud, the reality that Dauriel had always sought a great escape. Her tears fell, and she struggled to not collapse into sobs. "And it doesn't matter if we aren't together; I don't want her dead."

When Priestess Toria stood and knelt beside her, Tallora embraced her and wept in the priestess' arms. The last person she'd held was her dying momma . . . and oh what a sadness that was, to have no one. But Toria held her with all the kindness of her calling, and Tallora felt comfort for the first time in weeks.

"Tallora of Stelune, you are a brave and wonderful woman," the priestess whispered, "and Goddess Staella loves you. You haven't lost everything; you will always have her to lean on, no matter how dark your world becomes. She knows all your sorrows and will take them upon herself if you let her."

The words were not flippant; Tallora cherished them and their truth. She remained in the embrace for a time, and Toria did not rush her, merely let her cry. When she did finally pull away, the priestess smiled and said, "You'll come to the temple with me sometime, won't you? I think it would do you well to be around others who believe as we do."

Tallora nodded, touched at the offer. "I was training to be a priestess before Solvira kidnapped me. I lost my way for a while, but perhaps that's what I need to pursue again. My vestments are gone in the destruction of my home but . . ."

Sorrow filled her at the thought, to have lost something so precious.

"I think your home could use someone like you," Toria affirmed, and Tallora felt she truly meant it. "We write stories and songs of warriors and heroes, yet what becomes of the world when the wars end? The world needs mothers. The world needs healers. The tragedy of Yu'Khrall will pass, and when peace comes again, Stelune will need Priestesses of Staella to remind them where their humanity lies. Our calling is one of healing, and those who've known pain often become the best healers. You will be a great source of good."

"Thank you," Tallora replied, and for the first time she felt the mantle's full weight, what her lost vestments truly represented.

Perhaps as a frivolous youth, she had taken it for granted, but now it was a blessing, a purpose.

The future was dark, yet now a small light shone.

"Solvira said they would help?"

In the menagerie, Tallora found comfort and normalcy with Kal. After a nap in her room, she counted down the time to her official meeting with the council. "They did," she replied, and behind Kal was a rather surly sight.

King Merl hadn't smiled since she'd shown up. "But for the price of the water orb? They'll own us, all the same."

"Better them than Yu'Khrall—which, I do seem to recall is largely your fault."

King Merl's countenance darkened. "You wanted us in Solvira's grasp all along—"

Kal swam to float between them. "Father, Tallora—we're all angry. But we're our only allies here, so let's try and be polite. No use placing blame when the matter is already done with. We have to focus on solutions, and Tallora's is a good one."

"I simply want to know where her loyalties lie," Merl said, his frown ever-present, "given she seems to know a suspicious amount."

Tallora's fury rose, but Kal stared at his father alone now. "Stop provoking her. She came all the way here to try and save us. I'm just as guilty as she is in trusting Solvira, so if you need someone to blame, pick me. Please." He returned his attention to Tallora, ignoring his grimacing progenitor. "If there's anything at all we can do to help, tell them we'll do it."

"I will. And I'll be certain you're kept informed."

"Good luck."

Tallora left them, pretending to not hear Merl's muttered anger behind her back.

She ran quickly down the staircase, mildly winded when she reached the council chamber on the first floor. She was early, she knew, but better to be so than late—

Except, as Tallora opened the large double doors, there was Dauriel alone in the center, in the chair where Vahla had once sat. They matched eyes, and Tallora realized it was too late to back away.

Instead, she shut the doors as quietly as possible, taking a moment too long to admire the floor—black stone that sparkled in the light—and then the ceiling, which seemed to expand infinitely upward into an abyss.

Realistically, she didn't have a designated seat at the crescent moon table, but the impending awkwardness of standing silently before Dauriel quickly became too much. She sat herself at an end seat.

Every breath she took sounded like a tidal wave in the unnatural silence. She wondered if some spell had been utilized to prevent eavesdropping, but before she could contemplate that further, she noticed Dauriel watching her from the reflection in the shined table.

Tallora glanced to the Solviran monarch, who quickly diverted her eyes. Seated at the table, Dauriel kept a proud stance, despite the half-empty bottle between her thighs.

Rage certainly still boiled somewhere in Tallora's soul, but pity won out today, for the empress who held the world and yet had nothing. Now, it was Tallora who stared, who studied the false pride in Dauriel's posture. Her silver eyes held steel, yet her hands trembled as she gripped the bottle.

Dauriel caught her eye, and Tallora didn't bother to look away. Desperate to fill the silence, she said the least inflammatory thing she could summon. "I learned something today."

Dauriel's frown held no anger. "Did you?" she asked, hesitant and soft and oddly pronounced—likely trying not to slur.

"Khastra's afraid of water."

The frown at Dauriel's lip twisted into an unwilling smile. "It's because of her *'hoofs.'*"

Tallora snorted as a precursor to her giggling. *"Hoofs,"* she repeated, and Dauriel joined her in their tentative laughter.

The door opened. Their laughter immediately ceased as the aforementioned water-averse general entered, followed by Ilaeri and Adrael. Khastra spared a curious glance for Tallora and Dauriel but said nothing, merely took a seat between them, though Tallora suspected it wasn't personal—it was simply the largest chair in the room, clearly designated for her.

Thank Staella for Ilaeri and his incessant chattering. He filled the daunting silence with appall regarding a recent Theocracy diplomat's behavior, and Tallora felt free to merely exist instead of engage.

Priestess Toria soon joined them, offering Tallora a quick smile as she sat at the opposite end of the crescent moon table. Priest Rel followed shortly afterward, and when Neoma's priestess finally entered, Dauriel said, "Greyva, were you successful in communing with Neoma?"

An accidental stand-off occurred. Greyva eyed Tallora and her seat, who, in her infinite anxiety, misunderstood for a few seconds too long. Tallora awkwardly stood up, quickly stepping aside as Greyva wordlessly took her rightful place. "Empress Dauriel, I'm afraid—"

"Did I watch you disrespect my guest?"

Greyva stuttered, visibly taken aback. "S-She was in my seat. It was surely an accident but—"

Her words ceased when Dauriel stood quickly enough to tip her chair. "And now you would disrespect me with your justification?" She held the bottle in her hand, her steps the only sound as she walked to the end of the crescent moon. Tallora watched, horrified when Dauriel sat upon the table before Greyva, an unquestionable threat in her gaze. "Did you, or did you not *disrespect my fucking guest?!*"

Her cry echoed across the high ceilings. Light shone from her mouth, and Tallora knew it was fire. Khastra twitched in her seat.

Greyva's wide eyes held genuine fear as she dared to meet Dauriel's. She whispered, as skittish as a hermit crab, "Yes."

A *crash* sounded when Dauriel threw her bottle against the wall. Wine splattered, flecks of it managing to land on Tallora's dress, leaving deep stains. She hardly noticed, however—she swore her heart had stopped.

"I ought to sack you, you sorry cunt!" she screamed, and Greyva sunk lower in her seat, terror in her visage. "You'll give up your seat, and you'll kneel on the *fucking ground—"*

"Dauriel," Khastra said, and Tallora knew it was a warning.

"Go!"

Greyva accomplished a rather impressive feat, managing to slip out of her chair without standing and risking coming closer to the unhinged empress. She stumbled back, trembling as she walked backwards around the table, maintaining careful eye-contact as she stood before the council. Dauriel pointed at the ground; Greyva promptly knelt.

"Now, please," she said, spreading her arms wide, bravado in every word and gesture, "enlighten us with your bad news."

Greyva kept her gaze to the ground, fists bunching into her dress. "Neoma wouldn't speak to—"

"Look at me!"

Greyva obeyed, eyes snapping up. "She would only speak to you."

"See? That wasn't so difficult." She smiled as she looked to Tallora, her gaze withering and bloodshot. "Tallora, please, have a seat."

Tallora looked to Greyva, the urge to comfort the poor woman nearly stronger than her compulsion to rip this stranger of an empress to shreds. Neither impulse won. Instead, she glared as she took her seat, prepared to rain hell if Dauriel dared turn her ire onto her.

Dauriel looked to her council, all of whom were apparently as shocked as Tallora. "Anyone else?"

"I spent the afternoon in the war room, writing out a plan," Khastra said, withdrawing a scroll. "If you have finished your tantrum, I would happily explain it."

Dauriel's smile twitched. "Khastra, spare me the lecture."

"For now." Khastra unraveled her scroll, launching into her speech before Dauriel could retaliate.

As the half-demon spoke—jargon Tallora couldn't hope to understand—Tallora looked to Dauriel, who leaned against the wall beside her toppled throne. She appeared to listen to her general's words, even asking questions as appropriate, but a weighty mood lingered.

Tallora understood one wrenching piece—the ships would set sail in four days.

She wondered if this had been the nature of Vahla's rule, or if Dauriel Solviraes would become her own sort of tyrant. She looked to Greyva, the priestess' gaze back to the floor as she knelt, her hands clasped in what Tallora suspected might be silent prayer.

Half an hour passed, at least. Khastra rolled up her scroll. "So, with permission, I would send word to begin assembling supplies. It is only a few day's journey, so less food. More room for harpoons and men to shoot them."

"I'll write the edict myself," Ilaeri said, "if you can select the men."

"We will have to work quickly. As for Moratham, this is terribly inconvenient timing." Khastra exhaled a long breath, her frown permanently etched, it seemed. "You received another message. Greyva was able to remove the enchantment sealing it shut. General Shiblon of Moratham still wishes to speak."

"And I shall continue to ignore him," Dauriel replied. She straightened her stance, standing from her place at the wall. Greyva remained on the floor. "I think that concludes our meeting, then. Flitter on your way, please. I'll be off at the temple."

With swaying steps, Dauriel left, and Khastra followed quickly after. Tallora, however, went to Greyva, offering a hand as she stood. "Are you all right?"

Though she accepted, Greyva withdrew her hand quicker than polite. "I'm fine," she snapped, but then she looked to the door where Dauriel had left and visibly cringed. "I'm fine," she repeated, subdued this time. "Thank you for your concern."

Tallora summoned a nod and saw herself out.

In the hallway, she heard the unmistakable cadence of General Khastra's angry whisper from around the corner. Tallora crept closer, her vindictive heart curious to hear the inevitable reprimand.

". . . think you can go see Neoma in this state? She will have you thrown out."

"I'm the empress. I can do anything—"

"She is a goddess, and you are a drunk child. She will strike you down for insolence." Tallora heard a quick scuffle. "Come with me."

She heard footsteps and dared to follow, recalling both Dauriel's meltdown and Khastra's warning from before, to be gentle to the unraveling empress. Perhaps Khastra was exempt from her own rules.

They quickly ended up outside, for which Tallora was grateful—even in her white, albeit stained dress, the darkness would cover her. She paused in the door, however, grabbing the skirt of the garment and sparing a moment to inspect the stains, crestfallen to realize it was ruined.

She swallowed the emotion it brought, heartbroken to see the reminder of a glowing memory tarnished. She had stood at Dauriel's side, the symbolic gesture still beyond her own comprehension, but it had meant *something*. But now, with the dress splattered in deep red, she worried she might forget the joy of the night.

Would all her memories of Dauriel of disappear, doomed to be replaced by the brute seated on the throne? Tallora's skirt fell; her quarry was far ahead.

She followed them to the training ground, where the door had not quite shut. *"Get up!"*

"What in Onias' Hell are you—"

"You want to fight? Fight me!"

Tallora peeked through the door, aghast to watch Khastra throw Dauriel's weapons at her feet, her own sword aloft. "You are a coward, picking a fight with a vulnerable woman—prove you have a spine!"

Dauriel barely reached the general's sternum, and Tallora saw genuine fear flash in the empress' silver eyes. With trembling, gloved hands, she removed her cape, letting it fall into the dirt, and maintained eye-contact as she bent over to pick up her double blades. "Khastra—"

Khastra swung her weapon toward Dauriel's neck, a blow the empress barely parried. Tallora cringed with each blow—Khastra intended to kill, from the looks of it and the panicked defense of her protégé. Silver flame rose to cover Dauriel's swords, yet she could not come near the enormous half-demon and her longsword. When she ducked, Khastra brought her weapon down; when she came close, Khastra kicked her to the ground.

In the dirt, Dauriel spat blood, but when Khastra's moon-cast shadow covered her, she rolled aside before the half-demon could decapitate her. But she'd lost her swords, and Tallora watched her focus turn inward, waiting for Khastra to swing before she ran in and leapt—

And, by every god—she managed to grab Khastra by the neck, her own weight toppling the general. Khastra dropped her sword. On the ground, Dauriel screamed as she delivered punch after punch to Khastra's jaw, before she was thrown aside, landing with an audible thump in the dirt.

And though Khastra soon loomed over her, Dauriel didn't stand. Instead, she remained on her hands and knees, crying out as she beat against the dirt, silver flame rising, growing brighter, brighter—

Until, like a match, it extinguished. Dauriel devolved into agonized sobs. Khastra knelt and pulled her into her arms, holding Dauriel's head to her chest as she wept.

Khastra rocked her like a child, speaking gentle words amidst Dauriel's cries. "I will not leave you alone tonight. You will sleep in my room."

Tallora stepped back, knowing she had witnessed enough, and far more than she should have. Her soul felt raw from the display, her mind racing as she returned.

Oh, Dauriel—the mad woman of the castle, her lineage dooming her to a lifetime of brutality. Tallora knew she shouldn't pity her, yet her heart ached all the same.

Damn Dauriel. Tallora had cried enough for her, yet when she was alone in her room, she shed silent tears. Once, she had prayed for Dauriel's comfort and sanity—perhaps it had fallen onto deaf ears instead.

Or perhaps Dauriel had simply been doomed from the start.

Chapter IX

Tallora couldn't sleep, and so she wandered. The halls of the castle were too silent, yet to speak to Kal felt too loud. Tallora instead entered Solvira's Great Library, content among the quiet ambience of scholars. The sweeping walls and high windows would forever be magnificent, the knowledge harbored within perhaps limitless. She peered at figures high above, supported by lifts or ladders, admiring their contentment among the books and scrolls.

She thought of her people; she thought of all that was lost, their unwritten history vanishing with the tongues of the elderly fallen.

Sadness threatened to consume her. She left the main area, instead disappearing into a familiar hall leading to a room that filled her soul with dread for more reasons than one.

She shrunk before the ancient dragon skeleton displayed upon the ceiling, the memory of Yaleris' death too raw. At least his gruesome death meant he would never be shown off like some lifeless puppet. A hollow victory, that.

This was Rulira, and Yaleris had spoken fondly of her. The Solviraes had the orb she had once wielded, locked somewhere away. She recalled his sorrow at her death and wondered if his brothers and sisters felt the same for his. Would they care enough to try and save the world from Yu'Khrall or would they remain in their secret caves, content to let the world drown for its crimes?

Did they even know?

Upon the wall was the ancient mural of Yu'Khrall, but the great eye at the center was nothing to its living counterpart. Still, Tallora stood before it, hatred filling her as she contemplated what this monster had stolen—and for nothing, save a sick appetite.

She shut her eyes, tears filling them as she remembered her mother and their parting words. Tallora had been helpless to save her, at best able to sing a few hollow praises to their goddess as her spirit had slipped away into the Beyond.

Oh, to hold her one more time, to be held. They had been everything to the other for so long. *"Goddess Staella,"* Tallora whispered, for her soul was not too jaded to pray, *"I hope this is your will. I didn't know what else to do."*

The first of her tears fell as quiet footsteps filled the room. Tallora quickly wiped her cheeks, unwilling to cry in front of a stranger, when a familiar voice said, "I thought I saw you here."

Gasping, Tallora turned and saw a beloved face. "Mithal?"

Lady Mithal Redwood, the madam of the courtesans, wore elegant robes of silk with cascading hair of sunlight spilling down the front. The elven woman embraced her warmly when she approached. "A little bird told me that the mermaid had returned once more."

"I'm sorry I didn't come see you yet," Tallora said, but she saw no ire on Mithal's elegant face.

"You've been busy." If she saw any evidence of sorrow of Tallora's face, she was kind enough to not comment. "My condolences, for your loss. I know the pain of losing your home to a monster—years ago, The Scourge of the Sun Elves destroyed my village across the sea. And the world doesn't care. I know that pain too. I'm here if you ever tire of speaking to two-faced politicians seeking to profit from your heartbreak."

Tallora had wondered why an elf would be so far away from her home. She offered a grief-stricken smile. "I can always count on you to know every bit of information going through this castle."

"It's the unspoken responsibility of my job." Mithal's smile matched Tallora's—sincere, yes, but filled with sadness. "And my utmost sympathies for the death of your mother. Strange, how one tragedy among a thousand can sting the worst."

Tallora wiped the threatened tears from her eyes. "Did you also lose your mother?"

Mithal gently shook her head. "Instead, on the ship from Zauleen to Solvira, my daughter succumbed to illness. I had to bury her at sea."

"I'm so sorry."

"It was years and years ago—well before you were born. I haven't forgotten, but I have moved forward."

Tallora wondered if she would someday be able to do the same. Time had been a morass these past several weeks. "Thank you," Tallora said softly. "It's like you said—the tragedy feels so far away, and no one here can begin to fathom it. Solvira has agreed to help, but I may very well be handing the seas to them in return. I don't believe there's another choice, though."

"Solvira has always had aspirations to own the world, or so I was told once I came here. But across the sea, we'd hardly heard of them. The world is far larger than any one of us realize—larger than the ambitions of warmongering rulers and greater than even the tragedy beneath the Tortalgan Sea. I don't say that to belittle it. I mean only that you did what you must for the moment—there is balance in all things, and fate has a way to right it, in the end."

A small bit of comfort filled her heart. "Thank you."

"Solvira's gods have fought Yu'Khrall twice before. Perhaps they shall help once again."

As Tallora gazed about the Hall of Relics, saw artwork and artifacts as ancient and priceless as Solvira itself, she realized how little she truly knew of it all. "I hope so. I'm told Yu'Khrall defeated Ilune, and now with an orb . . ." Anxiety stole her words, her hope a candle facing a flood. "Perhaps if she returns, she'll actually kill him this time."

"That would spark a nasty war."

"I don't care," Tallora spat, bitterness staining the words. "He's killed so many. I don't understand why Neoma even cares to appease Onias."

"Walk with me," Mithal said, and Tallora obeyed, content to leave behind the filth the room brought to her soul. "There's more to that story than I think you know."

Mithal led her to the library's main sector, then detoured toward a staircase leading down into the endless pit of books. "You don't read well," the elf continued, apparently keen to remember every piece of Tallora's life—which she couldn't say was a comfort or disconcerting, "but there are children's books with illustrations that might suit your ability."

Tallora found the thought amusing, and when Mithal led her to the first of the descending floors, she was surrounded by a small sea of shelves. It felt secluded, save for the balcony behind them leading into the great pit. Her eyes skimmed the tomes, spotting the occasional familiar word, until Mithal withdrew one particularly ragged book—the cover peeled, the pages had yellowed, but Mithal led them to a table and gently opened it.

When she said nothing, Tallora squinted as she stared at the title page. "G-God of Death," she read aloud, pride filling her at her success.

"What do you know of Ilune?"

Tallora shook her head. "Almost nothing."

"There are a thousand mysteries surrounding Ilune and her legacy. She is the founder of Solvira and birthed the first emperor nearly four millennia ago, yet she has never revealed the child's father. She may be its most powerful goddess yet resides in the shadow of her mothers. But unlike the other gods of Celestière, she doesn't need a host to manifest upon our world; she is a necromancer and can possess and mold any corpse to suit her angelic body. It's how she got her masculine title. Morathma hates her, and he mocked her for her habit of possessing corpses of every species and gender. When he called her the God of Death, she embraced it to spite him.

"I am loyal to Sol Kareena," Mithal continued, "but Ilune is a goddess of great interest to me, if only for her ruthless endeavors." She carefully turned the brittle pages of the book, revealing more illustrations and words written in large text.

Tallora gazed upon the visage before her, finding it familiar to the likeness she saw in the temple. Ilune was beautiful, and here she held an infant child with the first hints of fire around its form. She looked at the caption and stammered, "The Con . . . *Conception* of a Kingdom."

"Very good," Mithal said, and then she turned the page again.

Tallora frowned at the next, for it showed Ilune standing before a demonic beast, monstrous and yet familiar in subtle, undeniable ways—the horns, the tattoos, all of it she had seen before. "Who is that?" she asked, and Mithal tapped one of the phrases in the caption. *"Bringer of War.* But that's not Khastra. It's . . . beastly."

"It is. Her blood powers allow her to turn into a great monster."

Tallora thought of Yu'Khrall, also the child of a god, and wondered if Khastra could fight him on her own. Perhaps not, because of her *hoofs.*

"Ilune bargained with the Bringer of War to come to Solvira, offered her glory and a legacy greater than she could dream of in Ku'Shya's court. She has been with Solvira ever since."

Tallora contemplated that as Mithal turned several pages, curious to know what would coerce a being like Khastra to pledge loyalty to anything. But Mithal revealed a daunting image—of Yu'Khrall, or something like him, facing the God of Death in all her glory. "People don't talk about grand defeats," Mithal said, "They talk about victory, and so very few know the story. It's said Ilune sought to slay him before he was a threat, but for reasons that are a mystery. She failed, and so she cursed him.”

“Cursed him?”

“Cursed him with an insatiable hunger. A fitting curse for a necromancer to place—no matter what he consumes, he will always be plagued with starvation. Some say it drove him to madness, and thus his rampage upon the sea.”

“And that’s when Neoma came?” At Mithal’s affirmative nod, Tallora said, “But why? Why would Ilune do that?”

Mithal shook her head. “Another of those godly mysteries we mere mortals aren’t privy to know.”

As Tallora gazed upon Ilune’s glorious image, she recalled the glee the God of Death had taken in stealing Vahla’s soul. Whatever morality she claimed, it held very different rules than Tallora’s. Perhaps she saw life from a higher plane, but perhaps it was merely the same brutal ambition as her progeny—for she was Dauriel’s ancestor, just as much as Neoma.

She remembered the dread she’d felt at Ilune’s gaze and knew it did not stem from good. She recalled what Khastra had said—that Ilune knew of the plot to free Yu’Khrall and had said nothing.

“It’s getting late,” Mithal said kindly. She shut the picture book. “Should I leave you?”

“If it isn’t too much trouble,” Tallora said, “I’d actually prefer the company. I won’t be sleeping.”

Mithal smiled knowingly. They spoke of happier things well into the night.

Chapter X

Dauriel was not at breakfast, for which Tallora was relieved. She heard nothing of the empress until afterward, when she approached the menagerie. A servant came to say her presence had been requested in the council room. Kal and Merl could wait, she supposed—Tallora obeyed, hiking up her skirts as she stepped through the hallway.

It was terribly annoying, feeling fabric brush against her legs.

In the council room, Dauriel sat slouched on the table, wearing an unreasonably attractive ensemble of black and red, her boots shined, a crown set at her hairline. Her eyes were brighter, or at least less bloodshot—perhaps she'd actually slept.

With her were a small gathering of guards and Khastra, whose face appeared unharmed despite Dauriel's volley of punches the previous night. But she couldn't ask of it, lest she reveal what she'd seen. Tallora merely entered and said, "I was summoned?"

Dauriel stood from the table, her stance subdued as she faced Tallora. "I wished to invite you to join me at the temple. Traditionally, when communing with the Triage for private business, one follower of each goddess is present. I do not know if Ilune or Staella will be joining, but I thought if you could plead for your people to Neoma directly, it might sway her to help."

Standing before the Triage had been a surreal moment in Tallora's life, to face her own goddess in all her glory—at home, they'd hardly believed it. It felt so daunting, to return, yet what was this but intercession? Tallora would be begging for mercy for her people.

"I'll go," she said, and Dauriel nodded in affirmation, then beckoned for her soldiers to move out.

Tallora followed, unsurprised when they were led outside. A carriage awaited at the gates.

Dauriel entered on her own accord, ignoring the attendant offering a hand. Tallora accepted the aid and muttered a quiet, "Thank you," as she entered the carriage and sat at the bench opposite Dauriel, who had pressed herself against the far wall, eyes fixed on the window.

When Khastra peered inside, she looked apologetically to Tallora. "Forgive me, Mermaid, but I will have to sit on that bench. I am too large to share."

Wordlessly, Tallora moved to the opposite bench, careful to avoid brushing against Dauriel. The half-demon settled as well as she could within the carriage, but she sat somewhat hunched, legs spread apart. "I am glad this is a short trip."

Tallora cracked a smile. "Do they have carriages built to accommodate you?"

"They do. But this one draws less attention."

The carriage rocked forward. The city approached. Tallora watched from the window, fascinated by uplander behaviors and keen to avoid accidentally meeting Dauriel's eye.

The temple soon appeared, the very same she'd met in months ago for intercession. Unity, she knew the sign said—the only temple dedicated to the entire Triage.

Dauriel kept her distance as they traversed the steps. Tallora stayed near Khastra, content in her shadow until the cathedral's covered them. The guards at the entrance bowed deep at Dauriel's approach, saying nothing as the three of them passed through.

The cathedral was empty. Dauriel marched to the altar, bypassing the spacious room without a glance. In her hands, Silver Fire flickered and burned; she touched them to the altar, muttering words Tallora could not quite hear.

The pedestals beyond glowed.

Three brilliant beams of light appeared, and Tallora knew them. She knew the fluid visages of the women before her, her love for the one at Neoma's right hand personal and sacred. With her brilliant wings and kind countenance, Staella held Neoma's hand in hers, unquestionable sorrow in her gaze as she met Tallora's eye. Tallora bowed, and Staella's smile was kind.

Tallora looked to the others who had descended with her—first to Neoma, whose severe gaze was reserved for the walls, contemplation in her visage. Power radiated from her stance, from every twitch of her body, the faint aura of silver around her ethereal form.

Ilune stood at Neoma's left hand, her own wicked gaze settling onto Khastra. Her staff, however, topped with its eerie, demonic skull, stared at Tallora, who withered beneath it. She was endlessly gorgeous, the culmination of her mothers' beauty, her sensuous form barely hidden beneath her silken dress, shamelessly teasing every curve and line of her angelic body.

Neoma spoke, her proud voice echoing across the high ceilings. "Greeting, Dauriel, and guests. There is much to speak of, yet so little to say. Onias refused to speak to me regarding Yu'Khrall. He said only that his words had been conveyed to the messenger."

Tallora recalled Harbinger's words and wondered if they were the same. But before she could speak, Dauriel stepped forward.

"So you do know?" the empress said, daring to stand tall before her progenitor goddess.

"My wife has heard enough pleas for help from her worshippers," Neoma said, taking her throne upon the pedestal. "We know all. The oceans weep for Yu'Khrall's rampage and for Yaleris' death. Yet there's only one who could have freed him."

A great many things happened in a few tense seconds; Neoma's bitter glare settled upon Tallora, who shrunk before her, but with that came Staella's own subtle glower to her wife. The Goddess of Stars whispered into Neoma's ear, who matched her gaze instead, silent words passing between them.

In the same instance, Dauriel looked to Tallora, her unreadable countenance scrutinizing above all. "What is she talking about?"

No condemnation; merely curiosity. "Only the Heart of Silver Flame holds the power to free Yu'Khrall," Tallora said, "and I was the heart of Neoma's chosen upon this realm. Chemon, King Merl's advisor, overheard your, um, mention of marrying me, and used my blood to . . . I swear I tried to fight him, but there were so many, and . . ." She frowned, suddenly cold. "H-He had a vision, or so he said. A vision that told him the Heart of Silver Flame wasn't Staella and who to look for instead. Goddess Neoma, I worry there's more to this."

"Indeed," Neoma said curtly. Yet her attention left her beloved's and drifted to Ilune instead. "Tell me more of it, Tallora. No detail is trivial."

Tallora said what she recalled—that the vision mentioned blood, that he'd awoken cold—what little she knew, and all the while Neoma said nothing at all; merely watched Ilune, who looked properly horrified at Tallora's words.

It was Staella's quiet heartbreak that spoke the loudest; she said nothing, revealed nothing, merely watched Tallora.

"I wish I knew more. If Yu'Khrall hadn't eaten Chemon, we could question him, but—"

"Is it true, though?" Ilune interrupted, her pouted lips twisting into a wicked smile. Depthless dread seeped into Tallora's soul, cold radiating through her limbs as Ilune looked to her. "Morathma came to meet with Yu'Khrall?"

The entire mood shifted. Confusion flickered upon both Neoma and Staella's countenances— apparently they had not been informed. Yet Ilune had somehow, and she had asked Tallora specifically. "It's true," she said softly, nervous beneath the pointed gaze. "Morathma came to Yu'Khrall and offered to help him.

He seemed to think..." She looked to Ilune, steeling her courage. "...that you would come to find him."

Ilune's expression didn't change; she kept her smile, her silver eyes wide and innocent.

Fury filled Tallora. "You knew," she whispered, deciding she didn't care if she were struck down for insolence. "Khastra spoke to you and told you what Harbinger said. You must have known this would mean his return."

Ilune placed a hand upon her heart, her gaze drifting from Tallora to the goddesses beside her, and then back. "Certainly not."

"You..." Tallora said, struggling to keep her voice subdued as realization struck her. Her jaw trembled; her blood pulsed hot. "You told Chemon about the Heart of Silver Flame. This is your doing."

"Tallora, you poor heartbroken thing," Ilune interrupted, her tone as sweet as sugar and utterly patronizing. "That's a nasty accusation. Whatever my ambitions, do you truly think I would condemn my mother's people?"

"I..." Her words failed her; her breath did too. "But then who else? No one else knew; no one but—"

She was stopped by a large, blue hand on her shoulder. Khastra leaned down and whispered in her ear, the subtle threat apparent: "Take care how you speak to my goddess."

"Ilune and I shall speak of this in private," Neoma muttered, disapproval etching itself into her beautiful face. "The affairs of Gods shall be handled in Celestière. Furthermore, if I must take this matter up with Morathma myself, I shall."

"Goddess Neoma," Tallora said, "I think I know the messenger of Onias."

Even seated on her throne, Neoma towered over her supplicants below. "Well?"

"Harbinger is the daughter of Yu'Khrall, and she'd been doing all she could to stop his return. When he did, she communed with Onias for a month to hear his will. All he said..." She searched in her memory, then spoke the words. "*'My word is law, forever and always.'* That's what he told her, when she asked how to defeat him."

To Tallora's relief, Neoma actually looked pleased. Her expression softened as she said, "Simple enough. It seems our old bargain remains. I cannot kill Yu'Khrall. That was Onias' demand from long ago. But I can subdue him as before." She looked to Dauriel, her stare nothing less than withering. "Dauriel Solviraes, blood of my blood, there is a way, but you must know the risks."

"I know the risks," Dauriel replied, willful and stupid enough to tell a goddess she knew best. "And I know the way."

"Do you know anything of my previous battle with Yu'Khrall?"

"You were channeled by Izthariel Solviraes, my ancestor of long ago," Dauriel said, reverence in her tone. "Together, you locked Yu'Khrall into his prison."

"Izthariel's godly blood was far thicker than yours, Dauriel, and he still succumbed to my presence."

Tallora's gut clenched, realization slowly settling within her. She looked to Khastra, whose demonic visage also held subtle horror. Mortals could channel gods. But Dauriel would only last so long.

"I know the cost, Goddess Neoma. But I, too, have a Convergence Orb. If I absorb its power as I channel you, perhaps I might have the stamina of my forebearer."

Tallora wanted to scream, to run to Dauriel and slap this insane notion from her head. When she might have voiced her objection, she saw Staella catch her eye and shake her head.

"It is not the fight itself that would destroy you—it is the power needed to place him back into his prison. You would agree to this?" Neoma asked.

"I would."

No, no, Tallora's mind screamed, tears filling her eyes when she blinked.

"Khastra has already orchestrated a plan without godly intervention," Dauriel continued, "but the promise of your aid would ensure victory."

"Actually," Khastra said, calculation in her words as she addressed Neoma, "with the promise of your aid, I can certainly make a few changes. Reduce the risk to all parties—including Dauriel."

"Forgive me for voicing what we're all thinking," Ilune said, leaning lazily upon her staff, "but the presence of Convergence Orbs does significantly raise the stakes. I do believe there was some mention of ice covering the ocean floor? It would be an absolute disaster if that were to spread, don't you think?" Tallora swore she saw the shadow of a smile upon the wicked deity's countenance. "Or worse—with every passing moment, who knows what mystery Yu'Khrall has managed to unlock. How soon before he floods half the continent or freezes the entire sea?"

Heat rose in Tallora's blood, Ilune's apparent amusement utterly appalling. And so she spat the words, "What's your point?"

Ilune looked directly to her, surprise in her glowing eyes. Just as quickly, it settled into vicious intrigue. "Only that perhaps I might be of assistance as well."

Khastra stepped forward, a warning in the brief glance she spared for Tallora. But skepticism raised her eyebrow, and Tallora wondered if she had any fear of godly authority. "Might you?"

"Come to Celestière and tell me your plans," Ilune said, conspiracy in her wicked stare. "I have a few of my own."

To Tallora's surprise, Khastra shook her head—which was nearly odder than the invitation. "If I were to spend a day in Celestière, nearly a week would pass here. I have much to prepare, Goddess Ilune."

"A fair rebuttal. Await my messenger, then—"

"You can't allow this!" Tallora cried to Neoma. Her anger spiked, and she no longer cared that Khastra loomed nearby, that she was about to lose her temper at a goddess. "Goddess Neoma, there's no one else but Ilune who could have done this—"

"Tallora," Ilune interrupted, saccharine and mild, "your outburst is very unbecoming. I understand you're mourning, but—"

"You awful, evil bitch!" Tallora marched forward, fully prepared to strangle a literal deity—and only stopped when Khastra physically held her back. "You did this! I don't know why, but you wanted this!"

Ilune merely smiled and shrugged. "If you're trying to get a rise out of me, you're wasting your time."

"How could you do this? To your mother's own people!"

"The vast majority of those killed were Tortalga's people. But I don't know, Tallora—why would I ever do anything so awful?"

There was an answer; there had to be. But faced with Ilune's indifferent mockery, the weight of her godly presence, Tallora's mind was empty of anything but rage.

"Tallora."

Tallora turned at the voice. Staella watched, her soft, knowing gaze cutting as deep as her soul. "Khastra, release her."

The half-demon obeyed; Tallora stumbled forward, nearly losing her balance.

"Tallora," Staella continued, "I feel your conflict. I know your pain. I want to assure you that I have heard every prayer you've sent and those of your people. My heart weeps for what has befallen Stelune. My deepest regret in this time of tragedy is that I know not where Yaleris' soul has gone to; he is a martyr for my people. I'm searching for him, but I fear the search will be fruitless. The dragons are from the time before, and there is so much even we in Celestière do not know."

The words reopened a wound only barely closed. Tallora blinked, her eyes growing misty.

Staella released Neoma's hand and stepped down from her pedestal. On equal ground, she barely stood taller than Khastra. "My heart aches with yours, for the tragedy of your people. They are mine, and they are Tortalga's, who I call my friend. And it burns me, down to my very soul, that what is mine and what is my wife's must be at odds." Staella's soft words held a poignant rage, and Tallora understood—she and Staella held the same hurt for Solvira's betrayal and the capture of Tallora's king and prince.

She couldn't face Dauriel. She knew the empress had heard it as well.

"And it burns me just as much," Staella continued, her voice as small as a mouse, yet impossible to forget, "that my own blood would take such amusement from the slaughter of so many." She looked up at Ilune, whose pouted lips revealed no remorse.

"I am simply here to find the hope in such tragic circumstances," Ilune replied, her smile sanguine and vile all at once.

Staella's form became smaller, until she was little taller than Tallora herself. She swept her up into a warm embrace, and Tallora held her tight, the feeling exactly as it had been in her dream a lifetime ago. Tallora's tears fell, but Staella enveloped her in her wings, blocking the world. "My heart weeps for your loss, Tallora," Staella whispered in her ear. Tallora's breath caught in her throat. "Your mother's soul awaits in the Beyond. I seek her still, and I shall not rest until I find her."

Staella pulled away only enough to face her, her countenance radiant yet not so blinding as the sun. The stars above beamed a gentle light and so did she. Tallora lingered in the embrace, for it was the motherly love she had missed so dearly.

"You shall have my blessing for this battle," Neoma said to them all. "And I shall await your prayer, Dauriel. I have not abandoned you."

Staella returned to Neoma's right hand. The Triage glowed like the stars before they vanished from the plane.

Dauriel was nearly out of the temple by the time Tallora's heart started once more. She ran, racing to catch up to the empress.

The shadow of the cathedral covered them. In the street, citizens went about their morning, some stopping to stare at the idle carriage before the temple steps, but Tallora paid them no mind as she cried, "Dauriel, you can't do this!"

She stood at the top of the steps, gazing down at Dauriel, standing at the crux of the shadow and the sun. "I beg your pardon?"

"You can't sacrifice yourself for this." Tallora hiked up her skirts as she marched down the steps. "Khastra's plan will work. You can't—"

"Why the fuck do you care?"

She knew that look—Greyva had been on the receiving end the night prior, but Tallora would not be so easily subdued.

"I seem to recall you having no sway on my life," Dauriel continued, "by your own admittance. Don't you dare pretend to care now that—"

"Oh, fuck you, you arrogant ass!" Tallora felt eyes from the street but fury won this day. "I hate you. I hate you down to the core of your stubborn, self-destructive soul, but don't you *dare* say I don't care. I wish so badly that hating you meant I didn't care, but I do. I do, Dauriel. I care, because I hate you, and I love you, and watching you implode is more than I can take—" A sob stole her words; Tallora shut her eyes, but tears streamed down her face nonetheless. She inhaled a shaking, painful breath. "I love you," she said, softer now. When she opened her eyes, Dauriel's watered. "I love you so much. Please don't do this."

Dauriel's gaze fell to the ground, quickly wiping her own tears with her sleeve. "I'm the empress of the world," she said, subdued and pained, "and with that comes the responsibility to defend it. Yu'Khrall is a threat to us all, but I can stop him."

"No," Tallora said, though it was barely a word, more an inaudible plea. "No. Your father could—"

"Eniah needs him. I won't take two parents from him."

"Dauriel, I'm begging you . . ."

But Dauriel held up a gloved hand, and Tallora's words faded away. "Izthariel Solviraes is a legend in my lineage. He lived over a thousand years ago, and his name is still revered. My name shall be even greater."

"A legacy isn't worth—"

"Isn't it though?" Dauriel's voice rose, that stubborn tone returning. "I shall have no children; I can't. I will abdicate my throne when my brother is of age and then live out my life as a forgotten advisor. But this . . . This is greater than a war against Moratham. This is greater than slaying a dragon. This is defeating a monster who nearly destroyed a faction of Staella's people—I'll be a legend. I'll be revered instead of pitied. People will speak my name in a whisper, lest they blaspheme a hero."

"Or you could live." Tallora bridged the gap between them, standing level on the steps. "You could live a full and beautiful life and be happy."

"Do I look happy, Tallora?" Dauriel let the phrase settle, its weight dampening the joy of the sunny day. "Don't berate me now—"

"Dauriel, please," Tallora pled, though it was far more a sob.

Dauriel shook her head and went to the carriage, leaving Tallora behind.

Tallora stayed on the steps, her composure hanging by a frayed thread. A shadow covered her—Khastra stood beside her. "This is her choice."

"She's reckless. She'll let herself burn out on purpose. You can't possibly be supporting this."

"The greater good demands it," Khastra said, as soft as Tallora had ever heard the general speak, "even though it shall break my heart."

She beckoned for her to follow, but Tallora shook her head. "I need to be alone. Let me walk."

Khastra gave a curt nod and ducked into the carriage. Tallora stood upon the steps as it rolled away, vision misting one more. She wiped her tears on her wrist, then took the final steps down, ignoring the stares of people on the street.

Damn Dauriel, and damn Tallora's admittance—it had been a revelation to them both. Her heart ached, but this was not the place to cry. Not here. Not with the hundreds of eyes watching as they passed.

Tallora swallowed her tears and disappeared into the crowd.

Her path meandered, though it maintained its course. Tallora thought of the past, of the day her destiny had been irreversibly changed, when a storm had hit the sea and she had saved the life of a princess. Fate decreed they should have never met, being born of land and sea, yet that impossible collision had occurred. They had hated each other. But slowly they had seen the souls behind the masks they wore, and while Tallora could not speak for Dauriel, she had seen something impossibly beautiful.

Somewhere, the gates to Neolan stood open. Tallora could leave. She could go home, for they needed all the help they could get. Toria had said her calling to be a priestess was a noble one, and Tallora felt the truth in that. She owed Solvira nothing; she could go.

And so, she ran. With hurried feet, she raced through the streets of Neolan, dodging people and horses and carriages, apologizing when she came too close but never slowing. The guards at the gate made no move to stop a single woman making an escape, and soon Tallora stood before a beautiful field.

At one spot beside the massive lake lay the skeletal remains of the amphitheater, where Dauriel had enacted her great betrayal. It lay partially disassembled, apparently taking far longer to take down than build. How Tallora hated it, hated Dauriel for building it, hated Solvira for utilizing it for so wicked a cause.

Tallora let it be, instead running to the lake's shore.

The breeze caressed her, offering freedom. The morning air was still fresh, and it was far more comfortable to run across a field of frost with boots. At the lake's edge, she stopped and gazed upon its beautiful surface, longing for what lay beneath.

She could go home.

Dauriel was going to die.

The mere idea crippled her, and Tallora sank to her knees and wept. Upon the lake's shore, she succumbed to anguish—Dauriel would die, and she was one of the few pieces of Tallora's heart that remained.

All the world was in disarray, her future a sandy shore smoothed by the tide, bearing no evidence of what it was before. Gods, she hated Dauriel. Tallora's anger had only grown in their time apart, to think how her life had fallen to pieces since. Yu'Khrall was not Dauriel's doing, but here she remained, holding to a grudge no one would fault her for. It was not a small thing, what Dauriel had done, but it felt so trivial compared to the loss of Stelune and its inhabitants, of her momma, even Harbinger . . .

Tallora decided she was a fool—a fool who craved normalcy and comfort.

A fool who desperately loved a condemned woman, destined to burn brilliant and bright—and die just as grand, for whom books would be written, songs composed, whose people would speak of her in a whisper.

With swollen eyes and misted vision, Tallora gazed upon the lake, still choking on her sobs. She could go home.

Every fiber of her being screamed to run and leave it all behind. The smallest whisper in her soul said to stay.

Tallora wept, yet the world continued.

Chapter XI

When her tears had dried, Tallora returned to Neolan. The sun remained low in the sky, not quite nearing noon.

She passed shops, all surely full of trinkets she'd adore, but she had no money, and her heart was too heavy to appreciate even looking. She wished she knew where there was a temple to only Staella, so that she might pour out her heart and feel her goddess' comfort. She thought of her six months of loneliness, when Kal had become her only confidant and friend and her heart had rejoiced at the reunion between she and Dauriel.

"I would have made you my empress."

The castle approached, and she entered its gates unhindered.

She traversed the stairs and saw the entrance to the menagerie. Kal and Merl were there, testament to Solvira's betrayal. She thought to speak to her dear friend, ask for aid in sorting her tumultuous thoughts, but as she lingered at the doorframe, a stranger said her name. "Lady Tallora?"

Not a name she'd ever been called before. When Tallora peered down the hallways, she saw a familiar face—High Priestess Toria, wearing robes of light blue. "Yes?"

"I brought you something," the woman said, and as she approached, she withdrew what appeared to be a long, beaded necklace. "I went to lead a worship service at the temple last night, and I recalled what you had said about losing your vestment; it broke my heart, to think how lost I would feel if I were you. This isn't quite the same, but I think it might help." She offered the necklace to her, and Tallora accepted, her heart already soaring.

It was entirely different, yes—not pearls and sea stars, but carved stars of polished green stone and little white beads between them. Yet it bore the weight and the message of what she'd lost, and Tallora clutched the gift to her heart. "Thank you."

"That's the style of vestment we use in the south, where I'm from—in Vaile, by the border. Silver and gold are common colors for worship in Neolan and most of Solvira, but this represents the earth and the stars and all life in between. I always thought the sentiment was lovely."

"It is," Tallora said, heart swelling in gratitude. "This is priceless. I can't possibly repay you."

"You're a priestess-in-training; it's your divine right." Toria's smile held kindness and light. "Are you well, Tallora?"

The question startled her, though she saw only sincere concern in Priestess Toria's face. "No," she said honestly. She bit back the rest of her words, surprised at her threatened tears but swallowed them.

Compassion shone from Toria's lovely features. "The world has fallen into a difficult cycle. I'm on my way to another war meeting with the council, and it's enough to make me weep, to fathom so much death. And look at you—you've already been through so much." Her voice lowered, hands clasping in front of her dress, demure and humble. "But I was quietly informed of Dauriel's proposed plan with Neoma. I take it you're hurting?"

Tallora nodded, yet found she couldn't cry; she'd cried enough at the lake. The lingering exhaustion of tears remained like a fog around her. "It's like I said—I don't have to be with her to not want her dead."

"I suppose all that remains," Toria said, thoughtfulness in every word, "is what you'll do about it. You can't control her. You can't control the monster who destroyed your home. But what will you do with what you can control?"

"Between you and me, I nearly swam home." Tallora gave a scoffing laugh, false and pained. "I went to the lake. I've done my duty, and Solvira will help.

There's nothing more I can do here." The hollowness in her stomach expanded; anxiety was her constant companion lately. "But here I am. I don't know if I'm empowered or a fool."

Toria shook her head. "Not a fool."

"Oh, I don't know about that." Tallora thought of the temple, of her confession on the steps, and felt anguish anew. She clutched the vestment close to her heart, her blinking heavy despite her exhaustion. "I told Dauriel I still loved her. I begged her not to go. I'm so stupid."

"Sometimes, changing fate is as futile as trying to stop water from flowing through your fingers," Toria replied gently. "But Staella teaches us to accept what we cannot change and find peace in that. Dauriel may be dead when the week is out, so what will you do about it?"

Tallora truly didn't know.

"In the meantime, I am late to my meeting. Would you like to join me? I doubt they would dismiss you."

Tallora nodded, and when Toria offered a hug, she accepted, struggling to contain her tears.

She was led to a spacious hall, rich in décor and priceless art. When Toria gestured to a particularly magnificent set of double doors, Tallora knocked lightly before entering.

Within, she immediately saw Khastra hunched over an expansive table covered in an enormous map of the continent. Surrounding her was the expected collection of council members who Toria quickly joined, as well as a few others—decorated soldiers Tallora did not know. The general spared her an idle glance, her words uninterrupted, but Empress Dauriel's gaze lingered, the bitterness in her stiff jaw paling to the exhaustion in her eyes.

"... continuing conflict at Cain will be abandoned. I care not for the foolhardy stubbornness of a final few men at the gates. Leave them; we will fly our banner in time. We need the troops for our next target—the Fortress of Seven Sons holds an enormous supply line for Andiamen. It will be a difficult siege, but when we capture it, the capital will risk starvation when the summer heat bakes them alive in their own homes." She looked to a well-built older man. "Colonel Joff, you will inform Marshall Helyn of this development. Send a message when the tower is in sight—then I will come to personally bash down the gates. Are we understood?"

There was a small murmur of 'yes,' among the crowd. Dauriel, however, spoke up. "You mentioned a message."

"Delivered this morning," Khastra said, handing Dauriel a scroll, tied with a small bundle dangling from the string. Tallora saw Morathma's symbol. "Enchanted to only open at your touch, but we can undo it if . . ."

Her words faded when Dauriel tugged the string anyway. The pouch fell to the floor.

"Glad to know your safety is as important to you as it is to me," Khastra said, and Tallora wondered if she'd ever had a fear of reprimand. The general stooped down to grab whatever odd parcel had accompanied the message.

"The first three were harmless," Dauriel muttered as she studied the written words. Her frown darkened. The silence lingered, the whole room holding its breath until Dauriel unceremoniously handed it to Khastra. "They still want to speak."

The general's own stare settled upon it. "Same reasons?"

Dauriel tore it in twain, content to let the pieces fall to the floor. "Yes. And they insist on speaking to me personally, hence the sand."

"And will you do that?"

Dauriel cast her gaze across the room, tension surmounting as she said, "Stand back against the walls. Or leave, if you value your lives. Moratham is known for honest combat, but there is always a risk. I wash my hands of your deaths, should you choose to stay."

No one moved. Tallora shut the door behind her to punctuate her own intentions. She swore Dauriel's frown sneered at the act, but the empress admirably kept her attention to Khastra alone. "Well. The honor is yours, General."

Standing against the door, Tallora watched as Khastra opened the small pouch and dumped what appeared to be a pile of fine sand into her palm. She blew it forward, to the space between her and the large table—but it did not scatter into the air.

Instead, it swirled with a life of its own, this miniature cyclone of sand. Guards readied their weapons; Khastra looked prepared to pounce. Dauriel, however, stood with her hands behind her back, poised as tall as a cliff face as the sand slowly took a form.

Amidst the tumultuous magic came order as the dust swirled together into a humanoid figure. It gained small details like fingers and a nose, but then color and shape—until, standing before Dauriel was a well-muscled man, a head taller than the empress, his own posture as tall as the skies.

Tallora did not recognize him, but Khastra greeted him first. "General Shiblon," she said respectfully, and the foreign general offered her a slight bow.

With every movement, sand filtered from his form, revealing him as a mere apparition and nothing more. "Empress Dauriel, I thank you for agreeing to meet with me."

"I have not agreed to that," Dauriel said curtly.

"Then I shall be quick, so as not to waste your time," Shiblon replied, his dark eyes and beard marking him as a handsome figure. "Surely you have heard of the tragedy of the Tortalgan Sea? With news of a leviathan ravaging the ocean comes the question of whether or not we set aside our feud. I would propose a temporary ceasefire. Our combined might would surely—"

"Stop."

Shiblon did, perhaps only for surprise. "Empress Dauriel—"

"What kind of simple sheep are you, to bleat into the night for my attention again and again?" Dauriel visibly seethed, and when she breathed, it was pure flame. "I will not speak with you. I do not need you. The only time we shall meet will be when I personally remove your head upon your surrender."

Shiblon's face twisted with each insult. "If you would look beyond your pride a moment, you would see that this is a matter that concerns us both. Staella's people reside beneath the waves—"

"All the more reason for me to spit at your feet!" And Dauriel did so—spat upon the apparition's shoes. "You offend me with your offer. Solvira needs nothing from you, save for your god to hang himself. I do not negotiate with Morathma or his followers—and should the world end for my pride, then I say *burn it!*"

"Empress Dauriel—"

Dauriel thrust her hand into the apparition, glowing bright as it faded into oblivion, leaving only a small pile of sand. Flame flickered at the exposed pores of her skin, fire rising at her feet as she breathed smoke. She kicked the pile of sand, and said, "Lying bastard."

The fire dissipated with each tense breath. Dauriel pinched the bridge of her nose, her continuing breaths ever deeper. "Leave us," she seethed. "All of you—save my inner council."

Khastra barked the order: "You are all dismissed! Joff, you have your orders. The rest of you, await my word."

Tallora stepped aside as the room emptied of soldiers and leaders, as well as the religious members of the council—Khastra and Dauriel remained, as well as Ilaeri and Magister Adrael. Tallora lingered, uncertain of her next move, when Khastra said, "You as well, Mermaid."

Tallora left, too exhausted to argue. The door shut behind her. She was once again left with lonely, confused thoughts.

"Neoma will fight Yu'Khrall?"

Tallora nodded, her soft smile genuine in the face of Kal's enthusiasm.

"This is grand news! It means our home will be saved."

"I don't know if 'saved' is the word, when it's already destroyed," Tallora replied, her melancholy stealing the joy from Kal's features.

King Merl watched from behind his son, contemplation on his aged visage. Kal swam close to the edge, and when he offered a hand, Tallora thrust her own through the barrier to accept it. "I'm sorry. I suppose I can't truly fathom the horror of it. Home feels a thousand miles away."

"It might actually be a thousand miles away," Tallora teased, and Kal's slight smile gave her hope.

"But you say they will not accept help from Moratham?"

King Merl's tone immediately sparked Tallora's fury. "Correct. The empress refused to speak with them."

"And we're supposed to risk certain doom all because a tyrant won't suffer her pride?"

Glowering, Tallora withdrew her hand from Kal's, letting water drip onto the floor rather than stain her dress. "It's a ploy," she said, "and you know that. Are you really so desperate to hate Solvira that you'd apologize for Morathma blatantly conspiring with the monster who destroyed your homeland?"

"Has it occurred to you that Morathma might be lying to Yu'Khrall?" King Merl's own frown appeared permanently etched as he glared at Tallora. "Perhaps they're simply handling this with tact instead of throwing it out the window for something so petty as pride. Perhaps if we heard them out—"

"The time for negotiations have passed! Our people are already defeated, and to even pretend to appease this monster means to insult the lives lost to his sick appetite."

"So you would disregard Moratham entirely?"

"They wanted Yu'Khrall all along, and they still do even after he destroyed Stelune. He murdered a bastion of *Staella's* people, and Morathma doesn't care because he thinks Yu'Khrall will still help defeat Solvira. And perhaps he will, but it won't be toppling an empire—it'll be genocide of the entire population. Moratham's leadership compromises their morals again and again to get what they want—"

"Assuming any of what you said is true," King Merl said, "how is that different than what Solvira did to you? Apparently Empress Dauriel loved you— enough for your blood to be the key to Yu'Khrall's prison—but she still betrayed your word and used you. The beast on the throne—"

"She's not!" Tallora slammed her mouth shut, refusing to show weakness to the man responsible for her people's doom. "She's passionate and ambitious and misguided at times," she continued, forcibly subdued, "but she does care. Her refusal to give an inch to Moratham doesn't mean she doesn't care for the sea—"

"But she—"

"She's giving her life for us, so *shut up!*"

Silence settled at her outburst. Tallora clenched her fists and left them. As she walked, she heard Kal's reprimand of, "Father, how could you—" But she shut the door behind her, rather than listen.

She leaned against a lavish wall, legs threatening to fail her. Shutting her eyes, she recalled her meeting with Staella, her words and her regrets. She thought of her momma, her soul still lost in the Beyond, and felt as aimless as she ever had.

Her mother had condemned her love for Dauriel. She had been right. Dauriel was brutal. She was everything the goddess Tallora loved was not.

Footsteps sounded. Tallora straightened her stance in time to see Dauriel herself round the corner. Alone, she still held herself like the top of a mountain—proud and daunting—yet deliberately did *not* look at Tallora. Not for a moment. Not a glance, even though Tallora's gaze followed for every step. Dauriel disappeared down the hall, and Tallora knew it led to the lift.

Tallora's shuffling steps held no pride as she walked toward the staircase. For not the first time, her aimless future lay scattered before her, a thousand different paths to take. She stopped at the floor with her guest room, yet went the opposite way, to Dauriel's suite.

Toria had asked what she would do. Tallora could not find the words to give it shape; instead, she entered the small foyer, then knocked on the bedroom door.

No one answered. She went inside anyway.

There sat Dauriel upon a plush chair, a half-filled wineglass in hand. She studied Tallora, who lingered in the doorway. "Are you drunk?" Tallora said, and Dauriel shook her head.

"Not yet."

Tallora shut the door behind her, hesitant as she approached.

Dauriel set the wineglass aside, her stubborn ire a distant memory upon her countenance. Instead, she looked merely weary. "What do you want?"

Tallora stopped before her, a great divide between them. With care to hold her stare, she placed her knees at either side of Dauriel's hips, straddling her upon her seat. The empress—*her* empress—sunk back, breath hitching as Tallora pressed their bodies together.

It was wrong. It was wrong. It was . . .

Their lips touched. In silence, she kissed her empress within the dark room, her hands cupping Dauriel's jaw and neck. She craved peace amidst this horrible storm, but instead, the empress shrunk back in the chair, frantically shaking her head.

Tallora sat back, then removed herself from Dauriel's lap when the empress' face fell into her hands. "I-I'm sorry," Tallora said gently, watching as the empress stumbled from her chair and to the bed, clutching the bedpost like the drowning woman in a storm all those months ago. In tentative motions, Tallora approached. Her hand settled on Dauriel's shoulder. "Dauriel—"

Dauriel shoved her hand away; Tallora flinched and held it to her chest. In Dauriel's gaze, Tallora saw anger and anguish, the battle raging in the ensuing silence. "What are you doing?"

"I'm loving you," Tallora whispered, praying her voice did not tremble. "Is that not what—"

"Stop." Dauriel stole a gasping breath, visibly pained as she held it. Her eyes watered, and Tallora's heart ached to see it. "I can't—I can't—" Tallora hardly had the chance to move before Dauriel released the bedpost and all but collapsed against Tallora, who managed to stand her ground and not topple. Dauriel shook as she wept into Tallora's breast, strong arms gripping her body.

Gently, Tallora wrapped her arms around her empress holding her tight as she wept. "I won't leave you alone," she whispered, and Dauriel nodded amidst her tears.

Tallora pulled Dauriel against her body, their souls held apart by only their mortal forms. She led her to bed, kissing her, stroking her hair as she cried, and whispering soothing words she prayed weren't sweet nothings: *"I'm here. I have you. I won't leave."*

And when Dauriel's cries finally stilled, when she merely trembled against Tallora's form, the empress whispered, "I love you."

"I know." Tallora kissed her hair, her own tears threatening to fall. "I'm not leaving you."

"Why, though?" Dauriel looked up, eyes swollen and raw. "Why this?"

It burned Tallora to speak the tragic words. "Because I couldn't let you die before telling you that I love you. You are so loved, Dauriel."

Dauriel's smile held tragedy at the unravelling seams. "By you, perhaps."

"And Khastra. She loves you, Dauriel. People love you."

"My people do not love me. They're afraid." Dauriel pressed her face into Tallora's neck. Her hands clutched Tallora's back, her grip nearly painful as she trembled. "Tallora, I'm sorry. This is all my fucking fault—"

"No, it isn't."

"If I hadn't captured your king—"

"He'd already given the order," Tallora soothed, though it lacerated her heart to say it. "King Merl gave the order to release Yu'Khrall if it all went wrong. His advisor overheard you and I talking and realized the truth." It burned her to consider it, but she stomped that feeling down—right now was for Dauriel. "It was his word that released a monster onto my people. Not yours."

"I hurt you," Tallora heard amidst Dauriel's tears. "I used you. I betrayed you. You shouldn't be—"

"You did hurt me," Tallora whispered, clutching Dauriel tight, as though it might keep her here, safe. "You used me. You betrayed me. You explained why on the shore, and I fucking hate you for it, but . . ." She swallowed her rising emotion, unable to give it a name—only that it threatened to cripple her tongue. "But as much as it hurts—and believe me, it does—I'm wondering if I'm the one who abyss wrong."

Dauriel stayed silent a moment, long enough that Tallora though she might have fallen asleep. Her words broke a heavy silence. "What do you mean?"

"I was so caught up in pulling my kingdom out of Moratham's grip that I didn't think twice about what I was asking of Solvira—specifically, when it came to negotiating with them." Tallora pressed her forehead to Dauriel's hair, content to breathe in her scent. "You aren't blameless. You're brutal, and it terrifies me sometimes. But my kingdom was conspiring with wicked men and listening to their lies. My kingdom had the plot to free Yu'Khrall and think he would actually listen to them." She brought a hand up to rub the back of Dauriel's scalp. "I'm still furious. You could have told me and my kingdom to fuck off and save face; instead you lied to me. If by some miracle you live past next week, I promise to scream and let everything out at you."

Tallora smiled, gratified when Dauriel glanced up to see it. "But my whole world has changed," she continued, "and not for the better. I don't know anything anymore. Nearly everyone I've ever loved is gone, my home is destroyed, and I'm probably stupid to be here, but . . ." Her own tears threatened to rise, but she forced them away, knowing that once she cried, she wouldn't stop. "You're one of the only things I have left, and now you're off to die as well. I can be angry once you're gone. I want to love you while I still can."

Dauriel trembled as she leaned up and kissed her lips, her tears staining Tallora's cheeks. When she pulled away, she held herself like a guppy before a shark. "I'll never lie to you again. I'll seal it in blood—whatever it takes for you to know I mean it."

Tallora touched her swollen face, stroked gentle lines upon it. "You can't make that promise. Not as empress. Not when Solvira is your priority."

"Tallora, I am so sorry." The empress' eyes glistened, her cheeks red and blotchy.

Tallora smiled as she cupped Dauriel's cheek. "I forgive you—"

"Don't," Dauriel said—mouthed, really, fresh tears stealing her word.

"Too late, Empress," Tallora said with a wink, but Dauriel fell apart in her arms nonetheless. As she wept, Tallora placed successive kisses upon her hair, content to cradle Dauriel forever if needs be. "I'm worried. I know more than you realize. I heard you crying to Khastra the night I caught you with the courtesans. I saw what happened last night—everything, Dauriel, from the council meeting until you collapsed in tears in the training grounds."

Dauriel's grip tightened, sobs shaking her form.

"I love you," Tallora said, vehement as she brought Dauriel's tear-streaked face to look at her. "Your sacrifice for the world will be the noblest of acts, but I'm worried you're being reckless because you don't want to be here anymore. Death was always your chance to escape—and now you've found a way."

Exhaustion fell upon Dauriel's countenance. Her hand came up to touch Tallora's face, sliding to the back of her neck as she held them together. "I'm losing my mind."

"You're hurting—"

"No." Dauriel stiffened, her tears still falling like gentle rain. "No, I'm losing myself."

Tallora's thumb stroked a tender line along Dauriel's jaw. "I don't understand."

Again, Tallora saw that shame, and she longed to kiss it away. "I don't know how to explain this horrible thing inside me. I've never been good at discussing feelings, but I feel like a nerve; I feel like a bloody, open wound, and all I can do is drink to numb it. My mind has always been dark, but lately it's screaming and I can't breathe—" Her eyes squeezed shut, anguish and shame twisting her features. "I'm sorry. I'm so sorry about those damned whores. You didn't—I just—I—" Dauriel's composure fell apart once more, but Tallora tried to catch her.

"I don't care," she pled, heart breaking when Dauriel wailed into her dress. "I swear to you, I don't care. Yes, it hurt to see, but we weren't together—"

But Dauriel sobbed, drowning out Tallora's words. Helpless, Tallora simply held her, her own composure barely holding on as the minutes passed.

Her memory welled a painful thought, of words her mother had spoken long ago—that to love someone broken could hurt as much as it healed, and that sometimes the only reward was to see another sunrise after a long night of soothing their aching soul.

When her empress' cries had dwindled into trembling, sniffling sobs, Tallora kissed her hair, sweaty from her exhausted state. "Let me help you," she pled, but Dauriel shook her head. "Dauriel, if there's anything I can do—"

"There isn't a monster to fight; not when the monster is simply me." She shut her eyes, setting her head against Tallora's chest. "Despite everything, I shall be my mother all the same. It's good I can't have children—they'd be as fucked as I am. But instead of ruining the lives of my people, I'd rather die as—"

"Please stop. You're not a monster, Dauriel." Tallora held tight to Dauriel, wishing so dearly she could chase her demons away. The whole world feared Dauriel, but this wasn't cruelty or narcissism. This wasn't a mirror of her tempestuous progenitors her kingdom had come to fear. Dauriel was vicious, but she'd always been just to her own.

This was despair.

"I've told you about my papa," Tallora whispered. "When I was a little girl, he told me there was a worm inside his head who whispered cruel things and made him sick—so sick that he'd sometimes stay in bed for days. That was how he explained it to me. I told him I'd fight it for him." She smiled, but it hurt—a wound that still ached on dark, lonely nights. "My papa's mind also screamed at him, and he was the kindest, sweetest man to ever live. He was worth fighting for, and my mother loved him with all her heart."

"Yes," Dauriel said, her words hollow and void, "and then he killed himself."

Tallora shut her eyes, jaw clenching at those terrible, damning words. Trembling, she pressed her lips against Dauriel's forehead, her breath escaping as a violent shudder. "What do you need? Right now—what can I give you?"

Dauriel whispered, "Just stay. For a moment."

"I'll stay forever," Tallora replied, and it frightened her so, to realize the truth.

What she wanted, she dared not contemplate. Instead, they simply breathed the other, drifting into a fitful rest.

They bathed in Dauriel's tub, living in quiet, tentative peace. Tallora was careful to not submerge her entire self, lest she transform; instead, she washed her empress' hair, kissed her tears when she softly cried, savored every precious moment with the woman she loved.

Dauriel clung to her in the warm bath, the water sealing their naked bodies together. Tallora lightly stroked her short hair, content to simply hear her breathe. The innocence of it warmed her heart, and she prayed Dauriel felt some comfort in their intimacy.

"In that meeting," Tallora asked, recalling Moratham's General and Dauriel's outburst, "what did you speak of alone?"

Dauriel shook her head. "Nothing particularly grand. My father thinks I'm justified. Toria thinks I should have at least heard the general out. Someday I shall issue an edict that states any council member who sasses the empress shall have their tongue cut out."

Tallora kissed her sneered lip. "While I do hope you live long enough to issue that edict, I think it would be taken poorly by the populace. Simply dismissing her is much less blood to clean up."

"Priestess Toria wondered if Morathma might be lying to Yu'Khrall. I think the notion is insane."

Tallora frowned. "King Merl said the same thing. What would you do if that was the actual truth?"

"Exactly as I'm doing now." Dauriel's frown hardened her handsome features. "I will not compromise. Not with Moratham, and not with Yu'Khrall—not after all the carnage."

Tallora kissed the side of Dauriel's mouth, but her empress pulled away, her frown still etched into her visage.

Dauriel was silent for a long time as she watched the subtle ripples in the bathwater. Tallora feared what her mind had wrought, but then Dauriel finally looked up, immutable sorrow in her features. "I'm so sorry about your mother."

Tallora shook her head, the words bringing fresh sorrow. "We're talking about you."

"Then I will be selfish and admit it's been plaguing me to think of you all alone after that awful calamity."

Dauriel's gentle gaze was an invitation, and Tallora spoke hollow, wounded words. "She didn't die in the destruction of the city. She died when I tried to rescue her from the ruins."

She told the tale—of Harbinger scrying to find her, of the survivors her mother had harbored, and of Yu'Khrall's onslaught, how he'd crushed her to death. "I held her hand as she died," Tallora finished, quiet tears streaming down her face. "And it hurts. I haven't felt like this since my papa died. My mom was my only family, and now I'm alone."

Dauriel pulled herself up, her hand cupping Tallora's face.

"I miss her, Dauriel. I miss her so much. She was my whole world for so long. After my papa died, she sacrificed so much to take care of me. And one of the last conversations we had was about you, and how she disapproved, and now here I am..." Tallora took a painful, heaving breath, heart aching at the terrible truth. "I'm sorry. I shouldn't have said that."

Dauriel shook her head, her grip on Tallora tightening protectively. "She wasn't exactly wrong about me."

"Whether she was right or wrong doesn't matter anymore. She's dead. Everyone's dead."

Tallora's sobs rose, wracking her figure. She clung to Dauriel, who held her tenderly, simply letting her cry. Oh, it hurt, the pain striking anew to think of her momma's hand falling limp, but Dauriel's gentle touch and strong arms became the whole world.

Her cries did quell, eventually. "She'd want me to be strong," Tallora managed to say. She wiped away her tears, stealing a gasping breath. "When my papa died, my momma told me to take it one day at a time. To think about the years ahead without him would drive me mad with grief. So one day. Get through one day. And then tomorrow, do it again. That's what I've done, even if I still cry most days, thinking about her."

"How can I help you get through this one?"

Tallora sniffed, still liable to collapse into sobs anew. "Distract me."

Dauriel kissed her cheek. "All right," she said, the barest beginnings of a smile pulling at her lip. It was the first Tallora had seen of it in so long; she loved it so. "All right—a distraction. How crass of a story would you like?"

Tallora managed to smile, recalling a time long ago when Dauriel had soothed her panicked heart all through the night. She stroked her empress' disheveled hair, adoring the dark locks. Savoring the touch, she thought only of this precious moment. "As crass as you'd like but make certain it's funny."

Dauriel pressed her face back against Tallora's breast, her hand sliding up to caress it, though there was no intention behind it. "When I was sixteen," the empress said, "Khastra caught me staring a moment too long at a maidservant's ass."

"That's a way to start a story." Tallora chuckled, gratified when Dauriel peered up to give her an exhausted smile.

With her hand still cupping Tallora's breast, she said, "I should add that I was actively fighting Khastra in the training grounds. The maidservant had been tending to one of the injured soldiers during practice—he was her lover, I think. But she bent over, and I was so shaken by the sight of her skirt tightening around her ass that Khastra whacked me on the back of the skull with her practice sword." Dauriel reached back to part her hairline, revealing a small scar among the dark locks. "I dropped like a rock. She panicked, thinking she'd killed me."

Tallora grinned. "That must've been hilarious."

"I wish I could remember it. I just remember the girl's ass and then waking up in bed with a pounding headache."

"That's a cute story," Tallora teased, but her empress shook her head.

"It gets better." Dauriel said, scooting up to bring their faces closer. "After that, I was banned from the training grounds for two weeks, in case there was any lingering disorientation. Khastra, of course, wasted no time in asking me what the hell went wrong—because it should have been an easy blow to parry." She stared away toward the window, subtle amusement in her smile. "I didn't really have an answer because I hadn't ever considered that I was attracted to women; I told her I was distracted. That might've been the end of it, but then the nurse attending to me entered while we spoke. She bent over to inspect my head and her blouse fell open—and she must not have been wearing a corset because I saw *everything*. Khastra said after, and I do quote this directly—" Dauriel then lowered her voice, providing a crude interpretation of the half-demon's accent. "'You stopped listening. You were staring at her breasts like a dog at meat.'"

When Dauriel grinned, Tallora chuckled and brought her hand to cup her precious face. "You are terrible."

Dauriel laughed, and Tallora's heart delighted to hear it. "I wasn't trying to be creepy—I'd never seen anything like it, except in artwork. But Khastra and I talked about it. She is old enough to have been married numerous times, to men and women both, so she was very supportive." She leaned up to kiss Tallora, her lips soft and welcome. "The end."

"You didn't know you liked women, though?"

Dauriel shook her head. "I was sick for years and missed a few milestones in my youth. Most girls start falling head over heels for boys when they're starting their monthlies—but I was crippled from pain and bedridden, so I never got to know either way." Her humorless laugh sank Tallora's tentative joy. "But, growing up as royalty, love was never something to pursue anyway. Whenever my mother was particularly annoyed with me, she'd threaten to find me a husband from Ilunnes and ship me off to live alone and pregnant in the swamp."

Tallora's jaw fell slack at that. "That's awful."

"It was, but I had an escape plan readied if she acted. Always kept knives at my bedside in case I needed to slit my own throat."

Tallora clutched Dauriel tight, heart aching for the little girl who had seen death as the only escape. "Well," she whispered, agonized at Dauriel's words, "she's gone now. She's gone, and you're mine."

"Is that what I am?" Dauriel asked, a certain softness in her words.

Tallora leaned in to kiss her, content to memorize her mouth and skin. "Yes," she whispered, the truth of it piercing her brutalized heart.

Their lips met, sweet and serene. Tallora let Dauriel lead, overjoyed to feel her mouth, letting her set the pace as her hands wandered Tallora's body.

Dauriel craved intimacy like a drowning man for a savior; Tallora knew this like her own skin. And so did she; in the aftermath of so much tragedy, she yearned for a moment of joy. They kissed with the softness of sunrise, their touch like lingering dew on petals, and when Dauriel pushed inside her, tears fell down Tallora's cheeks. The empress' tongue subdued her own, and Tallora loved to be owned, each thrust of Dauriel's hand pulling muffled groans from her mouth.

She savored the sensation, their slow fucking enough to bring her to the brink. When their eyes met in their lovemaking, Tallora said, "I love you."

Dauriel's eyes glistened as she placed kisses upon her cheek and neck, gentle trailing words of, *"I love you,"* at her lips. Little bites on Tallora's neck meant the world would know she was owned. But Dauriel owned the world, so what did their opinion matter? The gentle pace of their love never strayed, not until Tallora's pleasure peaked, the tender cry of, *"Oh, Dauriel...."* the one to soothe her through her body's erratic shaking. The empress' pace slowed as she rode her orgasm, finally withdrawing when Tallora stilled.

They lingered in the silence, the weight of Dauriel's soft breathing a reminder of the coming storm.

Tallora would be whatever she needed in their precious, final days.

Chapter XII

"Come outside," Tallora said, once her hair had dried. "The sun will do you good."

They appeared in the garden, a gentle falling of snow greeting them. There was a whole world outside filled with pain, a great cataclysm on the horizon, but for the moment, Dauriel was everything.

Evidence of snow covered the statues and skeletal remains of trees. "Winter doesn't come to the seas," Tallora said, adoring how the flakes fell upon her hair, reminding her of Yaleris' domain. "I think it's beautiful."

"I don't find many people who enjoy winter," Dauriel replied, her melancholy matching that of the scenery.

Yet, though they said winter was dreary, Tallora couldn't see it. She held out a finger, catching a single, miniscule flake, smiling wide as she stared at its perfect form. It melted, its beauty fleeting, but Tallora thought there was poetry to be found in that. She caught another, giggling as several collected upon her fingertips, then noticed Dauriel watching, adoration in her gaze.

Tallora kissed her shamelessly on the mouth. Dauriel returned the gesture, deepening the kiss with her tongue as they embraced in the winter gardens. Let the people see them; let them gossip. Tallora had seen tragedy, had witnessed death, saw how fleeting and beautiful life could be.

She would cherish it all, for as long as she had it.

Gloved hands caressed her hair and figure. Dauriel pulled her into a warm embrace. Tallora brushed gathering snow from Dauriel's doublet and hair, blushing when the gesture was returned. "When I was a little girl," Tallora said, "my father would tease me and say my hair was like the frost on the glaciers in the north. It wasn't until I was much older that I saw the truth in it."

"I've never seen hair like yours," Dauriel said, stealing a strand with her fingers, pure white against her black gloves. "When I first began falling in love with you, it was your hair that would linger with me—I once found a strand of it on my tunic when I was your keeper and couldn't bear to throw it away."

"That's terribly creepy," Tallora teased, and Dauriel laughed. Tallora squealed when Dauriel grabbed her and pulled her back against her chest.

"Oh, extremely," Dauriel said. "I've never felt a small emotion in all my life—I went from hatred to adoration to obsession quicker than I'd prefer to admit."

Tallora giggled, the hints of the asshole she loved peeking through in her safe moments. "Tell me more. You were obsessed with me?"

"I still am." Dauriel's cheeks colored red, and it certainly wasn't for chill. She released Tallora, who held her hand instead and tugged her along. "I simply try to keep it contained, otherwise I'd never stop ravishing you."

"Oh, wouldn't you?" Tallora grinned, overjoyed when Dauriel matched it. "Don't I get a say in this?"

"Certainly. You get to say 'yes.'"

Tallora swatted her lightly on the chest, enamored at her flirtatious words. By Staella's Grace—it felt so delightful to laugh. "I have a question," she said, her curiosity peaked, and Dauriel's mood stable for the moment. "And don't be self-conscious; I'm not casting judgement. But I genuinely want to know—what in the world were you doing to that girl? The one you were naked with when I walked in."

Dauriel's blush grew fierce, and Tallora feared she'd misjudged her love's temperament. When she finally spoke, it held boundless hesitation. "You wouldn't know, would you."

"Know what?"

"When I had sex with you as a mermaid," Dauriel began slowly, "it occurred to me that your anatomy limits the sort of sex positions you can do. And acts, for that matter."

Tallora couldn't say she understood where Dauriel was going with that, but she'd be damned before she admitted naivety.

"Women here will sometimes, um, wear devices that allow them to penetrate their lovers the way a man can."

Tallora's brow furrowed as she tried to unravel that bit of trivia. "So you were wearing a—"

"It's called a strap. It's a bit different than what you're thinking." Dauriel's blush hadn't faded, but an amused grin pulled at her lips. "I don't feel it the same way, though I hear there are spells for that. I get off on the power, and she gets off on me aggressively fucking her into the pillow. Sometimes that's all I need too."

Her lurid wink brought heat to Tallora's face, even if she still didn't quite understand. "So you wear a 'strap' and use it to have sex with women. That makes some sense." She frowned, struggling to articulate the bit that simply did not make sense. "But you were behind her."

Dauriel stared like she was still waiting for the question. Tallora pursed her lips, unsure of how to quite articulate the issue, when Dauriel suddenly snorted into laughter. "Never mind. I see."

"What do you see—"

Dauriel grabbed her, aggressive as she pressed Tallora's back against her chest. Her hands slid down Tallora's side and to her hips, where she kept her grip and whispered, voice dripping with lust, "Bend over."

Weak at her words, Tallora obeyed, bending as far as she could without toppling over. Dauriel's hips ground into hers, the friction sending unexpected jolts of pleasure through her body. Her gloved hand slid against the warm juncture between her legs. Tallora gasped when she pushed against her entrance, her winter dress between them. "There are advantages to being able to spread your legs."

"Point taken," Tallora said, breathless as Dauriel continued rubbing her hand against her entrance. "Looking to demonstrate?"

"Oh, that it weren't winter. I'd take you right here." Dauriel removed her hand, letting it slide teasingly before helping Tallora right herself.

With her back to Dauriel's chest, Tallora gazed up at her, her head spinning from the touch. "You are insatiable," she teased, sighing when Dauriel touched her lips to her ear.

"Simply obsessed, remember?"

Tallora turned over in her arms, pressing their lips together as they kissed with open mouths. When she finally pulled away, Dauriel's grin illuminated her countenance. "Look at you—smiling again."

"It's easier to pretend all is well when there's a gorgeous woman in front of me."

"That's the cure then? Anytime you're slipping, I just let you ravish me? I can accept those terms." She grinned, but Dauriel's smile faltered.

"You owe me nothing. I know I'm always teasing, but you can always say no if . . ." Her voice faded when Tallora pressed a finger to her lips.

"I know that. But I decided I trusted you long ago. I was your prisoner once, remember? You could have done anything you liked." She placed a kiss on the corner of Dauriel's mouth. "Besides, I've never lied to you. Why would I start now?"

"To protect my fragile ego?"

Tallora kissed her lips. "I love your ego, fragile or not," she whispered against her mouth. When Dauriel's shy smile returned, Tallora pulled away, stealing her hand instead. "So, do we tell people we're back in bed together? I'll be honest—I don't know what to tell Kal and King Merl."

"I don't owe my council anything." Dauriel looked to the castle, to the high towers and then the sky.

"Though the news will either make Khastra worry more or less. No in between."

"She asked me to leave you alone, initially." When Dauriel frowned, Tallora added, "Not out of malice. She asked me to simply ignore you rather than be unkind. I think it would give her peace of mind to know, honestly."

A pained groan escaped Dauriel's mouth. "Fine. Let's get it over with then."

But nobody knew where Khastra was. Not the servants nor the guards—and not Dauriel's father, either. "She has a workshop you might check," he said, when they found him in the hallway, his own suspicious gaze sparing their intertwined fingers a second glance. "That, or her bedroom."

"Khastra uses her bedroom for sleep, and that's about it," Dauriel said, once he'd left. Still, she led Tallora through the halls, until they reached a larger than typical door.

Dauriel knocked. Tallora heard absolutely nothing. "Does she have a suite as well?" she whispered, and Dauriel nodded.

The empress tried the handle, but it wouldn't budge. She knocked again. "Khastra?" She looked to Tallora. "We can find her at dinner—"

The doorknob twisted. Khastra's face appeared in the crack, opened only enough to reveal her horns and blue skin, slightly flushed with a hint of purple upon her defined cheeks. "Dauriel?"

Tallora glanced down Khastra's body, realizing she wore . . . a robe?

Dauriel looked equally confused as she composed herself. "Do you have a minute?"

"Exactly one."

"There's something you need to know, and I wanted to make certain you heard it from me. Tallora and I, we're . . ." Dauriel took Tallora's hand, interlacing their fingers. "We've set aside our feud."

"Oh." Khastra's expression softened as she leaned against the doorframe. "Not what I expected, but I am happy for you both."

Tallora looked to Dauriel and smiled. "I don't plan on leaving her side," she said, hoping Khastra caught the layered meaning.

"You have forty seconds left," Khastra said, then she looked back to whatever the door blocked. "Anything else?"

"No. See you at dinner?"

"You will not." Khastra shut the door.

Tallora looked to Dauriel, noting her confusion. "What the hell is she doing?"

Holding a finger to her lip, Dauriel pressed her ear to the doorframe. She lingered a moment, visibly straining to listen. When she finally pulled back, she whispered, "I hear muffled voices. Can't decipher a thing."

"So there's someone else in there?"

Dauriel furrowed her eyebrows as she nodded. "That's odd."

"Someone she didn't introduce us to and didn't want to leave for long? Did you see what she was wearing, Dauriel?"

Dauriel's expression remained the same as she stared at the door. "Very odd."

"I just want to know who."

"Me too." She took Tallora's hand once more. "Though she'll likely never tell. If I know anything about her, it's that she's secretive when it comes to her personal life."

"Even to you?"

"I'm used to it." Dauriel led her away, placing a small kiss upon her cheek. "I don't know about you, but I'd like to take dinner alone. Does that sound agreeable?"

Tallora grinned as she nodded, letting Dauriel lead her away.

They feasted in Dauriel's bedroom, a dinner of a roasted bird Tallora didn't recognize. It was delicious and light, but the better part was sitting with Dauriel in her room, both half-undressed from their winter clothing. Domestic bliss, Tallora decided, and it felt marvelous to eat her dessert seated upon Dauriel's lap and feel those lithe arms around her.

But Dauriel seemed less peaceful, here alone. She didn't drink, at least. Her smile frayed at the edges, unraveling entirely when she thought Tallora wasn't looking. When Tallora straddled her, Dauriel responded, but when Tallora looked into her eyes, their light had faded.

"Dauriel," she whispered against her empress' lips. She placed a lingering kiss at the corner of Dauriel's mouth, then another at her cheek before leaning back. "We don't have to continue." She brushed the lengthening strands of Dauriel's hair from her face.

Dauriel's hands settled at Tallora's waist, her thumb stroking lines along the fabric. "It feels like I'm wasting time if I don't."

"Spending innocent time with me is wasting it?" Tallora smiled gently, hoping it conveyed that she was teasing. "We've never had time to simply be."

"And we won't." Dauriel captured her mouth once more, her hands skimming the buttons of Tallora's dress, but Tallora gently extracted them and pulled away, interlacing their fingers instead.

The words jarred their future forward, but Tallora swallowed her grief. "I want you to hold me," she whispered. "You're welcome to hold me naked if you'd prefer, but I only want to be held."

With a smile as soft as the waning sunset, Dauriel stood, then lifted Tallora into her arms, cradling her as she took them to bed. "I can't be silent," she said, her expression quickly falling. "My thoughts are unbearably loud."

Tallora settled against the pillows and plush sheets, pulling Dauriel down against her. "Do you need to talk about it?"

Dauriel shook her head. "Let's talk about something else."

"Something else? Hmm . . ." Tallora kissed the top of her head, acutely aware of how Dauriel clung to her. "Your hair is getting longer."

"I'm tempted to shave it off."

"Oh, don't do that. There would be nothing for me to play with." Her fingers gently caressed the dark strands. "I'll cut it for you, if you'd like."

Dauriel's smile, however slight, was the most beautiful sight in the world. "I'd like that."

"Next time we bathe, remind me. I think it'll ease your stress, at least a little."

"I have to look good for my funeral," Dauriel replied, her wink unsettling Tallora's resolve, "assuming there's anything left of me."

Tallora shook her head, her grip tightening around Dauriel's form. "Please don't talk like that," she whispered. "I don't want to think about the future; I simply want to live for tonight."

Dauriel's face settled against Tallora's neck. "I'm still baffled you want to spend time with me at all, but I've accepted it."

"Good." Upon her back, Dauriel gripped her dress, a quiet desperation in the gesture. Tallora kept speaking, knowing the silence so quickly became daunting. "I don't know if I've spoken much of home. Or, rather . . " Her words filtered away, sadness filling her. The world was turned upside-down, and she had nearly forgotten. ". . . what's left of it."

"Memorialize it," Dauriel replied. She leaned up enough to meet Tallora's eye. "Tell me everything I don't know."

Tallora spoke, memories of her childhood and youth filling the somber room, bringing joy. Dauriel listened intently, the dullness in her eyes remaining, but she smiled as appropriate; she asked questions when needed.

Hours filtered by before her empress' eyes glazed over. Tallora bid her to sleep, though she still whispered stories for Dauriel to cling to.

It scared her so, to truly contemplate her empress' words, the illness in her mind. Tallora had been thrown into the trenches of a war she willingly chose to fight. She wondered if something so juvenile as 'love' might be of aid—perhaps not a cure, but something to soothe the worst of it.

Dauriel's breathing became steady and deep. Tallora held her, longing for the days when they'd bantered while she was in chains, as fucked up as that sounded. Life had been simpler. Life had seemed endless.

Dauriel might survive, and Tallora clung to that. There was still the possibility that Dauriel lived on, her legacy secured and so perhaps she'd be content. Perhaps not—Solviran ambition was limitless. But Dauriel's future was set in stone, either as a martyr or a legend.

It was Tallora's future that had been erased like the sands of the sea, an empty void of possibility, all of life in disarray. All she'd thought she'd known was gone. She shut her eyes, basking in the scent of her love's hair, and asked herself again . . . what it was she truly wanted.

"I would have made you my empress."

Tears welled in Tallora's eyes. The thought was impossible, yet it evoked so powerful a want that she fought an immediate sob. There was so little time.

Who was she to deny herself a moment of it?

She gently jostled Dauriel's arm, heard a confused groan escape the empress' mouth. "Tallora?" she mumbled, her sleepy eyes blinking into wakefulness.

"Marry me." She laughed at Dauriel's confusion, visibly processing the words. *"Marry* me, Dauriel."

"You'd marry a dead woman?"

"Don't you dare rescind your offer now," Tallora teased, joy and pain and other virulent emotions welling within her. "I'm saying yes. Marry me."

Dauriel nodded slowly, still noticeably sleepy, but a smile did cross her lips when Tallora kissed her. "When?"

"Tomorrow?"

Dauriel's silver eyes finally seemed to focus, her stare as mesmerizing as the glittering stars beyond. "Tonight."

"Tonight?" Tallora laughed when Dauriel nodded. "You mean it? By Staella's Grace—yes!"

"Get dressed," Dauriel said softly, visibly enamored at Tallora's enthusiasm, and oh, she loved it so.

She pulled on her boots, then ran to the mirror to smooth her dress, the thick fabric hopefully sturdy enough to protect her from the midnight chill—or whatever time it was. She primped her hair, quickly running a brush through the locks, as white as a wedding veil, when Dauriel approached, carrying a silver, embroidered scarf. She draped it over Tallora's shoulders, her smile unfathomably soft.

It glittered when Tallora swayed, as magnificent as the night sky. "This was given to me when I was twelve—my mother told me I'd wear it before my husband on our wedding day. Consequentially, I resolved to never touch it." Dauriel placed a lingering kiss on Tallora's cheek, watching her in the mirror's reflection. "Suits you much better. It'll keep you warm."

When she pulled back, Tallora realized she had changed into a black ensemble, her crown polished, boots shined, cape draped and billowing from her shoulders—and by every god, she looked gorgeous.

When Dauriel offered a gloved hand, she intertwined their fingers.

At first they walked, but soon they ran, their laughter spurring them onward. "Where are we going?" Tallora asked, once they stepped on the lift.

"To the temple, of course. It defies every tradition, but fuck it."

Tallora kissed her, capturing her lips until the lift stopped at the first floor.

They passed a few servants, but no one questioned their empress, even if her smile had become a rarity. The bitter cold nipped at Tallora's skin, but she pulled the scarf tight around her, surprised to find the thin fabric blocked the chill with ease. Suspecting an enchantment, she said nothing, simply let Dauriel lead, following suit as she nodded a farewell to the guards.

The moon shone high above. At the midnight hour, the city leisurely moved along, lanterns lighting the streets. Snow collected in the dark alleys, but Tallora saw men with shovels keeping it at bay. Those who recognized Dauriel quickly stopped and bowed, but so many simply passed them by, oblivious to the monarch in their presence.

Dauriel paid it no mind. Instead, she released Tallora's hand, only to settle upon her waist instead. She pulled her close, as close as they could be in the winter's chill. When they matched eyes, Dauriel's glistened.

They did not go to the Temple of Unity. Instead, Dauriel took a different path, through a quieter sector of the city.

A small church came into view, bearing stained glass and a single lantern lighting the front door. "What do those words say?" Tallora asked, pointing to the carvings above the door.

"For Whom the Stars Shine," Dauriel said. "This is a temple of Staella."

Tallora noted the stars within the abstract glass pattern. "I take it this isn't typical?"

"Not at all. But who better to bless our union than the goddess who chose to let us live?"

Tallora kissed her then and there upon the steps of the chapel, truly touched by the thought.

When Dauriel opened the unlocked door, Tallora saw rows of benches lit by dim candlelight. Flickering shadows revealed paintings and stone depictions of her beloved goddess, and she resolved to return and see it in the light.

A door opened behind the altar; an old woman entered holding a lantern, her clothing clearly a nightgown. "Can I help you?" she asked, though not unkindly. The temple was never locked, it seemed.

"Yes," Dauriel said, quickly approaching. When she neared, realization flashed in the priestess' face. She bowed, her grey hair sweeping in front of her face. "We need a wedding ceremony."

The priestess glanced from Dauriel to Tallora, eyes widening. "Right now?"

"Correct."

She nodded, though visibly confused. "Give me a moment to put on my proper garments. I'll return shortly."

She disappeared through the door.

Dauriel immediately swooped in and dipped Tallora down into a kiss, genuine joy in the gesture. "You're certain about this?"

"There's no one else, Dauriel." Tallora brushed aside her empress' lengthening hair. "There never has been and never could be."

Dauriel carefully lifted her back up, then stole her hands and led her to the altar. Tallora realized they stood in a wedding pose, with a depiction of Goddess Staella to watch them. "Vows, then?"

"Go ahead," Tallora said, giggling at Dauriel's grin.

"Tallora of the Tortalgan Sea, citizen of Stelune, and captor of my heart—the splendor of your breasts is matched only by the magnitude of your love—"

Tallora swatted her chest; Dauriel burst into a fit of laughter as she shied away.

"You're the worst," Tallora teased, grabbing her ass when Dauriel dared straighten her stance.

Their hands clasped once more, and Dauriel's countenance softened. "I'm not good at expressing my feelings, but I adore you. You are the cleverest, wittiest, most wonderful woman I've ever known. We never should have met; we only did because I committed an unspeakable crime against you, yet you found it in yourself to forgive me."

"You were willing to destroy your life to undo your crime," Tallora said, and Dauriel's eyes watered. "You're correct. If all were right in the world, we never would have met, but here we are, and by the Triage, Dauriel—I love you with everything I am."

The priestess returned, wearing a garb of pure white, gold embroidery at the edges bearing stars and filigree. "I can wait, if you're still—"

Dauriel shook her head. "Priestess, I don't want to waste a moment more of my life without her."

"I can skip the frills if you'd prefer, then."

Dauriel caught Tallora's eye, their silent exchange resulting in Tallora falling into giggles. "Yes, please."

The priestess smiled as she withdrew a silver thread from her pocket. "What's your name?" she asked Tallora.

"Tallora. They don't have surnames where I'm from, so it's only Tallora."

"For now," Dauriel said, her wistful smile melting Tallora's heart.

The priestess looked between the pair of them. "Taken from Goddess Neoma's robe, this thread shall bind your hearts, as it binds your wrists." She gently stole their hands, bidding them to clasp the other's wrist. She wrapped the string loosely around them, finishing it with a bow. "Dauriel Solviraes," she said, forgoing the title—for here, beneath the goddess' gaze, they were equals, "and Tallora, Mother Staella blesses your union. I pronounce you wed upon this beautiful night. Kiss, and seal your love."

They did, and it was as tender a kiss as they'd ever shared.

They bid the priestess farewell, their hands clasped as they left the chapel. Tallora could not speak for Dauriel, but her heart fluttered, her mind in a daze. They held each other in the cold, peace between them even in the emptying streets.

And when they returned to the castle, finally alone in Dauriel's room, they laid innocently in the other's arms, too exhausted to consummate their marriage.

Instead, Dauriel clung tight to Tallora's form, the words, *"Goodnight, Tallora Solviraes,"* nearly evoking a sob.

Tallora kissed her wife—by Staella's Grace, she had a *wife*—and held her until they fell into a serene sleep.

Chapter XIII

Tallora awoke to knocking and a blinding line of sunlight streaming between the curtains. Disoriented, she frowned when the bed shifted, unsteady as she sat up and saw Dauriel stomping toward the door.

She slammed it shut; Tallora cringed and rubbed her eyes, exhaustion weighing down her eyelids.

From beyond the door, Dauriel seethed the words, *"This had better be important."*

"M-My apologies, your majesty. But the hour is nearly noon, and General Khastra has called a council meeting. They are waiting on you—"

"I'll be there when I damn well want to—"

The words were cut off by her banging her outer door shut. Dauriel reentered the bedroom, ever the dragon as she breathed out the barest hints of silver.

Tallora beckoned for her, smiling faintly when Dauriel climbed back into the bed. "Good morning—"

Dauriel's lips stole her words. When she pulled back, her head fell upon Tallora's shoulder. A slight, yet constant trembling shook her hands. "Why must life move forward? Is it too much to ask for one quiet fucking morning with my new wife?"

"Considering none of them know yet? Yes." She placed a kiss on Dauriel's neck, running a soothing hand against her back. "Calm yourself, my dragon empress. One little meeting, and then we lock the doors and fuck the day away as wife and wife."

Dauriel looked up, her disheveled hair hilariously juxtaposed with her mischievous eyes. "Goddess' Grace, you're perfect."

Tallora placed a kiss on her mouth, content to savor her touch. When she pulled away, she whispered, "Let's get changed. Just imagine the scandal when you tell them the news."

Dauriel's grin conveyed nothing but fervent anticipation.

When they'd donned their day clothes, Dauriel led her down the hallway, her hand at Tallora's waist. Something different shone in her stance, a protective instinct that hadn't been there before—or, rather, it had exponentially increased. Dauriel looked prepared to pounce on anyone who so much as spoke to them, and Tallora wouldn't lie and say it wasn't stupidly attractive.

Dauriel was an ass, but Tallora knew it and loved it so.

They reached the council chamber; Dauriel threw open the doors, letting them bang haphazardly against the walls. Those at the table looked up—and among them was someone new standing before the crescent moon.

Unabashedly beautiful, this person held no clear race—she appeared human, yet her pale skin bore a lavender sheen, her eyes the same shade, yet as sharp as a knife. Her dark hair held an elaborate bun atop her head, revealing pointed ears, and her robes were as opulent to match, yet held no distinguishing marks of loyalty. Perhaps she was De'Sindai, but she was surely no mere visitor, and as she spared a glance for the general, Tallora held a few suspicions.

"My friends," Dauriel said bombastically, then she nodded to the interloper, "and guest. Before we begin this meeting, I have an announcement—or, rather, a reintroduction." She released Tallora, instead gesturing to her with pride. "I would like you all to meet Tallora Solviraes, my wife."

Tallora wouldn't say it was horror she saw, but varying degrees of shock met their gazes and no smiles—save one.

The mysterious woman laughed and clapped her hands. "Congratulations, Empress Dauriel. And you, Empress Consort. There are few mortal institutions finer than matrimony. I wish you many years of joy."

Many years of joy. Tallora swallowed the emotion those words wrought. "Thank you, my lady," she said instead.

"Who are you?" Dauriel asked, always straight to the point.

"My apologizes." She offered a hand, which Dauriel accepted. "My name is Maysonge deDieula, Herald of Ilune. I've come to explain a few . . . *addendums* to Khastra's plan. We've discussed it at length, she and I."

Tallora looked to Khastra, saw the fondness in her gaze as she looked to Maysonge, and wondered how much of the half-demon's inner life anyone truly knew.

"We're always happy to hear Ilune's will," Dauriel replied.

Ilaeri coughed expectantly, his smile all but painted on. "I suppose we should all give our congratulations on your matrimony, though perhaps with a few days' notice we could have provided an actual celebration."

"We're at war." Dauriel's hand crept back to Tallora's waist, trembling as she gripped her dress. "Sometimes things must be done quickly."

"Of course, of course. Once the issue of Yu'Khrall is dealt with, we can introduce her to the populace, though she might be infamous enough without that."

"Any person who takes issue with my wife can answer to me," Dauriel said, an unquestionable challenge in the words. "Whether they be from my own people or Moratham or the Tortalgan Sea—let them come."

Heat rose against Tallora's back, and she instinctively stepped away—Dauriel glowed from within, silver flame apparent in her mouth, smoke escaping her nostrils when she breathed. Tallora frowned, then dared to grab her arm despite the heat, her thumb soothing gentle circles against her sleeve.

"We're not here to discuss matrimony," Dauriel all but spat. "Lady deDieula, please, you have the floor."

Dauriel's grip on Tallora's dress remained possessive. She gestured to her seat, but Tallora shook her head. "Take it," she whispered. "I'd rather stand."

Truthfully, Tallora feared another outburst like the one she'd seen two days prior, so she let Dauriel sit and hopefully be calm. Instead, Tallora stood behind and placed a gentle hand on her shoulder. Dauriel's own snaked up to grasp it.

"Solviran Council," Lady deDieula said, grinning as her sharp gaze scanned the room, "Ilune is pleased. She sends her regards and her utmost praise at both your eminent victory in the desert as well as the handling of Yu'Khrall. She prepares to celebrate with you, but in the meantime, she offers aid."

"Aid?" Dauriel said, her interest apparently caught. "Do explain."

"Assuming you have no objections, Empress, I shall accompany your ships. Khastra and I have already discussed the intricacies of the journey, but once we arrive, I shall serve as the envoy of Ilune, wielding her designated power."

Dauriel's grip on Tallora's hand tightened. The council watched with intrigue, the words perhaps unexpected. "We would be honored to accept her aid," Dauriel said, "though while I don't question your power, Ilune does not even need a host to appear, so why would she not come herself?"

"There is contention in Celestière, regarding her offer of aid," deDieula replied, her grin conveying amusement. "Neoma does not disregard the usefulness of necromancy but has proclaimed that Ilune shall be absent from the fight. And so I, her most accomplished, shall be there instead."

"I'm curious, then," Dauriel replied. "What aid can a necromancer provide upon the seas?"

"Oh, a disgusting amount, I assure you. Khastra and I have discussed the necessary supplies, which we would happily relay to you alone."

"Oh?"

Lady deDieula's smile twisted, an ineffable wickedness in her countenance. "I would not insist if it weren't important."

Tallora felt a faint rise of heat in Dauriel's hand. She brought her own down to touch the back of Dauriel's hair, willing her to calm. The empress gave a brief, affirming nod. "What of the rest?"

Khastra answered, again devolving into jargon Tallora hadn't a hope to understand, but one thing did stand out as clear, as she went over numbers and plotting and such, that there was no consideration to collateral damage, and Tallora feared for what was left of her people.

And so, when a lull appeared in Khastra's words, she raised a tentative hand. Lady deDieula smiled brightly. "Empress Consort?"

All eyes turned to Tallora. "Forgive me, if it isn't my place to speak," she said, gently withdrawing her hand from Dauriel's, "but I do need to ask—what of my people? Will they be warned of the attack? So many have died already. I don't know if they'll be in Iids or by Yu'Khrall or if they ran or . . ." Tallora swallowed, the sudden rise of her tears unexpected. She warded them away, but deDieula filled in the silence.

"An excellent question, and it sparks a few more," the woman said thoughtfully. "Was I properly informed that Yu'Khrall has an appetite for merfolk?"

The question revolted her, and deDieula's smile suggested she already knew the answer. "Yes," Tallora replied, but appall stilled her tongue.

"An addendum," deDieula said smoothly, looking at Khastra with intrigue, and then to the rest of the council. "We send two fleets."

"You are vastly overestimating my numbers." Khastra's words were nothing less than unimpressed.

"General," she cooed, and it all but confirmed Tallora's suspicions regarding her place in Khastra's life, "I'm wounded. Hear me out. Two fleets. The second is all that you've brilliantly planned. The first is small. Pitiful. A legion of unseasoned heroes meant to foreshadow the coming storm. Perhaps they succeed; more likely, they fall, but Yu'Khrall has a taste for humanoid flesh. He consumes them, falls into a lull—then Solvira's true might crashes upon him from without . . . and destroys him from within."

Silence settled upon the room, the horrific truth of what deDieula suggested a poisoned cloud around them. Tallora's stomach sickened, and without thinking she said, "What?"

The woman frowned, though not unhappily—confusion marred her beautiful face. "Was I not clear? I will give undeath to the dead inside him and they'll—"

"You were crystal clear, don't worry." Tallora's fist clenched, jaw grit. "Lady deDieula, with due respect, that's barbaric."

"From a certain viewpoint," deDieula replied, apparently unoffended.

Tallora turned to Dauriel, desperation on her tongue. "You can't condone this."

Dauriel said nothing, merely stared thoughtfully at the table.

"Mermaid," came Khastra's voice, calm amidst Tallora's storm, "we cannot let emotion dictate our actions. War is not the business of soft hearts."

"She's proposing sacrificing these people! They won't even be warned—they'll simply be fuel for your fire. This isn't about emotion. This is about what's right and wrong—"

"You're a fitting follower of Staella," deDieula interrupted, no ire on her tongue; merely amusement, and Tallora couldn't shake the feeling that she was being mocked. "Full of dreams. What would you propose, Empress Consort?"

A cruel question, and Tallora felt the veiled insult in her words. She said nothing, because there was nothing she could say—she was no tactician, nor a warrior, not even a leader. Empress Consort—not a title of greatness, only proof that she'd married well.

"You'll be brilliant in peacetime," deDieula continued, her countenance almost kind. "You have the makings of being beloved in ways Solvira desperately needs—breathtakingly beautiful, charming and assured, a figurehead to adore. But in times of war, kingdoms need a stronger hold. You'll learn this in time."

Tallora's better judgement screamed to back down, but from a place beyond fear came the words, "Your title leads me to wonder what you'd possibly know of military tactics either. 'Herald' isn't synonymous with 'monarch.'"

Lady deDieula laughed, nothing of offense in the sound, despite Tallora's spiteful words. "All right, I suppose you have me there. Though I do have a few thousand years' worth of experience advising the goddess who founded the kingdom you've asked for help in dealing with your little tragedy—which, if I recall correctly, has the greatest military in the world." Her smile remained kind, which was somehow the greatest insult of all. "Why don't you leave the discussion to the adults, hmm?"

Given the choice between bursting into angry tears and leaving, Tallora forced a smile and walked out.

"Tallora?"

That was Dauriel, she knew, but she left the council chamber, nevertheless.

A horrible, crippling truth descended upon her; Tallora fell upon a pillar and wept in the hallway. Staella's Grace held no power here. Tallora held no power here. She feared she'd salvaged her heart in exchange for her soul.

She gripped the pillar, forcing her legs to support her. She stumbled as she walked, her eyes spilling tears. With no aim, she ended up outside in the garden. The snow had settled into a soggy path, ridden with dirt and deprived of the magic of a fresh falling. She wore no coat; the chill cut deep, but she couldn't say she cared.

Dauriel alone was who her heart craved. Dauriel Solviraes, empress of the fucking world, was the shadow Solvira lived beneath, and Tallora was a fool to forget it. Last night, all had seemed limitless, eternal, but the sun had risen and shined light upon her foolishness. Her momma had warned her of this; Tallora had left Dauriel because of this—

"Tallora?"

Tallora gasped at the name, surprised to see Dauriel approaching, her boots crunching against the dirty snow. She removed her cape in a single motion, immediately wrapping it around Tallora's shivering form. Dauriel embraced her, pulled her against her chest, and Tallora clung to the sound of her heartbeat. "I rejected the plan."

Tallora immediately pulled back, though she kept the cape secure around her shoulders. "You what?"

"You were right," she said, her words as soft as her silver eyes. "War begets unspeakable crimes, but the enemy is not my own people. I am here to lead; not to betray them for their loyalty. There is no justice in that."

Tallora studied this stranger's face and saw beauty unparalleled—both inside and out. Her tears fell quickly but she smiled.

"You mustn't cry in the snow," Dauriel chided, her own smile shy and tentative. "The tears will freeze against your face."

"Dauriel . . ." Tallora swallowed to mask her sob.

But Dauriel shook her head. "My mother's shadow lingers. It's a plague upon my people. She was willing to sell them to Moratham for power, and she would have done the same here—sacrificed her own to gain a small advantage. I'm not her. I'm better and will be remembered as such."

Tallora's lip trembled as she came forward again, accepting the offered embrace and warmth.

"You were right about warning your people. It would be a waste to defeat Yu'Khrall, only to have the denizens of the ocean die in the collateral damage. I would propose sending Prince Kal with a message and allow time for evacuation."

Tallora brought her face to meet Dauriel's, their bodies still touching with only the fabric to separate them. "You'd release him?"

"I'd release them both. As a gesture of goodwill and, well, as cruel as it is, your people aren't a threat anymore." Tallora couldn't argue with that, but before she could speak, Dauriel continued. "But they would listen to their king and prince. Assuming Yu'Khrall has not taken them captive, they might be able to orchestrate an escape."

"Why though? Why all of this? This goes beyond trying to erase your mother's memory."

Tallora watched the plethora of emotions pass Dauriel's face, saw conflict and contemplation and then . . . a semblance of peace. "Because there is no humanity in pure power. I can be ruthless without being cruel."

Tallora kissed her, because by Staella's Grace— she'd never been more beautiful. Dauriel's lips parted for her tongue, and they kissed in the chill afternoon, warmed by their hearts and the sun.

Suddenly, Tallora pulled back, recalling something concerning. "Also, Dauriel, Lady deDieula—" She lowered her voice to a whisper. "—I think she and Khastra are together."

Dauriel frowned, brow furrowed as she glanced back to the castle where the aforementioned woman was staying. "Strange."

"I don't like her at all."

"I wasn't going to brag, but I did politely tell her to go fuck herself after you left."

Tallora bit her lip to hide her smile. "What?"

"She insulted my wife." Dauriel placed a soft kiss into Tallora's hair. "I don't have to appease self-important advisors to goddesses. There's no one more important to me than you, and you have wisdom to offer."

Lips brushed against Tallora's cheek, stealing her focus. A fierce blush flared across her face, enamor filling her heart. "Dauriel—"

"I believe you said something about fucking the day away as wife and wife." Dauriel continued planting kisses along Tallora's cheek, her smile gentler than her words. "Food first. Can't have my sweet wife starving to death."

Tallora giggled at the word 'wife.' Never had she heard a more joyful sound.

When Dauriel removed her hands, Tallora stole one, still acutely aware of how they shook. She stroked a gentle line across her palm. "Are you unwell?

Cringing, Dauriel seemed to understand. "It's my penance for drinking—rather, for stopping. Nothing to worry about."

Tallora chose to believe her and kissed her lightly on her knuckles.

"I'll send a messenger to inform Kal and King Merl of the new development," Dauriel said. "My father can have a portal made to send them home."

"Might I go talk to them instead?" The slight wavering of the empress' smile spoke volumes. "Dauriel—"

Dauriel's gaze left her, focused on her mouth and chin instead. Something shifted in her demeanor, and Tallora sensed a bitter mood. "Of course you can."

Tallora brought a hand up to cup Dauriel's cheek, coaxing her empress to look at her. "What's wrong?"

"Nothing."

"Dauriel—"

"I don't like him, but it's irrational," Dauriel replied, her language oddly stilted for the oft eloquent woman, "and he's your friend. You should go."

"Dauriel, my dragon empress, you can't hoard me away—"

"I know," Dauriel said sharply, but her immediate cringe conveyed her regret. "I'm sorry—"

Tallora took Dauriel's hand, stealing her words as she stroked gentle lines upon it. "I need you to breathe," she said, and she mimed the motion with Dauriel, certainly noticing how smoke escaped with her wife's breath. "Why don't you like him?"

In the daunting silence, Dauriel clung to Tallora's hand tight enough she feared she might lose feeling. "Because the fucked up truth is your life would be so much easier if you'd chosen him instead of me."

Tallora frowned, shocked at the words. "That's not—He was never—"

"I know!" Dauriel released her hand, tense all over as she brought her whole stance inward. "I know, I know, but these are the kind of thoughts that scream in my head, and I wish—I wish *so badly*—I could shut them off."

"Dauriel, I married *you*—"

"And you can still annul it if you regret it—"

"I won't, and I don't, and I need you to please stop talking because you're spiraling." Tallora swore she watched a drowning woman, yet she could do nothing as Dauriel looked about to burst from tension. "Please, don't throw away your happiness because you feel like you don't deserve it."

Footsteps stole her words; they were no longer alone. Beside Tallora, Dauriel quickly forced her composure, though her eyes glistened. Ilaeri and Adrael approached from the castle.

When Tallora held her waist, Dauriel responded by pulling her close, protective as she said, "Father? Magister?"

"Empress Dauriel," Adrael said, "your father and I wish to discuss the details of your marriage. It is not exactly a small thing when a Solviraes takes a spouse, especially when they aren't of the bloodline."

"Or country," Ilaeri offered, though he sounded rather bored.

"Or species. And that isn't taking into account the political ramifications of you choosing a former prisoner as your bride. The amount of paperwork shall be—"

"Am I being questioned or interrogated?" Dauriel spat, releasing Tallora, who clung tight to the cloak around her shoulders. "The deed is done. Make it right. Give her a false lineage if you must to simplify your precarious jobs, but Tallora and I were married beneath Staella's gaze which, while unconventional, is still legal according to the charters of my kingdom, so cease your passive aggressive *bullshit* and do your fucking jobs."

Adrael looked appropriately offended, but Ilaeri simply held up his hands in defense. "No judgement from me. Though I was curious to know Tallora's parents' names so they might be included in the announcement."

Dauriel's fighting stance didn't shift. Tallora stepped forward lightly, eyes fixed on Ilaeri. "Tallor and Myalla—my father and mother, respectively. They've both passed away."

"Empress, the council would like to speak to you in private," Ilaeri continued. He gave a polite nod to Tallora. "With due respect to you, Empress Consort."

"Will Lady deDieula be present?" Dauriel asked, thinly veiled vitriol on her tongue.

Ilaeri shook his head. "Ilune's Herald announced her intention to return to Celestière until the day the ships are launched. She says she will speak to you then, instead."

Dauriel's scowl betrayed her dark mood, but Tallora spoke, braver with the affirmation of her place. "Your meeting can wait. We've made plans of our own. She'll call for you when she's ready."

"No," Dauriel whispered, defeat in her stance as her fury slowly seeped away, "I should go. Then this is done, and we can be free." For a heartbreaking moment, her glistening eyes showed pain. "But afterward, can we talk? Please?"

Tallora nodded and placed a chaste kiss upon her lips. "I'll be waiting."

They broke apart when Dauriel stepped back, silent as she followed her father and Adrael out. Left alone, Tallora drew the cloak tighter around her shoulders, stomach sinking.

She wished to speak to someone, whether it be Kal or even Khastra, though she was likely busy with her 'guest.' Lady Mithal was a friend, but Tallora didn't feel she could confide in her about this. And while Priestess Toria had offered support in the past, she would likely be in the meeting with Dauriel. Instead, Tallora returned to the castle, lonely beyond compare.

She didn't go to the menagerie. Instead, Tallora went to Dauriel's bedroom—now theirs together, she figured—cloak still wrapped around her body, the faint smell of its mistress comforting in her sullied mood. Exhausted from a night of little sleep, she laid down in bed and curled into the familiar scents and plush embrace.

Life moved on. She had married the love of her life, and now she faced reality—that this same woman slowly unraveled at her seams and would die in only a few days' time. The reality of it struck her like a knife to the stomach, and tears welled in her eyes. But who could she speak to? Kal was a friend, but it was strange to speak to him of this.

But there was someone; someone who always listened and loved. Praying she remembered the path, Tallora dressed in warmer clothing, tragically leaving Dauriel's cloak behind, instead donning the same wedding veil she'd worn the night prior. She took her gifted vestment of Staella, letting it display around her neck.

After a brief stop at the kitchens, she left the palace with no interruption, though she lingered before the council chamber, pastry in hand, wondering if Dauriel would explode and slay them all. Outside, the city moved along, oblivious to the dangers of the world, perhaps more concerned about the royal shadow they lived beneath. Solvira was fair, in theory, but its rulers were not known for kindness.

She went about unnoticed. The people knew her not as their Empress Consort, only as a girl in a particularly glittery and too-thin cloak. But she pushed her way through, the path not long, and soon she reached the Temple of Staella—the very same she had been married in.

The door was unlocked. She opened it, finding a few supplicants seated in pews, eyes closed in silent prayer. Peace settled upon her, the weight of the world lifted as she stepped through the door. Staella was the softness in this kingdom, the heart and the humanity. By the altar stood the high priestess of the temple, the same who had wed she and Dauriel, and with her, in hushed conversation, was High Priestess Toria, her presence unsurprising, given her role.

Though likely busy, she offered Tallora a quick and quiet smile. She returned it, and though Toria might've been an ear to listen, there was only one who could truly understand. Tallora stepped quietly down the aisle, taking a seat as the rest did, alone in her own pew.

She shut her eyes and bowed her head. Clear words floated through her mind, crystal in their clarity: *Goddess Staella, I'm so afraid.*

And within her, a strange sensation swelled, unnatural, though comforting. Beside her was weight, though she saw nothing when she peeked.

But not for me. For Dauriel, my wife. I cannot fathom her burdens. I don't understand her pain, but I've seen it. She may have only a few precious days left—what can I do?

The answer came with absolute clarity, as though it were her own thought. Perhaps it was. *Love her.*

A weight settled upon her shoulder, gentle and warm. But when Tallora peeked once more, still she saw nothing.

Tears welled in Tallora's eyes, her own impending loss ever looming. Her head fell into her hands. *She's going to die. She thinks it's the only path.*

She heard nothing. The presence waited.

If there's any way, any possible way to save her . . . how?

Nothing. But the presence lingered.

Perhaps it was the wrong question. *Can I save her?*

No, her mind said, and she mouthed the words unbidden. *But you can love her.*

They'd been ships meant to pass in the night, yet they'd collided like a tropical storm. Tallora wondered, for the first time, that perhaps they'd been meant to meet after all. That Dauriel's great purpose was to save the world . . . and Tallora's was to as well, but in a different sort of way. To walk with her to the end of the line and hold her before she took that final plunge.

Dauriel would die. Tallora felt no peace, but she felt . . . acceptance.

Her tears fell faster. The warmth on her shoulder enveloped her, bringing comfort as she sobbed.

Something soft touched her upper arm. "Tallora?"

Startled from her tears, Tallora nearly sobbed anew at the familiar face before her. "Leah?"

She was, her dark hair and features unmistakable, eyes stenciled by distinctive black powder. Leah looked as shocked as she, but at the sight of Tallora's tear-streaked face, she sat and wrapped her arms tight around her. Tallora fell into the embrace, weeping into her dear friend's shoulder. "What are you doing here?"

Tallora nearly smiled; the question held more weight than an ocean's worth of water. "I don't know where to begin with that." Wiping her eyes of tears, she sat up, grateful when Leah's arm remained around her shoulders. "It's been a long month."

"Last we spoke, you were only supposed to be here for a day."

Tallora nodded. "Have you heard the rumors of the calamity beneath the sea?"

"A few whispers, but I didn't give them any mind." Leah studied her broken stance. "Will you tell me? I want to hear."

Tallora relayed what mattered—of Yu'Khrall, of Stelune, of her mother's death, Harbinger's sacrifice—all in hushed whispers within Staella's temple. "And so I came here, to beg Solvira for aid. They've agreed to give it."

"I don't know that I can imagine a monster coming to genocide my people," Leah replied, lip trembling from sorrow, "but I do know how it feels to lose my country and my home. If I can be of any help, please let me. Do you need a place to stay?"

Tallora shook her head. She contemplated the truth, though it remained a secret to the public, and whispered, "This must be kept quiet for now, but I took the Solviraes name. I married Empress Dauriel."

Leah's eyes looked at least as large as Harbinger's, and Tallora nearly laughed to see it. "Was that the price of aid?"

"No! No, that has nothing to do with it. Her council didn't seem particularly happy, actually. We . . . eloped, in a sense. Married last night, here in this temple." She smiled, though it held sorrow. "I love her so much. Bu she's struggling. And . . . And I may lose her." Leah's wide eyes didn't understand, but she listened all the same. "I can't say much because it hasn't come to pass, but I may be a widow before the week's end, and Leah . . ." Her head fell into her hands, fresh tears welling. "I've never felt so helpless. Dauriel won't fight it. She won't consider any other options because" She released a quiet sob. "I'm sorry. I shouldn't burden you with this—"

"No, no," Leah soothed, kindness in her gaze. "Please let me help, if I can."

"She's hurting, and it's not as simple as just holding her when she cries," Tallora continued, wiping tears from her face. "She's explosive, and I don't have to be the one in the line of fire to be scared of it." She squeezed her eyes shut, willing herself to calm. "I love her so much, Leah. Seeing her little moments of joy makes it worth it, but now she's found her great escape, and she'll take it. It's the heroic thing to do, but . . . but . . ." She couldn't go on; she held in a sob.

"Oh, Tallora . . ." Leah's arms wrapped around her, holding her close.

"I came to the temple because I didn't know who else to talk to," Tallora whispered. "Little did I know I'd find a more tangible someone." Her smile became sincere when she looked to Leah, who matched it.

"It was so strange," Leah said softly. "I had dropped Mocum off with his tutor and hoped to catch up on housekeeping but something told me to come here. Just a prompting. I'm glad I followed it."

"Do you worship Staella now?"

Leah nodded. "I'd struggled for years to reconcile my religion with the one of Solvira—I told you that, once. Meeting you made me think more about Staella and her teachings. I spent a few months studying her and her legacy and decided she was someone I could devote my life to." She shrugged, though her eyes sparkled with joy. "It felt like a smaller step, if that makes sense. I don't know if Neoma is a goddess I can worship, but Staella is revered wherever you go."

"I've loved her all my life," Tallora affirmed.

Leah took her hand and squeezed it tight. "I wish I knew what to tell you. But I'm glad you told me. You need support too."

She gave a half scoff, guilt expanding in her stomach. "I feel selfish. Dauriel's the one who's hurting."

Leah shook her head. "It's difficult to take care of someone when you're all alone."

Tallora nodded, fighting the hope filling her. Dauriel might be dead within a week. It would not matter at all. "Enough about me. How are you?"

"I'm well," Leah said kindly. "Not much, except watching Mocum grow. My job is enjoyable, but not particularly exciting." A frown stole her good mood, slowly settling onto her brow. Her voice lowered. "Where did you get that vestment?"

Tallora held her gifted string of beads and carved stars. "It was a gift from the high priestess on the council. The one I had beneath the sea was lost."

Leah's scowl remained. "Is she from Moratham?"

"No," Tallora said, concerned at the segue. "She's from Vaile."

With some reluctance, Leah's expression softened. "I suppose that explains it. Vaile holds many Morathan immigrants."

"What are you implying?"

"When I lived in Moratham, I knew of Staella. I had visited Andiamen once as a child and seen a small temple to her glory. I think I told you once there's a very different worship of Staella in the desert and they pray for the day she escapes Neoma's tyrannical grasp."

Tallora nodded, her worry only increasing.

"I remember seeing that same style of vestment among the Priestesses of Staella in the capital. It symbolizes the union of Morathma and Staella, and the conjoining of their kingdoms—the earth and the stars."

Tallora felt suddenly cold. She tucked the long necklace into the bodice of her gown, secured within the corset. "But it was a gift. She gave it in good faith."

"I don't doubt that," Leah said, hands held defensively as she noticeably backtracked. "If she's from Vaile, perhaps that's simply what she grew up with. Nothing wrong with that. It's still Staella's symbol. It's a lovely gift, when you think on it."

Tallora nodded, still feeling strange at the thought. "I'll talk to her about it. As kind as the gesture was, I don't want to flaunt this if it makes people think . . . Well . . ."

"No, I understand," Leah replied. "But I don't know if anyone else would give it any mind, unless they were raised in Moratham like me."

"It just infuriates me, that anyone could bastardize Staella's worship." The coldness in her limbs fell prey to pulsing heat instead, her fury simmering.

"In their defense, they think the same thing about you. Indoctrination runs deep. It isn't something you unlearn overnight—some people never do, even when faced with proof."

Tallora hated that, couldn't fathom it at all.

"I have to leave," Leah said softly. "Mocum's tutoring is only an hour long, but can I see you again?"

"In two days—" Tallora swallowed that bitter truth. "—I'll be left alone for a while. Come to the palace anytime."

They embraced. Leah left her, but Tallora felt peace upon her exit. She shut her eyes, settling back into the pew. *Thank you.*

Within her soul, she felt warmth return. Perhaps she'd linger a little longer.

Chapter XIV

Tallora stayed for a long time, cherishing the peace of the temple. But there was somewhere else she was supposed to be. Long after her tears dried, she left the temple, realizing it would be sunset within the hour.

The unfortunate drawback of sleeping the morning away—she'd lost so much of a precious day.

As she walked the streets, she noticed the cityfolk were hustling more than normal—and actively leaving the marketplaces. Guards directed them, pushing them along. "You're all to return to your homes!" one cried, his decorated armor suggesting he might be in charge. "Executive order! The streets are to be cleared!"

She pushed her way toward one of the guards. "What's going on?"

"The city is under lockdown, my lady. You must return to your home."

"But why?"

"Empress' orders. We weren't told the details."

Tallora looked past him to the castle. She gave a brief nod, fortunately not stopped as she stepped past him, making her way toward home.

Her mind couldn't fathom this stroke of madness—were they under attack? Had the general condoned this? She hustled through the emptying streets, fighting against the current of people as she pushed her way through.

She had nearly reached the gates when she heard, "Stop!" From behind, a guard rapidly approached. "All citizens are to return to their homes."

"I—"

"Are you a servant in the palace, my lady?"

"No, but I'm—"

The guard grabbed her arm. She failed to wrench it away. "Then you cannot be here—"

"Stand down!"

They both turned, and Tallora recognized the pair of approaching guards—the duo at the front gate. The guard released her, visibly confused.

"She's the one they're looking for," one of the men said. "Tallora of the Tortalgan Sea, yes?"

Tallora swiftly nodded. "What's going on?"

"The city has been put under lockdown to find you. With due respect, your majesty, you'll be coming with us."

She nodded slowly, the words unsettling.

She was taken to the palace, the guards at the gate stopping their patrol and looking relieved to see her.

Tallora pulled the veil tight around her shoulders as the guards escorted her to the lift. She looked out the window to the empty streets, her heart palpitating. "Why though?" she finally dared to ask.

"Begging your pardon, your majesty," one guard replied—it seemed news of her new station had gotten out—"but you were missing for hours, and when a monarch is missing for hours, it's generally considered an emergency. While I won't put words in her mouth, Empress Dauriel seemed to believe you might be gone for good."

Tallora's heart sank. When the lift stopped, they faced the entrance to the throne room. She ran forward, the guards quickly following, and entered the expansive hallway.

As she traversed the narrow entry hall, she heard a ranting figure from the center, her heart sinking when she knew the voice. ". . . if the streets are empty, search the citizen's homes. If anyone is holding her, they'll face my wrath. The merfolk claimed to know nothing, but—"

Tallora locked eyes with Dauriel, who paced before her throne. Most of her council stood around her, though Khastra and Priestess Toria were missing, and a small plethora of guards flanked her. But

Dauriel's face held too many emotions for Tallora to decipher only one. "Where in Onias' Hell were you?!"

Dauriel rapidly approached. Taken aback, Tallora said, "I was at Staella's temple."

"You told no one!"

Tallora's pride bristled. "Did I commit a crime?"

Dauriel stopped a few feet away. Behind her fury, her jaw trembled; her eyes filled with tears.

Oh, Dauriel.

Tallora stepped forward, ignoring Dauriel's furious words of, *"You're royalty! You can't simply go off gallivanting! You could have been killed—"* and instead pulled her into an embrace.

Her cloak fell to the floor as she wrapped both arms tight around her empress, feeling the woman nearly collapse. "Call off the search," Tallora whispered. "We'll talk in private."

"Call off the search!" Dauriel barked, her composure quickly unraveling. "And get out! All of you!"

Her hold on Tallora tightened as the guards and the council left, leaving them alone. Dauriel took a breath to speak, but Tallora spoke faster. "I'm sorry."

Whatever Dauriel's words, they died in her throat. Her silver eyes watered as she stared at Tallora, still wrapped in her embrace.

"I should have told someone I was going. I didn't think of it because anyone I might've told was in the council chamber with you. But this is my fault, and I'm sorry I scared you."

Dauriel's lip trembled, a tragic whimper leaving her lips. Her tears streamed down her face. "After everything we talked about, I-I thought . . ."

Tallora gently interrupted her failing words. "You thought I was running away?"

"It was one of the many gods-awful thoughts in my head." Dauriel's face fell against Tallora's shoulder, where she wept. Tallora clung to her, content to be her lifeline in the storm.

"You're my wife, you dramatic, beautiful bitch," Tallora said softly, no ire in the words. "Tensions are high. But I love you so much."

Dauriel nodded against her shoulder, still crying. "I'm sorry," her empress said, and Tallora ran her fingers through her short hair. "I'm so sorry."

Tallora said nothing, merely continued with her soothing gestures.

They stood in silence, save for Dauriel's sobs. When they finally stilled, Tallora whispered, "Let me take you to bed."

Dauriel nodded, her face swollen and raw when she finally looked up. Fingers intertwined, they left the throne room, taking the lift down until they reached the proper floor.

Tallora escorted her to her bedroom, and once alone she placed successive kisses upon Dauriel's tear-streaked cheeks. "Oh, my wife," she whispered, and she clung to Dauriel in the dark room, then gently pulled her to the window and the balcony beyond.

With the falling night came a sea of stars, twinkling in the sky with all the brilliance of their goddess' glory. Dauriel stared out, to the meeting of sky and land, surveying the great kingdom she owned.

Tallora joined her, light-headed to think it was hers too. Her chest threatened to cave, but she asked a crippling inquiry all the same. "What will happen to me," she whispered, "when you die in your goddess' name?"

"You aren't of Ilune's blood and so will forfeit the right to rule," Dauriel said, her tone void of emotion. "But you will still hold influence among the court, should you wish to stay. You would be the first in line to take an advisory position to the new monarch. Or, you may return home and retire, supported all your life by the crown's treasury."

"I'd go home," Tallora admitted. "To what's left of it. They'll need all the aid they can get rebuilding."

"Solvira will help. My father has been instructed of that, and he will respect my wishes."

Tallora looked to Dauriel and saw nothing decipherable in her countenance. "What happened in your council meeting?"

"It largely devolved into me being reprimanded for acting rash in taking you as my wife." Dauriel's lip sneered, jaw steeling. "Because even though I could not have produced an heir, I could have married for diplomatic gain or money or even a treaty and simply kept you as a mistress, as all the Solviraes have done. Adrael and Rel were quite adamant about that, and my father begrudgingly agreed." Dauriel breathed, and Tallora realized she was slowly becoming accustomed to the presence of smoke. "But we did also discuss your people and Yu'Khrall. Kal and Merl have yet to be informed of their release—I was thinking tomorrow morning would be most appropriate now, given the hour."

"Did I mishear you, or did you say you'd interrogated them about my disappearance?"

Dauriel's stare fell to the balcony. She said nothing at all; she merely nodded.

Tallora wrapped her arms around her empress, taking a deep inhale of the night air. "Dauriel, I love all of you. Even the ugly parts. Even the things you hate. Just because my life might've been easier with Kal doesn't mean it would have brought me joy. You're worth it. And even if it's for only a few more days, I will never regret marrying you."

Dauriel remained limp, but she'd heard. Her trembling jaw revealed that much.

"I hurt when you're hurting, but your glowing moments have always made everything worth it. You're a mess, but I knew that. You've hurt me before, yes, but you're trying to be better. I've seen it." She placed a kiss in Dauriel's hair, lingering as she held her tight. She stole one of Dauriel's wrists, her thumb brushing a jagged scar. "Your worst enemy is in the mirror, and she might scream that I hate you until the day you die. But it's a lie, Dauriel. It's a lie, and I'm begging you to not listen. I swear to you, as your wife who loves you, that I'll remind you of that whenever you need it."

Dauriel didn't cry, though she visibly fought it as she squeezed her eyes shut.

Tallora whispered, "What do you need?"

"I don't know," Dauriel immediately replied, but Tallora shook her head as she again placed a kiss in Dauriel's hair.

"I need you to be introspective for a moment. How do you feel? And what do you need?"

Dauriel, again, faded into silence, but her stare returned to the sky. An arm wrapped around Tallora's waist. "I feel like a fool," Dauriel whispered, her grip growing ever tighter, slowly by degrees. "But it's like you said—I need reassurance."

"I don't think you're foolish." Tallora coaxed Dauriel's face to meet her stare, smiling tenderly as she stroked a soft line across her cheeks. Then, she brought their mouths together, kissing her beneath the starry sky. She quickly let it deepen, slipping her tongue into Dauriel's mouth, gratified when the woman moaned. Heat simmered between Tallora's thighs, but she couldn't speak for her love, didn't wish to push her for more unless she craved it too.

Dauriel's hand came up to her hair, stroked it as they kissed before the city's judgement. Her other went to Tallora's waist, gripping her dress as she pressed their bodies closer.

Tallora whispered, "I'm yours, Dauriel. I love you with all my heart. You have my full permission to touch me if that's the reassurance you need."

Apparently she had spoken true; Dauriel's hand left her waist and skimmed down her skirt. When she groped her, Tallora giggled, overjoyed when Dauriel smiled. "Predictable as ever," Tallora said, though she whined to punctuate it. Dauriel should know how desperately she was wanted. "We do still need to consummate our union."

"I have a thought," Dauriel replied, her voice low and wanting, "but let me touch you first."

Tallora grinned, Dauriel's warmth enough to stave off the cold night. Her lips skimmed Tallora's neck, placing slow kisses as she leisurely undid the buttons of her dress, letting it fall enough to untie her corset strings. Dauriel never broke pace with her kisses, clearly well practiced, and Tallora thought it terribly amusing.

When it fell away, she tossed it aside, and then the condemning vestment with it. Tallora stood half-dressed on the balcony, and Dauriel wasted no time squeezing her breasts. The fabric of Tallora's chemise shifted at Dauriel's touch, who held no reserve in pulling it down enough to expose her breasts to the night air.

Tallora groaned at the contact. The cold air juxtaposed cruelly with Dauriel's warm hands. When Dauriel took her breast in her mouth, Tallora nearly fell off the balcony when her knees failed her.

Fortunately, Dauriel held her, her strong arms a pleasure. Tallora looked up, half-dipped by her empress' touch, and gazed at the sky, sending her pleasured moans up to the stars.

Which was a rather awkward thought, considering she worshipped them, but Tallora sang praises to only one goddess this night.

Dauriel's hand lifted her skirts, touching the soft skin and fabric beneath. When her finger skimmed Tallora's thigh, she grinned, content to hold Dauriel against her breast still. "Oh, Empress," she sighed, then squeaked when said empress suddenly squeezed her ass. "Empress?"

Dauriel's mouth left her breast, the challenge in her eye enough to compensate for the sudden lack of contact. "Yes, wife?"

Heat flooded Tallora's face at the title. She crushed their mouths together, savoring Dauriel's hand on her ass, giggling when it stroked down to the warmth between her legs. The light touch brought a shiver down her spine as she helped slip her underclothes to the ground; Dauriel then hitched her thigh over her hip and touched lightly against her clit.

Tallora's whine punctuated the silent night. Dauriel's arm was all that supported her—and so when she was gently led down, her back touched the edge of the balcony.

Dauriel pushed inside. Tallora gasped, eyes opening at the unexpected entrance. She smiled as she moaned, savoring the touch and the crass delight in her wife's eyes. "Dauriel, my empress . . ."

Her empress moved slowly, more stretching than thrusting, and Tallora loved it so, the connection to her love. Dauriel knelt before her, both of them nearly on the ground now.

The minutes passed slowly by, and Tallora's body stayed in absolute bliss at the gentle, tender motions. She mourned the withdrawal, when Dauriel suddenly pulled away. Her hand emerged from Tallora's skirts. "It's freezing. Let's go inside."

Boneless, Tallora couldn't articulate a coherent reply; simply a mild, "Uh-huh," as Dauriel led her back into their bedroom.

She collapsed onto the bed, grinning like a fool as Dauriel lit a candle on the bedside table, illuminating Tallora's half-naked form. Her empress's eyes luxuriated over her as she said, "Wait here. Touch yourself; you might as well enjoy those tits of yours too." Dauriel's wink was nothing less than obscene, and oh Tallora loved it so.

She left Tallora wanting and waiting in the warm bed. With no shyness, Tallora removed her dress and all her underclothes, purposefully laying to reveal her cunt. Despite the clinging chill of outside, her body pulsed with heat; she touched herself gleefully, praying Dauriel returned quickly to enjoy the show.

She thought of Dauriel, a few suspicions rising as she waited, until the empress peeked her head out, pupils widening as she gazed at Tallora's body.

"I was waiting for you, Empress," Tallora said, breathless and desperate for her wife's touch.

Dauriel had kept her shirt but removed her trousers, instead emerging wearing what Tallora could only presume was the 'strap.' Strips of fabric were tightened around her ass, and the protrusion from between her legs seemed to be made of hardened leather. "You look beautiful," Dauriel said, and Tallora's blush reached as far as her toes. She stepped forward, her expression somewhere between enamor and *ravage.* "This is your first time, so I want you to be in control. You're going to, uh..." Dauriel's blush darkened her cheeks as she crawled into bed. "... sit on it."

Everything uplanders did was strange, and this was no exception. Tallora bit her lip at the admittedly large leather piece and nodded skeptically. "And it's going to fit?"

"I have a smaller one if it doesn't." A sheepish grin stole Dauriel's confidence. "This just isn't one I've used before yet, and I don't feel quite right, um ... Well I haven't used it with the courtesans, I mean—"

"Oh, hush," Tallora said, purposeful as her hand slid down to her vulva. She caressed the edges, then parted the folds to reveal her entrance. "I want to do what you did with that whore. That's what's been in my head."

Dauriel's eyes followed her hand, pupils wide and starving. "If you insist. Hands and knees."

Tallora giggled and obeyed, her body in agony as excitement pulsed through her blood. As Dauriel knelt behind her, she shook her hips in the air, grinning when her wife gripped her ass, groping her shamelessly.

Yet the entire mood shifted when Dauriel's hand touched the lips of her vulva. "You'll tell me if anything hurts, all right?" She stroked against the seeping wetness from within, then brought their hips together—

Tallora gasped, pained and yet *wonderful* as Dauriel slowly pushed inside her. Oh, she'd never felt so full, and when hands grabbed her hips, she managed a breathy, *"Yes."*

Dauriel pushed inside her once more, the motions steady as Tallora's body adjusted to the intrusion. Mouth slack, she turned her head back, nearly finishing from merely the lurid desire in Dauriel's eye. She shut her eyes, content to bask in the sensation as Dauriel continued thrusting, her motions ever increasing. Pleasure jolted through Tallora, the contact of their hips as glorious as anything she'd ever felt. "Oh, Empress," she whined, her mind quickly unraveling as Dauriel claimed her.

Her breasts bounced with each thrust. Behind her, she heard Dauriel's own faint groans of pleasure. Tallora let her cries fly freely, knowing her love adored hearing it. She wondered idly if she sounded better than the whores, and somehow didn't care.

Each thrust welled heat within her. From behind, she heard a breathless, *"Fuck,"* and loved it so. Dauriel's groans were wonderful to hear. When Tallora looked back, everything in her countenance bespoke bliss—until she met her eye, that was, at which point Dauriel winked—

And lightly smacked her on the ass.

Tallora squeaked, uncertain of what that meant, but Dauriel's ensuing grin held such crass enjoyment that she giggled and said, "You can do that again, Empress."

Dauriel obeyed, and the sharp sting melded with her pleasure. "Gods, you're something."

"Only something?"

"The light of my life? The thief of my heart? A fine set of tits and ass?"

Tallora balked at the words, then grinned despite the rhythmic fucking. "I knew I liked you."

She gasped when Dauriel suddenly leaned forward, grinding their hips together. When she grabbed Tallora's breasts from behind, she squeezed and said, "Only like?"

"You're ridiculous—" Tallora's words cut off when Dauriel pinched the delicate buds. When Dauriel released her, Tallora whined, pouting as she batted her eyelashes, only to cry out when their fucking resumed—harder this time, and she swore Dauriel's hands would leave marks on her hips. Oh, she was perfection, and Tallora so loved her crass words.

They continued at a smooth pace, each thrust pulling desperate cries from her lips. When Dauriel suddenly gasped and moaned, Tallora looked back again, watching ecstasy flash across Dauriel's perfect face, saw her tremble and shudder as her pleasure peaked—and to actually see her undone was the most glorious vision of all.

Dauriel kept a slow pace, perhaps sensitive after her orgasm, but one of her hands slipped around Tallora's hip. Her empress' body pressed close against hers as her finger rubbed against Tallora's clit, the touch and the fullness within her enough to quickly push her over.

Tallora cried out, her arms nearly failing as she finished. Pleasure coursed through her limbs, her quivering form finally stilling when Dauriel removed her hand. They remained still a moment, their heavy breathing all that filled the night. Then, Dauriel withdrew, and Tallora felt an empty ache within her.

Dauriel fell down beside her and immediately grabbed her, held her desperately, their bodies sweaty and heaving from pleasure.

The strangest sound met Tallora's ear—an endearing blend of laughter twisted with tears. Kisses fell like rain upon her head, and the understanding of what this meant to Dauriel nearly drove her to tears as well.

Tallora returned the yearning embrace and slipped her hands beneath her shirt, delighting in Dauriel's muscled back, uncaring of the sweat. "I love you, my empress," she replied, boneless as Dauriel held her, thighs trembling, cunt aching. "And I approve of your method of consummation. You've been hiding this from me all along?"

When she looked up, Dauriel smiled, exhaustion etched into her blushing features. Her eyes had rimmed in red. "There never was time before. And I didn't know if it would be too strange for you."

"So you waited until we were legally bound so I couldn't leave?" She let the statement linger, just long enough for Dauriel's panic to manifest upon her darling face. Tallora laughed, grinning like a fool at her love's palpable worry. "I'm teasing, you silly thing. That was wonderful."

Dauriel pulled her close. "I hope you know I don't actually only see you as—"

"Hush. I love knowing you find me attractive."

"Yes, but while I've seen many fine asses and tits in my life, none of them were part of quite so witty and wonderful a woman."

Damn Dauriel and her precious smile. Tallora rolled her eyes, her blush hot against her face.

Dauriel kissed her cheek and laughed. "I can show you a few more methods of consummation, if you'd like."

Tallora's body ached, yet by Staella's Grace— she wanted it all. She bit her lip as she nodded, then giggled when Dauriel sprinkled her with a shower of kisses.

Chapter XV

Tallora awoke to soft breathing and gentle streams of light through the parted curtains.

Her wife slept, sprawled naked on her back, and Tallora curled around her, content to savor her heartbeat.

Tomorrow, the ships would set sail.

Tomorrow, Dauriel would leave. And they might never see each other again.

Tallora swallowed back tears, determined to push those horrid thoughts aside. Dauriel slept. She desperately needed it, so Tallora remained still, simply basking in her presence.

She ached, a muted pulsing lingering between her thighs. The strap hung up in the washroom, cleaned of pleasure. They, too, had bathed, and Dauriel's scent remained subtle and perfect upon her—something rich, something warm, and the subtle, ineffable aura of sweetness Tallora was told magic brought. The world turned beyond, oblivious to Tallora's crumbling heart. She slid one hand to rest upon Dauriel's sternum and contemplated today, refusing to think a moment beyond.

What would they do on this final, blessed day?

The minutes passed in near silence, Dauriel's breathing soothing to her mind. When a hand fell atop Tallora's—the one between her wife's breasts—she looked up to meet a sleepy gaze. "Good morning," Tallora whispered, and on Dauriel's countenance was peace.

Her empress smiled, her sleepy eyes half-lidded. "How long have you been awake?"

Tallora merely shrugged, then snuggled closer, placing a kiss on Dauriel's shoulder. "What would you like to do today?"

"Besides this?"

Tallora grinned. "We can do this as long as you'd like, assuming you have breakfast sent up."

Dauriel placed a lingering kiss into her hair. "Realistically, I have meetings. Final preparations for tomorrow. But as my wife, you're welcome to join me. The council can fuck themselves."

"Dauriel . . ." Tallora sat up, scooting so her bare chest was pressed against Dauriel's. Her fingers traced invisible lines along her wife's face. "I'm going to be selfish and ask you to forget all that. Stay with me today. Please. It might be our last."

When Dauriel's hand cupped her face, tears welled in Tallora's eyes. "My first duty is and always must be to my people. My second is to you." A wry grin cracked across her face. "My council is very near the bottom of the list, and they'll survive perfectly well without me. I'll defer all decision-making to Khastra."

Tallora beamed, and Dauriel's smile matched. "What shall we do, then?"

"I've always wanted to see the Painted Cliffs of Tholheim. The Valley of Neoma is traditional for Solviraes newlyweds. I also hear Chaos' Sorrow is a spectacular sight. It's a cliff all the way in Zauleen."

"I'm sure all of those are wonderful," Tallora teased, "but we have a day—not months of travel."

"And I have a father who can channel the Silver Fire into inter-planar travel."

Tallora waited for the jest, but when Dauriel's countenance remained the same, she laughed. "All right. So anywhere we'd like."

"Where have you always wanted to go?"

Tallora thought a moment, then whispered, "Anywhere I've ever wanted to travel to is below the sea."

"What about a beach, then? You can show me your world."

Dauriel smiled in earnest, her endearment infectious. Tallora blushed. "There's a beach in the far south—south of Moratham, even—where they say the sand is pure white and the water is as crystal blue as the sky. It's called 'Cove of Callaria' My father promised to take me when I was a little girl, but a lot of dreams fell away when he passed. I think it would be wonderful to go with you."

Dauriel kissed her, lingering at her lips as she whispered, "Get dressed."

Tallora scrambled to obey, habitually selecting a corset, before Dauriel stopped her. "You won't want that on a beach. May I pick something lighter for you?"

Tallora nodded, curious at Dauriel's words, and when she emerged from her closet with a light, flowing gown, Tallora accepted it with care. "This is lovely. And it'll fit without underclothes?"

"It technically is an undergarment, just a fancy one," Dauriel teased, and she helped her put it on.

Once Dauriel had also dressed, far more casually than her title would typically allow, with her billowing shirt and worn boots, she said, "There is one task we may wish to oversee first."

Tallora glanced to the open closet door. "Oh?"

"Yesterday's plans fell away. Kal and King Merl still need to be sent home with instructions." Dauriel looked to the rug beneath the bed, subtle shame in her demeanor. "But I'd like you to accompany me, if only to reassure them that you're alive and well."

Tallora nodded, unwilling to ask what precisely had been said the day before, lest she poke a festering wound. "I'd be happy to speak to them," she said, her smile reassuring and bright.

When they approached the menagerie, Dauriel's hand rested upon Tallora's waist. The empress stopped at the door, her deliberate steps quieting as she stole a single breath.

"I'll talk to them," Tallora said softly. "All you need to do is loom menacingly." Her wink brought a small smile to her love's face. Tallora took her hand; they stepped inside as equals.

Kal immediately swam to the edge of the tank at their approach, his eyebrows raised at their intertwined fingers. "Tallora, glad to see you're safe."

"I was at the temple," Tallora said, and then she spotted King Merl lurking in the background, glowering at the empress. "And I come with news."

She explained it all—the plan, the ships, Ilune's aid, even Dauriel's purpose in it, though she refrained from mentioning the sacrifice, lest her heart break. Kal listened with utmost interest, nodding at the appropriate intervals. "And so we need you two," Tallora said, "to lead our people to safety before the armada arrives. By any means necessary. The future of our people depends on it."

"Absolutely—"

"Whose plan was this?" King Merl finally swam forward, ire in his stare. "Solvira's? How do we now this isn't a trap?"

"It was my plan," Tallora spat. "I care very deeply for the safety of my people."

Merl glared past Tallora's shoulder, to Dauriel lurking behind. "Don't think for a moment that I trust you."

"Then don't," Dauriel replied, and Tallora fought a grin at her utter indifference. She wondered if the king had ever been so dismissed in his life. Judging by his sneer, she doubted it.

"Just as likely," Merl continued, "we'll be fed straight to the leviathan's maw—"

"I don't have to let you go." Dauriel's damning phrase lingered; when Tallora looked back, she saw no smoke, but it in no way lessened the threat. She held a powerful stance, arms crossed as her silver gaze bored through the magical barrier. "I will send Kal alone. He's a far worthier ruler than you."

"Then you'll be exactly the sort of tyrant this traitorous slut claims you aren't!"

Tallora's eyes widened at the remark, though not for offense—she watched Dauriel's composure twitch, her jaw suddenly grit. "Perhaps you're right," Dauriel replied, the first hints of smoke escaping her mouth. Tallora saw her grip on her arms tighten, and she wondered if Silver Fire could burn fabric. When she glanced at Kal, his expression matched her own. "I rescind my vote, lest my reputation be so horrendously sullied. Instead, I shall defer to my wife. Empress Consort Tallora Solviraes," she cooed, and Tallora adored that wicked glint, "what say you?"

Tallora grinned at Merl's horror, his eyes nearly as wide as his slack jaw. Kal also appeared appropriately shocked—but not unhappy, to her relief. But business was at hand, and Dauriel was quite sincere, she knew. Tallora's amusement faded as she studied her king—but was he? What was a fallen king to the empress of the world and her wife? "The only traitor I see here is you," Tallora said, fists clenching. Merl had condoned the release of the leviathan, he had tortured Harbinger for his own gain, and had chosen to risk his people's lives. "He can stay here."

Merl rushed to the edge of the barrier, stopped by the undulating water. "How dare you!"

"How dare *you?!*" Tallora cried, fury suddenly spiking. "What kind of hubris must you have to release a monster onto your own people?! Countless people are dead! My mother's blood is on your hands! There was never a risk to Moratham; whether they knew Yu'Khrall could be controlled or not, it was our people standing as the barrier, not theirs—"

She was stopped by a hand on her shoulder. When Tallora glanced back, a victorious smirk twisted Dauriel's lip. "Gods, you are perfect," she whispered, and Tallora released a sigh, her anger seeping out. Dauriel looked to Kal. "You'll be sent back alone to warn your people and lead them to a prosperous future; your father will be returned once the matter is done to face whatever justice the Tortalgan Sea would grant him. My father will create a portal for you. Solvira will offer what aid we can, once Yu'Khrall is dead."

"Thank you, Empress Dauriel." He looked to Tallora and smiled. "And you, Empress Consort Tallora."

There was finality in the phrase. Tallora thrust her hand through the barrier and clutched his own, as close to a hug as she could give. He covered hers. "Congratulations on your marriage."

"Be safe, Kal," she replied. "Save our people."

When she released him, she felt a lingering sense of peace. Dauriel suddenly swept her feet from beneath her, instead holding her in her arms. Tallora gasped, then laughed as she was carried from the menagerie and once away, she kissed her wife on the cheek, noting her glower. "Dauriel—"

"No worries, wife." Dauriel scoffed, careful as she placed Tallora back onto the ground, helping steady her. "What matters is he'd cower like a dog if I ever thought he'd be stupid enough to fight my claim to you."

"He wouldn't fight—"

"Shh," Dauriel cooed, malicious intent in that salacious grin. "Let me fantasize."

Tallora rolled her eyes, allowing Dauriel to lead.

Dauriel packed a bag full of towels and clothing, then detoured to the kitchen, demanding a basket full of food for a picnic.

The cooks, of course, scrambled to obey their empress' request. Tallora held Dauriel's hand all the while, overjoyed to simply share her presence.

Ilaeri was found in his study, signing paperwork. Eniah sat on the floor, drawing a loose interpretation of a cat upon parchment.

And when Dauriel told him her terms, he didn't argue. "You'll be leaving us to sort out this mess alone?" he said, sounding nearly bored.

"I will. And you'll help, or—"

"Or my position is forfeit, I know," he replied, resignation in his uninterested voice. "Where are you going?"

Before Tallora could answer, Dauriel said, "You're not fighting this?"

"No need. I fully believe that you'll sack me if I don't obey, dearest daughter."

There was little love in the title. Still, when Tallora told him the name of the beach, he was able to identify it on a map.

Within minutes, he had summoned a portal in the study. Tallora's stomach lurched in its presence, but Dauriel seemed unaffected. "Take this," Ilaeri said, offering a strange, smooth stone. "Ignite it with Silver Fire once you're ready to return home. Then I'll know to find you."

Dauriel nodded, accepting the gift and placing it into her pack. "Thank you. You'll hear from me at nightfall. Or later." She grinned at Tallora. "We shall see."

Without a farewell, she took Tallora's hand and walked her through the portal.

Tallora stood among a sea of stars, floating like she might beneath the ocean. But then, the scenery solidified; her feet touched sandy ground in tandem with her stomach lurching from nausea.

The air smelled of salt and ocean spray. Gone was the winter's chill—here, the sun shone cheerily upon a beach of sand as white and blinding as Tallora's hair. Rock formations blocked the beach from the rest of the land, though the foolhardy could likely try to scale them. Vibrant green plants grew near the cliff's base, thinning as they approached the beach until there was merely sand. And the water, as crystal blue as the sky, was clean enough to see the rainbows of fish within its waves.

Dauriel offered a wistful smile as she set down their things. "It's beautiful—What are you—?"

Her confusion likely stemmed from Tallora herself, who had already removed half her dress.

"We're all alone," she said, not shy to reveal her breasts to the open sea. When her dress was a pile upon the sand, she spread her arms wide, offering her pearlescent body to the sun. "How I've missed the sea."

"You're adorable," Dauriel said, and Tallora ran for the ocean, her heart yearning for its familiarity.

Instead of bolting to the beach, she climbed up a rock formation, scaling it with ease on her nimble feet. She stood atop it a moment, basking in the sun and spray before diving into the sea. The cool water enveloped her; her legs felt first of jelly and then they were sealed—when Tallora opened her eyes, she saw her magnificent pink tail and laughed from pure joy.

She swam in view of the beach, waving at her dearest wife who stood shirtless and struggled to remove her boots. "You like me in pink, right?" She flicked up her tail, a spray of water rising with it. She swam nearer to the shore, the sand cushioning her torso as she emerged. But her tail—or most of it— remained beneath the waves, and so she kept it.

Dauriel ran to her, holding down her breasts with her hands—a sight Tallora laughed to witness. "Look at you, Mermaid," Dauriel said, coy and assured as she revealed her body. She placed her hands on her hips; Tallora rolled over, the water lightly lapping her revealed breasts. "As lovely as when I met you."

"You mean when you kidnapped me?"

Dauriel winked and took a step into the water— then immediately withdrew. "I was expecting that to be cold."

"It's perfect," Tallora said, using her tail to pull her into deeper water. "Now, come on. It's my turn to hold you."

It was a joy to do so—after some coaxing, Dauriel finally submerged herself into the waves, and Tallora carried her far from the shore. She beckoned Dauriel to hold her breath and dove deep with her, showing her the fish, the coral, and all the beauty beneath.

Only in little spurts. Dauriel had to breathe, but Tallora explained it all when they returned to the surface.

"Can you talk to fish?" Dauriel asked, after a particularly brave little flounder had let her pet its scales.

Tallora laughed. "That's like if I asked you if you could speak to your horse."

Dauriel attempted to splash her, but Tallora released her first—the waterlogged empress was forced to keep afloat instead.

There was plenty to do above the waves as well. Tallora used her legs to admire the plants along the cliff's base, enamored with the rainbow of flowers dotting the scene. "Do you know their names?" Tallora asked as she bent over to admire them.

"I don't." Then, creeping hands slid down Tallora's bare ass; she squeaked when Dauriel pinched. "My favorite flower is right here."

Tallora smacked her shoulder as Dauriel fell into a fit of giggles. "If you're going to try that, lay down a towel first."

Dauriel, of course, happily complied.

It was a day of genuine bliss, spent exploring and playing and fucking above and below the waves. Here, Tallora had her Dauriel—the one she loved, Dauriel alone. Her laughter was a precious thing, her joy so rare. Away from politics and the great, looming palace, Dauriel was free.

At sunset, Tallora, with her tail idly floating in the water, sat upon the beach, Dauriel at her side, the water gently lapping against them. The tide came in; the water reached much farther now. As the sunset flickered through an arch of rock formations, it cast a picturesque view.

Tallora leaned her head against Dauriel's shoulder. Her empress spoke tragic words. "We could disappear," she said wistfully, the light breeze tousling her dark locks. "I could throw my stone into the ocean, and we could run."

Their time had nearly ended. Tallora felt it like a knife in her stomach. "Is that what you want?"

Dauriel stared into the fading sunset, the whispered words, "Duty over heart," leaving her lips. The burning sky clung to the day, but night would fall all the same. It always did.

When Tallora looked up, Dauriel had begun crying, silent tears streaming down her face. Tallora kissed her cheek, then placed herself in Dauriel's lap, clinging to her empress.

But Dauriel did not return the gesture, her hand idly touching Tallora's tail instead, the sunset reflecting the fuchsia hues. Her stare remained a thousand miles away.

The sun faded. The last vestiges of light became a memory. And Dauriel's words, when she finally spoke, were as soft as the whispering waves. "All my life, I sought to escape. I searched for my glorious death. I finally found it, but . . ." Her lip trembled; she shut her eyes, seizing control of her emotions. ". . . I also . . . finally . . . found a reason to live."

Tallora kissed her tears, the taste of salt strong on her face. "For so long," she said, recalling her sentiment at her goddess' temple, "I thought we had upset fate in order to meet. I don't believe that's true anymore. Perhaps this was always your fate, to channel Neoma and save the world. And perhaps it was always mine, to hold your hand until that final plunge."

"Fate is cruel, then, to give me joy just to take it away."

"If this is the end . . ." Now, Tallora's tears welled, the first falling quickly. "Then it's as we always feared—that we're doomed to spend the afterlife together, given our respective goddesses."

Dauriel laughed, though her tears still freely fell. "If only it were a fate worse than death, to spend my life with you—instead it shall be eternity."

It brought a shattered, broken sort of hope, the pieces of which Tallora vowed to hold to all her life.

Chapter XVI

They returned, for they were not meant for paradise. They bathed, scrubbing salt from orifices they'd rather not admit to. Though exhausted from swimming and the sun's light, Tallora lifted a pair of shears and said, "Sit down. Let me do this for you, please."

Dauriel relented, her smile endlessly soft as Tallora snipped away the small bits of growth, a gentle rain of black and burgundy falling to the floor. All the while, she placed tender caresses upon Dauriel's face and in her hair, adoring this final semblance of peace.

And when she was done, they embraced, holding each other in the silent washroom, soon filled with quiet tears.

Tallora awoke in the morning to a tender kiss on her cheek. Her eyes fluttered open—she realized the sun had yet to rise and that Dauriel was dressed. "Sorry to wake you. But I had to say goodbye—"

Her words were cut off by Tallora's embrace. She pulled Dauriel back into bed, still too asleep to cry but awake enough to know this was the end. "Let me see you off, please."

"Get dressed quickly, then."

Tallora did so, throwing aside her nightgown and pulling on one of her crumpled dresses. Dauriel assisted, and something choked in Tallora's throat—for this would be the final time she ever did. She smoothed her hair in a mirror, sparing Dauriel a glance when she caught her empress watching. "Yes?"

Dauriel shook her head. "Nothing. Just committing you to memory."

Despite the somber mood, Tallora 'dropped' her hairbrush onto the ground, certain to lift her skirts as she bent over. With her ass in the air, she looked to Dauriel. "Silly me. But did you see enough to remember it?"

When Dauriel laughed, she stood straight, grinning when her empress swept her into her arms. "Gods, I'll miss your wit on the sea."

"You could take me with you."

But Dauriel shook her head, dashing that idle hope. "To what end? You'll only be in danger."

Tallora didn't argue, because she knew it was true. Any reason for her to join was merely to keep Dauriel company and be there at her end.

The somber reminder stole her joy. She wrapped her arms around Dauriel and held tight, breathing in her familiar scent, savoring the safe embrace.

All was quiet. The world beyond meant nothing.

When Dauriel finally pulled away, their fingers intertwined. The empress led her out. In silence, they walked through the quiet halls. Tallora held her as they rode the lift down, her head pressed against her leather doublet.

They went to the council chambers. A small collection of people turned at their entrance—the Solviran Council and Lady DeDieula. Ilaeri spoke first. "Empress Dauriel, this is for you." He offered a small wooden box, engraved in filigree patterns. When Dauriel opened it, Tallora was surprised to see a glass orb, with a swirling pattern of blue and yellow gas within.

Realization struck her. This was Rulira's orb; the perfect counterpart to Yaleris'—the one Yu'Khrall claimed.

Dauriel removed her glove, flexing her fingers before grasping the ancient artifact. Immediately, it glowed with life, subtle sparks of lightning flickering from the orb. But more daunting was the subtle silver light surrounding the empress, the slow breath she exhaled to dissipate it.

Then, she tossed it lightly into the air, nonchalantly catching it—as one did with priceless artifacts of depthless power.

"Can Neoma wield the orb?" Tallora asked, and Dauriel nodded.

"More likely, though, she'll absorb its power and redirect it as Silver Fire."

"If all is settled," Ilaeri interrupted, "you're the last to arrive. I can summon us a portal."

Dauriel gave an affirmation. As Ilaeri worked, Tallora watched Khastra and the strange woman known as the Herald of Ilune. They did not touch, but the adoring glances from deDieula as Khastra surveyed the room were almost sweet. Tallora wondered at that, at the apparent love affair between them, but then her stomach lurched. She nearly fell into Dauriel's embrace.

A portal appeared at the center of the room, a literal rip in space.

Was this it? When Dauriel stepped forward, Tallora tugged her back. "Is this the end?"

Dauriel didn't answer; Khastra did. "No," the general said, lingering at the portal's entrance. "I will not be joining this mission either, so you may return with me." She offered deDieula a hand—the two stepped through together.

Tallora and Dauriel shared a glance, then stepped through.

The feeling of flying through space would never be normal. When Tallora's feet touched solid ground, she nearly cried for relief. She stood upon a wooden dock, and as she glanced about the port city, she realized she knew it—this was where she had been taken when she'd been kidnapped all those months ago.

Before them stood a fleet of grand ships, some already setting sail toward the rising sun. Beside Tallora, Khastra and deDieula gently clasped hands, pure adoration in their eyes. "Be careful," Khastra said, her words as soft as her smile.

Lady deDieula beamed beneath the general's gaze. "Are you worried?"

"Yes. But my worry is not greater than my faith in you." She bent down to place a lingering kiss upon deDieula's brow, perhaps as affectionate as she would be in public, then released her hands. Lady deDieula's smile remained as they parted. With graceful steps, she approached the ship, then blew a final kiss.

Tallora and Dauriel shared a glance, and oh—how she wished they had time, even to gossip about something as silly as this. Instead, finality settled upon her; Dauriel tucked the orb away into her cloak. She looked between them, lip trembling when Khastra knelt and took her into her strong arms, shorter than the empress for perhaps the first time in their lives. The general's glowing eyes expelled tears as they held the other, and Dauriel's fell to match. "Thank you," came Dauriel's whisper, "for everything."

"I love you, Dauriel," Khastra said, and when she pulled away, she gripped Dauriel's shoulders in her large hands. "I am so proud of who you have become."

When Khastra tried to release her, Dauriel leapt into her arms a final moment, weeping in her embrace. The general lingered, parting only when Dauriel initiated.

When Tallora stole her, Dauriel held tight. "Whether it be in this life or the next," Tallora whispered, her own tears falling fast, "you will see me again."

They didn't kiss—they had done enough of it in private, and Tallora knew it would only bring more heartbreak. Instead, their hands lingered as they parted, and Dauriel visibly struggled to not break down and sob anew. "I love you."

"I love you, my empress," Tallora replied, and Dauriel left, sparing glances back as she walked up the plank.

Tallora slowly crumbled, soft sobs escaping her throat as cries sang to set sail. A presence appeared beside her—Khastra placed a hand on her shoulder, silent and strong as she watched the ship, her own tears still falling.

A familiar silhouette appeared upon the back of the ship—Dauriel gazed down, remaining even when the boat left the dock.

Khastra squeezed her shoulder. "We should go back."

Tallora obeyed, the final image of Dauriel, silhouetted by the sunrise, giving her the illusion of angelic wings.

Tallora lingered by Khastra as the portal dissipated, daring to ask, "What now?"

There was softness in the half-demon's gaze, a certain empathy Tallora clung to. "You stay busy. You drink. You pray, if you think it will bring comfort."

Khastra left her, the mood somber and heavy.

Tallora wandered. With quiet steps, she moved lightly through halls of a palace she now claimed. Solvira was hers, and that reality had yet to fully take meaning. She had married someone the world feared would be a tyrant, but Tallora still believed she could be more.

Yet now that same tyrant sailed toward her chosen death. Tallora felt numb.

Exhaustion struck her in time, her early waking hour colliding with the sun and spray of the previous day. She returned to her shared bedroom, wondering if it were odd for Solviran monarchs to actually share a space with their spouse. They had broken form, marrying for love and not money or political gain. But Dauriel would do as she had always done and spit in the faces of any who tried to control her.

Tallora shed her clothing, wishing for a nightgown instead. But as she went to Dauriel's closet, there sat a small, foreign box. Before it lay a scrap of parchment bearing beautiful words—*Tallora Solviraes, all my love.*

Within was a pearl wedding ring.

Chapter XVII

Tallora lived in a haze of dread. She curled up in bed, falling in and out of sleep, unable to stand even when her bones ached from lack of motion. But so long as she remained in comfort, her face pressed into the final traces of Dauriel's scent, the world needn't turn. Even when her stomach panged from hunger and light faded from the window, she clung to Dauriel's pillow, though soon enough it was soaked with tears.

When loneliness threatened to overwhelm her, she studied her wedding ring. It was not an undersea tradition; only the very rich decorated their fingers, a sign they had better things to do than work, but she'd stolen one of the many dainty necklace chains in Dauriel's room and strung the ring through. Knowing Dauriel, it would last beneath the ocean, much like the shears from months ago.

At some painful hour of night or morning—she couldn't say—she left the room to forage for food. A few kitchen servants bustled about at the late hour, preparing for breakfast. They stopped at her entrance, quickly bowing.

"I'd like some food, please," she said softly, and she was quickly, if coldly accommodated. Not for malice, she decided as she sat alone in the private dining hall. But she was their superior now, even if the word was bitter.

What a lonely existence. Surrounded by people, yet unable to connect. Tallora had once had countless friends.

Most were dead now. She felt it like a festering wound.

Her fog continued into the next day, after a fitful few hours of sleep. She laid in bed, wondering if she'd ever find the will to move again, when a knock sounded on the outer door.

She couldn't stand. "Come in," she managed instead.

She didn't recognize the servant who peeked her head in. "Your majesty, there's a visitor for you."

Tallora sat up, rubbing her swollen eyes. "Who?"

"She says her name is Leah."

Tallora bid her to enter. Upon seeing her friend, she nearly burst into fresh tears; she resisted long enough to hug her in the doorframe. "I stopped by to see Mithal on my way here," Leah said, holding her tight, "and she told me where your wife went. If I'd known, I would have brought wine."

Tallora laughed, though it nearly led to her sobbing anew. "You're a treasure. Where's Mocum?"

"Oh, he's um . . ." Leah's smile faltered, but it held, though painted on. "He's staying with friends. All is well. But won't you come with me?" Leah pulled away, though she kept her hands on Tallora's upper arms, squeezing reassuringly. "Mithal would love to see you."

"Is everything all right?"

A genuine smile replaced her false one, but Tallora couldn't help but recall that Leah had spent years of her life faking smiles to please men. "Yes, he's fine. I'm nervous leaving him alone for the night."

"For the night?"

"You think I would abandon you when you need me the most? I'm staying." She took Tallora's hand, who followed, touched at the thought. Perhaps she still had a few friends left in the world.

Warm greetings met her at the doorway. Mithal embraced her. "Congratulations on your wedding, Tallora," the elven woman whispered, and relief filled Tallora's heart to hear it. "I was surprised, but there's never been another person in the world who could ground Dauriel quite like you."

"Thank you." When Tallora pulled away, she noticed the sorrow in Mithal's eye.

"Forgive me, but I pride myself in knowing all the happenings of this castle," Mithal continued, "and have reason to believe your happiness may soon be cut short."

Tallora nodded, but she could say no more.

"Wine it shall be, then."

Bless her. Tallora greeted other women she recognized, though hadn't quite known. One stood away from the rest, and Tallora's gut churned to realize she'd seen her before—a week ago, moaning as Dauriel had thrusted inside her. Judging by her blush at Tallora's approach, the woman—unbearably beautiful with her long, blonde hair, nearly white, and vibrant eyes—recognized her as well.

Tallora hurt, but she couldn't stand to hold any grudges. Not for a woman who'd only been doing her job. She shyly offered a hand. "Hello."

The woman accepted, her handshake a bit limp. "Your majesty," she said with a curtsy, but Tallora shook her head before she could say more.

"I'm Tallora," she said, drawing her hand back, "and I'd like to know your name too."

"Phira."

"Phira, I can't imagine a more uncomfortable beginning for us," Tallora said, offering what she hoped was a reassuring smile, "but I'm happy to set that aside and . . . be friends?"

Phira smile held palpable relief. "I'd also like to forget that."

Tallora invited her to join their little circle, and Phira graciously accepted.

Warmth surrounded her. With Leah at her side, Tallora didn't feel alone at all. These women had once helped her through the most frightening era of her life. Now, through her heartbreak, perhaps she would be supported again.

But by Staella's Grace—it still hurt. Tallora drank the offered wine, weeping to a supportive chorus. What use was there in hiding it when it could no longer be stopped? "Even though I knew it was coming," she said, giving no cares to the tears falling into the wineglass, "I wasn't prepared for the dread of waiting."

Leah knelt behind her, braiding her hair into intricate designs, the motions soothing. All listened as she spoke of her wedding night, their elopement before Staella's gaze. She kept Dauriel's suicidal nature to herself—even her drunken tongue could withhold that much—but spoke of what she could. "When she dies, I'll go back home," Tallora continued. "They need all the help they can get, beneath the sea."

"You said that . . ." Leah's shy voice trailed off, and even Tallora's tipsy sight saw her blush. "You said that Kal was returned home?"

"Yes," Tallora replied, her own smile regretful. "I'm sorry you didn't get to see him."

Leah shook her head. "I doubt he thinks anything of me."

"Well that's not true at all." Tallora giggled as she told Leah the bits of truth she did know, that Kal had mentioned her more than once in the time after. "If the stars align, he'd be charmed to see you again."

Leah's grin was infectious. "You'll say hello for me, won't you?"

"Who's Kal?" Phira asked.

Of course, surrounded by a bunch of gossiping women, Leah told the rest of her encounter with Kal, her tongue loosened from alcohol as well. "Just a sweet thing," she said, giggling at the memory. "I've never known a royal who was so precocious. Didn't think that was possible."

Though Tallora shied at the more explicit details of her best friends' tryst, she listened when others chimed in with their own 'royal' encounters. Plenty of stories of men, but on the occasions a nameless woman was mentioned, Tallora internally rolled her eyes.

"I need to ask," she said, after at least the fifteenth mention, "how many of you have slept with my wife?"

More than half the room raised their hand, including Leah and Phira, of course.

Tallora didn't know what emotion filled her, but it manifested as chortling laughter. And then a few more tears. Might've been the wine though. Phira shyly raised a hand. "If it's any consolation, Empress Dauriel called me your name more than once."

There were two or three other commiserating nods, and Tallora merely sighed. "Oh, my sweet, idiot wife." She sipped her drink, finding her second glass nearly empty. "Can we talk about something else, please?"

The conversation drifted into more humorous topics, the sort that sent Tallora spiraling into fits of laughter. Soon she couldn't see straight, much less speak. She wasn't the only one, and when her vision started blinking in and out, she remembered Leah helping her to a couch, content to let the darkness take her.

Next she remembered, something sharp pinched her side. When she blinked her bleary eyes open, her head pounded, tongue fuzzy and dry. In the darkness, she sat up, wondering if she'd imagined it, when a shadow froze across the room. She stared at the dark figment, wondering if alcohol still muddled her mind.

It twitched.

She stole a breath to gasp—

The shadow rushed. She screamed—it was no figment, but a man wearing black, the bottom half of his face covered by a cloth. Below her on the floor, Leah stirred, but Tallora's shallow breaths stopped entirely when cold metal touched her throat.

Lights came to life all around them. Disoriented, the man stumbled back—then tripped over Leah, who joined in Tallora's screaming.

And before he could hit the ground, a figure held an arm to his neck and a knife to his back. "Drop your weapon," Mithal said, and when the man struggled, he elbowed Mithal in the stomach—

But not before she slid her knife between his ribs. He fell to the ground, breathing labored. Mithal knelt atop him, one knee upon his spine, and cried, "Someone fetch a guard! We need this man interrogated before he passes—"

He did speak, but not in a tongue Tallora recognized. She clutched the blanket around her figure, heart pounding, half-blinded by the abrupt lights, but Leah sat up, listening intently to his frantic words.

When she spoke to the man, her words matched his. His eyes spelled shock as he answered. Their conversation, brief and curt, held as much tension as Mithal herself, forcing him prone with her very body.

Leah looked to Mithal. "He is from Moratham. He was sent to capture Tallora."

"By whom?"

Leah spoke, and whatever the man replied with seemed unhelpful. "He won't talk until he's healed—"

Leah's words cut off when the man suddenly cried out—Mithal had twisted the knife between his ribs. "Ask again," the elven woman said, and now guards filtered in, as well as General Khastra, still wearing day clothes. Mithal held out a hand, silently bidding them to wait.

With some trepidation, Leah repeated her phrase to the man, this time listening intently as he managed an answer. "He says he took his orders from the Speaker of Morathma."

"Ask him why," Tallora said, finally able to find her voice amidst her panic. She spared a brief glance to Khastra, who listened intently, grateful for any familiarity in this sudden skirmish. "My marriage hasn't been announced to anyone outside this castle. Moratham was told explicitly that I'd died, so how does anyone know I'm here?"

Leah repeated the words in her tongue. The would-be assassin groaned, then managed a few curt words. "He says he was not given a reason. He was following orders."

"But how did they know I was here," Tallora whispered, because all this meant something—something deeper than even a war against a hated kingdom.

The assassin spat blood—and then he collapsed. Mithal lifted the man's hand and let it drop. It hit the floor with no resistance. "He is either dead or passed out," she said as she stood.

Khastra stepped forward and knelt beside the man. She placed two fingers to his neck, frowning. "He is not dead yet," she said thoughtfully. "Guards, take this man to the healers. If he passes, we can ask Priest Rel to question him further. Death never stopped a necromancer."

Shaken, Tallora clutched her blanket as Khastra spoke quick words to the guards. Leah sat and put an arm around her. "Are you all right?"

"Someone in this castle is colluding with Moratham," she whispered. "Who knows what else they know."

Mithal stood as the guards came to take the unconscious man away. "General, a word," she muttered, and the two women made a vicious sort of eye contact—two powerful woman who ruled domains of very different sorts. "I have reason to believe this is more than it seems."

Khastra frowned, but not from anger. "Explain."

"Tallora is correct—Moratham doesn't know she's here, and if they do, they found out from one of ours. If there's a mole, it's a very close one, considering this man knew to look for her *here* of all places, well away from Empress Dauriel's chambers. And how terribly stupid, to try and kidnap her with so many witnesses asleep around her. It means he was desperate or operating on a rigid timeline—or both."

When Khastra sat beside Tallora on the couch, the entire seat shifted for her massive bulk. "I must speak to the council," she said to Mithal, sparing a glance for the pool of blood staining the carpet. The final few guards left at her word. "Do not clean that up yet. Instead, keep the mermaid hidden. Send your girls to their rooms."

Tallora realized they had attracted quite the panicked crowd.

"We must be careful of what we say," Khastra added. "For all we know, it was one of them."

"Leah, hide Tallora," Mithal muttered. "The general is right—we can trust no one."

Tallora followed, exhausted and confused and parched. Leah helped her to stand, then beckoned her through a door Tallora had never been inside.

Small and dark, bearing only a couch for comfort, light filtered in from cracks in the wall. Muffled sound came from beyond, though Tallora couldn't quite understand any of the words. "Call it creepy it you want," Leah whispered, coaxing Tallora to looked through one wall of cracks, "but this room was designed for eavesdropping."

Tallora peered through the wall and saw a lavishly decorated bed, but no one within it. "You watch clients through here," she muttered, realization settling in.

"It wasn't something we did often," Leah replied, "but if we had any reason to believe a client posed some kind of danger, we would put him in one of the rooms connected to this one for Mithal to keep watch. But come here."

Against the wall, connected to the main room, Tallora could eavesdrop here as well, eyes wide as she watched Khastra and Mithal engaged in a hushed conversation—but if they'd spoken louder, it would've been trivial to overhear.

Tallora watched with interest, the reality that someone close to her had tried to have her kidnapped finally settling in.

The first to enter was Prince Ilaeri, immutable shock on his sharp features. Mithal bowed, but he said nothing at all as he stared at the bloodstained floor, then brought a slow hand to rest on his cheek. "Is he dead?"

Khastra said, "Not yet. He is in custody."

"Be that as it may," Ilaeri said, and then he cut himself off, looking to the guards who had brought him. "I want my son checked on immediately. Guards will be posted in his room for the rest of the night. If the castle was breached by one, it might as well be a hundred." The guards scurried away, leaving Ilaeri alone. He took a few steps closer. "Where is Tallora?"

"Somewhere secret."

Adrael appeared then, immediately cringing at the blood staining the carpet.

Tallora heard a soft whimper beside her. "Tallora . . ."

When she turned, Leah was near tears, visibly trembling. "Tallora," she repeated, "there's something I need to tell you."

The rest of the Solviran council filtered in, but Tallora paid them no mind, apprehension filling her at Leah's opening. "What's wrong?"

Immediately, tears filled Leah's eyes, the barest hints of light through the slats glistening upon them. "Please know that I love you so much, and I'm sorry."

A cold wash of dread coursed through Tallora's blood. "What did you do?"

"I had no choice. They have Mocum."

Tallora's heart clenched. "Leah—"

"The night after we met at the temple, Mocum was stolen from his bed. The ones who took him held a knife to my throat and said . . . they said . . ." Tears streamed down Leah's face, and Tallora's dread faded into rage.

"Tell me everything."

"Dauriel's room has specific protections placed upon it to stop unwanted visitors—all the royals have it, to prevent this kind of thing from happening. So I was told to lure you out. I took you here because I thought they'd have the least chance of succeeding."

"Who is they?"

"Someone in Moratham. I don't know anything beyond that. But now that they've failed, I worry . . ."

Leah's head fell into her hands as she quietly cried, and Tallora spared a glance out the slats to be certain they hadn't been overheard. "They alluded to there being an informant in the castle who would know if I tried to warn you, but I don't know if it was to scare me or not. All I could do instead was try and wake you when they came."

So something sharp had pinched her and awoken her from sleep. Tallora watched the Solviran Council through the slats. "Khastra is loyal to Solvira and to Ilune. She's the one person I'd trust to not be colluding with Moratham. We should try to . . ."

The beautiful High Priestess Toria stood beyond, looking despondent at Khastra's words. Toria, who was kind and had listened when Tallora wept. Toria, who had seen them together at the temple. Who gifted Morathan vestments. Who had come here within the last few months.

The terrible truth slammed Tallora like a crashing wave.

"Leah, I think I know who the informant is," Tallora said, the bitter cold of betrayal pulsing through her limbs. She grabbed Leah's hand, offering a reassuring squeeze. "I believe you. And I forgive you. I'm so sorry you were put in this position. But if we want justice, we have to prove it." Tallora glared at the priestess, disgusted at the mere idea of it. "It's Toria. I'm sure of it. We have to get her to confess, but more than that, we have to know what she's planning. Are there other exits out of here?"

"No," Leah whispered. "What are you planning?"

"I'm going to lure Toria out. As soon as we're gone, you're going to beg to speak to Khastra—alone. Like you said, we don't know who we can trust. Tell her what you told me. And tell her I'm going to talk her into confessing—if I'm wrong, and she's innocent, we've lost nothing. But if she's corrupt and all goes according to plan, Mocum will be safe."

Leah looked wounded, but she swiftly nodded.

Tallora crept to the door and left alone.

"... how was he stopped exactly?" Adrael said, his scowl likely permanent.

"Mithal stabbed a dagger through his back ..." Khastra's words trailed off at Tallora's entrance. "Mermaid? You are supposed to be hiding."

Tallora could not quite fake tears, but after the long night, her watery eyes were genuine. "I-I'm sorry," she said, adding a slight quiver to her lip. "I just ... I've had such an awful scare." Too melodramatic, she decided. "Honestly, I'm nearly panicked. Might I ask Priestess Toria for a blessing?"

"You have your free will," Khastra replied, but her obvious scrutiny showed her actual opinion, which settled somewhere between confusion and 'all right, stupid,' but Tallora couldn't explain.

With demure, she approached Toria, eyes wide and hopefully innocent. "I-I can't be here," she stammered, and Priestess Toria put a gentle arm around her.

"Come with me, you poor thing. Staella is a goddess of comfort—I'm certain you know that very well."

Tallora nodded as they left, then swallowed her residual panic. She had everything to fear, but her ploy would hopefully save Mocum and answer a few damning questions, should she move forward just right. As Priestess Toria led her away, Tallora whispered, "I really do need to speak to you in private."

Toria looked at her oddly, but not with any notable suspicion. She directed Tallora to a vacant sitting room. Once Toria shut the door, Tallora sat on a couch, hoping it conveyed her ease. "Toria, hear me out before you act—you helped orchestrate this, didn't you."

To Toria's credit, she did not react in the slightest. "I don't know what you mean—"

"You're helping Moratham. You told them I was here and that Leah was my friend. You have Mocum hidden somewhere, and I'm asking you to please return him, because I'm going to come with you."

Toria's airs faded, revealing nothing sinister, no, but calculating. Her lips lost their habitual smile, instead pulling into a line. "Explain yourself."

"I'm not Solviran." Tallora bit her lip; now was the moment her entire plan hinged on. "And I don't know if I accept their view of Staella."

Toria kept her stare, eyes narrow as she studied Tallora's demeanor. "I'm surprised, if only because of your recent marriage."

"Dauriel has always been a temptation." Tallora blinked, willing tears to well, but she still couldn't quite conjure them. She thought of Dauriel and the betrayal she was about to speak, feeling the first rise of something. She dug far back into her memory and recalled the wicked words Amulon had used to describe the love of her life. "I pity her. I do. And I care for her, I think. I married her because she was going to die, but now that she's gone, I'm so confused. Deep down, I know that what I'm feeling toward her is . . . *unnatural.* I need help."

Toria frowned, but not for unkindness, no. "Oh, you poor, sweet thing," she said, and she sat beside Tallora and embraced her. Tallora breathed out a heavy sigh of relief, which was thankfully misinterpreted. "Staella loves you and will forgive you."

"After everything Solvira has done to me," Tallora whispered, bitterness she had long ago released dancing through her mind, "I don't know who I can trust. I feel so confused, as I said." She summoned her courage, as well as a convincing sob. "Perhaps I've been on the wrong side of this war."

Toria held her tight, and it might've been comforting were Tallora's heart not pounding for her lie. "Let me take you to them," Toria whispered, pulling a handkerchief from her pocket. She dabbed the tears welling in Tallora's eyes—they hadn't pooled enough to fall. "You would be invaluable to the war effort.

Morathma would proclaim you exalted. And when the Goddess of Stars returns to him, you'll be one of the first she thanks."

Her words disgusted Tallora, but she forcibly kept her despondent countenance, nonetheless. "Why were they trying to kidnap me?"

"Bargaining. You were to be taken to the ocean to cut Dauriel's resolve when she goes to fight Yu'Khrall."

It was so simple, yet so brilliant. Tallora had to admire it.

"Whatever her strange proclivities, it seems she's ill enough to think she cares for you, given your blood was what released Yu'Khrall. Your presence would subdue her enough for Yu'Khrall and Morathma to defeat their fleet."

"Morathma?"

"With the Herald of Ilune joining Neoma in the fight, Morathma has pledged to help Yu'Khrall. Once they're victorious, they will come to Solvira and build it anew."

Which was certainly a polite way of saying 'destroy it,' but Tallora fixated on a different, more condemning piece—Morathma would be there.

"Take me there," Tallora said, praying Leah had done her part. "The plan is brilliant. But we must hurry—they'll come to find me soon."

Toria held a finger to her lips and beckoned her onward. "I want to believe you have good intentions, and I swear upon my honor as a fellow follower of Staella that if you come with me, Mocum shall be returned. But if you betray me on our journey there, it will only be his head."

"Of course—"

The moment Toria opened the door, she was bombarded by a wall of blue, tattooed muscle. Khastra immediately strutted inside, Priestess Toria held by the hair. A plethora of armored elites followed, and Leah was the last to join—she shut the door behind them.

When Toria tried to scream, Khastra's hand engulfed her entire face. "If you scream, I will crush your skull."

The priestess stopped struggling, and when Khastra released her, she collapsed onto the ground, staring with wide, fearful eyes. "What is the meaning of this?"

"You confessed. I heard it. She heard it." Khastra nodded at Leah and then to the soldiers. "They heard it. The empress consort heard it—that's damning enough for a trial."

Realization manifested as horror upon Toria's face. When she looked to Tallora, her expression was nothing less than pitiful. "How could you?"

"How could *I?*" Tallora balked, the anger she'd subdued now freely spewing from her mouth. "What you preach is infantilizing—*dehumanizing*—to my goddess. To me. To my wife! You're the one who's betrayed the morals Staella preaches—and to put an innocent little boy in danger? How sick are you?"

A flicker of regret flashed across Toria's face. "The greater good said—"

"The greater good said to steal a child from his mother?" Tallora saw her weakness and latched on— Toria might still be of use. "If you have any semblance of humanity left, you'll tell us where he is. Your crimes are your own, but Mocum is innocent."

"It was never supposed to go this far. I was merely an informant, but then they started asking for more." Toria looked to the door, then to General Khastra looming above, before finally settling back onto Tallora. "You could still go to them. Everything you said—"

"I adore my wife, you zealot bitch. There's nothing unnatural about it, so keep your bad opinions to yourself." Tallora looked to Khastra. "If she won't talk, what do we do?"

Khastra crossed her arms, enhancing the already threatening aura of her musculature. "I could declare martial law and kill her. Then Priest Rel could use necromancy to interrogate her." Toria's face became as white as snow, but Khastra continued. "Or I simply torture her until she tells us the boy's location, and I arrest everyone found there—"

"That won't be necessary," Toria muttered, looking defeated, and she spoke an address in monotone. "He's there. He's safe. The men who contacted me weren't the sort to murder small children without reason."

Khastra looked to one of the men nearest her. "This is a highly sensitive situation, and so I shall accompany the envoy myself. Send your most trustworthy to escort this woman to the dungeon— keep it secret."

"Wait," Tallora said, and the general held up a hand to her men. She stood before Priestess Toria, this corrupt woman, and asked, "Why? Did they promise you anything? How—" She swallowed her anger, though she could not hide the sneer of her lip. "How could you do this and still claim to love Staella?"

"I . . ." Toria's lip quivered, but she shed no tears. "I do love Staella. I did this for her."

"But how—"

Tallora was stopped by Leah's hand on her arm. "When you've been told one thing all your life," she whispered, "it's the hardest thing you'll ever do, to see it as something wrong. She genuinely believes it."

As Tallora gazed down upon Toria, all but seeing the cognitive dissonance battle within her, she felt pity, which was a much kinder thing than before. "She should go to trial," Tallora said. "You can take her now."

Khastra motioned, and the man she'd spoken to before beckoned for a few to follow. Toria didn't fight as they took her away.

"I was just like her, once," Leah said, stance defeated as her hand clutched her wrist. "And I might've stayed like her. It's because of you that I looked a little closer at Staella and saw her as Solvira did instead."

Tallora offered her a shy smile. Dread flooded her, however, and she looked to the general. "Khastra, Morathma is going to meet Dauriel with Yu'Khrall. They have to be warned."

"They do," Khastra said, her lips a thin line as she stared at the wall. "Dauriel chose to forgo any communication devices, lest she lose her resolve. There is no way to reach her."

"What about Prince Ilaeri? He could create a portal and send someone."

"I encourage you to ask him," Khastra said. "But the more pressing matter for the moment is rescuing Leah's child."

Leah's eyes watered at the phrase. Tallora placed a hand on her waist. "I'll talk to him."

Khastra didn't leave immediately; instead, she turned her scrutinizing gaze to Leah and said, "Technically, you should also be arrested for treason. What say you, Mermaid?"

Taken aback, Tallora said, "What? No!"

"I need no justification. I will simply not repeat what she told me."

Then, she left.

Chapter XVIII

In the same room as Toria's arrest, Tallora sat with Leah as the latter wept from worry. Blubbering apologies spilled from her lips, but Tallora dismissed them all and simply held her, let her cry.

A sane person would be angry. Tallora just wanted her to smile again. "There's no one in the kingdom more competent than Khastra, and she's personally helming this. Mocum will be found; I'm sure of it."

Strangely . . . she truly was.

But her mind spun at the rest of it. Morathma would be fighting alongside Yu'Khrall. Neoma's plan already held risks; would this topple the scale?

As she contemplated the dark twist of fate, Khastra entered, evidence of blood on her armor—and a small boy held in her arms, unharmed despite the evidence of swollen eyes and tears.

Leah's wailing cry held anguish and relief both; Khastra placed Mocum into her embrace. Both mother and son cried, and Tallora nearly joined them, for one small piece of the world was right again.

"I did try to question the men holding him hostage," Khastra said, then she gestured to the blood on her armor. "But they died. Highly unfortunate. Your boy did not see it, however; I sent him from the room."

Leah simply cried, keeping a protective hold on her son.

When she finally calmed, Tallora announced her intention to speak to Prince Ilaeri; Leah and Mocum joined, as did Khastra.

In the courtesan wing, Ilaeri sat upon a couch, watching as servants cleaned the carpet of blood. When Tallora explained the reveal and the plan to send someone, he responded by shaking his head.

"Not feasible," Ilaeri said, his attention on his wine. Tallora's hope seeped away at his words. "The ship is not a static object and we don't know where they are. The chance of failure is astronomically high—more likely, whoever we send would drown when they fell into the open sea. Even if I were close, a few miles might as well be the length of the sky for as far as they'd need to swim."

There was truth in the words—a truth so heavy that Tallora nearly lost balance. "Send me," she whispered. Ilaeri caught her eye, visibly intrigued. "I can't drown. If I'm submerged in water, I'll turn into a mermaid."

"If you're willing, I do see the merit."

Though lightheaded to consider the task ahead, Tallora knew she was the only one. When Ilaeri stood, she looked to Leah, who held her boy in her arms. "This is it, then."

Ilaeri stood apart from them, glowing slightly in an unmistakable, silver hue. But Leah shook her head, worry etched into her features. "This is exactly what Priestess Toria wanted—for you to be in the ocean."

"Yes, but Dauriel never would have attacked the Morathan fleet if I were on their boats. Instead, I'll be on hers, or I'll swim farther away once I've spoken to her. It's not a perfect plan, but we have no other choice. I'm the only one."

Leah looked ready to cry anew, but Khastra gave a resigned nod. "I am worried, but you are correct."

Tallora gave a brief glance to her company and removed the underclothes beneath her skirt. "I don't want to know what happens if I try to transform while there's something between my legs," she said sheepishly.

"Be safe," Leah said, though her smile trembled.

"You get all my things if I don't return."

Leah embraced her. Tallora melted into the gesture, craving the comfort, content to stay until her stomach sickened.

Before her, a portal grew—first a line and then it stretched into an oval, sparking at the edges like lightning. "I don't know precisely where this goes,"

Ilaeri said. "We don't know where Yu'Khrall is, so there's every risk this will lead you straight into his clutches."

Tallora nodded, swallowing her creeping doubt. "I understand."

"Good luck, Tallora," Leah said, and her smile was genuine.

General Khastra offered a hand, which Tallora accepted. "Your tenacity is worth admiring. If you die, I will mourn."

The strange compliment oddly reassured her. "Thank you. Both of you."

Tallora clutched her wedding ring where it hung from her neck, praying for courage. She stepped through the portal . .

. . . and fell from the sky.

She gasped, the rush of air overwhelming. She twisted, facing the approaching water—

And plunged.

Familiar cold engulfed her. Her dress weighed her down, but her body sang joyfully at the reunion. The now-familiar sealing of her legs resulted in the return of her beloved tail. Finally breathing, she freed herself of her clothing and let it float away, keeping only her necklace.

Behind her in the darkness, she saw the barest hints of the canyon leading to Stelune. Something odd reflected the light, but she hadn't the time to investigate. Idly, she wondered if Kal had succeeded, though her heart ached to think he might've failed—

Within the black morass of water, Tallora's keen eyes saw something move.

Gasping, Tallora's powerful tail pushed her forward. She darted through the waves, cold water rushing past. When she glanced back once more, her eyes had not betrayed her—great tentacles rose in an ever-increasing mass.

He had only one eye, but if it spotted her, Tallora's life would be forfeit. The urge to scream nearly choked her. Behind, she caught a glance of that horrid yellow eye and panicked.

She dove into a craggy alcove. The rocky wall pressed against her skin, threatening to tear the tender flesh. But she cowered, trembling as the mass blocked the minimal light. Did he know she was here? Would he search for her?

She took vain comfort in the idle thought that his tentacles were too large to fit into her crevice. She shut her eyes and breathed. *Goddess Staella—*

Darkness covered high above. By Staella's Grace, the beast was close.

Goddess Staella, please.

She remained against the wall. Only her heartbeat counted the passing time, and she prayed the leviathan couldn't hear it.

Light appeared.

Clenching her fists, Tallora forced herself away from the wall, daring to peek up to the sky. She saw a clear sea—enough to even witness a blur of distant stars through the watery scene.

She emerged, taking care to look about the top of the crevice before tentatively emerging. Clear oceans surrounded her on every side. No sign of Yu'Khrall.

She offered a silent prayer of gratitude and swam to the surface. High above, the stars were familiar, but beyond, Tallora saw a ship. Her heart sped, but though her body jolted and longed to join it, an urgent cry of *no* sang through her mind like her own thoughts.

No?

Frowning, she did swim a few degrees closer, enough to spot a flag bearing a crown and stars—

And the barest hint of a leviathan.

Instead, she looked back to the constellations above and swam toward where Solvira would be, knowing she would surely find the correct ship in time. Though with less urgency now, she continued onward, little on her mind save her pulsing blood and her burning arms and tail.

She could not stop. Hours passed.

When the sun burst over the horizon, with it came the silhouette of an armada. Invigorated, Tallora swam faster, the hope of rest and of seeing Dauriel spurring her onward. She knew not which ship was Dauriel's—they all bore the same flag and decorations—but when she finally neared and risked being shattered upon the hull, she screamed her lungs out, willing someone to hear.

Someone did. A sailor peeked his head over the railing of a ship. Tallora frantically waved her arms, relieved when he barked out an order and a rope fell over the side.

She clutched the knotted rope with all her might, her arms burning to hold her body as they pulled her up. But once her tail left the waves, her legs split, the pain merely a dull ache. Her feet settled upon a knot.

When rough hands helped her climb aboard, she immediately cried, "Which ship has the empress? I must speak to her immediately!"

"Who are you?" one well-dressed man said, and Tallora instinctively covered her nakedness as best as she could.

"My name is Tallora Solviraes. I married your empress not four days ago, and I bear news that will determine the fate of this mission. Please."

The man muttered quick words to another next to him, who immediately ran up a set of small stairs. Tallora's entire body shook as a thunderous horn sounded from the vessel she stood upon.

A beam of light shot up in the air from a distant ship behind them. As Tallora stared upon it, she realized it was no mere figment—but a person.

Lady deDieula dove toward them, the ethereal grace of her figure paling to the magnificent *wings* behind her back. They bore the tendrils of jellyfish and floated just as gracefully as she landed on silent steps.

They glistened, pure ethereal light, then faded and disappeared from sight. "Tallora? What a surprise."

"Lady deDieula," Tallora said as she dared approach, "I have to see Dauriel immediately."

Lady deDieula held her arms out. "May I?"

Tallora nodded, allowing deDieula to gently lift and cradle her like a child. Her touch felt odd, as cold as ice, and though the morning was chilly, Tallora felt no end to it—no warmth within her at all. So close, Tallora felt pulsing power in this woman's veins, and as they flew through the air, though her stomach lurched, she knew there was safety to be found here. One did not become the favored of Ilune without their own well of power, she supposed.

When their descent slowed, a familiar voice cried her name: *"Tallora?!"*

Tallora looked out and saw Dauriel—her beloved, her wife—remiss of finery. Upon her tanned, sun-kissed body, she wore simple pants and a shirt, the jerkin upon her torso half-unbuttoned. Were it not for the broach of the moon at her breast, she might've been just another sailor. Lady deDieula helped her to stand, those wings somehow disappearing, but Dauriel just as quickly swept her into an embrace, preserving her modesty with her body. "What are you doing here?"

"I have to speak to you and Lady deDieula," Tallora replied, her wife's presence surreal. Dauriel smelled of sweat and salt and ocean spray, and Tallora wouldn't have had it any other way.

Dauriel spoke, the words gently vibrating against Tallora's body. "We'll go to my quarters. Once we find my wife something to wear, we'll discuss all of this in private."

With every step, exhaustion settled, the reality that she'd swam for literal hours finally hitting her bones. She leaned against her wife, practically carried by the time they descended a set of stairs leading below deck.

The room they entered held small pieces of finery—a full bed, a dresser half-open, the drawers displaced by the waves, even a small window. One drawer glowed, and when Tallora peeked inside, she saw the orb unceremoniously laying among a pile of underclothes. Dauriel helped Tallora sit on the mattress, her smile soft when she spotted the ring around her neck. She grabbed a clean shirt and leggings. "I don't have anything to better suit your taste."

Tallora shook her head as she accepted the offering. "This is perfect." As she slipped into the pants and loose shirt, she noticed deDieula gazing beyond the window, introspection in her distant stare.

"What has happened?" Dauriel asked, joining Tallora when she sat again upon the bed.

"A man from Moratham tried to kidnap me." When Dauriel placed a protective hand against her waist, Tallora leaned into the touch. With each breath, her senses slowly caught up to her—here she sat below the deck of a ship, seeing her love again, about to deliver news that might be a death sentence. "Obviously he failed. But there's more. Moratham wanted to use me against you in the upcoming fight—there's a ship here. Morathma himself will be joining Yu'Khrall."

From the window, Lady deDieula frowned. Dauriel's expression matched. "Explain."

"Priestess Toria was an informant for Moratham. They know we're coming, and Morathma intends to make certain Yu'Khrall won't be defeated this time."

Lady deDieula's expression had darkened, her lavender gaze severe. "The only thing larger than his thick head is his hubris."

"Priestess Toria, you said?" Dauriel asked.

"She was working for Moratham," Tallora continued, and at that, deDieula turned and approached, intrigue twisting her frown. Tallora told the rest of the story—of the attempted kidnapping, of

Leah's tearful confession, and of Priestess Toria's betrayal. "I had to say awful things for her to believe I was sincere," Tallora whispered, guilt filling her at the memory. "Dauriel, my love, my wife, if she tries to use anything I said against me or you, please know it was all lies."

Dauriel didn't ask; she simply nodded and listened.

"But she's in prison now. We have to focus on the threat at hand. Morathma will be there. I was the only one your father could send, since I can't drown."

Dauriel held her. Tallora might've drifted off to sleep, but Lady deDieula spoke. "I don't fear Morathma. Perhaps this shall be the excuse my lady needed all along—to finally slay the Desert Sands."

The darkness in her tone filled Tallora with a strange and familiar dread—though she struggled to name it. "Can we?"

"What are gods but angels with superiority complexes?" deDieula laughed, the sound lovely to hear but unnerving all the same. "Angels are immortal, but they can be killed. And while Dauriel was successful at removing Morathma's host's head and banishing him back to Celestière, I can tear out his soul." Her gaze suddenly sharpened, a glower sneering her lip. "Still, the presence of Yu'Khrall does make that difficult."

Tallora frowned. *You* can tear out his soul?"

"I told you, Tallora," deDieula replied, her patronizing tone thinly veiled, "Ilune granted me a portion of her powers."

"I don't fear Yu'Khrall," Dauriel said, her hands stroking soft lines against Tallora's skin and hair. "We have Neoma. We have the orb. We have an armada of trained men prepared to sacrifice their lives for the opportunity to harpoon this bastard. I have no desire to defy my goddess' wishes and slay Yu'Khrall, as much as he might deserve it, but even with Morathma here, we have every chance of success."

"The fastest course of action would be to simply banish Morathma," Tallora said. "A few harpoons through his body and he's banished, right?"

Lady deDieula stared at Tallora with all the intensity of the sun, even as Dauriel said, "Possibly," the empress said, "and it's a likely enough chance that we should take it."

"Or," deDieula cooed, a grin twisting her perfect lips, "Dauriel, you get to be known as the Solviraes who slew Morathma." The words lingered; Tallora swore she felt all the air leave her wife's body. "I would have to strike the killing blow, yes, but you would be the mortal who killed a god. Imagine it—*Empress Dauriel Solviraes, Slayer of Gods, Destroyer of the Desert Sands*. First you take his life, and then his kingdom. What better gift for your goddess, and what better legacy for you than Morathma's head?"

Tallora sat up and held Dauriel's face between her hands. "She's right, but . . ." Tallora's gut churned, but she forced her words, knowing they must be said. "What of Yu'Khrall? We can't forget what we came here for."

"We'll defeat him too," Lady deDieula said, but her attempt to literally wave away Tallora's words with her hand only infuriated her.

"I don't think any of you truly understand what Yu'Khrall is. I watched him kill and *eat* a dragon. He's literally as large as the city he destroyed. He's the son of a god and can't be treated like an afterthought."

"Don't forget," deDieula said, "that Ilune fought him before—"

"And *lost.*" Tallora let the word linger, hoping it conveyed enough strength. "He was subdued by a god, but he also defeated a god. It was always a roulette, even with two against one. Now it's two against two, but if we banish Morathma, we have a chance to succeed."

Ilune's Herald shook her head, actively fighting a grin. "You've been studying history, you clever girl. A fitting follower of Staella, to offer mercy to that bastard—"

"It's not mercy! I'd also happily have Morathma's head as a trophy, but we have to consider the greater good. Yu'Khrall *destroyed* Staella's people."

"Well, they were predominantly Tortalga's people, but I digress." deDieula didn't appear even a little bit angry, which only infuriated Tallora more. "I have every intention of killing Yu'Khrall. In fact, leave him to me. Let it be a climactic battle between Dauriel and Morathma—"

"We're not killing Yu'Khrall," Tallora said, unease welling in her stomach.

Lady deDieula waved off the remark. "I misspoke. Anyway, while you fight Morathma, I subdue Yu'Khrall, then, you channel Neoma, if you haven't already, and lock him away. I grasp Morathma's soul, tear it from his body, and destroy it." She held out her hands, as though presenting a fine cake instead of battle plans. "I would happily bestow all credit to you—it would be your victory. It's brilliant. And we may never have this opportunity again."

Dauriel had said nothing; Tallora might've forgotten she was there, except that her touch was a constant presence. Her gaze drifted down Lady deDieula's body, the strange coldness of it suddenly cast in a different light. "You're not the Herald of Ilune." Tallora said. All of this, every meticulous puzzle piece, slowly formed an image she feared to face.

"Am I not?"

"Lady deDieula isn't real, is she." Tallora swallowed her dread, the words damning, possibly literally so. "You're Goddess Ilune."

There was no change in her countenance—all remained the same, from her coy smirk to her palpable amusement—yet it somehow shifted from teasing to malevolent in a single moment. "You're very clever."

She transformed before them, the grotesque shifting of her host sickening to behold as the flesh twisted and changed. Maysonge deDieula—or rather, Ilune—became a Celestial woman of unbearable beauty, pale and delicate, with rich black hair flowing down her back. Wings of translucent light floated behind her.

Tallora knew this image, though now she bore the color and substance of mortality, instead of her angelic light. "My herald is a real woman," Ilune said, her grin spreading wide, eerily so. "The real Maysonge is fine, don't worry—simply instructed to stay at home and lay low."

When Tallora forced her gaze away, though Ilune drew her attention like a black hole, she saw that Dauriel, too, stared at the God of Death, her own expression indecipherable. "Goddess Ilune," Tallora said softly, "your mother said— You're not supposed to—"

"Would my mother be foolish enough to banish me in the middle of a fight? She needs me; I've invited myself."

When Tallora merely stared, Ilune laughed. "Find the flaws in my plan. If I can't defend it, then dismantle it, please. But I do stand by what I've said. I won't command it. I'm Dauriel's ancestor, but I'm not her goddess. Besides, it would ruin the valiance of her victory against Morathma, if she did it by my decree." She smiled at Dauriel with that sanguine gaze, and it made Tallora sick. "Think on it. But not too hard—your new bride is here. Make love to her while you can."

Again, Dauriel said absolutely nothing as Ilune saw herself out. The words lingered, leaving a cloud of dread in the air.

Tallora touched Dauriel's face, coaxing her to look away from the window and to her instead. "Dauriel," she whispered, the weighty mood nearly suffocating, "Ilune is manipulating you. She wants something, but I don't think it's as simple as Morathma's death."

Upon Dauriel's familiar countenance was quiet contemplation. "She's right, though." Dauriel's gaze filled with light. "I could slay Morathma. What greater legacy is there than that?"

"Under any other circumstances, I would welcome this," Tallora whispered, "but this was never about Morathma. It's about Yu'Khrall—"

"Isn't it, though? If it weren't for Morathma's influence, Yu'Khrall would have never been released. And for him to help Yu'Khrall after his genocide of your people? What better reason to slay him is that?"

"There are a thousand and one reasons to slay him, Dauriel," Tallora pled, though it tore her heart to shreds to do so—it was all Dauriel had ever wanted, and Tallora sought to take it away. "But we might do away with him in moments if we only seek to banish him. Then we would win. Yu'Khrall has an orb."

"So do I—"

"Losing means to condemn the whole world!" Tallora shut her eyes, furious at herself, at Dauriel's ambitions, at Ilune and her pretty words. "There are times to take risks. But you don't understand the threat of Yu'Khrall. You haven't seen it. You haven't had that gods-awful eye turned on you and known he was about to eat you. You don't understand, because the world doesn't understand, and your hubris is going to get you killed. If you die, Neoma is banished, and then what? Yu'Khrall turns your entire kingdom into a frozen wasteland. Are you willing to risk the lives of your people for a title?"

For a blessed moment, Tallora thought she'd spoken words enough to sway her bullheaded lover. A blessed and beautiful moment, as Dauriel shut her eyes and sighed. "Morathma is the true threat," she said, the words dashing Tallora's hopes like waves against jagged rocks.

"No, Yu'Khrall is. We can subdue Morathma another day—"

"Tallora, I don't want to fight with you—"

"Then, *listen!*" Tallora was too furious to cry, too furious to even form cohesive words, much more inclined to throttle her love than try and explain. "This is a dream for you. I know that. And I'm the bitch wife pleading at your feet for you to give it up. But you just don't understand. My mother was killed, and you can comfort me sincerely in that. But my people are dead. They're *gone,* and with them has died the dreams of thousands—do you know what that looks like, Dauriel? The sudden death of thousands? It's a literal fucking bloody cloud. You see it; you breathe it; you taste it in the water. And if you don't want that to be Solvira, you have to put their needs first."

Dauriel glowered, but she did not yell. "Ilune would never concoct a plan that condemned her people."

"If she's as stupidly short-sighted as you are, she would." Oh, that was nasty. Tallora shut her mouth, regretting it all as she stood up. Dauriel grabbed her hand; she batted it away. "I need to be alone," she managed to say, and then Tallora ran from the room, her tears already falling.

Early daylight did little to warm Tallora. A cold breeze whipped across her face, and she wrapped her arms around her figure, savoring the subtle smell of her wife in the shirt and breeches.

Tallora loved her so, and tomorrow she would be dead. Within hours, they would come across Stelune. Ilune would fight Yu'Khrall; Dauriel would fight Morathma. Tallora would likely die in the collateral damage, but if she didn't, there was no use for her back in Solvira.

She should be with Dauriel. She should be comforting her in these final hours, lavishing love upon her. But tears streamed down her face as she watched the horizon—tears caused by politics, ancient feuds, and her stubborn wife.

Instead, she stood at the edge of the railing, the salty air familiar and comforting. When a shadow passed over her, she ignored it, but then a figure appeared. Ilune joined her as she gazed upon the path ahead. Tallora's soul felt dark in her presence, and she shied away.

"Care to unburden yourself?" Ilune said, sweet and smooth.

"Not to you," Tallora whispered, uncaring if she blasphemed. She'd likely be dead in a few hours—and if she was not, Dauriel would be—so what did it matter if she were rude?

Fluttering laughter left Ilune's lips—bright like a bird and just as charming. "My mom always was the better listener. Both of them, really."

Tallora swallowed her tears, wiping the few still trailing down her face. When she looked up at Ilune, she was reminded of how the goddess could walk the plane without a host—this body was no living being. "Why do you care so much about Yu'Khrall? I understand your feud with Morathma. He was cruel to you and hates you for all you are."

"He hates me because I'm not his," Ilune whispered, and there was cruelty in her smirk.

"You've fought Yu'Khrall before, yet no one knows why. You cursed him—why?"

"I'm a goddess of many mysteries—"

"But this one has an answer." Tallora glared, uncaring if she were struck dead.

Her smile lost that wicked edge—not kind, no, but amused. "You must think I hate you, but I really don't at all. You frustrate me, and you dare to challenge me, but I respect you all the more for it. Not many have the spine."

"Certainly not Khastra," Tallora muttered, and to her surprise, Ilune burst into a fresh fit of laughter. Frowning, she watched Ilune's amusement—she had to clutch the railing lest she fall. "Am I that funny?"

"No, no," Ilune replied, wiping her eyes as though there were tears—there were not. "Well, yes, you are, but no. Khastra certainly has the spine, though she can be easy to talk in circles. I do try not to though. Feels wrong. But Khastra will absolutely tell me if I'm full of shit." Her smile softened as it had days ago on the docks, and Tallora thought it the strangest sight of all. "I'm the luckiest woman alive, to have her."

Though fascinated, Tallora refused to follow the distraction. "You never answered my question."

Ilune's smile disappeared, though its shadow remained. "You're very persistent. You'll make a fine monarch—"

"Are you going to tell me or waste my time?"

"Now, now," Ilune said, chiding her as she might a child. "I like you, but I'm known to change my mind." She looked back to the sea, and Tallora spared a moment to admire her wings, their translucent undulations like an undersea creature. "Yu'Khrall is of grand interest to me. He's a person of powerful blood, yes, but it's his body that makes him unique. He's the largest leviathan to ever swim in the seas. I am a woman who takes what she wants. And I wanted him."

Tallora cringed at the implication. "You *wanted* him . . ?"

Ilune laughed, Tallora's discomfort apparently hilarious. "Oh, no—not like that. While I have had strange men, Yu'Khrall is much more valuable dead than alive. I want him dead. And then, I shall grant him new life."

Realization settled, the reality oddly more horrifying than the prospect of Ilune engaging in intercourse with a gargantuan eldritch monster. "You want him undead. Then you can control him."

"And then Solvira well and truly owns the seas." Ilune's smile held wicked intent, that same vicious glint Dauriel had been granted. "When I failed to slay him, I cursed him so my mother would be forced to put him down. Silly me, assuming that him rampaging through the seas and consuming its citizens would be a reason to kill him."

Tallora stared in horror, unable to form a reply, but Ilune laughed and continued. "Congratulations, however—you were right. I did send the dream to the merfolk advisor once I learned his plan. But I didn't tell him enough for it to be damning to me—not according to my mother's laws, at least. Who am I to deny myself another opportunity to succeed?"

"She still banned you from coming here," Tallora said, seething as Ilune merely smiled at the horizon.

"I don't fear my mother's wrath. I don't fear anyone. I certainly don't understand why they're both keen to appease Onias. With our combined power, of course we could destroy him. Perhaps they'd let me own him as well. That's the thing about death, Tallora—it's the great equalizer. If I deem you unworthy of the Beyond, it's no stretch of power at all to pluck your spirit back. It does not matter what you achieve in life; you all die in the end. Then you become mine. Even gods. Even Dauriel. Even you."

Ilune's apparent indifference only enraged Tallora more. But there was nothing to say, so Tallora merely spat at her feet. "You'll fall for your hubris someday. I don't know when. I don't know how. But I'll be the first to laugh and slander your name."

"I was imprisoned for hubris before," Ilune said, her smile wicked and lovely and enough to make Tallora sick, "and I'd do it again."

Tallora could say nothing to that. She could say nothing at all and instead backed away, too disgusted to speak to this monstrous woman—who had founded the very kingdom Tallora might rule and whose blood ran through the woman she loved.

When Tallora returned below deck, Dauriel hadn't moved. She remained at the edge of the bed, her face blotchy and red, evidence of tears apparent even as she tried to wipe them away.

Whatever else Tallora felt toward Dauriel, underneath the anger and pain, there was pity. Pity for the woman who had no aspirations except to die.

They didn't speak. Tallora gathered her wife into her arms and pressed her face to her chest. It was as Dauriel had said—she did not want to fight.

Tallora clung to her, letting one hand trail up and gently thread into her hair. When Dauriel pulled away, their mouths met. Tallora kissed her gently, no urgency despite the looming heartbreak rumbling like distant thunder. Instead, they kissed like summer rain, warm and soft, immune to any faraway storms. When they fell into bed, they touched as the meeting of the sun to the horizon, shining bright despite the oncoming dark.

Their space became peace, a realm for them to rule as lovers, as gods, as equals, and when Tallora let Dauriel inside her, it was a meeting of souls.

Outside, the world turned. They clung desperately to peace.

Chapter XIX

The midday sky became as night. Upon the deck of the ship, Dauriel held an orb of depthless power, and high above, clouds gathered to block the sun. Thunder rumbled, an omen of the battle to come.

Tallora stood beside her, wearing her wife's clothing and a blanket from her bed to protect against the whipping, winter winds. "That was once the dragon's power?" she whispered, her gaze drifting between the artifact and the sky.

"Just as Yu'Khrall stole Yaleris' orb," Dauriel whispered, giving an affirming nod, "this was taken from Rulira."

"And so you've truly become my dragon empress?" Despite the tease, Tallora struggled to smile, the coming conflict churning her gut. "My dragon empress against a demi-god wielding a dragon's power?"

Dauriel smirked, vicious and cruel. Her body glowed, the orb flashing, crackling with lightning as silver flame rose at Dauriel's feet. High above, thunder rumbled; when Tallora looked up, dark grey clouds slowly swirled to cover the sun. "I'll be a god, even if it's only for a moment."

Tallora could hardly breathe as she took in the visual. "So Rulira was a dragon of . . ?"

"The sky," Dauriel finished. "Just as Yaleris was water and ice, Rulira ruled the skies. All her power rests in this orb."

The armada had spread wide, separating lest they be swept away by Yu'Khrall in one swipe of his tentacles. Something sparkled upon the horizon, but Tallora's eyes could not quite make sense of it.

Not until a shining star flew through the air to join them. Tallora clung to Dauriel as Ilune descended, victory in her grin. "Not much to see," she cooed, her wings unquestionably magnificent as they spread wide, nearly bridging the width of the ship. She hadn't bothered to resume her disguise. "I'm expecting a surprise."

Tallora squinted back upon the sparkling object on the horizon, realizing it might be . . . ice?

High above, the dark clouds slowly swirled, an expansive whirlpool in the sky. "How shall we continue, Empress Dauriel?" Ilune said, and Tallora sensed the weight of the question. This was Dauriel's moment. Or at least, the beginning of it.

Dauriel looked at Tallora, regret in her gaze. The flame at her feet died; her body lost its shine, though clouds still gathered above. "We would be foolish to not expect a trap. Morathma may not realize we know of him, and so he will likely try to surprise us." She stared into the orb, and even Tallora could feel the radiant power it emitted. "Yu'Khrall is our priority, but I will instruct our ships to shoot at Morathma as soon as he appears. Hopefully, it'll banish him. If not, he's your priority, Goddess Ilune."

Tallora gasped, relief flooding her. Beside her, Ilune's smile faltered, but she didn't care. She stepped forward, hesitant to embrace her wife given what she held. "Why, though?"

Dauriel's gloved hand clutched the orb tight as her arm fell slack. She stared at the ground, and every word held pain. "Because if by some miracle I actually live through this madness, I want to be someone worthy of you."

Tallora dared to take her hand, rapidly shaking her head. "You're more than worthy."

"I wouldn't be if I put myself before my people. Before yours. Before you." Dauriel squeezed her hand, then wrapped her arm around her, mindful to keep the orb away as she clung with all her might. Tallora held her, the finality weighing her down like an anchor. "My soul is heavy," Dauriel whispered, "but when I think of you, I feel peace. Even on my darkest days, I feel I have something to live for."

"I love you," Tallora said, and when Dauriel kissed her, by Staella's Grace, it was with all the passion in the realms.

The water churned. Tallora and Dauriel stumbled apart before clinging to the other. From beyond, a rapid expanse of *ice* crawled toward them. "So it begins," Dauriel said. Her silver gaze settled onto Tallora. "Find safety. Stay below deck or swim away, I'm begging you."

"I want to help you if I can."

"You can't. And I can't be distracted worrying for you."

Tallora nodded, knowing in her heart that Dauriel was right. But as she stepped away, a great wave rose from the depths. The ship tilted precariously. From beyond, Tallora heard screaming.

A massive tentacle rose from the ocean, shadowing an unfortunate vessel in the distance. The single appendage was nearly as wide as the ship, and when a second rose to match, all the world paused. Tallora watched, transfixed upon the sight.

The tentacles crashed down. The ship shattered. Men's screams filled the air.

"Prepare harpoons!" Dauriel cried, and her ship scrambled to obey. "If you spot Morathma, fire at will, but in the interim Yu'Khrall is your focus—if you see his eye, don't hesitate!" She looked to Ilune, who radiated wicked glee. "You know what you need to do." The goddess gave a swift nod and rose into the air, flying off to some distant ship.

Dauriel looked to the sky, holding up the orb as the gathered clouds crackled with lightning. She spared a single glance for Tallora, then looked to where Yu'Khrall had vanished.

Their ship nearly capsized as a massive tentacle rose before them. Tallora stumbled, gripping the mast of the ship for support, but Dauriel stood tall, serenity on her features as she watched, waiting.

When the tentacle rose to its full height, the orb flashed. Tallora screamed as lightning burst from the sky, striking Yu'Khrall's appendage. It flailed and retracted, the massive burns upon the scaled skin bearing fractal patters.

Dauriel looked again to Tallora. "Go!" she cried, desperation in her voice. Tallora obeyed, though it ripped her very soul in twain. She disappeared below deck, stumbling as the ship tilted wildly.

She managed to find Dauriel's room, unsure of where else to be. Water soaked the bottom, a few inches deep—Tallora spotted the open window. She ran to it, taking care to hike up her trousers, and shut it. Beyond, the dark sky flashed—a bolt of lightning struck the sea, and the hair on Tallora's arms raised in response.

One of the ships came precariously close, and Tallora wondered if it would strike them. But from the sides came an outpouring of . . . people?

A beam of light rose into the sky—Ilune shone as a magnificent beacon, her godly form made manifest. Her laughter rang through the sky, echoing off the clouds. "I heard you missed me," she said, her voice as pervasive as the mist from the sloshing waves, and from her hands came a purple glow. It consumed her whole figure, this strange purple flame.

Below the water's surface, Tallora heard and felt a deep rumble. A cry of pain—it reverberated against the hull of the ship. She peered out the window, a strange discoloration blossoming beneath the surface.

The people throwing themselves overboard swam despite the waves. Some sunk, but a few managed to stay afloat, and Tallora wondered what madness had coerced them to act. Yet their movements were unnatural, frightfully so, and as Tallora squinted, she saw horrid patches of raw flesh on some, others lacking limbs or eyes.

Ilune, the Great Necromancer, The God of Death. So this was the sensitive cargo they had cryptically spoken of; Tallora's stomach churned, both from the rocking motions and the realization. The undead bit and tore into whatever flesh they touched.

Boils covered the next rising tentacle. Horrid pustules ravaged the smooth surface, seeping black ichor and a gaseous purple flame. Was this Ilune's doing? It shone in the same shade as her magic.

Ilune's attention suddenly shifted. Tallora swore she felt that dreadful smile. "Hello, Snake," her voice boomed.

Morathma had come.

The water beyond slowly swirled, not unlike the clouds above. Countless tentacles suddenly burst from the center, sending raucous waves across the water. A sheet of ice spread from his body—one ship became trapped by ice, then it was engulfed.

But thunder rumbled; lightning struck. Though the ice still slowly expanded, Yu'Khrall flailed. The great, swirling waves broke the ice apart, leaving precarious chunks to ravage the ships instead, small glaciers in the sea. A wave of cold suddenly struck Tallora, and when ice covered her window, she stumbled back, then shrieked as it crept inside.

She scrambled to the bed as the floor froze solid, the inches of water now a slippery trap. When it rose to consume the walls, panic stole her wits—she ran from the room, taking care to avoid the ice's path.

Deeper down in the hull of the ship, the icy sheen spread fast. Wood creaked. The temperature rapidly dropped. Tallora sought direction, but when she tried to descend the stairs to the bottom of the hull, filled with cargo, the ship shook.

Tallora lost her footing; she tumbled down the stairs, landing on an icy sheet. Bruised and battered, she grasped a wooden crate as she tried to rise.

The ship tilted, reverberating as if struck. The crate she clung to slid—she let go, lest it crush her—

Only to be smacked by yet another crate. She stumbled into standing, clutching the wall now as she slowly inched back toward the stairs. There was no use in winning this fight if Tallora were killed by the ship's cargo.

By some miracle, she reached the staircase. She clutched the rail, even as the ship tossed and turned, managing to slowly rise, step by step. Back in the hallway, she slipped on the ice, barely managing to direct herself. Rumbling thunder and booming cries sought to deafen her, but here she fought her own smaller battle—simply trying to not be crushed and consumed by ice. She could survive being thrown overboard, but not being frozen to death.

She saw the stairs leading to the deck. Hands on the wall, she slowly moved forward, though her feet ached from cold. Twice, she slipped, but she stumbled along, nearly sobbing from relief when she grasped the railing of the stairs, not yet frozen from ice.

Tallora pulled herself up the stairs, only to stare into hell.

A gargantuan whirlpool had formed, the armada dotting the sides, slowly being sucked into an abyss of death. Centered was evidence of Yu'Khrall's body, his tentacles darting up from the water to consume ships at random. Great chunks of ice, larger than the ships, joined the swirling mass. When lightning struck the center, it radiated out, sparks dancing across the waves.

Ilune floated high above, pristine despite the storm. She faced a monster of water, a massive humanoid figure, though not so large as Yu'Khrall. It rose a watery fist, launching it toward Ilune—

Only for her to vanish before it could strike. Her laughter sang loudly across the battlefield, despite the thunder and waves, before she reappeared as a sparkle of silver and purple beyond. From one of the ships, a harpoon shot toward the watery figure, only to burst straight through—had Morathma turned to water? Tallora didn't understand.

She stumbled forward, then saw Dauriel consumed in silver flame, the orb held before her. She directed an orchestra of death, her hands moving in rhythmic succession, tossing lightning from the sky like her fire, yet in massive form. Her face bore perfect focus—if she noticed Tallora, she didn't acknowledge her. Sailors rushed about, but Dauriel Solviraes was at peace.

A sparkle in the sky stole Tallora's attention. Ilune appeared, nearer to the center of the whirlpool, evading yet another of Morathma's blows. "Is that all you have? I'm surprised you've come this far at all—the ocean is not your domain."

Morathma struck; Ilune evaded with another fit of laughter, and Tallora's gut clenched, realizing the game. Ever closer to the center, yet she seemed to hardly notice—there waited Yu'Khrall.

Tallora ran up the stairs to the front of the ship, then cried at the top of her lungs, *"Ilune, watch out!"*

Lost in the winds and rain and rolling thunder, her voice was a drop in a bucket. Tallora screamed as one of Yu'Khrall's tentacles burst out—

And grabbed the God of Death.

Horrible purple smoke rose from the coiling tentacle, but though Yu'Khrall screamed he did not release her, instead pulling her back. Ilune disappeared beneath the waves.

The world became quiet, despite the deafening storm. A glow shone behind Tallora, as blinding as the sun. When she turned, Dauriel's body filled with glorious light.

Her body morphed and grew, expanding to accommodate this new being. Brilliant wings burst from her back as she rose into the air, as translucent as moonlight and just as bright. Hair flowed down her back, tightly braided at the top of her head—her face was Dauriel's, yes, but not, ineffably changed to match her progenitor. The flame at her skin rose, consuming her, brilliantly burning to outshine the villains before her. Yet Tallora saw the figure within the fire, a powerful goddess, exalted above the rest.

Neoma didn't speak. She clutched the orb, tiny in her hands. It was not lightning that burst from her fingers, but a torrent of silver flame.

As wide as Yu'Khrall's tentacles, it burst through Morathma's figure, yet not dispelling in the water—instead, Morathma cried out as steam rose from the hole in his form. The relentless silver flame continued its onslaught to Yu'Khrall—fire burst from the center, steam rising amidst his rumbling cry.

When the fire dissipated, Neoma held a small bit in her hands, caressing it like a pet as it rose and grew and swirled around her hands. "You disgust me," she spat, the words booming within the cloud cover.

Her gaze was fixed to Morathma, and the elemental figure finally spoke. "Delightful to see you too," he said, the words deep yet wispy, like sand caught in a desert breeze. His tone held no politeness, but a sharp, piercing ire.

His watery fist rose to strike Neoma, but she stood her ground; she held up a hand, the silver swirling in a torrential, fiery whirlwind. The water did not touch her. Steam rose around her; Morathma's fist burst into rainfall, then the fire struck his face.

Tallora marveled at the display, the beauty of her magic as she effortlessly tossed it around her hands and blasted the Desert Sands. Not true flame, though it burned hot and could become it—but pure magic. When he moved to touch her again, she simply glowed like the moon. At his touch, her light became blinding, then burst, sending silver flame across the gargantuan whirlpool the world had become.

Tentacles rose; Neoma's wings brought her higher into the sky as she blasted smaller balls of silver fire at each appendage. All the while, Morathma attempted to barrage her with his own mysterious power, but though Neoma dodged and absorbed what she could, Tallora's heart raced with panic. Helpless on the deck, she gasped when a burst of jagged ice jutted from the waves to impale the great goddess—

By Staella's Grace, she dodged—or perhaps Neoma's own grace—but Tallora's gut churned at every blow, at every gorgeous display of flame and water and ice. Morathma sought to drown her, yet

Tallora noticed substance within him, something darker, murky—mud? Sand?

She stared a moment too long before realizing he looked not at Neoma, but at her. His great fist came down upon her ship—Tallora screamed as it cut in twain. She grabbed the mast on instinct, then looked up at the sky. Neoma stared, stalled in the conflict—

And was then swatted by tentacles. Neoma tumbled through the air but righted herself. Her flame rose once more.

The bisected ship sank slowly. Sailors scrambled about, some managing to grab hold of the ship and others falling into the sea. Tallora quickly shed her clothing as the water came to greet her. But a shadow covered her; Yu'Khrall's tentacle crashed down—

She plummeted deep below the waves.

Though surely bruised, Tallora lived, and she nearly hugged her tail for joy as her legs sealed together. Yu'Khrall was a mass before her, but his golden gaze was reserved for the world above.

Swim away, her gut screamed, yet far below Yu'Khrall was Stelune.

Instead of the familiar towers of home or even the toppled ruins, Tallora saw a great expanse of ice. Enormous, formless sculptures grew within the once great city, creating a jagged dome around the valley— the top of which was shattered, as though recently broken through by Yu'Khrall. She dove deeper, drawn to her former home. The world above became quiet. Beneath the depthless waters, Tallora moved in a trance toward the shield of ice . . .

Only to see a graveyard.

Tallora lost feeling in her tail, yet she slowly continued onward, stunned by the silence, the peace amidst the nightmare around her. A thick sheet of ice coated the ruins of Stelune, and frozen within were the faces of her kin. Survivors of Stelune lay in stasis— either dead or sleeping, she did not know—along with citizens of Iids. She swam over the translucent surface, horror slowly twisting her gut. Perhaps they had rejected him. Perhaps this was the price of pledging. Perhaps it had been a lie all along—Tallora didn't know.

The floor sloped, revealing more. Not merely her own people—the Onians who had come to aid them, punished for their kindness. All around, Tallora was surrounded by ice, yet the chill outside was nothing to the chill within her soul.

One stood out, trapped in an outcropping jutting from the center. That bluish mop of hair was unmistakable, and those eyes—bright and filled with light, even in stasis—stared beyond her, seeing nothing at all.

Tallora placed a hand upon the ice before Kal, an agonized cry escaping her throat. It echoed loud among the silence, reverberating across the high, broken dome. Despite the turbulence beyond, peace remained here, the quiet eerie and damning.

Tears filled Tallora's eyes, escaping and freezing into tiny, sparkling droplets as they joined the sea. Within her blood, something hot and furious pulsed, and within the ruins of a city she had once loved, surrounded by the bodies of her frozen loved ones, Tallora whispered the beginning of a prayer. *"Goddess Staella . . ."*

Whether it was within her or behind, Tallora could not say, yet a new presence settled, one she had come to know.

"I have to do something," she thought.

They merely sleep. They can still be saved.

Tallora removed her hand from the icy wall. *"How?"*

It is not a small thing, what you ask for. You know the price.

The words held sorrow, yet Tallora felt only conviction. "Use me," she said out loud.

It shall be a noble end.

Searing heat filled her. Tallora gasped, burning yet not, tingling as *something* settled inside her, filling her own limbs with theirs. She grew, body twisting as light radiated from every pore. Brilliant wings burst from her back, gently floating among the waves, yet her tail remained, and when she blinked, she saw the universe—facets of light, cracks in the world leading to others, even tendrils of magic. She knew it all like her own skin.

"Be free," she said, but they were not her words, and in the wall of ice, she caught the barest flash of her reflection and saw divinity glowing within.

Then, her mirror shattered as a thousand cracks split through the ice. Like a spider's web, it spread wide, growing up and then down, scattered all across the floor beneath—

When it burst, she heard the gasping breaths of countless voices, heard children cry, yet it filled her with hope. Her lips smiled as the figure within her did, yet it was her own words that spoke to the familiar boy before her. *"Kal!"*

Kal swam forward, precocious as his gaze traveled up and down her body. He seemed so small—perhaps half her size. "Tallora?"

"Yes," she replied, and it was two tones, two voices melded together—one familiar, the other musical and soft. *"Kal, Yu'Khrall is fighting Neoma as we speak. You have to lead your people away immediately."*

"I will. I tried before, but they were already—"

"It's all right." She smiled—it was her own doing this time. The presence within her waited. *"Go. Save our people."*

He nodded, his gaze lingering a moment before he sped away and called for order.

Tallora.

The voice was within. Tallora froze.

Time is of the essence. We must go.

Where?

To save Solvira and the sea.

Tallora placed a hand upon her heart, the rapid beating beneath her skin unnatural. *Will there be enough time?*

You are stronger than you know. You have life enough in you for this.

Tallora immediately rushed through the water, sparing a final glance for her people's exodus. They would be safe; that much she knew.

When she burst through the waves, her wings spread wide. She hardly noticed the pain as her tail split in two. Oh, the air felt marvelous. A glorious sensation of freedom flowed through her—not her own, though. These were Staella's feelings, her own elation filling Tallora with joy.

The storm raged on, but the combatants stilled in her presence. High in the air, Tallora gazed upon the gargantuan whirlpool capable of swallowing a city, saw the remaining ships still battling the great leviathan. That golden eye peered straight up, fixed upon her. The two battling deities watched, their own tempestuous battle having waned in her company.

Then, Staella dove, and Tallora, a stranger in her own body, watched that eye grow ever closer. Tentacles flailed, daring to swipe at the Goddess of Stars, but at their touch, Staella blinked out of sight. The world shifted as Staella crossed the barriers between worlds seamlessly, from here to what her possessor's knowledge said was Celestière, and back again, only to repeat it at Yu'Khrall's next swipe. In rapid succession, she blinked in and out, the world changing back and forth from peaceful and white to the raging storm, and when the eye came too close, it vanished before they could touch—

Then Staella reappeared beneath him, in the waves. Tallora's tail reformed as countless tentacles swirled around them in a violent mass. *Search with me,* said the voice in her head, and Tallora kept her eyes peeled as Staella navigated the undulating mass, blinking in and out as necessary—a sensation both nauseating and invigorating.

The black mass seemed endless, and Tallora swore her eyes had dulled, when a flash of light beside her gave her pause. Staella approached, finding a wispy wing poking out from a curled mass of tentacles. She touched it.

They appeared in a different realm, one filled with pure nothingness, only white, endless mist. Ilune collapsed to the ground, coughing as water ejected from her vessel's lungs, her earthly coil a stolen one. Evidence of tears stained her face, and an outpouring of love shook Tallora, pained her. Staella gathered her daughter in her arms, and Tallora felt relief unparalleled, as well as peace. Ilune gazed up at her, her countenance twisting into an exhausted, mischievous smirk, and Tallora felt that she'd adored this smile for thousands of years. "I should have known you'd come."

"Are you well enough to rejoin the fight?"

"I wouldn't miss it."

Staella helped Ilune rise, then kept her grip on her hand as water suddenly consumed them. She held Ilune to her body, expertly dodging the array of tentacles, blinking in and out, until she finally left the mass.

She burst into the air, then released Ilune, whose wings spread to catch her. *"Lure Morathma away,"* Tallora said, though it was not Tallora, and the sensation was still so strange. *"I shall greet Yu'Khrall."*

"But, mother, I could—"

"No." Tallora felt love unparalleled, yes, but also vast anguish for the daughter her goddess adored. It churned her stomach, so deep it welled. *"You've done enough damage to him."*

Their eyes met, and Ilune grit her jaw and nodded. She flew away, toward the tumultuous battle of fire high above. Staella, however went to the leviathan, stopping above his great eye. He flailed at her approach, his tentacles whipping at her form—but Staella floated serenely, radiating peace as she blinked in and out of the world to avoid him. Tallora swore the storm calmed, that the battle beyond them stilled. Even the whirlpool slowed.

Staella said, *"Yu'Khrall, Son of Onias, I weep for you."*

The leviathan spoke for the first time; his tentacles docile, though rising high enough to match her. *"Goddess Staella."*

"Let me help you," Staella said, and it was a whisper, for everything she said was soft and hushed, yet it echoed far and wide enough for the whole world to hear.

"You . . . cannot."

Staella gently floated down, close enough to show good faith. *"I am a breaker of curses, a savior to those in bondage, a soother of spirits. Let me help."*

The tentacles followed, ominous as they lingered. *"You . . . You shall only imprison me again."*

"There must be justice for what you've done," Staella said, and sorrow filled Tallora at the words—her own, and her goddess'. *"But there must be justice for you too. The one who hurt you has served her penance, yet the wrong was never rectified."*

A single, massive tentacle came close, and Staella touched it gently, stroked a soft line down the scaled skin. Tallora felt . . . pity. Pity and charitable love from a part of her soul she knew was not her own, yet it was so real, so *vivid,* this desire to help a monster who had destroyed her people.

Staella kept a hand on his tentacle, coaxing it down as she floated closer to the water's surface. The whirlpool hadn't ceased, but it actively slowed, no longer fueled by the orb's power. Her feet touched the water's surface, and she walked as though weightless toward the eye of the beast. It watched, that golden gaze as wide as she was tall. With one hand still holding his tentacle, Staella reached her other toward him.

. . . and took his curse upon herself.

Oh, it *burned,* pure fire in her veins, and Tallora fought to not scream. Within her, a hollow welled in her stomach, rapidly expanding, never ceasing, boring away all notions of sanity and thought and driving her mad.

Staella stood tall, merely shutting her eyes, but though Tallora housed her, it took all her will to not double over and weep. It was anguish; it was pain; it was *agony;* by every god, she was *starving—*

It ceased.

Tallora breathed as Staella did, her godly blood burning the final vestiges of the curse's essence away.

Before her, Yu'Khrall stilled, his tentacles slowly returning to the sea. He said nothing at all, but soon it was only the tentacle gently held in Staella's grasp . . . and then a second.

He offered her Yaleris' orb, secured in the center of one of the massive suckers on his appendage.

Staella shook her head. *"That is yours by right. You slew Yaleris."*

"There must be a penance."

In his leviathan rumble, though it reverberated against her bones, Tallora heard regret. *"It is yours to defend now,"* Staella said, *"against any who might try to steal it."*

"I . . . agree."

That great eye looked beyond her—when Staella turned, Neoma approached, her wings supporting her as she levitated above the ocean's surface. *"Grant him a gentle cage,"* Staella said softly, and Yu'Khrall did not move or argue. *"I will help."*

Neoma offered a hand, and when Staella accepted it, Tallora felt only Dauriel's touch. Staella released Yu'Khrall, then the duo poured their power into one brilliant burst of light and let it settle and coat the leviathan.

Yu'Khrall did not fight. The spell was painless, Tallora knew instinctively, and she watched as the great leviathan became smaller.

Not tiny, but when the steady shrinking ceased, he was far from city-sized. *"You shall stand watch over the orb,"* Neoma said, echoing her wife's sentiments, *"as well as the Ruins of Stelune. A hundred years for every life you consumed—and then you shall be free."*

Yu'Khrall's rumbling voice no longer frightened her. *"So it shall be."* He sank into the sea, his body disappearing by slow degrees, soon leaving only bubbles.

As the sea settled into tranquility, Tallora saw the graveyard the battle had become—shattered remains of ships scattered across the sea, heroes who knew the futility of this fight yet chose to come along all the same. Beside her, Neoma glowed, Rulira's orb held in her hand, and her smile was Dauriel's—wicked and all she adored. *"How do you feel?"* Tallora asked, upon her own volition.

Neoma's smile softened, adoration in her gaze. *"Like I can go a little longer."*

They flew up into the sky, hand in hand.

Ilune waited, and across from her was Morathma himself, the final remains of mud and water falling into the sea, revealing his angelic body hosted by the Speaker. Tallora understood it now, Staella's own knowledge combined with hers—that his power lay in the elements of earth, but that Yu'Khrall had granted him more.

"I concede," Morathma said, his hands held out in deference.

"I'd still happily fight," Ilune spat, but Neoma floated up beside her and placed a hand upon her shoulder.

"Oh, that I could kill you in this realm," Neoma said, her sneer all Dauriel yet it truly was the goddess who spoke. *"Crawl back into your hole."*

But Morathma did not. Instead, he looked to Staella, who slowly turned her head away. *"My deepest condolences, for the tragedy of your and Tortalga's people,"* he said softly, so kind and sincere, and the rage filling Tallora was certainly her own, but something quiet simmered with it—anger that was not her own; anger that was ancient. *"None of this was meant to hurt you. I simply did what I had to."*

Tallora fought to seize control, to yell and scream and fight Morathma, but a gentle voice inside her head said, *Say nothing at all. Do not even look at him.*

Tallora obeyed. She simply stared upon the horizon.

It is the only way to deal with people like him. Give him nothing.

She remained there, floating, until Morathma's light went out. When Tallora did turn, a mortal man, already cold and stiff, fell into the ocean.

Far beyond, on the horizon, the shadow of the Morathan ship sailed away.

A few ships remained, and the Triage flew to the nearest one. Ilune settled upon the deck, disheveled but in good spirits as Neoma joined her. "Did she die?" she asked Neoma, and Tallora scoffed at the bluntness of it.

"*No,*" Neoma replied. "*I did not strike the final blow, as I'd intended. What power I did use, Staella supplemented. Dauriel shall live.*"

Neoma slowly shrunk, her wings blinking out of sight, her light fading out until it was only Dauriel on the deck. The orb plopped onto the ground; Dauriel fell into Ilune's arms, groaning as she was led to the floor. "Oh, I hurt," Dauriel said, and she puked on the deck.

"There, there," Ilune said amidst her heaving. "A long nap, and you'll be fine."

Tallora.

The voice whispered inside her head.

I am all that anchors you here now.

Tallora floated down, her wings as much a part of her as anything else. When Dauriel met her eye, those beautiful silver ones widened, as though noticing her for the first time. "Tallora . . ?"

Tallora blinked, and with it came a welling of tears. "*Dauriel . . .*"

With Ilune's help, Dauriel managed to stand. She stumbled forward, her shaking legs holding as she gazed upon Tallora's godly visage. "No, you can't—" Dauriel's lips trembled, a sob stealing her words.

"*Duty over heart. It was the price to save my people,*" Tallora said, and a heartbreaking sob tore from the empress' throat. "*Dauriel, my love—*"

Her words cut off at Dauriel's embrace. With no hesitation to hug her mother goddess, she clung to Tallora with all her might, as though it might hold her here. "You can't go. I . . . can't go on without you."

"Yes, you can," Tallora pled, though her own anguish steadily rose. *"You're so strong Dauriel. Every day of your life, you fight to live, and by Staella's Grace—don't give up now.* Tallora's own tears fell, her hold on Dauriel an anchor. *"You're going to do great things. I want you to. I want you to live. Don't view it as a lifetime without me— simply one day. Take it one day at a time."* Her lip trembled; she struggled to speak, but each passing second was worth more than gold. *"When we see each other again in the Beyond, I want to hear about every moment of your beautiful, brilliant life. Please."*

Tallora . . .

"I have to go," Tallora said, and though Dauriel trembled, her hold softened. She placed a lingering kiss upon her wife's brow, this final gaze between them Tallora's most precious possession. *"I love you, Dauriel."*

"You are the love of my life," Dauriel replied, but then she shut her eyes, tears falling fast. "I'll make you proud. I swear it."

Tallora felt a new embrace around her—Staella herself beckoning her home. She followed.

All the world turned to light.

Chapter XX

"*T*allora . . ."

If Tallora didn't open her eyes, daylight wouldn't come. She cherished the dark embrace of night, of her warm bed and pillow.

"Tallora, you sweet thing—open your eyes."

"Five more minutes," she mumbled, but then the blankets drew tighter around her, squeezing gently. The strangeness of it coaxed her to open a single eye.

She saw a world of white mist—the very same as when she had aided in saving Ilune. How long had it been? Had she even slept? Tallora groaned and held her head, groggy as her memories slowly returned.

She realized, then, she was being held. Gasping, she looked up to see the smiling face of Staella, her beloved goddess. *"Your soul is safe with me, but it is normal to be disoriented."*

Tallora managed to nod. Staella sat within an endless void of mist. "Where are we?"

"The Beyond. I did not want you to linger here for long, but . . ." Staella looked at her oddly. Not frowning, but with furrowed brows. *"You did not tell me you had two lives within you."*

Taken aback, Tallora said, "What do you mean?"

"To channel me stole all the life you have, but there was a second one, simply waiting, not a drop of it spent. As for how it got there, you tell me."

Tallora sat up; she had her tail and realized she could float freely in this strange realm, as weightless as in water.

A second life? Tallora swam in slow circles, unsure of what to make of any of it, thinking back upon her life and remembered . . . "Harbinger," she whispered, realization settling in. "The price for me to transform from mermaid to human was a life—Harbinger gave me a lifetime."

Staella smiled. *"That would do it."*

"That means I can go back, right?" Tallora's hope spiked, but while Staella did not disagree, regret showed in her features.

"The price must still be paid. A lifetime has gone, and while I can do many things, the realms have rules even I must follow. You have to choose."

Tallora frowned, nervous at her tone. "Choose what?"

"You must choose which life and what you will be—a mermaid or a human girl."

Breath hitching, Tallora's limbs grew cold, though it must have been in her head—she had no body here.

The path diverged. And now, she could truly never go back.

Her future beneath the sea had become shattered glass, but with it came life anew—the chance to rebuild her people. She had a duty; she had died to save them and give them their lives back. She thought of her home and all its beauty, how the upper world paled to the great coral reefs and rainbows of fish. She thought of Kal, her friend, of her momma, who had passed.

Home was lost, but it could be found again. The ocean remained vast and beautiful, and her people would find a way. The Onians had already offered to help. For a brilliant moment, hope filled her at the thought—the world had ended, yet her people still lived. What better way to honor the goddess who had saved them than to finally become a priestess? The Temple of Staella had been decimated in the calamity, and Tallora might be the only one left.

But Dauriel . . .

Tallora's face fell into her hands, weeping to think of her. She remembered their goodbye; and oh, the change in Dauriel before that great and final battle. She wanted to live, and by Staella's Grace—Tallora's heart soared for that.

She had made a vow, to love her forever. And sometimes loving Dauriel meant to hurt alongside her, but oh, how fiercely her empress loved in return.

To live in Solvira would be a difficult life, the duties of being crowned empress more than she could fathom here in the Beyond, and her very soul shirked at the thought. But home would be a life of strife as well, rebuilding all she'd lost. Duty said to become a priestess and bless the people she loved. But her heart . . .

Two paths diverged, and both would be difficult, rewarding lives.

"What would you choose?" Tallora whispered, and though she sought to cry, her tears didn't fall. She had none.

Staella watched her as only a loving mother could, with understanding in her eyes. *"I would choose what brought me joy."*

Tallora's jaw trembled at the thought.

"Forget your duty, and forget your heart. What do you want more than anything? This is the chance to start anew."

Tallora knew, but she couldn't say it. It felt like a betrayal.

Staella's smile held all the kindness in the realms, and Tallora cherished it so. *"Once upon a time, I had all the world at my feet. I was a goddess to a land of people who adored me, embraced in the arms of a man who loved me, and held duties I enjoyed immensely. I was the Goddess of Stars, the Light that Glitters above the Desert Sands. My life should have been perfect, but I knew in my quiet moments that something was wrong. Meeting Neoma . . ."* She looked wistfully at the sky, reminiscence in her countenance. *"Meeting her wasn't instant clarity, but I began seeing the cracks in my perfect world, all the things I overlooked so I could be happy in a life I hadn't chosen. The price of compliance—sometimes you're young, you let life happen, and others make decisions for you."*

When Staella shut her eyes, Tallora saw only peace. *"I made the first decision of my life—to leave my duty behind and love Neoma. I think you know the story is more complicated than that, but that's the part that matters: I didn't do what I was supposed to do. I saw the future I wanted and grasped it tight. I've never let it go, and while my life is not perfect, it brings me unparalleled joy."* Staella looked again to her, quiet peace on her beautiful face. *"What do you want, Tallora? What will you grasp and never let go?"*

Tallora thought a moment, imagined leaving her beloved world behind to stay at Dauriel's side and be the empress consort—for what other option was there? The title was not at all what she wanted, but she couldn't betray her marriage vow, just as she couldn't abandon Dauriel if there were any hope to stay. But though she could plead for Dauriel to live for her, it cured nothing. Dauriel was hurting, bearing shackles of gold and a crown she'd been destined for, yet never truly given the choice to—

And then, a thought came, a tiny spot of light in an otherwise dark sky. An impossible thought, yet it filled her with hope.

"Goddess Staella, what if this question isn't meant for me? What if there's someone else who might choose between duty and love?"

Dauriel had spent all her days seeking a great escape. Perhaps fate might allow that after all.

"I know I must choose, and I will. But you once gave me legs with no cost to me. Could you ... Could ..."

Her words failed, but Staella smiled, and it was sweet yet nearly impish—as though this were the answer all along. *"Neoma will object, but we never dismiss the free will of our people. Dauriel must make the choice, but—"*

Her words were stolen by Tallora's sudden burst of sobs. Staella embraced her when she fell apart. *"I love you, my Tallora. I shall quell any potential storms that might arise from this decision, but I believe you have chosen the greatest part. I shall see it done."* She traced soft lines into Tallora's hair as she wept—though there were no tears, and it felt so odd. *"A final question, before you go: Your mother has been found. She lives a wonderful afterlife among like minds—your father included. Is there any message you would like me to give them?"*

Tallora shut her eyes, knowing she could write a novel of thoughts but had to pick only one. "Tell them," she whispered, her sobs finally waning, "that I'm happy. And I shall be so all my life."

"They'll be delighted to hear it." Staella released her but kept a hold of her hands. *"Are you ready?"*

Tallora nodded. She shut her eyes, and all the world went dark.

Epilogue

In the early morning, High Priestess Tallora of New Stelune chanted the final refrain of the prayer with fellow worshippers of the Goddess of Stars:

Mother Staella, hear my plea
Grant me love and serenity
Bless my home with joy and light
I shall not forget your gentle might

They concluded the prayer with a murmuring *amen*. Fading starlight signified the sun would soon come, and Tallora waited near the surface, greeting those who came to thank her for the service, granting blessings to those who asked. And there was true magic in it, a small portion of Staella's power granted to her through the sleek little fish always at her side—a lovely, vibrant thing of purple and red and brilliant yellow. 'Fairy,' Tallora called her, and though her familiar did not speak, there was affection in the way she bumped against Tallora's cheek, how she slept in her mass of white hair.

Dawn had arrived by the time the final few worshippers cleared the scene. Tallora dismissed her small group of priestesses-in-training, then spared the waning stars a final goodbye, admiring a particular constellation, when a familiar voice sparked joy in her heart. "Tallora!"

To her bafflement, there floated Prince Kalvin, Ambassador of the Tortalgan Seas, his familiar navy hair flat to his head above the water. She swam to greet him, quickly embracing his decorated form. Across his chest was a sash of braided kelp, signifying his new duties beneath King Rek'Thir and Queen Narissa's reign—Kal's sister's marriage to the Onian Prince had sealed a new era of peace. "What are you doing here?"

"I'm visiting the local magistrate to discuss new building plans for the capital—we need more houses, as always, and the orphanage could use an expansion. But I couldn't come to New Stelune without seeing an old friend."

"How long are you in town? I'm exhausted from leading worship, but we would love to have you come over for dinner."

"My wife and I will be here for a few weeks, actually. I've been instructed to supervise these new plans by my mother."

The Queen Mother did not hold power anymore, but she held influence. The world had not forgotten her bravery when she had led her people from Stelune. And when King Merl had been returned to the people of the Tortalgan Sea, his fate at their mercy, she had shed no tears when announcing his execution for treason.

"I shouldn't tell you this, so keep the news quiet, but my sister is expecting," Kal said, and Tallora's heart soared for that. "She's asked if you would be willing to come to the capital after the birth and grant the baby a blessing of Staella."

"I can't think of a greater honor," Tallora replied. "Tell her I'd be happy to."

Kal looked up to the sky, his knowing smirk nothing less than impish. "She's the brightest one up there."

With a wistful smile, Tallora gazed up to one of the remaining constellations, the collection of stars a clear image to those who knew what to look for. "Dauriel wouldn't have settled for anything less."

Memorialized in the sky was Dauriel's image, the commemoration of her sacrifice in the great battle with Yu'Khrall, so that all the world might remember. Near it was a mermaid's tail, and Tallora knew it was no coincidence.

When she and Kal bid their farewells, Tallora gave him an address and told him to visit any time.

They embraced and then they parted. She grinned as she swam her way home, followed closely by Fairy.

New Stelune lacked the grandeur of its predecessor, yet it held something far more valuable—*hope*. In the five years since its founding, Tallora had watched something beautiful come from the ashes of her home, reborn like a phoenix of old. No longer in the valley, no, but instead they had settled farther north, away from the memories of destruction and murder. Here, they could become something new.

In the early morning hours, most sane people were asleep—except for worshippers of Staella, who pledged to the stars every dark moon. As Tallora passed newly built homes, she spared a glance for the distant sky, the dark waters leading to a realm she never tired of. Though tempted to bid farewell to the final few stars before sunrise, home called to her.

She did not live far from the temple, her home a gift from the city when she had accepted her calling as High Priestess. With ease, she rolled aside the stone before her humble abode, unsurprised to hear only peaceful silence.

She removed her vestments and laid them carefully upon a table, leaving her in only the chain bearing her wedding ring. With a kiss, she whispered, "Go rest, sweet Fairy," and the little fish swam to her alcove. Tallora went to the single bedroom.

There lay Dauriel, fast asleep.

With her deep maroon tail and cropped black hair, Tallora thought her the most wonderful sight in all the world. In peace, Dauriel rested posed to show her tattoos, her scars, every perfect piece of her. Everything was different, yet it was all the same; all Tallora loved and adored.

Gently, Tallora floated into bed and embraced her wife from behind, wrapping their tails together and placing a lingering kiss upon the back of her neck when she stirred. "Good morning."

Dauriel rolled over in her arms, her silver eyes heavy from sleep. "Good morning," she mumbled. "How was worship?"

"As magical as ever," Tallora replied, delighted when Dauriel kissed her lips and smiled. "Kal and his wife are in town. I invited them over."

"Of course you did." Dauriel hummed contentedly as she settled in beside her, their bare chests pressed together as she shut her eyes anew. "Well, I'll cook something. Or, rather, the mermaid equivalent of cooking." When she snapped her fingers, a small spark of light flittered from her thumb—the Silver Fire was not true fire, but it burned hot beneath the sea.

Tallora giggled. Dauriel's mishaps in maintaining her façade of just another refugee were frequent, but no one had found them out yet. She was not Empress Dauriel Solviraes, the most powerful woman in the world. Empress Dauriel had died that fateful day in the battle against Yu'Khrall. This woman was merely Dauriel, who went by a new name in public, who worked in city planning and was campaigning for the position of magistrate and had earned a reputation for being vicious and relentless in her negotiations.

And she was happy.

Tallora kissed her forehead, her adoration for her empress—for Dauriel would always be her empress—only growing in their years together. "Go back to sleep, love. You have a few more hours before the world will want you."

Dauriel didn't need to be told twice, and within a few minutes, her breathing resumed its deep, comforting pattern. She had a peaceful life; it was all she'd ever wanted.

Tallora rested beside her, sleep evading her a few moments more as she reflected upon her new, impossible life. Duty brought rewards unparalleled, and Tallora was adored both in the city and beyond, the speaker for Staella herself, when necessary. Staella was both a mother and a friend to everyone, and

Tallora had happily chosen to devote her life to the Goddess of Stars as a thanks for the greatest mercy of all.

Ilune had told Khastra the truth, or so Tallora had been informed, and the general had mourned but understood, joyful in that bittersweet way to know Dauriel was alive and happy. Kal knew the truth, for he knew Dauriel well, but had shown his commitment to secrecy over the years. The rest of the world spoke of the legend of Empress Dauriel Solviraes in a whisper, her great sacrifice the noblest end. The history books would remember the brutal woman who had defeated both Yu'Khrall and Morathma in a battle as superb as the world had ever seen.

With both the Speaker and Solvira's Empress dead, the war had met a quiet, anti-climactic end. Certain to be resumed by future generations, yes, for the conflict was eternal. It would remain so, for as long as the Stars glittered by the Moon's side, and the Desert Sands lay restless in his own realm.

For now, the affairs of gods would be their own.

Tallora held her sleeping wife, her exhaustion finally overtaking her as the sun rose to warm the waters of her new home.

The history books would write of a brutal, heroic end, for Dauriel had always been meant to burn brilliant and bright. But the unspoken epilogue would be a gentle secret for only them to know.

Quiet joy filled Tallora as she joined Dauriel in sleep. They deserved to rest.

End

Acknowledgements

Sea and Stars began as a silly 'what if' story between my wife and I, but it quickly evolved into something more. The story felt special. I couldn't have anticipated how large of a project it would become. It was meant to be a standalone novel, but I couldn't for the life of me decide on an ending. And then, one day, I realized it wasn't supposed to end—and so books two and three were born.

But it takes a village to write a book. I couldn't have done this alone.

Big thanks to my readers, new and old. Not a day goes by where I don't feel your support and love.

Special thanks to Jaylee, who put up with my incessant chattering at the gym as we tried to piece together the details of Death's Abyss' ending.

Thank you to LaRae—the cheerleader I need.

Thank you to Andi—who saved the ending of Heart of Silver Flame.

And thank you to Ruth—who wasn't afraid to tell me what parts sucked.

Thank you to Jerah, to Mars, and to Jade, for being the artistic masterminds behind the scenes.

Thank you to my wife, who understands that I rarely live in the real world.

And, finally, a big shoutout to my feline companions, Mulan, Jasmine, and Elsa, who did everything in their power to distract me from finishing.

To my wonderful readers—thank you!

If you liked what you read, kindly leave a review! That's the best thanks an author can get.

Sea and Stars may be complete, but the magic isn't over! I have two FREE short stories available exclusively through my newsletter—one involving a certain General of the Solviran Army (being technically demoted and going on a date with an oblivious angel) and another about the protagonist of the FALLEN GODS series discovering she's a witch and spending her days with her wolf mentor. Go to sdsimper.com for more info!

Also, check me out on social media! You'll get all the latest updates. Plus you can meet other fans of SEA AND STARS, FALLEN GODS, and more! I'm @sdsimper on Facebook, Twitter, and Instagram.

Up next—*Fallen Gods 4: Tear the World Apart.*

See you then!

-S D Simper

What happened after Tallora's great sacrifice?
Find out from Dauriel's point of view!

Aftermath

A Patreon exclusive novella
by SD Simper

Keep turning pages for an exclusive sneak peek!

Dauriel had thought she'd known despair, had watched the love of her life swim away—twice—had bid her farewell a final time before boarding a ship and sailing to her doom, had kissed her before the end of the world . . .

No. Dauriel had never known pain before—not like this. She had lived but at an unbearable cost.

She felt nothing, save the crushing weight of anguish and the cold body in her arms.

Salt water and tears clung to those precious white locks, as limp as the rest of Tallora's precious body. Gods, Dauriel was haunted by those glassy eyes, but she couldn't bear to shut them, couldn't bear to never see that crystal blue again. Sunlight broke through the storm clouds, casting light upon her pearlescent skin, her fuchsia tail, and Dauriel memorized it all as she held Tallora's hand, comforting even in death.

Tallora was gone.

Shifting light revealed the one witness to her tragedy, Ilune's gold and silver wings casting their own illumination. She waved at one of the few surviving ships—and Dauriel felt so endlessly selfish to mourn this one person when so many others had fallen.

Ilune paced, her quiet steps no louder than Dauriel's soft weeping. "I could bring her back as a ghoul. I'll even stuff her spirit in there. A little crass, disrespectful to some, but you'd have her."

"Don't tempt me," Dauriel mouthed, for necromancy was not a power to trifle with.

"That ship will be here in a few minutes," Ilune continued, pointing in the distance. "I hate to sound insensitive, but you do need to decide what you'll do with her—and I don't mean regarding necromancy. I mean if you wish to bury her at sea among her people or in Solvira. She is the empress consort, so a royal funeral would be appropriate, but this was her home."

Dauriel knew, but her very soul tore at the thought. She forced the words, nevertheless, though fresh sobs came with it. "She should be buried here."

Ilune withdrew a knife from thin air. "Take this. Cut a bit of her hair. Something to remember her by. You'll regret it later if you don't."

Dauriel could hardly touch it, could hardly see from her renewed tears blinding her vision. Trembling, she accepted the weapon, but despite her shaking hands, she became still as she neared Tallora's skin, not daring to mar her. She cut a lock about half the length of her long hair and gently wrapped it around her fingers. She held it to her heart and supposed there was small comfort in it.

So enigmatic, this wicked goddess. Just as comfortable sacrificing entire legions of people for her cause as she was providing thoughtful gestures in times of tragedy.

With Tallora splayed in her arms, Dauriel tucked the precious hair into her pocket, then held her a final time to her chest, her grief numbed in the face of duty. Tallora would want this. Tallora loved Dauriel, but she held no love for Solvira. Instead, she had always cherished her home.

Dauriel caressed the damp hair from her face, lip trembling as she placed a lingering kiss on her brow.

And when she withdrew, Tallora's eyelashes fluttered, the glass fading from her eyes.

Dauriel froze, transfixed upon her face as anger spiked within her. "Ilune—"

Tallora gasped for breath, chest heaving as she surged up, pain in each heaving inhale.

Dauriel looked to Ilune for some explanation, for this didn't bespeak necromancy, and the God of Death simply shrugged.

"Dauriel?"

A voice Dauriel had thought she'd never hear again.

Dauriel stared a moment into Tallora's eyes, cupped her cheek, unable to even breath as her mind wrapped around what she was witnessing.

Then Tallora smiled, and it was unbearably her, so impish and kind. Dauriel's mind became blank—all she could do was weep.

Amidst her cries, she felt Tallora's embrace, heard her own precious name muttered from Tallora's lips. "I'm here, Dauriel. It's me."

For all her anguished cries, nothing compared to this. Dauriel did not know whether to laugh or cry, but she managed to smile, responded to the impassioned kiss upon her lips. Her breathing became labored, but she managed a few words: "How can this be?"

"When Harbinger turned me into a human, she sacrificed a lifetime and gave it to me. So when I died, that life still lived within me." The sensation of Tallora's fingers in her hair both invigorated and grounded her, her wife's surreal presence still a dream.

Dauriel barely understood, her shock still leaving her cold, but Tallora was here, her body warming with every second.

"But there is something we need to talk about—quickly." Tallora drew their gazes to meet, though Dauriel could not have looked away even if she wished. "I had to choose whether to be a mermaid or a human. I can't be both. Not anymore."

It came like a punch to her stomach. As the implications fell together, Dauriel's hand came to rest upon Tallora's beautiful scales. "I-I understand," she said, but her tears fell anew.

"But you can come with me."

The words meant nothing. "What?"

"Goddess Staella has offered to let you come with me. She had the power to turn me into a human—and she's agreed to turn you into a mermaid, if you wish it. No cost, except you can't return."

In the ensuing silence, Dauriel contemplated a great many things.

Solvira, her people—they needed her. Yet she had already agreed to leave them, to die for their survival.

Neoma . . . what would Neoma say? Yet Staella had offered?

She thought of her home, of her family, of Eniah and her father, of Khastra . . . Yet here was Tallora, who had sacrificed her home for Dauriel.

The time ticked ever-forward. The oncoming ship would take her home—or deliver news of her death.

The words were not hers, yet they came from her mouth. "I'll come with you."

The joy on Tallora's face was worth it all, even if Dauriel felt nothing.

She looked to Ilune. "You'll tell them I died. Neoma's power burned me out, as expected."

Amusement twisted Ilune's grin. "All of them?"

"Yes, why wouldn't—" The truth fell together gently, for her father and brother needed to think she was gone forever but . . . "Tell Khastra I love her. Tell her the truth, but bid her to tell no one. She'll understand; she has to."

A glimmer of sincerity settled upon Ilune's countenance. "She will. I can tell you without a doubt in my mind that this is what she would want for you."

"Thank you." Dauriel looked to Tallora, to her radiant smile, and managed to summon her own. "I'm coming with you."

Tallora kissed her, and with it came unparalleled joy.

A lifetime ago, Princess Dauriel had plunged beneath the waves during a storm. She recalled her racing fear, her shock, the cold, the darkness of the ocean's depths.

And then an angel's face had appeared and changed the course of her world.

Today, she plunged beneath the waves anew, no longer a princess, not even an empress, yet as scared as she had been during that fateful storm. The endless expanse of ocean surrounded her, grey from the lingering storm. Wreckage from ships slowly sank, and massive shards of ice rose, but none were as jarring as the corpses bobbing with the waves, suspended and weightless. Dauriel gasped, panic filling her as the cold ocean did too, yet her body took in air.

Remnants of a kingdom coated in ice stood ominously below, and Dauriel caught a glimpse of a massive tentacle coiling away from it—harmless to her, supposedly, docile now in the punishment that Neoma—that she—had enacted.

Gods, her mind still reeled at it all, of Neoma's spirit filling her and knowing she would die, only to live . . .

And as panic might've stolen her anew, beside her came Tallora's face—watching, waiting, her smile as surreal as the bubbles leaving Dauriel's lips.

Dauriel shut her eyes, and for a moment she saw only Tallora's collapsed form, dead and cold upon the deck.

When she opened them, Tallora's beautiful countenance remained, but Dauriel was sinking. Instinct drove her to try and kick her legs—but of course that was impossible. She didn't have those anymore.

Instead, her tail—maroon and scaled—pushed her forward. Too far forward. Dauriel tumbled, stomach churning, and every motion seemed to only make it worse. She couldn't breathe; she couldn't stop—

Tallora stilled her endless spinning. Like the night they first met, Tallora held her by the waist, the quiet reassurance in her gaze heart-stopping.

For a moment, Dauriel lost her breath, as she usually did, when blessed to see her wife's face. Sharp, clever eyes, yet large and doe-ish all the same, and her dainty nose, her hair—oh, her hair, billowing beneath the waves—and Dauriel momentarily forgot the world.

They were wives, and Dauriel still wondered what she had done to find exaltation.

"Your tail is stronger than you think," Tallora said, placing a quick kiss onto Dauriel's cheek. "Try to keep your motions slow and steady when you're treading water."

Tallora released her, but thankfully kept her arms encircling her, a barrier without touch. Dauriel tried to do as she said, focusing on her abdomen as much as her tail—but rose anyway, until Tallora stopped her. Heat flooded her cheeks, in tandem with her rising anger. "They'll think I'm broken."

"You'll figure it out." Something feisty twisted her smile, and Dauriel loved to see it. "Or you let them think you were injured in escaping Stelune. I can carry you."

"I don't want to make you do that—"

Tallora's finger pressed against her lip, stealing the words away. "Hush. You're a stranger in my world. Let me teach you."

"I simply hate feeling like . . ." Dauriel swallowed her pride, the admittance difficult for reasons her twenty-four years had never let her decipher. ". . . like I have no control."

Something unbearably soft settled into Tallora's countenance. "I know," she whispered. "And I swear upon my pledge to Goddess Staella that you will learn. It will simply take time. In the meantime, can you trust me?"

A pit welled in her stomach, the same one that always formed whenever Tallora manage to pierce right through to the center of her pain—and puncture it.

Dauriel kissed her, the taste of salt incomprehensible behind the sweetness of her lips. "I trust you," she whispered, and with those words one of Tallora's arms took her by what would have been her bottom and held her like a child. The water did not make her weightless, but near enough, and Dauriel thought a moment to that blissful time upon the beach, to what was supposed to have been their final day. Tallora had carried her then, too.

Tallora carried her often, even when she didn't know it.

Dauriel looped her arms around Tallora's neck as she swam, daring to peek down and steal a look at those perfect breasts—and tried to ignore the sight of her own. Nakedness was fine in private, with beautiful women, with lovers, but this was open sea. Despite the aforementioned perfect breasts—pearlescent pink, perfectly peaked, gods—she caught a glance at something that made her breath catch.

A scar upon her own abdomen, exposed for all the world to see.

She loosened her hold from around Tallora's neck by small degrees, and there were her tattoos, runic and flowing with magic, but beneath them was shame.

At the first welling of her tears, Dauriel clenched her fists and slowly placed her face into the crux of Tallora's neck, feigning exhaustion. She was, but not so much as she was . . . furious? Betrayed? Goddess Staella granted her a tail and a new life, yet left the scars from the old one? She had power enough for one—why not the other?

She stole a breath, but it was more a gasp. Curse it; Tallora slowed. "Dauriel what's wrong?"

No sense in hiding her weepy eyes, but how strange, to watch the sea carry away her tears. "A lot is changing all at once," she said simply, and Tallora smiled sweetly.

"Don't take this the wrong way," Tallora said, swimming with ease. The ruins of Stelune were left behind, as well as the monster now designated to guard it, and it was only a matter of time before they caught up to the survivors. "But I'm glad that even though my world is broken, that you get to come as my wife, instead of my prisoner."

That really was easy to take the wrong way. Dauriel feigned a smile, but Tallora's own became stale.

"I just mean," she amended, and despite Dauriel's sudden rise in guilt, she admired how easily Tallora spoke, "that I don't want my home to be a place of fear for you. I'm so . . . so happy, Dauriel. This is a dream I never thought to consider. Having you here, even though the world's gone to hell, it makes me feel like everything will be all right."

Dauriel stroked her thumb along the curve of Tallora's neck, adoring her soft skin. "The danger is over. We just have to survive."

"And we will, especially with Kal around to help keep order."

The name was a slap in the face. "Kal?"

"Yes, Kal. He saw me possessed by Goddess Staella, so I know he's safe. He . . ." Realization stole Tallora's words. ". . . He knows your face."

"Tragically, Goddess Staella didn't grant me a new one."

"It'll be fine. I'll talk to him. He won't say anything." Uncertainty colored her words. But Tallora smiled, gorgeous and full, even if her eyes hid panic.

"The worst that happens is he has me executed, and we had already anticipated my death." Dauriel's chuckle failed to uplift her wife, whose countenance had fallen. "More likely, he'll have me imprisoned."

"Stop talking like that. If it isn't fine, then we run. We find some small town far away from Stelune and start over."

The words sunk like a rock in Dauriel's stomach. "No, you'll go with them. It's what you want—"

"I want you, Dauriel."

"I'm not worth giving up your home for—"

"I was already willing to do it once."

"Tallora—"

Tallora's hands suddenly left her body, leaving her floating. Anger stiffened Tallora's lip. Yet her words were as serene as the sea in this aftermath of destruction—though danger lurked, all was calm. "Dauriel, please stop."

Dauriel didn't dare to move, lest she tumbled anew in the waves. Instead, she slowly floated down, a cold hand gripping her chest.

Though Tallora's tears could not seep as they did on land, Dauriel recognized the welling softness within her eyes, the tinge of red. How tragic she looked when she cried. It wrenched her heart—always had. "I died today," Tallora said, floating down to match Dauriel's descent. "I said goodbye to you forever. So I'm a little raw right now, but I need you to listen and believe me when I say I want to be with you. If my people won't accept you, there are other places for us to go. But Staella wouldn't grant us this mercy and then abandon us—whatever else, trust in that. Neither of us expected to live past today, yet here we are with a brand-new start."

At the conclusion of her speech, Tallora's arms came around her anew, the duo floating together down to the outskirts of the destroyed Stelune. There they lay, and Tallora immediately wrapped her into a tight embrace.

Dauriel clung to her, those vicious voices in her head relentless in their tirade. "Do mermaids have tattoos?" she finally asked, cutting through the vitriol— not that the question was necessarily soothing.

"Yes." Tallora looked up from the spot between Dauriel's breasts, then took her hand, curious as she studied the tattoo on her wrist.

Every instinct within Dauriel screamed to flee— like always, her shame never yielded. But now she did not have the luxury of gloves or sleeves. Instead, she was exposed at every angle, forced to reveal her body to the world.

But Tallora rubbed her thumb along the ink, the scar beneath it tender even now. "These are Demoni characters, right? Good thing we're meeting with the Onians. Of all things to be suspect, this isn't it. Most people didn't know Empress Dauriel Solviraes had tattoos. Certainly no one here."

"No, but many more knew about my other scar."

As Tallora extracted herself, Dauriel shut her eyes, refusing to shed her tears. She had cried enough, and for far more important things. Her self-image was nothing compared to the pain of losing this woman, her wife.

Her throat closed to even consider it.

She was brought back by Tallora running her hand across the thin, raised line between her hips. "Different," Tallora said, and how kind was her gaze, "but not unexplainable."

Dauriel could not meet her eyes—not until Tallora cupped her cheek. How beautiful, those white, fluttering lashes. So different than anyone she had ever met before. "What's bothering you?" Tallora asked, for she always knew.

But though Dauriel wished so dearly to deny it, Tallora was her sanctuary, her home, more than Solvira had ever been. "I'm vulnerable. I'm exposed. And not ten minutes ago, I was weeping over your dead body, so perhaps I'm simply not all right." She forced her smile, but Tallora held her anew, gently breaking her damn of tears.

Her anguish rose, but Dauriel found stability in Tallora's soft skin, in the rise and fall of her chest. Her wife was alive, not the cold corpse lying on the deck of the ship.

"I'm right here, Dauriel," came Tallora's fervent whisper. "And I'm sorry—I'm trying to push all that aside to get us to my people, but I didn't think what this would do to you. We can slow down. We have time, I promise."

Dauriel shuddered at the touch of her lips on her cheek, shivered as she caressed the short locks of hair at her neck. "I can't even swim."

"You'll learn. I promise."

Tallora shifted, and Dauriel failed to not be acutely aware of her bare breasts. But at Tallora's smile, her whole world shifted to those beautiful lips. It was not lust that brought her to kiss them—she was introspective enough for that small thing—but the need to know this was not simply a dream, that she wasn't still collapsed on the deck of a ship over her wife's lifeless body.

Countless times she'd dreamt of Tallora in salacious ways. Both in her presence and far away, even once before they'd even kissed—which had been uncomfortable and left her aching all day. But dreams had never compared to the vibrancy of reality, to how soft and warm Tallora's body was, to how precious it was to feel her lips, and at the release of a small, perfect hum, Dauriel could not deny it was real.

When Tallora pulled away, there appeared that precious, submissive look in her eyes—that one that sweetly asked, What do you need?

Perhaps it was because her body was new and raw, or perhaps because they were lost upon the ocean floor, exposed in the middle of nowhere, but despite the constant craving for validation, sex was not the answer.

"Just hold me, please," Dauriel said, a plea to a goddess she had vowed to love for all her life.

Tallora took her back into her arms, into the very heart of love, and stroked her hair. "Talk to me."

Dauriel unburdened the tenderest parts of her soul.

When the sky darkened, Tallora coaxed Dauriel to rise.

"Do you want to try swimming again?" Tallora asked.

Though uncertainty filled Dauriel, it was better than her despair of before. "I'll try."

Tallora took her hands, gently leading her. "Don't use your tail yet. I'll pull you along. I want you to simply feel the water, all right?"

Dauriel nodded, even shutting her eyes as Tallora tugged her along. The water enveloped her, and Dauriel's tail's tendrils undulated with the motions.

But the genius of Tallora's plan slowly unfolded, as Dauriel felt patterns in the waves, the natural synchronizations in the ocean, and though it felt like letting go, she let her body simply respond.

The initial tumble pushed her ahead, startling her. Her eyes opened, revealing rocky terrain and Tallora's startled face. "Whatever you did," Tallora said, those bright eyes filled with pride, "do it again."

With their fingers intertwined, Dauriel flicked her tails as before, unsteady in the water but at least not tumbling. "I think I'm starting to feel it."

Tallora kept her stabilizing touch, her laughter utterly radiant. "Dauriel, you're doing amazing!"

Dauriel had cried enough, yet that choking sensation in her throat returned, causing her words to falter. But a semblance of freedom returned to her world, the ability to navigate without aid, and when Tallora's touch tentatively loosened, Dauriel breathed through her fear.

"You'll be darting about with ease in no time," Tallora said, spinning in loops around her. "And if we keep this pace, we'll catch up in no time."

Dauriel winked, though anxiety did rise with her next words. "We'll keep this pace because I don't know how to stop."

Tallora's delightful laughter returned, so impish and free. "Watch me."

She zoomed ahead, to where Dauriel could see, then pulled her body upright, her momentum ceasing immediately. "You try!"

Dauriel obeyed, pulling her body up—and continued tumbling, resuming her spiral.

But before she could be ill, Tallora's arms came around her, slowing her down. "You'll get it soon."

The farther they swam from the Ruins of Stelune, the less dusty the world became. The greys gave way to spots of color, signs of life, little fish that caused Dauriel's breath to catch, but it was all stolen away as they emerged upon a massive reef.

She tried to slow; Tallora helped her stop. Even beneath the night sky, the colors were vibrant to Dauriel's eyes—perhaps a gift that came with her tail. But the brilliant coral shone in gorgeous shades of pink, the fish shining in a rainbow of colors, some luminous under the stars. Like the gardens of home, there was method to the layout, nature creating natural patterns of color, and with Tallora's aid, Dauriel swam closer, amused as many of the fish darted away.

But just as many did not, and Dauriel stroked some silver creature, uplifted to feel its sleek body. A few came close to her face, as though to inspect her, the interloper in their lands. Others stared curiously beyond, not shy as she sought to cup them in her hands.

"Why are they so friendly—" Dauriel's words ceased when she caught Tallora's stare—and beaming smile. "What?"

"You are so cute."

Taken aback, Dauriel released the fish she'd apparently charmed. "And how?"

"You don't have to try hard," Tallora said, her wink drawing heat to Dauriel's cheek, "but the fish like you, and that's terribly cute. Reminds me of Solvira, with those puppies."

Dauriel chuckled, the memory a blessed one. "I've always liked animals. I trust them more than people."

"Given the quality of most of the people in your life? I'm not surprised."

The thought came with sorrow, and Dauriel faltered in her admiration of the reef. Home was far away, and while the thought of never seeing it again was not a sad one, she still wondered for her father, for Eniah. Ilune had said she would tell Khastra, who would understand, but it hurt, nevertheless.

But what hurt the most . . . No one but Khastra would truly miss her. No one from her council cared. And as much as she wished to say, "fuck them," and move on, her stomach churned at the idea.

"What are you thinking?" came Tallora's precious voice, shining through the somber clouds.

"No one misses me."

"Khastra does."

"She's one among thousands."

Tallora took her hand and wove her through the reef. "Well, fuck them."

Dauriel loved Tallora's spite and strength.

"Do you want to know who is proud of you?" Tallora continued.

"I presume the answer is 'you?'"

"Well, yes, but no." Tallora slowed, supporting Dauriel once more as they treaded water. "Neoma."

Dauriel scoffed, that bubble of shame still aching inside her. "According to you, Staella said she wouldn't be thrilled by my decision to abandon my throne and people."

"It doesn't change that you were courageous enough to sacrifice your life for Solvira." Tallora brought them close, grounding Dauriel through touch, through running her fingers though her hair. "I can't imagine that meaning nothing to her. But you said the other part—that Staella is proud of you too."

That one was more difficult to argue with, though Dauriel struggled to smile.

"When I pray before bed," Tallora whispered, "I will inquire to see if Staella knows anything more. She's shown she's willing to talk to me. I can't imagine she'd stop now."

Dauriel managed to nod, though nervous at the thought. To assume Neoma was disappointed was one thing; to know was another entirely.

She was brought back to her body by a kiss on the corner of her mouth, gentle and chaste. "It's beautiful seeing my world through you. I love my home, and I can't wait to show it off."

As Dauriel gazed into her wife's crystal eyes, saw the love refracted there, perhaps it was worth Neoma's disappointment after all. She brought their lips together, immediately parted Tallora's mouth with her tongue, and kissed her deep, savoring this rise in intimacy.

Strange, to feel arousal in parts she hadn't had before. Heat pulsed through her at Tallora's whine, her soft femininity all Dauriel craved. Strange, to be naked against her outside, taboo wherever you went on land. But Tallora's breasts were pressed against her skin; her skin was open for Dauriel's touch. For now, Dauriel's hands settled on her waist and in her white locks of hair, more aware of her own body than Tallora's—for once.

Her pleasure welled subtly below the juncture of scales and skin, where she knew from experience was where a mermaid's cunt lay hidden. Did she fear it, as she had in her human body? Her answer came when Tallora stroked along her waist—no panic, but that visceral sensation of wrong lurked beneath the surface, if she touched any lower.

Tallora never would though, had never intruded on her boundaries. Dauriel feared she would forever wonder why Tallora didn't abandon her for her insecurities, but the kinder part of her accepted it.

A slight bite on her lip drew her back into the moment. "What's going on in that head of yours?" Tallora whispered. "You aren't here with me."

"I'm sorry—"

"There's so much happening, Dauriel. I'm not upset, but I'm going to keep worrying."

"Thinking about me," Dauriel admitted. "Thinking about this body."

Tallora's gentle visage suggested she understood, or at least tried to. "I think, once we have a place to rest, touching yourself alone might be good for you. I know from experience that a new body is a lot to come to terms with. But you know I'm always here, and we can explore whatever new boundaries you want to set."

Dauriel kissed her once more, for she was comfort and joy.

Tallora grinned against her lips. "Though if you want to explore sooner, we're all alone."

A strange thought. "Do merfolk often engage in public indecency? Is that not taboo?"

"Of course it's taboo, but it wouldn't be my first time." Tallora's wink only fueled the rising heat within Dauriel.

She glanced down at the reef, noting the alcoves down below. "Do we have time?"

"We can make time. Kal and the refugees will move much slower than us." Tallora soothed her hair, the tender gesture sending chills across Dauriel's skin and scales. "Come make love to me."

Oh, her soft words, her smile—Dauriel was weak and enraptured. "Lead the way."

They held hands, Tallora gently guiding them below the reef, to the rocky terrain below. A small cave offered privacy, and as Tallora floated down, she released Dauriel's hand, instead cupping those beautiful breasts of hers. "Woe is you. You'll have to get used to seeing my tits on display all the time."

"Woe is me, indeed," Dauriel replied, her focus torn away by the motions of Tallora's hands, watching them tease herself. She came beside her, finding it strange to aim her descent so she landed on top, but she gleefully stole Tallora's breasts in her hands, the gratification immediate.

Fuck, she was stunning.

Tallora's hum was all she sought—gods, what a joy to touch her. "You'll be seeing all sorts of tits on display, actually. Woe is you."

With her favorite tits in hand, Dauriel froze at the words. "Oh, shit."

Tallora laughed. "It's all right. I was just as startled to know you silly Solvirans covered them."

Discomfort rose within Dauriel, threatening to drown her. She pushed it off, praying Tallora could not feel her tension. "Yes, but I am much more worried about becoming a pervert."

Gentle hands caressed Dauriel's back, drawing her closer. "Your thoughts don't matter. Only your actions do. As long as your hands are all for me, I don't care what you do with your eyes."

Admittedly, the words helped. Dauriel kissed her anew, cherishing those pliant breasts, the feeling utterly primal, pleasure embodied. Her arousal surged, the growing pleasure on Tallora's countenance an absolute joy. The very center of her world, and when Dauriel twisted those darling nipples, Tallora's gasp drove her mad.

With her hands busied with Tallora's breasts, Dauriel kissed her smooth neck, the small bruises bearing the signs of their previous lovemaking—heartbroken upon the ship.

No, no—not something to dwell on. Not now.

Instead, Dauriel's mind fell away into a lull of sensation, her lips kissing down to Tallora's collar bone, then to her breasts, deftly pleasuring one with her tongue. Tallora groaned, her fingers twisting in Dauriel's hair. Chills scattered across her skin, Tallora's touch a joy, and there she remained, the world simply quiet.

No thoughts. Just tits.

Tallora's nails spread pleasure across her scalp and back, the touch a comfort as much as it aroused. "Oh, Dauriel . . ."

The sound of her name brought color to her world, her very skin illuminate. Dauriel touched down to the juncture of skin and scales, caressing the shift in texture. Still different than what she knew, but she cherished Tallora's body in any form—and mermaid cunts were just so damn exciting.

Dauriel stroked soft lines against her scales, amused to feel them part at her touch. She kept her mouth on those tits; no need for sight as she softly touched the outer rim of Tallora's cunt, the tender skin twitching beneath her fingers.

Tallora's cry surged through her body, as dramatic as though Dauriel had pressed inside her—

but that was simply how sensitive this glorious body was. "Fuck, Dauriel. You're an awful tease."

"Are you suggesting merfolk simply plunge inside?"

Tallora's laughter was tainted with pain—the sort of pain that pulsed heat through Dauriel's limbs and tail. "We're built differently, but that doesn't mean I don't love how you touch me."

Dauriel kept her tantalizing motions, Tallora's face twisting in ecstasy. "Could you finish without fucking?"

"Perhaps? I don't know. I-I've never tried. Dauriel—"

Her words were stolen by a moan; her fists pounded the ground, frustration rising to match her want. "Dauriel—"

"Shh," Dauriel cooed, delighted at the display. "I'll tease you all I want."

"Oh, fuck you," Tallora whined, but nothing in the words said to stop. "Or fuck me, rather. Oh, fuck me, please."

Instead, Dauriel's mouth finally left her breast, kissing down to where her fingers made torturous work of Tallora's body. Her lips, swollen from pleasuring those gorgeous nipples, instead placed the gentles of kisses at the outskirts of her cunt, teasing the scales. She licked the sensitive skin around her entrance, savoring how Tallora convulsed. She was so beautifully open, and Dauriel loved to simply look, to study those tender ridges, to gaze upon her most intimate parts. Tallora had said her clit was inside, and if Dauriel peered closely, she swore she saw the little node.

"You're just wicked," Tallora said, breathless and wild. "Wicked and vile. Gods, I love you."

"It's not my fault you're so fucking beautiful down here."

"Flattering won't get you out of trouble. Fuck me, you ass."

"I will gladly fuck your ass, but I think you'd rather I finish this first."

Scandal set Tallora's mouth agape. Dauriel responded by pressing her fist inside her.

Tallora's gasp held relief, her body tightening around Dauriel's hand and wrist. Dauriel needed no other incentive than that, thrusting her hand within her. Fuck, it was unreal, being so fully inside her. Her trust, her vulnerability—not to mention, those carnal cries.

Dauriel attention deviated to her breasts, watching them bounce in rhythm with her fucking. How merfolk functioned with tits constantly on display, she still struggled to guess, but in the meantime, Tallora's were hers; Tallora was hers.

Tallora, her precious wife.

"Harder, damn you!"

Dauriel obeyed, bicep burning to match the heat between her . . . well, not legs, but she struggled to find the word. Positively sinful, to watch Tallora's body shift with her motions, to be buried so deep within her. The idle thought of "could she leave if she even wanted to?" passed through her head, wondering of the complexities of mermaid bodies, but Tallora screamed and convulsed around her, drawing her back into the moment.

Tallora finished with a few powerful motions, Dauriel thrusting to match. Upon its conclusion, she lay still upon the ground, simply breathing. Dauriel stroked her hand along the side of Tallora's body, outlining her breasts, her waist, her hips. "So beautiful," Dauriel whispered, and Tallora's smile was as sacred as their cherished act.

Her body loosened, allowing Dauriel to withdraw. But Dauriel lingered, savoring the bond. "Do I have to take it out now?"

The question reflected oddly upon Tallora's countenance, as though something new. "No. You can stay. But try not to move too much—I'm sensitive."

Dauriel rested her head on Tallora's breasts, absolute bliss in their weight against her cheek. "So if I touched myself where I touched you . . . would I open up?"

Tallora's hands fell into her hair, completing Dauriel's whole world. "I would think so."

"That's . . ." Dauriel winced at the thought, struggling to speak of it. But here she was, safe upon beautiful breasts, buried inside her wife, and she managed to breathe through the panic. "I don't think I'd like being so open."

"It's an odd sensation. You barely notice in the moment—you're a little too focused on wanting it filled." Tallora chuckled, her nails sending chills across the back of Dauriel's neck. "We don't ever have to explore it if you'd rather not, though."

"I think I simply need to be emotionally prepared for when I inevitably do brush against it," Dauriel said, clinging to Tallora's body, to the feeling of her skin.

"If you want to stimulate it yourself so you're prepared for accidents, you know you're safe with me."

There was no question of that in Dauriel's mind, and she planted a kiss on Tallora's sternum. "Not today, but you're right."

Tallora hummed, her thumb stroking farther down, to Dauriel's back. "I like this. You staying inside me, I mean. It feels special."

Heat rose against Dauriel's cheeks, the tender words unexpected. "Special?"

"It's more innocent, and yet . . . not." Tallora's chuckle bounced her breasts, which Dauriel was very keen to notice. "I don't know. But after the intensity of sex, it's wonderful to be intimate."

"Would this arouse you again?"

"Eventually, I suspect."

Dauriel smiled against her skin, every part of this perfect. "I love you."

"Stay a little longer. I'm happy to rest."

Dauriel obeyed, cherishing the sacred moment.

Want more *Aftermath*?

You can continue the saga at patreon.com/sdsimper,
or by following the QR code below!

About the author:

S D Simper is a bestselling horror author, award-winner of fantasy romance, and understands that the true secret to writing great villains is living with cats. She and her wife share a home with four cats, a Great Dane, and innumerable bookshelves.

Visit her website at sdsimper.com to see her other works, including *The Sting of Victory*, the dark, seductive tale of a girl who falls in love with a monster.

9 781952 349034